Needles

William Deverell

ECW Press

Published by ECW PRESS
2120 Queen Street East, Suite 200, Toronto, Ontario, Canada M4E 1E2

NATIONAL LIBRARY OF CANADA CATALOGUING IN PUBLICATION DATA

Deverell, William, 1937–
Needles / William Deverell

ISBN 1-55022-543-X

1.Title.

PS8557.E8775N44 2002   C813´.54   C2002-903343-8
PR9199.3.D474N44 2002

Cover and Text Design: Tania Craan
Production and Typesetting: Mary Bowness
Printing: Transcontinental

This book is set in Bembo and Imago

The publication of *Needles* has been generously supported by the Canada Council, the Ontario Arts Council, and the Government of Canada through the Book Publishing Industry Development Program. Canada

DISTRIBUTION

CANADA: Jaguar Book Group, 100 Armstrong Avenue, Georgetown, ON L7G 5S4

UNITED STATES: Independent Publishers Group, 814 North Franklin Street, Chicago, Illinois 60610

EUROPE: Turnaround Publisher Services, Unit 3, Olympia Trading Estate, Coburg Road, Wood Green, London N2Z 6T2

AUSTRALIA AND NEW ZEALAND: Wakefield Press, 1 Parade West (Box 2066), Kent Town, South Australia 5071

PRINTED AND BOUND IN CANADA

ECW PRESS
ecwpress.com

BOOKS BY WILLIAM DEVERELL

Fiction

Needles

High Crimes

Mecca

The Dance of Shiva

Platinum Blues

Mindfields

Street Legal: The Betrayal

Trial of Passion

Slander

Kill All the Lawyers

The Laughing Falcon

Non-Fiction

A Life on Trial: The Case of Robert Frisbee

Everything one does in life, even love, occurs in an express train racing towards death. To smoke opium is to get out of the train while it is still moving. It is to concern oneself with something other than life or death.

JEAN COCTEAU

FOREWORD

In the 1970s, a Chinese cartel, known as the Ch'ao-chou, secured a monopoly over the Asian heroin trade, hauling to its refineries, by elephant and mule caravans, hundreds of tons of opium from the poppy fields of Asia's infamous Golden Triangle.

In 1978, the Ch'ao-chou penetrated the markets of the New World, and began flooding the United States and Canada with a potent strain of heroin called White Lady. The gateway was Vancouver, British Columbia. The syndicate was notoriously ruthless.

The sole hope of breaking the back of the North American network resided with one man. This is his story.

Many of the events and characters are drawn from real life — though altered, for obvious reasons — and are based on the author's three decades of practice as a criminal lawyer in Vancouver.

Saturday, the Third Day of December, at Eight O'Clock in the Evening

It was warm in the room, and there were smells of sweet sauces. A naked bulb near the front door illuminated a route past the counter, into the back. In the dimmer light there, the room seemed densely populated but still, as if a tedious cocktail party were in progress. Most of the figures casting thin shadows were suckling pigs and whole swine carcasses and plucked ducks, aging for taste. A long shadow was cast by the Surgeon who worked deftly between two assistants, his fingers dancing and probing. There were human noises: murmured entreaties, then gasps, the sounds of air being sucked in suddenly.

And then a scream from the fat man on the chopping block. A shriek that shivered the stillness and echoed wildly among the animal corpses.

The two assistants stood at either end of the long block intently observing the art of Dr. Au. They were bodyguards, junk brokers, hard jacks-of-many-trades. They were both short, sturdy, agile. They were veterans of Dr. Au's campaign to extend Ch'ao-chou markets in the New World and wore scars of battle, like emblems.

One assistant was bereft of hair, bland of expression, and retarded of mind. He had old cuts on the skin covering his skull, which, by fortunate chance of genetics, was thick and hard. He had fought in Vancouver's tong wars, and he brought to the service of Dr. Au, his great khan, much natural skill with hands or weapons. Au controlled him like a dog, with simple commands and piercing looks. He was Charlie Ming.

The mind of the other assistant was quicker and crueller and more devious. He was fierce-looking with his old-country drooping moustache and a knife scar that ran over the bridge of his nose and just under the right eye. That eye was partially paralyzed and rarely moved in concert with its partner. He was a gunman, a dead shot either from or into a moving vehicle, but lacked a little in courage. He watched Au's technique with a keen interest, and every twenty minutes or so he popped a white pill into his mouth. He was Laszlo Plizit.

Between them, and in contrast to them, Dr. Au appeared handsome. In his fifty-first year, he was ten years older than Ming and Plizit. They wore rough clothes; he wore an English-tailored three-piece suit, conservatively cut, with a fine light stripe. The grey of the suit met the shade of his hair at the temples and the silver of his eyes, which were intense and brilliant and cutting. His face and body were clean and smelled gently of musk. He was slender and tall, and he moved with a fluid grace. There was only one outward blemish: an inch of flesh and cartilage had been torn from his right ear many years ago, and the ear looked patched.

None of the men in the room was a heroin addict, although the man outside was. That man wore a raincoat and a narrow-brimmed hat, and squinted through the smoke of a cigarette, which hung limply from the side of his mouth. The mouth was outlined by thin lines of lips below a pencil moustache. The man was tall and sinewy and nervous and cold. He was leaning against a telephone pole, checking his watch from time to time by the light from the window, light which glistened on the black car nearby. He winced when he heard the scream from within, and he squinted into the dark tunnel of the street. But saw no one. This man was Jean-Louis Leclerc, and because supplies were plentiful and free, he was doing six or seven caps a day, enough to stay straight and get a little buzz on top. He had burned out two veins in his left arm.

There was reason for this gathering: it was a solemn inquisition into a charge of treason. The accused was the fat man. The inquisitor was Dr. Au. The trial was by ordeal.

There had been damages suffered. Several of Dr. Au's runners were in jail, and networks below the border were in jeopardy, and the arrests had cost Au nearly a third of a million dollars in payments to next of kin. Such business losses can be endured, but disloyalty to one's patron cannot — the Ch'ao-chou say that thieves in a household are hard to guard against — so Jimmy Wai Fat Leung, naked and roped spread-eagled to the chopping block, related the final chapters of his life between bursts of pain that ignited his body.

In recital, Dr. Au was an artist, a master.

He tinkled the piano of the fat man's torso with a clean and delicate touch, and composed toccatas of pain. Improvising, he discovered chords of anguish that caused his trussed patient to render dissonant songs of confession and repentance. The touch of Dr. Au taught Jimmy Wai Fat Leung the wisdom of speaking truth, and for truth this plump plaything, this hapless Pavlovian dog, was rewarded by release from pain. Au's hands knew the points of the human body where pain nerves surfaced, and they knew where touch brought surcease from pain and where it brought pleasure, as Au willed. The long fingers of Dr. Au could strike flesh percussively, or could soothe as they transmitted the learning of centuries of Chinese healing.

Those fingers lacked the accuracy of needles but were more sensitive, and they returned to the sender messages that were honest, messages that inspired Jimmy Wai Fat Leung to continue his broken dissertation of past and present treachery. Jim Fat (as he was called by his friends and by the police) was made of jelly. He was no stoic, and no more reticent in his choking pleas for relief than he had been in his conversations with a certain narcotics officer who had blackmailed him — quite properly by standard RCMP procedure — and taken information from him.

Au was serene. It was unseemly in his family to exhibit anger or make a show of seeking revenge. While still a novice in his school of acupuncture he had been tutored in business by elders of the Ch'ao-chou, who believe that one can gain an edge if one goes about his affairs without passion. The Ch'ao-chou hold that the mind must be unfettered by feelings: that "the mind must be as clear as a mirror." Looking inwardly at himself, while his hands studied the undulating structure of Jim Fat, Au observed that the emotion he least mastered was a tranquil sorrow born of the need to engage his friend and follower in such painful physical conversation. A balance was nicely achieved, however, by the pleasure that Au's work had given him this evening, for in two and a half hours he had drawn from Jim Fat, in the dialect of the Ch'ao-chou, a nearly complete history of his clandestine relationship with Corporal Cudlipp of the Royal Canadian Mounted Police, a senior man in its Asian heroin team.

"My parents," he cried in a jerky sing-song, "are elderly."

"I respect them."

"Ai, ai, I beseech you, Au P'ang Wei! I am their only support. . . . Ai, please listen! Twenty years in jail were spoken of. Or life — the remainder of my pitiful life. I could not face my ancestors in heaven. . . . My parents would have starved, Au P'ang Wei. It was . . . it was with respect for my parents that I came to such arrangements."

"You are unworthy of them, Wai Fat Leung," Au said. "It distresses me that you did not respect my generosity, the more so because it is known that I allow no family to suffer in such circumstances." The dialect varied much in pitch, but Au's voice was modulated and without inflection of anger. Au did not feel anger.

"Do they have any of our Kowloon people?" he asked. "Do they have the Bangkok people?"

Au's finger again found the touch point for the head pain, and Jim Fat groaned and hoarsely begged to be freed from it.

"You will avoid this by answering quickly," Au said.

"In complete sincerity," Jim Fat said, panting, "I assure you I gave no names. I gave only dates of some small deliveries, and these you know."

"Yes, Wai Fat Leung, I have those from you. Chang last spring. Pin Low and Yen T'saio-po in June. Four friends in August, and one was Sorenson, whose markets in Cleveland, Detroit, and Buffalo are gone." Au contemplated those losses for a time.

Normally Au P'ang Wei could not enjoy the luxury of such long discourse with patients, and when time was limited he would move more quickly using needles of gold or silver or platinum (or cutting instruments, with which he was equally deft). But he was as learned in the art of the *an na*, the use of hands and fingers, as in needling, and his fingers could balance *ch'i* — that energy whose flow is ordered by the interplay of *yin* and *yang* — as well as stop *ch'i*. (The Chinese phrase "to stop *ch'i*" means to bring death.)

The essence of Taoist medicine was love of humanity, and Au scorned this. He had taught himself the darker side of the old arts and had discovered the points of pain and the meridians of death. He understood the twelve death-touch points of karate.

In Canada he had become a businessman, but prided himself that he had not become a dilettante at acupuncture, using his gifts wastefully. In fact, he used them to further profits and protect against loss. Jimmy Wai Fat Leung had squandered Au's profits, investing foolishly by selling information to the police for no return but his own worthless freedom, and Dr. Au's fingers — sensitive computers of human frailty — ingested that information.

He had found a place five centimetres above the left knee where he could cause alternately a drumming pain in Jim Fat's back brain and an electric shock in his kidneys. The middle finger tapped that point, and it was as if a lightning bolt cleaved Jim Fat's kidneys, and he arched his back, and piss spurted from him.

"We have everything except the last three months," Au said in the silence that came after the screaming. "How often did you meet after August?"

"Ai, ai, Au P'ang Wei, I have . . . I have spoken in perfect candor. One meeting, only one meeting in September. . . . Ai! Then I grew afraid to meet with Cudlipp — ai, patience! — because he is not trustworthy, in my poor opinion."

Au set about to master the sadness that had again insinuated itself into his heart, because here was Jimmy Wai Fat Leung, who had worked for him for eleven years and who, although in extremity, was failing to be honest. He removed the mist of sorrow, cleaned the mirror of his mind, and placed his hand gently on the comfortable shape of his old friend's abdomen, feeling turbulent movement from within the man.

Au said: "It is taught that one does not employ a person one distrusts, but one must trust a person one employs. I gave you my trust, and even now you hold yours from me." Au caressed the belly, and the trembling within ceased. "You met alone with Cudlipp on five occasions after September. The last such occasion was two days ago, when you drank whiskey with the policeman in the back room of Archie's Steak House. Cudlipp gave you a package wrapped in a newspaper. Yesterday, I am unsure of the time, you placed his package under the front seat of my automobile, which was parked at a meter near the Hastings Street office. You were aware that I had intended to drive it to my home alone. There is heroin in the package, and a box of condoms and a one-ounce weight. I find it most displeasing that I cannot drive my car. It sits and collects parking tickets."

Au favored his former ally with a delicate suggestion of a smile, and moved his hand down the slope of his abdomen. "I bore you by relating these concerns at such length," he said. "Perhaps I have misconceived certain matters. Favor me by showing enlightenment."

He stabbed a finger deeply where the stomach met the pelvis. Jim Fat roared and vomited, and Au dispatched Charlie Ming to the basement to find a mop and pail. Even such a simple task would take Ming a while.

After much crying and stuttering, Jim Fat said: "I beg . . . beseech you . . . I was faced with no alternative, Au P'ang Wei. Corporal Cudlipp, in his treachery, made me know that if I did not help to jail you, he would speak to you of my earlier indiscretions — and that you would kill me."

"Corporal Cudlipp demonstrates thereby a nice appreciation of the realities of our business," Au said. He knew Laszlo Plizit understood nothing of the conversation, so continued: "It will be of interest to you to know that Corporal Cudlipp has been more forthright than you in his dealings with me. He has spoken to me of the danger to me should I attempt to take possession of my automobile." Au remained serene in expression. "Because it appeared advisable to make more than a token contribution to his personal welfare, I have suffered a financial loss that will be recovered only after many weeks."

Au patted Jim Fat on the cheek, and was rewarded for this gentle gesture by a sharp bite on his palm, his patient finally rebelling, having given up the last remnants of hope.

Au remained serene. He held out his hands, palms up, to Plizit, who pulled a pair of rubber surgical gloves over them. Au reached into his bag and took out his greens and put them on. Plizit tied the gown at the back and handed Au his scalpel. There were cleavers nearby, and any manner of knives for butchering, but Au, who had studied surgery in England — the practice of which had been his dream before misfortune deflected his course — preferred to cut with instruments designed for use on the human body. They called him the Surgeon. And that pleased him.

"I will first take out your tongue," he said. "You will be well advised to spend the remaining three minutes of your life contemplating the enormity of your deeds and recalling the wisdom of the old saying that the mouth is the primary source of calamities. After you have utilized those three minutes, I shall remove certain glands that adorn you poorly, then cut your throat. I shall do so quickly and without pleasure, for although deterrence is necessary in maintaining integrity in business affairs, I feel a rare compassion for you, and do not wish to prolong your suffering unduly."

But the compassion would not distract Au, who had good training and moral strength. Au believed gentle expressions of feeling, always appropriate for poets and artists, were not misused upon the infrequent occasion of concluding an association with an old business friend.

Across the street, in Suite C on the second floor of a poor rooming house, Dugald McTaggart was attempting to bolster a weak queen-side attack. He moved knight to queen's rook four, daring Selwyn Loo to play a centre game. Loo was unafraid, and moved his king pawn forward to begin a double attack on McTaggart's underprotected queen pawn. Loo was not about to be deterred by the activity on his right flank and, without the queen's knight there to hamper him, he planned to pour all his resources right down the yawning open king file.

McTaggart was a bit deaf and did not hear the screams coming from the building across Chungking Alley, but Selwyn Loo did and, while waiting for his turn, memorized the scene outside through his thick heavy glasses, donated grudgingly by the Department of Human Resources. Without glasses, Loo's eyesight was as poor as McTaggart's hearing without hearing aid. For McTaggart, age was the thief; for Selwyn Loo, disease. His mother, an aging prostitute who lived and often worked in the room across the hall, had suffered from syphilis eleven years ago when Loo was being nurtured in the womb.

As Loo opened the window, the screaming was heard louder. He motioned to McTaggart to turn up his hearing aid, and the old sailor came to the window on wobbly knees. They saw dim light shining through the front window of H-K Meats and a man outside flipping the butt of a cigarette to the curb beside a long black car. The screams sounded choked; then they ceased. Loo and McTaggart saw curtains part in the lit window opposite and a man's face appear briefly, framed in the light. That man made a gesture with his hand to the man outside.

Loo felt a lump of hate swell within him as he studied the face in the window.

There was a third rented room — Suite D — on the second floor of the old frame house, one of many such houses in Chinatown. In it, on a sway-backed bed, were two sleeping lovers, Billy Sam and Millie Redfeather, bonded with the glue of stale sweat, spilled wine, and deep affection. They snored, each with a separate rhythm.

On the clock, it was three hours later in Baltimore. There, in a twelfth-storey room of the Plaza Towers, Jess Flaherty, in an old denim jacket and bell-bottom jeans, was concluding a deal for the purchase of a hundred and fifty grams of bulk heroin.

"Turkish ain't worth camel shit no more, but I'll give you the ten — which it ain't worth anyway — and half a big one as a bonus," Flaherty was saying.

The dealer, vaguely relating to a late rush of paranoia, studied his buyer for a moment and said: "You're not a cop, are you?"

"Oh, fuck off!" They both laughed, and Flaherty counted out $10,500 and passed it to the connection, who, still chuckling, handed over a package wrapped in brown paper. Flaherty opened it, smelled it, tasted it, snorted a little just to make sure, then pulled out a gun and arrested the man.

An hour later, back in the offices of the Drug Enforcement Administration, Agent Flaherty — an undercover specialist — was on the telephone with Superintendent Charrington, internal security, Royal Canadian Mounted Police. Charrington was a crooked cop hunter, and he wanted someone with special ability for a delicate task.

"See you in Vancouver, love," said Flaherty, grinning.

"Yes, yes, of course," Charrington said. Audacious, he thought. But after all, the agent *was* American.

Monday, the Twenty-third Day of January, at Ten O'Clock in the Morning

Corporal Everit Cudlipp, reeking and hung over, his pounding head held together by a set of headphones, shifted uncomfortably in his chair, doing battle in a losing cause against flatulence. His growing paunch had been nurtured by a daily quota of beer, and there were sounds hissing and popping within it. No one heard these noises, for all Cudlipp's neighbors also had their ears enclosed in headphones. They were members of Special I, the bugging squad. The only sounds in the wiretap-monitoring room were the whirring noises of reel-to-reel recorders.

The annual winter roundup of West Coast heroin traffickers was underway, and Cudlipp's job was to listen for leads to dealers still at large. The two men talking on the tapped phone were rambling on about friends caught in the scoop — or rodeo, in the argot of the trade — but soon went on to other things.

"Danny got scooped. Buncha other guys I don't know. Danny got popped in the rodeo last year, too, so he won't get his bail."

"Son of a *bitch*."

"And I think we've had a little steam up this way, just hanging around, you know, so watch it."

"Yeah."

"Danny got loose, I tell ya. I seen him. He was fuckin' lunch bucket on Friday down at the Homer booze can. Heat comes in there. I seen a coupla big gazoonies, looked like they had a piece of something under their jackets, just sittin' around, yackin' with him. He's giving this rap about the good shit he's got, and he's wired, dozin' off. Two days later he gets made. I don't know, man."

"Heard there's lots of ladies down there."

"The new booze can? My man, it's like a sugar daddy's trip in a penthouse. Picked up a sweet little chick up from L. A., up here to check out the scene, and she was hangin' around lookin' for action, you know? So we went flyin' out of here in my new wagon — seen my new El Do-ra-do? — for a little tour around the park with her. Man, she did *not* take in the scenery, unless you count the old bazooka, which is now so red and sore I can't tell ya . . ."

Cudlipp gritted his teeth in resentment. He would have loved to have been driving a new El Dorado around the park, some sweet little chick from L. A. giving him head. Still . . . there *was* Alice, his steak house waitress. Insatiable Alice Carson, who urged and goaded him in bed, and often marked his back with her fingernails.

But surely he deserved a handsome chariot as well, a sleek Cadillac with Alice Carson clinging hungrily to him as he swooped down the freeway. It would come. Alice would be his permanent old lady. A ranch house in Adelaide. The means for wealth and a fresh beginning were at hand, and the hand that held them out was the hand of Dr. Au P'ang Wei.

Somehow, in the middle of this cruel and dreary winter of his thirty-sixth year, Corporal Everit Cudlipp had got caught up in a hopeless tangle of love, avarice, and double-dealing. He wanted out. But he also wanted Alice Carson. He could not have Alice Carson unless he had money. He could not have money unless he travelled down the trail with Dr. Au. Cudlipp was on it, stepping carefully and watching his back.

He was doing a lot of drinking along the way, and it showed. His nose was blotchy and his body puffed and slack. His finest feature, a resolute chin, was slowly retreating behind the cover of jowls.

Slouched now in his chair, he halfheartedly gave ear to the voice on the dealer's phone:

"... It dazzles me. If you can take the hassles, Billy, if you can take the fuck-ups, the bums, you can wear diamonds. ...."

Everit Cudlipp had joined the Royal Canadian Mounted Police when he was nineteen. The pattern of his sixteen years on the force was out of the archetypal mold for a career officer: a short period of training when he actually learned how to ride a horse, endless series of two-year shifts in dreary towns in the Prairies and Northern Canada, highway patrols, radar traps, Christmas roadblock. Calls to break up brawls in beer parlors. Lectures to teenagers about beer. Visits to lonely women peeped by toms. Cudlipp mastered the technique of two-fingered typing, then endured the policeman's purgatory — endless hours of composing reports without number. He learned well the mechanics of the courtroom, and he served in barren little Legion Hall courthouses as clerk, as prosecutor, as friend and adviser to the local lay magistrate, and occasionally as informal counsel to the smiling, obsequious town drunk. Later he undertook courses in Ottawa and Regina on refined aspects of criminal investigation. Ten years ago he finally graduated from his uniform into plain clothes and graduated from the country into the city. He became a narc.

For six months, he was a hippie. He worked undercover for the soft-drug detail, and was to be seen frequenting dope smokers' haunts of Vancouver's Fourth Avenue, wearing a dirty Mexican serape from which exuded the rich stink of shared mattresses in the co-op houses where he crashed. He smoked pot and collected names. He cultivated his garden of potheads, buying from everyone who had a spare lid to sell, spreading his largesse broadly and evenly, buying dime bags, nickel bags, even only a joint or two if a friendly freak could be persuaded to part with a little of his own supply.

Cudlipp had not enjoyed that time. He had felt easier with the straight criminals, the muggers and smugglers and embezzlers, the young toughs with big mouths who learned their lessons in back alleys or up against the hood of a police car. Cudlipp believed the hippies represented a greater danger to his preferred way of life than did the bandits and bunco artists who shared society's concern with material values. So it was with pleasure that Everit Cudlipp, brandishing his lists of traffickers, came in from the cold of the counter-culture and triumphantly led a police sweep — a hippie rodeo — through the rows of seedy co-op houses near Fourth Avenue.

He was famous for a few days. Newspapers and radio talkers heralded the bravery of a dedicated cop who had survived for six months behind enemy lines. He received a written tribute from the commissioner's office in Ottawa, thanking him on behalf of his country for his bravery in the trenches of the drug culture. He made corporal.

Everit Cudlipp had peaked then, at the age of twenty-five. Somehow, his star stopped rising. He was moved to heroin control. The addicts were easy targets, although sometimes a little jumpy. But the jumpiness made for more excitement. A careful cop could enjoy a little workout occasionally, especially if it became necessary to prevent the suspect from swallowing the evidence.

Now he spent his days in the anesthetizing routine of electronic listening devices, whose demands dulled body, mind, and soul. Cudlipp had been at it today for two hours, and he was dying. His mouth was parched, his system was dehydrated, his head throbbed, and his stomach heaved.

Cudlipp's wiretap target, a middleman, a bundler who ran his own back end, had his own complaints.

"He wants us to cuff him two whole fuckin' bundles," the middleman's partner said.

"No way," the middleman replied. "He don't get cuffed until he pays for the last one. I ain't gettin' behind no more on this sucker. Tell him we want the cake on the line."

"Yeah."

"We ain't gettin' ripped, right?"

"Yeah."

"Uh . . . the new came in last night."

"Yeah?"

"Yeah, well, we were up all night with the mixer. Then we did a tester out to Gabe. He said the blast is okay, but it don't hold so good when you level off. You couldn't nod on it or nothin', so we're gonna have to beef it up a bit. Last time you guys cut it with a buff that was too heavy, like snow, and Gabe got off too heavy on the tester. Came onto him so strong he got into the hots, and he sweat so bad he took his shirt off. He said —"

"Yeah, well, we found —"

"He said it was procaine, you know, for buffing coke."

"Yeah, we figured that out. But it was *dynamo* White Lady. It'll sell like ice cream in August. It means champagne, Billy, two-hunnerd-dollar hookers every night."

Everit Cudlipp had been head of a Special I unit for a year now, manning the taps, listening blearily each day, listening to the dealers, listening to their ladies, listening to their voracious gossip, hearing about the good times. Cudlipp's long hours of panning for gold sometimes paid off with a few nuggets of information, but his guts wrenched with envy at the knowledge that for some, crime was paying well. He heard tales of money ("beans," "cake") passing hands in amounts so large that he began quietly to curse a world where honest men like Everit Cudlipp were forced to accept gifts.

Cudlipp's relationship with Dr. Au went back to 1969, when the Surgeon had begun to emerge as a leading importer of number four white heroin from Burma via Bangkok and Hong Kong. The relationship was strictly official: a cop trying to make a crook. Cudlipp watched Au for a few years and finally put together a reasonable case of conspiracy to traffic, charging Au, his mixer, and three of his middlemen. Later Cudlipp sullenly agreed to a deal proposed by the federal prosecutor, following discussions with defence counsel: the middlemen would plead guilty to trafficking, and charges would be dropped against Au and his back end (the mixer, the man who cuts the dope eight to one with manitol and fills the gelatin capsules). Cudlipp was certain that palms had been well buttered and that Au had supplied the butter, but he did not resent Au for that. It was business.

Cudlipp abhorred some criminal types: child molesters, pimps, political weirdos. But as athletes respect the skills and abilities of high-scoring players on opposing teams, Cudlipp respected the skill and ability of Dr. Au P'ang Wei. After the conspiracy charge was dropped, Cudlipp began to visit Au regularly, and although the visits were official business, Cudlipp enjoyed them. Au always expressed interest in the health, happiness, and financial well-being of his visitor.

"Drug Enforcement in the States claims you've been meeting with some of the Chicago people," Cudlipp said on one occasion.

"Corporal Cudlipp," Au replied, "one who acts upon rumors is, in our words, chasing the wind and catching the shadow."

"They say the meet was in Vancouver, at the airport Hyatt. A mafioso captain and a couple of strong-arms, Dr. Au. They were being followed."

"No doubt I was mistaken for another, my friend. I have heard that we all look alike to Westerners. At any rate, the agents of the DEA cannot find a door in an empty room. I am relieved to know that in this country the police, so well represented by yourself, have a reputation for being more efficient, and for being fair as well. In the United States of America, by comparison, one may not adjust his hat under an apple tree or tie his shoelaces in a melon patch without suspicion attaching to him. Please sit awhile. You are on duty; therefore, I shall offer you only coffee. You must bring me up to date upon the atrocious demands being made upon you by your wife. Perhaps I can sweeten the coffee. There is an excellent brandy . . ."

The friendship grew. So did Cudlipp's bank overdraft. He was up to his armpits in debt from misadventures with penny stocks and owed fat sums to his ex-wife. Ultimately he decided that his current financial needs might be met through the discreet sale of valuable information to Au, and he knew he possessed in Jim Fat the vehicle to perform the task.

More than a year earlier, Jimmy Wai Fat Leung had been unlucky. Armed with information from a disgruntled customer of Jim Fat, Cudlipp was waiting near a railway-station locker when the little dealer came by to secrete a pound of uncut heroin. Cudlipp cheerfully took him in tow and in a discussion over coffee told his suspect that for such amounts the practice of the judges was to send Orientals away for life. Jim Fat, a family man, agreed to exchange information for clemency. The two men began to meet regularly.

For several months Cudlipp so damaged Au's business that the street price of heroin was driven up by ten dollars a capsule. The result was a junkie panic, a fifty-per-cent increase in house break-ins, and the death of three shopkeepers who unwisely ignored the danger of guns held in shaky hands.

Cudlipp basked in a brief resurgence of former glory, but his bank manager was unimpressed. So he called again upon the services of Jimmy Fat. The offer was this: if Jim Fat would take a small package and place it under the driver's seat of Au's Continental, he would be released forever from the threat of prosecution for his pound of heroin.

That was insufficient inducement. Jim Fat feared the Surgeon's knife. But Cudlipp's ace was this: Jim Fat's parents had recently arrived from Hong Kong as immigrants — after he had made suit to the immigration department, guaranteeing they would not be a burden on the state — and Cudlipp made Jimmy Fat know that if he did not help, not only would he go to jail for life, but his mother and father would return to the colony in disgrace, and the wan face of Jimmy Wai Fat Leung behind the screen of a visiting room would be their memory of their favorite son and provider.

So Jim Fat took the deal.

Without giving away too much information, Cudlipp assured junior narcotics officers on his team that he had been tipped that Dr. Au, upon entering his car, would be found in possession of heroin, enough to end his career. The heroin had in fact come from exhibit locker 3-C, maintained by the Southeast Asia heroin section, RCMP.

There was little likelihood of Cudlipp's transgression being bared. Exhibits went missing all the time, for one reason or another. But it was wise to be careful, because the brass were currently trying to keep the force's collective nose clean while royal commissions inquired into police practices. However, no one was going to miss four ounces from a two-pound bag. Once weighed, amounts were never questioned.

The deed done, Cudlipp called Au, and they agreed to meet at his office.

"There is a sadness about you," Au said. "Does your personal situation continue uncomfortable?"

Cudlipp told him his wife had won a court order for arrears of maintenance. That had come on top of some losses in private speculations. He also said an investigation was under way which would almost certainly result in Au's arrest, but exposure to risk might be avoided. Au inquired as to the extent of Cudlipp's obligations to others. The policeman would be able to make ends meet with twenty-five thousand dollars.

The safe was opened. Bills were counted out. Cudlipp gave information. The young policemen working under him were likely, he said, to withdraw surveillance from the automobile after two or three days.

That automobile, said Au, was always kept locked, and only a selected few had access. Would the officer care to speculate as to how entry into it had been made?

Cudlipp regretted that such matters involved confidential police information. Au went back to his safe.

The twenty-five thousand dollars in hand would pay Cudlipp's current debts. Forty thousand more, given to his wife as a lump sum to satisfy all future claims, would free him forever from her mercenary grip.

Au paid ten thousand dollars down. They talked.

A few days after Jim Fat's death, an envelope containing the further thirty thousand arrived at Corporal Cudlipp's door.

"...With all these suckers getting scooped, there's gonna be a panic around here with the whole town's veins poppin' out."

"Well, can we get something out on the street by tomorrow?"

"There's the pound those jokers delivered, but they tried to whiz me."

"Oh, yeah?"

"It's a choked pound."

"You sure?"

"My calculators don't corrupt, man. They took the hog. There's a unit short. They came by in their old beat-up frapped car and just threw it at me."

"Well, Jesus, a guy best make what best ventures."

"Yeah, we'll get the pound up fast, cut it all down by tomorrow...."

Cudlipp made notes while his stomach rumbled. Tonight he would lie in the arms of his sweet waitress, who would have cold beer waiting for him in the fridge. She would talk with him about going farther down the road with Dr. Au. About how far they would go. And what price they would ask.

Friday, the Seventeenth Day of February, at Eleven O'Clock in the Morning

The secretary heard gasping, the noise of turbulent wrenching of the throat, muted behind the closed door, and she felt her own throat muscles constrict in sympathy. It sounded like the dry retching of a man whose guts had been emptied of all loose matter. Each day it got worse; each morning at nine when the boss arrived at the office, his face was more ashen, his lips more the color and consistency of chalk, his eyes more red and damp. Two weeks ago, when she had first started to work for him, he had looked well enough — at least he did not throw up — but in the last few days he had gagged and retched for two or three hours at a time. And yet by noon he would emerge from his office in good condition, talking to her in that clipped, cool way of his: casual, relaxed, confident.

She had known alcoholics before, but none as strange as Mr. Cobb.

She had little to do and was bored. Cobb was a trial lawyer with an empty waiting room. She knew he had been a prosecutor for twelve years, and she recalled seeing his name in newspaper accounts of murder trials. Before he went on the bottle, he had been a court-room lawyer of high reputation. On his own now, without clients, was he on a downhill run? Was it a mistake to have answered his advertisement? Damn it, he had seemed so capable and self-assured at the interview.

For the first few days she had allowed herself to daydream about him, about what it might be like to be with him. She told her girl friend that he was kind of cute — sort of early 1940s Gary Cooperish but with blond straight hair, cut sharply at the collar. Tall, kind of loose-boned and thin-assed. Super little pot belly which he kept trying to hide under his belt. Sad eyes, but crinkly at the corners. Somewhere late thirtyish? Cute, really. But did she want to get it on with an alcoholic — a *married* alcoholic? Mooning about his wife. . . .

Mind you, he hadn't made a pass at her yet. That would come in time.

This morning she had taken only one call. From Cobb's wife (stuck-up, she thought, with her flashy looks and flashy clothes). "Hello, dear," Mrs. Cobb had said. "This is Deborah. You had better be warned: he is just very damn forgetful. Put this in his diary for two weeks from tonight — dinner at Ed and Martha Santorini's at seven. And let me speak to him." The balance of the call, casually listened to, was about bread, milk, and coffee, to be picked up by Cobb on the way home. Mrs. Cobb's voice sounded imperious, and her husband's strained. Obviously a *b-a-d* marriage.

After Cobb hung up, she heard another bout of dry choking, and suddenly his door opened. She quickly put down the receiver as he hove into sight in his doorway, materializing from a cloud of smoke. The boss did not even look at her, but walked funereally past the waiting room to the hallway, leaving a trail of heavy smoke from his blazing brier pipe.

After several seconds he re-appeared, carrying a paper cup with water. Through teeth clenched hard on the mouthpiece of his pipe, he mumbled something like, "Don't put anything through to me for fifteen minutes." He looked like a man biting a bullet.

"Your business cards have arrived," she said.

He paused, picked one up, and grunted. "More crap to carry around." And he disappeared inside his office, wreathed in smoke.

She heard him lock the door.

The phone rang.

"This is Ed Santorini. Put me through to the useless tit." She remembered Santorini from a visit when he had copped a feel of her rear, saying: "Can't help it. Hot Italian blood." He was chief prosecutor for Vancouver, and her boss's friend.

She went to Cobb's door and rapped on it. "Will you speak to Mr. Santorini?" she asked.

"No calls!" came his hoarse reply, followed by some mumbling.

She turned to the phone. "He's in conference now. Can I get him to call you back?"

"You mean he's finally got a client? Don't let it go to his head. I'll get back to him. Hey, how you doing, sweetheart? I hope you're not scared up there all alone with him. Guess you heard: he's a homicidal rapist."

"I haven't seen that side of him yet, Mr. Santorini."

"Don't take dictation on his knee. He goes a little strange." I'll bet, she thought.

Again came the rasping sound from the inner office. Trying to ignore it, she busied herself with typing particulars in an impaired-driving case for one of only three clients who had been in this week. One had made frequent visits: a sallow-faced man, thin and nervous. All she knew was that his name was Benjamin Bowness and that Cobb called him Bennie Bones.

Fishing inside his desk, Cobb found his silver coffee spoon, and he studied it gloomily. He put it back, then pulled it out again. In his other hand he held the business card. He put it to the window, holding it up to the gray light of a murky, sunless day.

FOSTER L. COBB, M.A., LL.B.
BARRISTER AND SOLICITOR

The words shimmered in lightly raised gold lettering on cream, discreetly, elegantly, and, he thought, pompously offering his professional services to those luckless enough to have been caught at crimes, preferably crimes of murder, robbery, or corporate fraud. The trick was somehow for the cards to find their way into the pockets of prospective murderers, robbers, and swindlers. He was having difficulty seeing the card through the veil of wet film on his eyes, a veil which made the pupils look like glass beads. The air of his office was musty, stale with pipe smoke, and he breathed heavily in it. His pipe was burning out now in the ashtray beside the cup of water. It had finally become too bitter in his mouth.

There was a knock on his door. He heard the sweet, gooey voice of his secretary, a mousy woman enveloped in her daydreams, who seemed to stalk him like some merciless animal of prey. "Will you speak to Mr. Santorini?" she said.

God *damn* her. "No calls!" he shouted. He cursed quietly. He resented her prying and obtrusiveness.

For the first two hours of his working day he had hidden out in his office, gagging and spitting, desperately smoking a strong mix, at intervals swivelling his chair about to stare out his ninth-storey window at the forest of buildings that loomed through the grey unyielding mist. Vancouver was submerged in its winter torpor and Cobb in his own self-pity.

The call from Deborah had been blunt and businesslike, and it had done him in. She always had that knack. If she had not called, he just might have made it. . . .

Cobb was desperately trying to quit, or at least cut down. He paid for such efforts with pain.

His cramps tore through him again, and he held his head over the waste basket while his abdominal muscles contracted and pulsed, delivering nothing. If he kept up, he would be spitting blood.

Cobb put the spoon down on his desk, the bowl suspended over its edge. He placed a copy of *Martin's Annual Criminal Code* on the handle. Then he unlocked the second drawer of his desk and removed a metal box from it, and unlocked it. There were seven number-five gelatin capsules in the metal box. Cobb opened one, tapping the fine white powder into the bowl of the spoon, into which he also poured a little water from the paper cup.

It was the last work day of his meagre week. The call from Deborah meant that she would be home tonight, not at Whistler. God knows if that meant there would be dinner. Probably she would be going up the mountain early in the morning. If he wanted to spend the weekend with her, he could go too. If he could get himself together. If he could handle it. If he could take the bitching and the pain.

On his third try, Cobb got a flame from the lighter and heated the bottom of the spoon for a few seconds. Still standing, he undid his belt and took down his fly, letting his trousers fall to his feet. Then he drew his shorts down and he stood, hating himself, hating the absurd trial lawyer, in suit jacket, dress shirt, and tie, naked from hip to socks. He sat down and took from the metal box a syringe. He drew the warm, pale fluid into it, through a wad of cotton batten which strained impurities. Then, with his fingers, he massaged a scarred vein in his crotch, where his inner left thigh met his groin. There were more prominent veins — in the inner elbow or on the feet — but tracks in the groin would not be seen except by the most astute and indiscreet observer. (It was not a territory frequented even by his wife. At least of late. Deborah did not know he was back on the wire.) Finally the vein came up, and he inserted the needle. It missed, and he cursed softly. He tried again, and this time blood backed into the syringe. He squeezed the plunger and sent the pink solution flowing into his bloodstream, pouring its sweetness into his flesh and muscles and organs as it found pathways up his spine and into the cortex of his brain.

It was an instalment his rapacious body demanded at least twice a day.

Just before noon, Santorini called again, his voice full and booming and ineffectively disguised.

"Is this Mr. Cobb, the lawyer?"

"Yes."

"I've just been busted for cheating at cards."

Cobb beat him to it. "Sounds like a trumped-up charge," he said.

"Hey, you goddamn deserter, how's it hanging?"

"Ninety degrees to the horizon."

"Got the invite for March third? Cocktails at seven. Nothing fancy. Just a bunch of lawyers with good political connections" — Santorini was actively seeking a federal judgeship — "and their spouses. Might have Judge Foot-in-Mouth over so we can all truckle up around him and pick up a few gold stamps. Hey, tell Deb not too much cleavage — I don't want people drooling in their glasses. Pomerol '66. Drool makes it go flat."

"Your Lordship will be stocking a Pomerol '66. Isn't that a little ambitious — even for someone who's judge-bound?"

"I dream of the day I can cite your ass for contempt, Cobb. So. Anyway. What are you up to now that you're out of my hair? You got anything to do down there beside goose your girl and smell your finger?" Santorini would make a different kind of judge. "How busy are you? — that's what I want to know."

"I've got people lined up all the way down to Granville Street," Cobb said. "I'm giving away a free Big Mac for every new client." Cobb paused and drew a breath. "Aw, Jesus, Eddie, actually it's lonely up here, and it's nice to hear a human voice. Even yours."

"Don't be too sure. I could be a recording. Speaking of which, I've got a new *Don Giovanni*, featuring that great Italian soprano Joan Sutherland." Santorini was an opera nut. "Maybe we can get into it after the deadwood has left the party. Okay. Enough chatter. Got a big case. Just for you. *The* big case. Special assize and all. I mean, look, who's playing games? I figure you need the money, and we've got an okay from Victoria to use a private prosecutor. Regular ad hoc crown rates plus sixty bucks an hour preparation."

"The Surgeon."

"Yeah, right, brilliant."

"Eddie, I hate losers."

"Who knows? Maybe it's *his* turn to lose. He's batting something like six out of six. The odds gotta catch up to him."

"Eddie, I'm trying to put together a private practice. I'm trying to live down my reputation as a crown counsel. I can't do that by putting people in jail. Send over some criminals, for God's sake. I'm doing a special on shoplifters next week. I'll take anything. Pedophiliacs, corn-holers, flashers. Red Army kidnappers. Crooked politicians. Loudmouthed prosecutors of Italian descent. Commit a crime, for Christ's sake, then phone me."

"Yeah, well, Jesus, Fos, you know you don't have a beggar's tin teacup worth of business. Start making a living, then you can afford to be proud. You'll make it, given time. 'Good counsellors lack no clients': *Measure for Measure*, Act One, Scene Two. I hate to feed your ego, but you're the best goddamn starving lawyer in town. A court-room brain, you got. Like they say, you talk good."

"Suck a little harder, Eddie."

"Aw, Fos, this isn't my idea of a personal bequest to the Foster Cobb Starvation Foundation. Homicide wants a special prosecutor for Dr. Au this time. Honcho Harrison doesn't trust the department regulars to put enough jam into it. He wants this one so bad his bicuspids ache." Harrison was a senior city homicide detective who specialized in hard cases. The end of Au P'ang Wei's career was his dream, and although he was past voluntary retirement age, he stayed on, waiting for one final crack at him.

"I won't take it," Cobb said. What he meant, and could not say, was that he didn't know whether he *could* take it unless he kicked junk.

"Aw, shit, you'd just *love* to fire a few harpoons up his clammy ass. You itch after Dr. Au just about as much as Honcho does."

Cobb recalled the scene in the prosecutor's office two months earlier when Detective Harrison, told that Au had been released on $150,000 bail, erupted and spewed lava all over the green young man who had appeared for the crown at the bail hearing.

"It's only three weeks away," Cobb said.

"Aw, *Jeez*, Fos, don't play coy. You'll earn ten thousand for two weeks in court. Maybe more — I'm not going to study your bill too hard. Not that you wouldn't earn it. I know the kind of hours you put in with a jury. Or maybe you'd rather spend them standing in front of some grinning hyena at the provincial court zoo copping out hustlers and junkies." Cobb flinched inwardly. "You told me you wanted another crack at the Surgeon. You got it. Go for it." Santorini sounded petulant, as if Cobb were refusing a generous gift. Cobb knew the senior prosecutor was beleaguered — his inexperienced and underpaid staff of salaried lawyers had been scored on recently by quicker-thinking defence counsel, many of them graduates from his own office.

"Maybe I should hold out for Dr. Au's phone call," Cobb said. "He doesn't pay by the hour."

"The position, as you know, is filled. The Surgeon uses the high-priced spread. Smythe-Baldwin can buy a small country with his retainer." Cobb could hear him sigh. Santorini liked money very much. "Okay, Fos, don't say yes, don't say no, don't say anything. Sleep on it. Honcho wants to know today, but sleep on it. He says you're his man. Look, we'll provide junior counsel. We can dredge up some bright light around here."

"Fat chance. Nobody down there knows his asshole from an indictment. Even if I have to say no, thanks for the offer. I don't know if I have my shit together right now. Give my love to the slaves."

"Mine to Deborah."

Cobb had followed the latest Au case: murder in the barbecued meat plant. Au P'ang Wei had cut an old friend up and left his usual calling card — surgical removal of the testes. Over the years, Au had slipped a half-dozen convictions and was suspect in five unsolved homicides — all by knife, all involving castration. There had not been enough evidence to get information sworn in these cases. Narcotics police had given Au the code name of White Lady — not in deference to his precise, charming, almost effeminate side, but in recognition of his excellent merchandise. The heroin that Au's syndicate handled — delivered at the docks of the port of Vancouver by Chinese merchant seamen — was known in Hong Kong and Taipei as White Lady, and was ninety-seven per cent pure before delivery to the back end. Au had built, with singular devotion, a profitable trade route: Burma, Bangkok, Hong Kong, with links to North America through Vancouver; he had mercilessly expanded captive markets in the New World. He killed off his competition. Literally.

Cobb, cooled out now after his fix, feeling easy and just drifting a bit, sat back in his chair, which he had again swivelled to allow him to stare out the window at the dark clouds of winter. The dope that Bennie Bones dealt to Cobb was rich and potent. Bones was an old friend of Cobb's and warranted his goods as pure as possible. And it kept his head in one piece, kept him together while his marriage was falling apart. The thought that the stuff was probably White Lady from the factories of Dr. Au made him feel dirty, because the thought of the man was a stink in his nostrils.

He remembered the hard lump that had sat in his gut for months following the acquittal of Au in their one previous encounter, ten years earlier. Cobb had then been the junior prosecutor assigned to assist a senior counsel poorly equipped for his task in a case against Au involving the wounding and mutilation of an attractive call girl. Her clitoris had been removed neatly and antiseptically. The woman had been a poor witness, poorly prepared, terrified under the calm gaze of Au's brittle grey eyes. She had been caught — stumbling, correcting herself — in several small lies during Smythe-Baldwin's cross-examination. During the clitoridectomy she had been blind-folded, but she testified she knew the touch of Au's hands. Au did not take the stand, was found not guilty, and walked from the courtroom after a polite bow to the judge and a quiet smile in the direction of the prosecution table. His eyes met Cobb's briefly, and Cobb felt with discomfort that he had been sized up quickly as an ineffective opponent.

Another call. Detective Harrison was on the line.

The Honch was not wasting time.

"I'm working for the bad guys now," Cobb said. "Fighting crime does not pay."

Harrison's voice growled through the phone, as if filtered through a bed of gravel. "Fos, I don't want a screwed-up job. Santorini, now I know he's a friend of yours and all, but he just don't have any smart people down there, he was gonna pawn the case off to some jerk who'd forget to prove what year it was, or some fucking thing. The last time, we had Dr. Au on an attempt on some guy who was trying to muscle into the territory — you remember the case? — and our brilliant witness, some RCM-piss-up, picks out the wrong Chinese guy in court. That's just a lousy job of coaching by some prosecutor who can't clean the snot from his nose and who thinks the most important part of his job is going to the bank twice a month to cash his cheque."

"Prosecutors don't coach," said Cobb, getting a word in.

"Don't lay any of your holier-than-thou lawyer bullcrap on me, Fos. Any good prosecutor will do what he has to do. Anyway, the Surgeon probably paid off the narc. He wasn't a real policeman, he was a *Moun-tie.*" Harrison said the word with a little-girl accent. It was his bleak view that officers of the law, Harrison alone being the exception, were ultimately corruptible. Cobb said nothing, waiting for the sales pitch.

"We got the goods this time," Harrison said. "It's tight. I can get a bank loan on what we got. We got honest witnesses, a juvenile chess champion, smart little son of a gun, and an old seaman. We got an *eye*-fucking-witness, one of the Surgeon's goons by name of Charlie Ming, bit of a loser, and he's backing off, but we got him signed and sealed. We got weapons all over the fucking place, it's a Chinese butcher shop. We got wiretaps. We got a bite mark on the killer's fucking *hand*."

"He's got Rear Admiral M. Cyrus Smythe-Baldwin, Q.C., V.C., and OBE," Cobb said.

"Yeah, well, he's a sly shyster, but he's over the hill," said Harrison.

Cobb knew Harrison would not admit to being scared of Smythe-Baldwin, but he had been mauled by the lawyer more than a few times.

"Smythe-Baldwin is a hell of a lawyer," Cobb said.

"Yeah," said Harrison, "he's a good lawyer, but you can beat him."

He's going for my pride, Cobb thought. Honcho Harrison understood trial lawyers: the good ones are driven by their egos.

M. Cyrus Smythe-Baldwin, now nearly seventy years old, had always demonstrated a deadly precision in locating the jugular in the crown's case. He had had the clear edge on Cobb in the half-dozen occasions they had paired off — something like five to one, Cobb admitted to himself, galled. But Cobb loved the old man. Thirteen years ago he had pried open the gates of the legal profession and got Cobb inside. Newly graduated from law school, Cobb had learned that his criminal conviction — for robbing a service station for cash to buy a fix — might deny him the right to be admitted to the bar. Smythe-Baldwin, laughing off Cobb's attempts to pay him a fee, convinced the benchers of the Law Society that Cobb had accomplished a miracle of rehabilitation. Cobb was in fact off drugs at the time, and he stayed off for thirteen years.

Six weeks ago he had gone on the wire again.

Harrison, sensing victory in the silence at the other end of the line, stalked his quarry. "If you want a big win over the old man, I got just the vehicle. Front page. Good start for a good lawyer just getting his practice off the ground."

"Clients don't take cases to famous prosecutors," Cobb said.

"That's bullcrap. Smart crooks with money look for class. They know lawyers are all pimps who don't give two tiny turds where their money comes from. Smart crooks hire pimps with class. You got class."

"Thanks," Cobb said. "I needed that. I'll look at the file, and I'll promise nothing."

Relentless, Harrison said: "I'll bring them up before I go off shift — witness statements, record, bail transcripts, exhibit lists, police reports, the whole pisseroo."

"Okay," Cobb said. "I'll send out for the ice."

He hung up, stared at the telephone for a long moment, then opened the impaired-driving file, which his secretary had brought him, and began to read the summary of evidence. But his unresisting mind ambled slowly off to the trial of Dr. Au P'ang Wei. Could he do it? With his high-wire shakes, could he handle it?

Cobb knew the fundamental truth about junk, a truth all junkies keep in their hearts: once wired, you can never get free. You can stop using; you can lay the spike aside for years. But you're never free. The wire keeps you hooked until the day of your death.

Friday, the Seventeenth Day of February, at Half-past Ten O'Clock at Night

"This," said a despairing Cobb, flinging the files on his desk, "is a poor pile of manure."

Harrison merely smiled. He was used to hearing lawyers carp. He felt he had served up Dr. Au on a silver plate, dressed and done to a turn.

"Do you think a jury is going to give us a conviction for this pigswash?" Cobb asked with a theatrical flourish of his arms. He was drunk. Honcho Harrison had brought a quarter of Johnnie Black with the files as a bribe. That bottle had gone dry, and the two men were working their way through Cobb's Ne Plus Ultra, kept for entertaining important clients, should any pass through his door.

"We've got a butchered body hanging from a meat hook, with his tongue and nuts cut off — the jury's going to have a collective coronary — no fingerprints, no motive, no physical evidence that Au was there. . . ."

"He owns the buildings. Rents it out. He's got a key. We got witnesses."

"You have two witnesses, bless their law-abiding hearts, one blind and the other deaf. They see Au's face in the window. I'm expected to ask a jury to put the guy away because his face was in the window? Aw, come *on!*"

"Charlie Ming. We got his written statement. He and the Surgeon pick Jimmy up at home, take him to the butcher shop." Harrison, a tall, red, and round-faced man of fifty-seven, was beaming and confident.

"He doesn't see fuck *all*," Cobb shouted. "He's off getting a mop and pail, comes back, no sign of Dr. Au."

"Well, we picked Charlie up right away, got a statement."

"A retard tong gunman: our best witness. And now Au's got to him somehow, and he's turned tail on us, claims his statement was false, made it because he was scared of a certain homicide cop."

"Aw, they always come out with that kind of bullshit," Harrison said. Cobb turned his eyes to the ceiling and snorted. "He'll come around before the trial, don't worry," Harrison said.

"Au will give us the finger; and walk out of court whistling 'So Long, It's Been Good to Know You,'" Cobb mumbled. "What else have we got? A telephone tap — you said there was wiretap. I don't suppose we have the Surgeon on the phone naively planning a killing."

"There was a problem about the wiretap," Harrison said. He had not been able to pry a transcript loose from city narcotics. All Harrison knew was that the taps came after Jim Fat's death, and Au was mentioned in them. The tap was placed by the city police, and Cobb assumed that the secrecy had something to do with the close-to-the-vest poker game that city police liked to play with their competitors, RCMP narcotics.

The night's business done, Harrison took Cobb home, recklessly driving with courage given by drink and by the knowledge that every traffic cop on the street was terrified of him.

Harrison watched Cobb sway up the walk to his front door. He sighed, and drove off. Well, sure, he thought, it's a tough case. But then, Foster Cobb, he figured, was the toughest courtroom tactician on the Coast, a sharp cross-examiner.

There was only one problem. And it could be a great mother of a problem: Cobb was carrying a monkey again. Inside Harrison's jacket pocket was the silver coffee spoon he had picked up from the floor of Cobb's office.

Harrison figured he might take it to the lab tomorrow to have it analyzed. Just to make sure.

The monkey was first introduced to Cobb when he was sixteen, a high-school student. An older student, Paul Quade, contemptuous of others' weaknesses, turned him on, gave him his wings, in the language of the trade. Cobb was unsure about doing it, but he had no choice. It was a matter of confirming loyalty, proving virility. Two girls looked on, giggling and thrilled, as Quade heated up some junk in a bottle cap and loaded a set of works. The heroin hit Cobb with a whoosh, and, embarrassingly, he threw up. But a few seconds later he was blasted, flying, omnipotent, free.

After that, Cobb did up when he could, using hard drugs as a high, as a trip. For a while he merely chipped, still hanging out with Quade and a few other young braves. The chemistry of Cobb's body was slow to form the mysterious compounds that create the dependency effect. To get a better rush, Cobb began to shoot in the mainline, and by the time he was in first-year university it dawned on him that he was wired. Hooked. Full on the spike.

His connection found him a part-time job as a short-order cook and waiter in a greasy spoon where addicts hung out at night, drinking beer and smoking reefers in the back booth and cranking heroin in the washrooms. He became a part of the scene, fixing friends who were too dozy to shoot themselves in the line, banging them in the arm in exchange for a free hit for himself.

Benjamin Bowness was twenty-one then, a few years older than Cobb, and they became sidekicks. They would sit together, bullshit, get loaded, then tear around town.

Soon, there wasn't enough junk being laid on Cobb to satisfy his thirsty bloodstream, and he started to listen to Bones's brave talk about how easy it was to make a big score. One night, fearless with dope and vodka, they hit a service station for seven hundred and thirty dollars and change. Bones held the unloaded gun, and Cobb scooped the till. Twelve minutes later a traffic cop pulled Bones over for running a light, and found the money and gun in the glove compartment.

Cobb was eighteen, and the magistrate let him off with a sentence of four years. They put him on methadone and weaned him from it in jail, and he got parole after fifteen months. He went back to university, completing his arts degree in the daytime while managing a pool hall at night, often doing shifts in the back room to relieve the boss, a friend and rounder who ran poker games there. Enthralled by the study of history, he expanded his major into a master's degree, and entered law. He had quit his job at the pool hall, but by now was skilled enough at cards to be able to parlay his way through three more years of university.

Cobb was hired into the prosecutor's office, and for some months was put on show as a kind of symbol of the rehabilitative process. He discovered he had a gift for the courtroom. He could use words well and argue persuasively. An addict now for history, he enjoyed digging through old casebooks for buried ancient precedent. He grew fond of law's fragmented logic. He learned how to assess the humor of judges; he learned their weaknesses, prejudices, and strengths. The legal community soon forgot his past.

Four years after joining the prosecutor's office, he met, wooed, and married Deborah Fletcher.

He met her through her father — a law professor then, and now a judge, a man of erudition and culture, and the first strong male figure in Cobb's life since his own father died when Cobb was a boy. A deep affection grew between the two.

Deborah was eighteen then, a prize-winning skier with a supple, athletic body. She was red-haired and strong-featured, her eyes hot and darkly green, her mouth expressive and full. Before her, there had been casual encounters and short romances. No one seemed special to him. But Deborah Fletcher blew his mind.

And she was infatuated with him: he seemed burned raw by life, mature, and deep. Her first impression of him — as her father's dinner guest at home — was as a tall blond man, loosely strung together, with pained eyes that seemed to cut through her.

She gave him a ski lesson one weekend. They went for drinks. And he seduced her with his mystery, his cool, his theatre: rounder-turned-prosecutor. In a borrowed ski cabin they made a fire in the fireplace and love on the rug.

A month later they married.

And now it was all coming apart.

The seams had started showing about three months ago, and it was unravelling faster day by day. She wanted excitement in her life. He was content to smoke his pipe and watch his hockey games and read his books. She wanted to disco. He wanted tickets to the chamber-music season. Those were symptoms. Cobb didn't understand what lay beneath.

Their home — a twenty-fifth storey condo near Stanley Park — had now become an arena where Cobb and his wife staged caustic and sulking duels. The separate bedrooms frequently were separately occupied.

And Cobb, six weeks ago, had bumped into an old acquaintance on the street. One Bennie Bones, who had painkiller, medicine for the heart.

Cobb began to find his orgasms in the pit of his stomach, where the mainline rush is felt.

Cobb lurched into the apartment, feisty with liquor and ready for battle.

Deborah called out: "Did you bring the coffee, bread, and milk?"

"I am doing a murder," he announced.

"Legal aid? Or do you get paid something?"

"Deb, it's a hell of a case. Dr. Au. The Surgeon. He slashed an informer's throat. I'm prosecuting it."

"Did you," she repeated, "bring the coffee, bread, and milk?'

"God*damn* you, Deb!"

"Cobb, you are drunk."

Corporal Everit Cudlipp marvelled at his beautiful waitress's ability to achieve repeated deep orgasms, and he felt powerful as her lover. Alice Carson came once again, then clung to Cudlipp, holding him inside her. Her hair was dark and very long, and was sprayed across the pillow and over her face. It was a pretty face, but the nose was perhaps too small, the eyes calculating and not kind.

Cudlipp knew Carson had been a prostitute some years ago, when, as she admitted to him, she had had to live by using the tools that God had granted her. Cudlipp was forgiving. She had repented her past, and it would be replaced by a future as Mrs. Everit Cudlipp, a future hopefully to be found in South Australia. The burden of his debts was off his shoulders now, but there was one last score to make before he quit the force.

"Make him pay big, T-bone," she whispered hungrily into his ear. "Tell him a hundred and fifty. No. Bullshit. Tell him two hundred. Two-fifty. I'd be worth another hundred thousand. I'd be good." She bit his ear lobe until it hurt. "I was serving. You had a T-bone steak. I remember."

Cudlipp merely grunted. He did not like to talk after having sex.

"Don't go cheap, baby," she went on. "Make him pay. He *has* to pay. You can sink him, baby. You can do him in."

Yeah, he thought, I *can* do him in. *I* set the price. He looked into her eyes. She was almost *too* smart, and that made him a little uneasy. For a woman, she had a hell of a business head.

"We'll have a little cocktail bar in Adelaide," she whispered. "I can run it single-handed. They brew good beer in Australia. You'll be my best customer." She worked her tongue into the interstices of his ear, and felt the little hairs there.

"Hey, that tickles. Get out of there."

"Just trying to get you going, T-bone."

"Jeez, Alice."

"Not man enough?"

"Just give me a minute, damn it."

"Tell him two-fifty. Maybe he'll settle at two."

He looked hard at her again. Real smart head on her. For a woman.

Dr. Au P'ang Wei stroked the silky hair of Prince Kwan, his favorite Persian cat, with whom he felt a kinship. The chair upon which they sat was a Louis Sixteenth, gilded and softly plush. Red velvet curtains with a thick napped surface shut his room off from the outside, and there was time and solitude for reflection.

A matter somewhat bothersome: it has been suggested that there were witnesses. But who? Some effort must be made to find out who they were. It must be done quickly; the trial was three weeks away. Perhaps some work could be performed by Mr. Plizit. . . .

A slight pain drifted across his eyes, and he pinched a point in his left ankle along the gall-bladder meridian, which travelled to the cortex. The pain disappeared.

Another problem: Old Ma Wo-chien had sounded petulant on the phone. Were there conspiracies in Hong Kong? Are they envious of my success here? Why had he asked about my health?

But there is work to be done. Eastern Enterprise III, out of Taipei, was due at Centennial Pier at noon tomorrow, and there would be three and a half pounds of number-four white aboard, which must be sent immediately to the back end.

So: there were impositions always upon his time, and there was so little that could be spent with Prince Kwan, his brother in spirit.

Wednesday, the First Day of March, at Eleven O'Clock in the Morning

Cobb was straight now. He had fixed an hour ago and was working quickly and easily now, putting together a synopsis of the evidence of witnesses he had interviewed. The phone rang.

"Hello," he said.

"Hi. I'm Ms. Tann." Unmistakably: Miz. "I've just joined the prosecutor's office."

"Yes," Cobb said. "Ed Santorini told me. We haven't met." That seemed unnecessary to say.

"Let me warn you, I'm as green as a bean. I mean, I was called to the bar only six weeks ago. But don't panic, Mr. Cobb, I'm full of go, and I'll learn." The voice was lilting, almost gushy. Cobb groaned inwardly. He prayed she was not a gusher.

He frowned resentfully at his telephone. "I am sure I will enjoy having you work with me," he said in his most formal manner.

"Well," she said, "I am sure I will enjoy having me work with you, too." Now *that* sounded like a typical bit of female sarcasm.

Damn! Cobb thought. Santorini — some form of practical joke? — had sent him a courtroom virgin.

The Au case, with its cruel letting of blood, was no place for a faint heart, and Cobb had hoped his assistant would be competent, tough, professionally distant, capable of working late hours and sharing hard liquor. Well, he would have to resign himself.

"I guess you had better get to know the cast of characters," Cobb said. "I will want you to read over the file."

"I read it last night," Tann said. "The boss gave me the file copy. I don't know *that* much about it, but it could be a little tough." It was said as a question.

"It's tough," he said.

"The man, this Au, is a heavy-duty operator. Is he nuts? He collects them, doesn't he? Nuts, I mean. Not meaning to sound crass. Do I sound crass? I'm sorry. But he sounds like he has a . . . what . . . a fetish? Will he go down on this one, do you think? Can we nail him?"

She had a breathless way of talking, and did not leave much space between her words. Cobb would have to live with this for about three weeks. He had a picture of her: a babbling, bright-eyed innocent with an over-large mouth.

"We need to fill in some gaps before I could be confident of a conviction," he said. "We don't have a knife to put in his hands, but we *should* be able to get him into the building where the killing took place. The meat market. The trouble is, in addition to Au and Charlie Ming, there was a third man involved, maybe a fourth, and right now I'd have to say there may be reasonable doubt as to who killed Jimmy Fat. So there's a big piece of evidence missing. We have an outside chance."

"What sort of outside chance?"

"Well, we're going for the bomb with the clock running, and it's third and ten on our own twenty."

"Third and what?" She did not sound like a great outside receiver.

"We have just over a week to get this case into shape. If we get all our witnesses together, if old Mr. McTaggart and the Loo kid come across, if Charlie Ming tells the truth, if we can force Dr. Au onto the witness stand and stick it to him in cross-examination, if we get some rulings from the judge — well, if all of those things break for us, we might pull it off." But Cobb knew he needed more than these. He needed direct eye-witness evidence of Dr. Au wielding the murder weapon. As far as Mr. Justice Horowitz was concerned — well, he would display an even temperament, would lean neither way, and would rule fairly on questions of law. He would be affable and gentle and would seek compromise on issues of evidence.

Cobb told Tann of the meeting with the judge and Smythe-Baldwin that afternoon. "Are you free to come, Miss Tann?"

"Sure. It's Jennifer. Where and when?"

"Two o'clock. Meet me at the courthouse outside Mr. Justice Horowitz's chambers."

"Mr. Cobb, I don't know why I was picked to junior you — except maybe because I'm Chinese-Canadian, and Ed Santorini thought I'd give the trial some balance."

"Balance?"

"You know — all you white hordes coming down on some poor ignorant Chinese immigrant trying to make his way in a new country."

At the top of the courthouse steps, M. Cyrus Smythe-Baldwin, seeing Cobb send his taxi away, waited like a reception committee, beaming at his adversary.

"Well, if it isn't Colonel Sanders," said Cobb, trotting up the stairs. "What's the good word, Smitty?"

"The good word is innocent," said Smythe-Baldwin. "You seem chipper, Foster, for a man whose task is to try the impossible." Smythe-Baldwin, ruddy, stout, goateed, and immaculate in his three-piece black suit (Colonel Sanders with a Canadian accent, dressed for mourning), reached an arm around Cobb's shoulders with almost fatherly affection. "And so, after ten years of public service, you have joined the rest of us workers scratching the soil for a few seeds."

"The seeds have been well picked over," Cobb said, "by the big roosters."

Smythe-Baldwin smiled grandly. "What they've handed you to prosecute, my young friend, is known to us roosters as chaff." He leaned toward Cobb's ear, and his voice became conspiratorial. "I take it some sincere thought is being given to your entering a formal stay of proceedings so that we may all go about our honest ways and relieve the hard-pressed taxpayer of an unnecessary and wasteful trial."

"I have a case against your man, Smitty. All I ask is a chance to get him on the stand and drill him a little bit."

"Whether the good Dr. Au takes the stand is his choice, fortunately, and not yours. It grieves me that I must remind a practitioner of your ability and experience of the simple civil rights that are enshrined in our jurisprudence." Smythe-Baldwin's arm was still about Cobb as they entered the building, the door being held open by one of the old lawyer's juniors.

The commissionaire inside the doorway snapped to attention as the lawyers walked by. Smythe-Baldwin greeted him like an old friend: "Eric, you are looking *very* well. I trust your kidneys are treating you a little better."

"Yes, sir," Eric said. "Good to see you again, sir. And you, Mr. Cobb."

The entourage, small but led in kingly fashion by Smythe-Baldwin, glided through the corridors to Mr. Justice Horowitz's chambers. En route, clerks, sheriff's officers, and court reporters in turn enjoyed the beneficence of recognition by the senior counsellor.

At the door to the judge's chambers, Cobb stopped short. He felt a sinking sensation in his chest cavity. On the street, or in a casual bar, or at a country dance — anywhere but in a courthouse — Ms. Tann would have looked . . . well, appealing. In fact, she was delicately attractive — slender and tall, with dark Oriental eyes and straight shining black hair that hung loosely to about mid-waist. She wore huge hoops in her ears, a loose embroidered blouse, and a full-length skirt of rough materials that, to Cobb, looked suspiciously homespun. The whole effect was uncomfortably bohemian, in his view.

"Hello," she said, "I'm Jennifer Tann." There was something mocking about her smile.

"I'm Cobb."

"I suspected."

She did a bird-like twist of her head, looked over Cobb's shoulder, and squinted at Smythe-Baldwin.

Cobb introduced them, and Smythe-Baldwin's broad face opened up in a wide smile. "And what," he asked, "is a lovely young lady like you doing in a place like this?"

Tann raised her eyebrows. "My *God*," she said softly, then shook her head.

A dark cloud of embarrassment settled over the men, relieved only by a strangled little chuckle from Smythe-Baldwin's junior and some mumbled words from Cobb: "Um, she's going to be with me for the trial."

Composed and still smiling, Tann gave Smythe-Baldwin a hard look. "What are you doing this for, defending this butcher? He's off centre, really."

What, Cobb asked himself, have I done to Santorini that he has done this to me?

"Young lady," said Smythe-Baldwin with icy aplomb, "every man is entitled to a fair trial in our courts. Every man is entitled to the presumption that he is innocent until proven guilty beyond a reasonable doubt —"

"Every woman, too?" she interrupted.

Smythe-Baldwin refused to be deflected. "These principles hold true whether the sin of the man — or the woman — be murder or smoking marijuana. That's a lesson you would do well to learn early in your career."

"Well, I guess I could accept that — if everybody charged with a crime could afford the best defence that money could buy," she said.

Cobb broke in. "Let's see the judge," he said, and held open the door leading to the desk of the judge's secretary. Smythe-Baldwin, his features now set, strode through, followed by his junior, then Jennifer Tann, who whispered as she passed Cobb: "I think I got to him, hey?"

The secretary took them immediately to the private chambers of the judge.

Selden Horowitz was an old hand in the court system, good at his job, and he liked to move things along quickly. He could be expected to leave the arena to the combatants.

He rose from his desk as the lawyers entered his room, and when introductions had been made, he motioned everyone to a seat.

"I understand we have a trial coming up in less than two weeks," he said. "I have asked you here to see if we can iron out any problems beforehand. I will want to know if there will be any pre-trial motions, any problems with the evidence — *voir dire* and that sort of thing — anything we can handle in advance of the trial. We don't want to inconvenience the jury by sending them out of the courtroom too often."

Cobb knew Smythe-Baldwin would use this forum to seek information about the crown's case. Normally, a preliminary hearing would have been held and the defense would have questioned all crown witnesses. But a decision had been made by Santorini to proceed by direct indictment to trial.

"Mr. Cobb," Horowitz said, "do you foresee any problems?"

"No," Cobb said. "We may have eighteen or nineteen witnesses, not including lesser lights such as ambulance drivers and coroner's technicians. I should assume my learned friend will not put us to the task of proving trivia. We may have to make an application to cross-examine a witness hostile to the crown. We will have some law on that, and the jury may have to be out while we argue it. There will be no issue as to any statements made by the accused to the police — for the simple reason he made none, no doubt having been recently advised by counsel. There will be some technical evidence — fingerprints, none from the accused; blood samples; the autopsy report. We will have the case before the jury within four days."

Horowitz, looking over rimless spectacles, gave Cobb an expression that suggested he was being over-optimistic. "It *sounds* straightforward," he said.

Smythe-Baldwin met his cue and drew a deep, audible breath. "I wish it were," he said. "My learned friend Mr. Cobb, like a man ashamed of tarnished underclothing, is afraid to disclose his case to the defence. I presume he is acting under orders from on high, because I have known Mr. Cobb to be a generous and fair man when empowered to make his own decisions." Smythe-Baldwin had begun speaking quietly, but his voice continued to rise. "I am confidently assured by the crown that witnesses exist who claim to have seen the accused in a window of the building where the murder was alleged to have been committed. It is egregious to suggest that the defence is not entitled to the names and the evidence of these witnesses. You are aware, my lord, that the crown, impelled by motives that in my simple way I cannot pretend to appreciate, has deprived my client of the right of a preliminary hearing. The least we are entitled to by law and by any standard of fairness is a digest of the evidence of these so-called witnesses, and should my friend persist in his stone-walling ways, I intend my thoughts on the matter to be put on record in the courtroom — in a form in which they may be perused ultimately by a higher court, should an appeal unhappily become the vehicle whereby justice is delivered. My first course of action, however, will be to apply to adjourn the trial to some later assize, to permit the crown sufficient time to provide the material which will allow us to make full answer and defence." Smythe-Baldwin spoke now with defiant force, and his words rumbled about the room for a long moment of time.

Horowitz, impassive, swivelled in his chair, and seemed engrossed by the view of parked cars outside his window. "Mr.

Cobb, what do you say?" he asked softly. "We are less than two weeks from a murder trial, and the defence seems to be in the dark about one or two things."

Cobb would show a large and open spirit. "He has a right to their evidence, my lord. Not only am I prepared to give my friend copies of the witness statements, I will be pleased to permit him to interview them — in my presence, of course. But I have reason to believe — and I won't go into this deeply unless Mr. Smythe-Baldwin challenges me — that these witnesses could be in grave peril from the accused." The judge's eyes went up over his glasses again. Cobb continued: "My suggestion is that the information be provided to defence counsel within a couple of days before the trial begins. As of that point I will arrange for police protection for them until their evidence has been heard in court."

"Mr. Smythe-Baldwin?" said the judge.

The lawyer let out his breath slowly. His words marched out, hard and emphatic. "Your lordship knows — and my learned friend knows — that I am not a follower of that less-than-professional practice followed by some inexperienced members of the bar of beginning preparation for a trial only a few days in advance of it. I begin when I am retained. I have been retained for three months. I am not prepared for trial. I will not be prepared for trial until I have examined, digested, and considered every aspect of every word written in every statement taken from every witness. If I am not in possession of the material which we are discussing within the week, I shall formally bring on the adjournment application."

"All right," Horowitz said, turning back in his chair to face the lawyers, "the crown will just have to provide by this weekend whatever police protection is deemed necessary for these witnesses, or a secure place for them to live in the meantime. I'm prepared to make an order to that effect in open court to avoid an adjournment."

Cobb shrugged. "We'll do it," he said. "We wish no delay."

"I thank my friend most graciously," said Smythe-Baldwin, his voice sweet like honey now. "Then perhaps we can deal with another vexing question — wiretaps. I am led to understand the crown claims to be armed with taped telephone conversations, the contents of which have not even vaguely been made known to me. If it is the intention of the prosecution to adduce such evidence, I pray that my learned friend will display sufficient generosity of heart to provide the defence with reasonable notice. If courtesy does not demand production of the transcripts, the Criminal Code will. We are all familiar with Section 173 of the Privacy Act." These words were spoken with stentorian, measured cadence. From behind him, Cobb heard a quieter voice.

"I believe you will find the section is 178 decimal sixteen, subsection four," Jennifer Tann said.

Smythe-Baldwin paused. Cobb waited for the inevitable squelch, then realized the defence lawyer was ignoring her and ploughing ahead. "Of course, if my information is incorrect, and there are no tapes — and I have reason to believe their existence is a figment of someone's fertile imagination — that is an end to it. Perhaps Mr. Cobb can shed some light on the matter."

"I am told there are tapes," Cobb said. "I have warned Mr. Smythe-Baldwin of the possibility. I have not heard them or read transcripts. I am given to understand that his client's voice is not identified, and therefore there will be no attempt to use them as part of the crown's case. Whether they contain material to be used in reply or in cross-examination of his client, I cannot say as yet. My learned friend has no right to disclosure of evidence not a part of the crown's case."

"My friend no doubt will be prepared to argue the issue should the occasion arise," Smythe-Baldwin said primly. "I know of no authority that suggests wiretap evidence can be used even in rebuttal or cross-examination without sufficient notice being given of their contents."

Again the quiet, calm voice from behind them. "Regina versus Sundawa Singh and Lamton, just reported, in the *Western Weeklies*, I think," Tann said.

Cobb now found himself suppressing a smile. Smythe-Baldwin seemed to be giving way to bluster: "In the appropriate arena, and at the appropriate time, I will be only too happy to engage my learned friend in battle over the issue. He will need all the support he can get from that young walking compendium of current Canadian law who is assisting him."

The judge broke in. "I'm not interested in chasing shadows. We'll deal with the issue if it arises. There is nothing more, gentlemen?" No one answered. "The trial will commence with jury selection at ten a.m. Monday, March thirteenth. This is a special assize, and we will have a panel of forty-five prospective jurors. Thank you for coming in."

Outside, in the corridor, Smythe-Baldwin drew Cobb aside, away from the others. "Stay the charge, Foster," he said. "Save yourself a good deal of needless embarrassment."

"How so?"

"We have under subpoena a perfectly reliable witness, a man beyond challenge, who was in the company of our Dr. Au for three hours until and including the time of death of poor Jim Fat, some six miles from the scene of death."

"I'll take my chances with any witness the Surgeon pays to alibi for him," Cobb said. "Even Dr. Au can't afford the price of an honest man."

"Ours is a witness no jury will dare disbelieve," said Smythe-Baldwin.

"The Surgeon was having tea with the Anglican archbishop? Come on, Smitty, I've been hanging around you too long to back away from a bluff."

"I think you may be too good a poker player to call me on this one, Foster. I hold a royal flush."

"We'll see. It can safely be assumed that you are not about to tell me who the paragon is."

"Normally, I would not. Normally, I would tell you, as I have heard it put, to urinate up a rope. But because I respect you and do not wish to endure an old friend's shame, I will bare my Roman breast and full disclosure make."

Smythe-Baldwin paused for effect. Cob saw himself in the role of that consummate courtroom loser Hamilton Burger, waiting for Perry Mason to announce the arrival of the inevitable surprise witness.

"Corporal Everit Cudlipp, senior officer, narcotics division, Royal Canadian Mounted Police."

Friday, the Third Day of March, at Twenty Minutes to Noon

A Special I man came into the monitoring room with a scribbled message from the receptionist and shoved it under Cudlipp's nose. The corporal was listening on his earphones to a slave copy of overnight recordings, and he read the note quickly: "Ev: A lawyer, Mr. Cobb, wants an appointment to talk to you. Left his number. D.M." Cudlipp scribbled his answer: "Tell him I'm on surveillance, can't be researched." The message bearer left the room with the note.

Cudlipp did not want to talk to the prosecutor. If Cobb were going to come at him in court, he would have to do it cold, unprepared. And Cobb would have a damn hell of a time finding Cudlipp during the ten days before the trial was to begin — he was about to take two weeks' holiday leave.

He was apprehensive about the trial — Cobb had some kind of reputation as a needler, a cross-examiner with an array of hooks and jabs. Cudlipp was not going to give him an edge by letting him have the whole alibi in advance. On the other hand, Cudlipp was feeling pretty good about the negotiations. With Alice Carson stiffening his back, he was going for the bundle, the big score. Two hundred and fifty big ones.

A new voice on the recorded phone tap intruded upon his thoughts:

"Hello."

"Yeah, hi."

"Yeah, who's this?"

"Bennie."

"Bennie?"

"Bennie B. Jesus, do you want me to spell it?"

"Oh, Bennie! Long time, Bennie. Hey, how are ya?"

"Okay, okay. Lot's happening. Busy, you know. How you doin', guy?"

"Alive, you know. Despite the heat."

"Yeah, despite the heat."

"So what's up, Bennie?'

"Ah . . . you know, the well's gone dry down my way. You know, the sweep, the rodeo."

"Some folks aren't too hard up."

"You got?"

"I do, I do."

"Bundled?"

"Yeah, but I can't front ya."

"I know. I got the cake."

"Okay. Say, six o'clock, Eighteenth and Alder. Green El Dorado. Got myself a brand new wagon, Bennie."

"Okay, meet you for a —"

"Yeah, for a few beers. How many beers you figure you can consume?"

"Oh, three, I guess. It's good?"

"Dynamite."

"Right on. Lookin' forward to it."

Cudlipp knew that caller's voice, and decided he would put a tail on Bennie after the pick-up and try to catch him dealing. It would be a sawbuck in the can for Mr. Bones, a three-time loser.

"Got the sucker by the short and curlies, old boy," said Flaherty with a slow, sexy wink. Charrington flinched. He knew the undercover officer had performed on the stage before joining the DEA, but did the role have to be so over-played?

"Are we ready to move?" he asked.

"Couple of weeks. Don't get your ass in a knot. I want to play out some more line and see if the fish will run."

The thin moustache on Charrington's stiff upper lip seemed to bristle. Flaherty lacked the decorum that Charrington expected from the regular members of the force. The style was outrageously gauche.

The Organic Apple, where Jennifer Tann persuaded Cobb to come for lunch, was obviously her local, her hang-out. She joked with the staff and some of the customers — a leather, beads, and denim crowd. Cobb dined on an avocado-and-bean-sprout sandwich, while Tann played with a small salad and chatted gaily about herself, about her travels (she had been in the Far East, searching for her roots), her hobbies (jade and delicate Oriental watercolors), her forms of recreation (yoga, swimming — she had been a lifeguard — and, predictably, backgammon). She gaily tripped through one topic after another, pausing only sometimes to catch her breath. Cobb listened less than he watched, and it was her face he watched: expressive, open, her almond green eyes flashing and brilliant.

She turned the subject to the meeting two days earlier with the judge and defence lawyers.

"I think I took a little stuffing out of his shirt," she said. "I don't *dislike* the old guy. I guess he's okay — with his big successful image and all *that* rubadub." She shrugged, with a bird-like twist of her head that seemed to be her trademark. And she laughed: a light, giggling, tinkling sound that Cobb decided he liked. "It's that stuffy pinstripe image that I can't dig," she said. "I mean, I used to go out with a lawyer in his firm. They're *all* like him, over-bearing, preening themselves like prize roosters. This dude, his lawyer, took me home to meet his mom one day. Fat-cat Shaughnessy family. You know the scene — storekeeper's daughter obviously gold-digging in the family mine, and mommy's stuck-up little nose crinkling as if she smelled fish and onions on my hands, if you know what I mean. You don't talk much, do you, Mr. Cobb? You just sit there being bored while I rattle on like some spinny over-age teeny-bopper, all mouth, no brain. She said, hoping he will disagree. Do you think I'm spinny? Do I rattle on too much?"

"I'm hanging on every word."

"I'll bet." She laughed and shook her loose hair back from her face. "So anyway, my boyfriend. My last-ditch effort at making him human was to try to turn him on at a party where there were a few joints floating around. He went white and sort of fainted, and I looked at him, just sad, and said to myself, I said, hey, J.T., there's no hope. The man is *super* straight."

Cobb was looking at her with one eyebrow raised.

"I can see by the supercilious look on your face that you do not approve. Dope-smoking hippie — take away her licence to practise. Do you think that is a terrible thing, Mr. Cobb? You, with your disapproving scowl. Obviously you've never turned on. Too bad. Loosens you up." Her eyes flashed green at him, laughing.

Cobb just looked at her blankly, searching with his tongue for a bean sprout stuck between his molars.

"Are you going to turn me in?" she said in a plaintive, teasing voice. "Will I be running my daddy's vegetable store for the rest of my life? Do I shock you? Tell me if I am evil. Do you think I'm evil? Look me in the eyes."

The reason Cobb had not been looking at her eyes was that his were absent-mindedly studying the gentle curve of small, high breasts, outlined in taut detail through her thin blouse. Suddenly he was aware that the words were no longer rolling from Tann's mouth. In the shock of silence, he took his eyes away from her body and looked up with a start, with a red-faced grin.

"Hi," she said.

Cobb shifted back in his chair and decided to relax.

"Why," he asked, "is so unlikely a person as you working in the prosecutor's office? Prosecutors are supposed to be stuffy old crocks, like me." The comment was meant to be self-depreciating but somehow came out self-pitying.

"I'm just learning the ropes — do I call an old crock like you 'Mr. Cobb,' or what? — so I'll know what happens on the other side of the fence when I start defending people. When I go out on my own. Eventually. Also, I need the bread. Mom and Dad barely make it working all day and night in a little store — and I mean a *little* store. A *Chinese* corner store, if you know what I mean. And it's the same store my grandparents ran before they died. And *their* parents came over as contract laborers on the railway. I'm a fourth-generation Canadian," she said proudly. She paused to take a breath.

"Foster. People call me Fos. You can call me 'Fossil.'"

"Is it a game? Are you modest, or are you really putting yourself down? I mean, old crock? Fossil?"

"I guess I'm hoping you will tell me I am not all that bad." He smiled.

She studied him hard, then smiled back. "Well, maybe you *are* an old fossil. Mr. Fossil Cobb, the barrister." She reached out and touched his hand softly. Cobb's impulse was to jerk his hand away, but he stilled it, and her fingers touching him were long and fine and cool. "And I being too forward?" she said, withdrawing her hand and slapping it in mock punishment for her transgression. "I'm sorry," she said. "I touch a lot."

"It's too late," Cobb said. "Now you'll have to marry me."

"Oh, yeah? You aren't already taken?" She leaned toward him like a conspirator, one of her eyebrows arched, and spoke in a stage whisper: "But does your wife understand you?"

No! Cobb wanted to shout. Instead: "Currently, we are undergoing a re-evaluation of our respective marital roles within the framework of connubial stress."

"Ah, so, said the Chinese detective, you are breaking up. A chance for the Dragon Lady to move in." She batted her eyes at him comically, then pushed her empty plate away and leaned forward on her elbows, holding her face in the palms of her hands. "Tell me true, Fossil, are you unhappy in your marriage?"

After a few moments he said simply: "I would have to say I care for her."

"Then I'll just be your heartbroken friend. Tell me about her. Do you think I have any business asking you these questions? No, you don't. It's none of my business, is it?"

He could think of nothing to say. Deborah was beautiful, tough, sexy, charming to others, and cruel, it seemed, to him. She had moods that left him outside her, unable to touch her. He wanted to make the marriage work. But why? Out of stubbornness? What could Fossil say about his red-haired queen?

Finally: "She's a ski instructor."

"So she's a jock." She said, then studied him for a reaction. "Was that unfair? Do you not react? Do you always sit there like a big grapefruit? Do you have to wear that awful Clint Eastwood dead-pan? Are you always so WASPY? God, no feelings. You'd make a great judge — you're pompous enough. Are you pompous? Or just mysterious? Am I bugging you with all my prying?"

"Yes."

She gave him a look that said she was disgusted, giving up on him. "Okay, you want to talk business. Here's Jennifer Tann, very business-like." And she picked up her briefcase, withdrew a thirty-cent ball-point pen and a pad of paper, stuck a pair of wire-rim glasses on her nose, crossed her legs, and sat poised, wearing a sour stenographer's face.

Cobb grinned, and finally broke up.

"Good God," she said, "he's human."

Cobb found his eyes had slipped again to her blouse. He shook his head as if coming out of a coma, and reached down into his briefcase, pulling out a file.

"All right," he said, "let's start with Charlie Ming. He's a reluctant witness. Au or one of his top men got to Charlie after he signed his statement, so he's now changed his story, and he will probably deny that Au was anywhere near the H-K Meats. I have to interview him yet, and maybe he'll come across, or maybe we can get him declared adverse. Get me a brief on the law of hostile witnesses, applying it to the circumstances of this case."

He paused. "Is there coffee in this place, or do they consider that part of an imperialist conspiracy to keep Latin-American dictators in power?"

Tann laughed, again the cheerful giggling sound, a sound that made him want to make her laugh. "Comfrey tea is what you want," she said, and yelled to the kitchen: "Comfrey tea for my friend and me!"

"Number two," Cobb continued. "Wiretaps. The city narcs, not the RCMP, have a tap on someone's line, and they've been listening to people talk about the Jim Fat murder. I don't have the transcripts yet, but Au's name, or some reference to him, shows up. Can we use anything like that in cross?"

"In cross?"

"Cross-examination of Au, if his lawyers decide to put him on the stand. Anyway, you know the law there. Obviously."

"I did a paper on wiretaps. First thing I plan to do when I get out on my own is have the whole wiretap law ruled unconstitutional, contrary to the Bill of Rights, the Magna Carta, the UN Declaration of Human Freedoms, and the Ten Commandments. Anyway, I'll get together a brief on that."

Cobb returned the file to the briefcase. "I guess that's all for now. The whole key to this trial will be to put together a strong enough case to force Au to give evidence, to expose him to my cross." He paused, put his hand to his forehead, and closed his eyes. Then he looked up. "There's a missing link — a third man in the room, I think, in addition to the guy who was outside standing watch.

Maybe all Smythe-Baldwin has to show is that someone else had the same opportunity as Au to kill Jim Fat, and there's his reasonable doubt. We think the motive has to do with Jim Fat turning informer, but I have not been able to nail that down."

Cobb paused, sipping his hot comfrey tea. "Our main problem is that Smythe-Baldwin claims he has a cop who will alibi for his client."

"He has a what? A cop to give evidence for him?"

"Yes. I don't know him. A Corporal Cudlipp. A Mountie in narcotics. I've been trying to reach him — no success. All the drug prosecutions in this town are handled by federal prosecutors, so I have never seen him on the stand. I'm going to try to get some kind of book on the guy. He may have been paid off."

"A corrupt narc?" she said. "God forbid. Who *can* you trust?"

"Narcs, my poor innocent, rub shoulders with all sorts of not-so-innocent folks — and some of these folks have big money to throw around. And sometimes it rubs off on them."

"Heavy," she said.

"Yeah," he said, "it's heavy."

The psychiatrist sighed and shook his head. "All right, you're on the needle. I hope you sterilize it. Dirty needles cause hepatitis and tetanus. You'll end up sick, and I'll have to send you to a *real* doctor. Two caps a day. That's what you tell me. Two caps a day. Yeah, sure. Who can believe a junkie? I've never known an honest junkie. It's four caps, isn't it, Fos?" He threw his hands up in disgust.

"So what am I going to do?"

"I don't *know* what you're going to do. Figure it out for yourself. I've got my own problems. Your trouble is you came off the tit too soon. You know what I figure? The hypodermic syringe is a big tit. When you shoot up, you're breast-feeding. Only problem is, you don't have a mother to wean you, so you have to do it yourself. Listen, Foster, I laid this on you ten years ago. The craving starts up in times of crisis. I warned you about psychosexual crises. Just control your intake, or you'll develop too much tolerance. Keep the level within bounds, and you can handle your trials."

"And how am I supposed to resolve it? My so-called sexual crisis."

Dr. Broussaud leaned toward Cobb and looked hard into his eyes.

"Let me lay something on you, Foster. This comes more from a friend than a psychiatrist. As far as your marriage is concerned, you're simply going to have to decide whether you want to fish or cut bait. You suffer from a trial-lawyer syndrome: you hate losing. You can't handle the thought that you may be losing your wife. If you want the marriage to work, *you* are going to have to work at *it*. But I don't know if you do. The two of you have been winging off in different directions ever since you met." He paused, bit his lip.

"Okay, look," he continued, "the movie started off great — eighteen-year-old college queen meets jailbird-junkie turned crown attorney. She's infatuated. But she's twelve years younger than her husband. He's had *his* excitement: a poker-playing pool-hall shark who got hooked on dope and pulled a robbery. He settles down, puts that all behind him, retreats to his den, surrounds himself with his pipes and law books and Mozart and Vivaldi, and she's *bored*. She can't *drag* him out to a discotheque or a party."

"Yeah, well, she won't go down to the pool hall with me, either."

"That's supposed to be sardonic, but it's probably typical of your relationship. Anyway, what has she got? She's got a guy who's just like her father — a stuffy law professor. She's not quite ready to marry her father. But of course Foster Cobb worships her old man, and the two of them can sit around for hours talking about jurisprudence and listening to the professor's Schubert."

"Bach. He likes baroque —"

Broussaud cut him off. "Bach. Whatever. But here's one of the problems: You can't *bear* the thought of the hurt your beloved old mentor would suffer if his favorite and only son-in-law breaks up with his daughter. So the marriage drags on, because you feel responsible, not to your wife, but to her father."

"Jesus," said Cobb softly.

"Oh, yeah, she had a program for you: politics, a lucrative private practice in a big firm, an acceptable level of fame and fortune. You say the hell with that; you're happy where you are. And it gets *more* boring for her. She tries for a family, but her periods continue to arrive as faithfully as the month's new moon. So the cheerful-homemaker trip is a failure. She takes up skiing again, and you and your friends the Santorinis buy a condominium at Whistler, and she's up there every weekend giving ski lessons. And *you* stop going with her because you complain you can't keep up to her on the hill. Well, it's almost as if you're asking her to fuck around up there —"

"That's crap!"

"— because you're looking for some evidence, so you can blame *her* if the marriage fails. 'That's crap,' he says. Well, it's not a very heroic masculine trip to set your wife up to do the dirty work in a marriage break-up, so you're not going to admit *that* to yourself."

"Aw, c'mon."

"Well, what do *you* think she's doing up there, Fos? Drinking hot toddies and twiddling her thumbs? Ah, shit, I shouldn't even be doing this. If the psychiatric association found out, they'd revoke my licence."

"Well, goddamnit, Jack, I love her."

"You don't even know what love is at this stage. It could be some kind of dependency trip." Broussaud reflected for a moment. "Yeah, in a way, she's always been some sort of crutch for you. You didn't need junk when she was around for you."

"Well, I don't think she's screwing around on me." Cobb folded his arms and looked stubbornly at Broussaud.

Broussaud exploded. "Well, why the *fuck* do you think you're wired again?"

Cobb reeled back, stunned.

Broussaud sighed and shook his head.

"Sorry, Fos. Look, you try to think some of this through, and we'll get together in a week or so. I think you're going to have to get into your head and pump out some of the shit that's blocking you from dealing realistically with the marriage. All right. I've got people waiting outside, and they're crazier than you."

Cobb took in a full lungful of air and slowly breathed out. "Okay," he said. "Yeah, okay." Then he paused. "Look, Jack, speaking of crazies, just before you fire me out the door: I've got a murder I'm prosecuting, and there's a letter from the crown shrink suggesting a sociopathic personality with some sexual dysfunction. The guy's into some weird kind of castration thing."

"That's a good one. Okay. Sociopath. Psychopath. Same guy. No loyalty, no guilt, no conscience. But usually no big sex-kinkiness factor, unless he has some kind of sadomasochistic hangup." He paused and reflected. "Now, there is a kind of psychopath, when he's exposed to stress, he can develop a paranoid psychosis, delusions of persecution, that sort of thing. Centre on some guy as a mortal enemy."

"Dangerous?"

"Depends. Could be if he gets into some wild psychotic trip. Charlie Manson-ing around your drawing room. Get a guy like that, with a tendency for a little violence, you might want to head for the fort, draw the gates and man the cannons."

Friday, the Third Day of March, at Six O'Clock in the Evening

Cobb dragged his tired body and aching head into his apartment, seeking solace. Unfortunately, this afternoon Cobb had drawn — in the lottery of the provincial courts — one of the lesser lights of the lower bench, and his impaired-driver client, doubtless guilty but not proven so to Cobb's mind, ended surrendering his licence and five hundred dollars.

Deborah was in the bathroom, making up. At its doorway, Cobb sipped a glass of water and watched. She was naked, softly damp from the shower. Her movements were liquid. The hair dryer buzzed softly, blowing into the plastic cap over her hair and ears. He watched her a long while, and she glanced at him through the mirror and must have seen the longing in his eyes. She even smiled, and that was a very good sign, he thought. He scanned the curve of her body, her breasts, her buttocks, and felt a dryness in his mouth and sexual tension surge through his system.

She smiled again at him, through the mirror, not turning around, and it seemed the smile was an honest one, so he stepped behind her, close, and put his hands on her, caressing her.

"When do we have to be at the Santorinis'?" he asked. "Do we have time?"

She did not move away from him, but attentively applied eye makeup, seemingly oblivious to his hardness against her. "I'm sorry," she said. "I can't hear you. The hair dryer."

"I said," he called, "do we have time — before we have to be at Eddie and Martha's?"

She switched the blower off and smiled a third time — significantly? — saying: "Why don't you get undressed and get into the shower? You're all sweaty."

What was that? A yes? A maybe? A gentle tease? Cobb did not risk clarification, and began undressing. Deborah switched the hair dryer back on and continued to work with an array of cosmetic tools spread across the tile counter. Inside the shower Cobb washed away the day's toil and sweat, the hot water beating over his skin and over his stiff erection. Through the shower door he could see his wife's body shimmering. He breathed heavily with the need for her. Three weeks had passed since they had last made love, and there had been a month before that. So far, it had been a barren year, broken only by fleeting occasions of union.

Cobb towelled himself, stepped from the stall, and approached Deborah again, moving his body into the warmth of her back, his cock hard against her buttocks, his hands sliding about her hips to the front of her, along the gentle lines of her belly, and under her breasts.

She appeared, or pretended, not to notice.

"God *damn* you, Deb, let's stop the games and let's get it on. Or let's just call it quits."

But he knew she could not hear him.

Again she turned off the blower. "Cobb, I've spent the last half-hour getting ready. I don't want to ruin my face."

She leaned away from him, toward the mirror, applying lipstick. "Maybe after we get back," she said. "I just can't hack it right now."

"Jesus, Deb, we can be a little late. We don't have to show up panting on their doorstep at exactly seven o'clock." His hips undulated lightly against hers, but met no responding rhythm, yet Cobb was drawing hope from her failure to physically reject his advances. He bent his knees slightly, and his penis felt the softness of her hair.

"I need you," he said. "It's been nearly a month. You must feel the same."

She sucked her breath in sharply. "Christ!" she said angrily. "Then do it! Do it! Get it over with! You're already half-way up my cunt. Do it, goddamnit!"

Cobb flushed and backed up, trembling with anger. He hissed at her: "What is making you so frigid? Does it *all* get used up on Whistler Mountain?"

She wheeled, slapped him, and ran from the bathroom, tears already beginning to discolor the makeup.

Cobb slammed the bathroom door shut, locked it, and angrily masturbated.

The Cobbs were more than fashionably late arriving at the Santorini residence, a flat, rectangular structure spread across a manicured lot in the British Properties — a prosperous subdivision in the lower reaches of the North Shore mountains. Below the house, the lights of Vancouver blinked across English Bay through the cold March night.

Martha Santorini greeted them at the door. "My God, what a relief," she said. "I was beginning to think the big-time criminal lawyer had decided to snub us."

The muscles of Cobb's face pulled together a smile, and he gave his coat. In the living room he could see about ten guests, all lawyers and spouses, seated on heavy furniture around the fireplace, eating buffet-style and chatting brightly.

Ed Santorini's voice called from the kitchen, where he was attending a sirloin-tip roast. "You guys decide to come by bicycle or what?" he shouted. "I was just going to apply for a bench warrant. You're both charged with failing to appear." He guffawed, the laughter that of a practised host. "Come in here. The roast is hot; the wine is red; the canapés are eaten. Shuck your coats and pick up your plates. It's a twelve-pound monster, so eat your hearts out." Again the braying laugh.

Cobb was sullen, prepared to dampen all conviviality. Deborah, however, seemed prepared to make up his deficit, hugging and kissing Martha and cheerfully waving to the guests. Despite the cheerless drive from their home, she was now radiant. She apologized with a lie: "Sorry, folks, Foster got so wrapped up at his office he was an hour late getting home." Her face carefully repaired, she was wearing a backless, braless, ankle-length gown.

Five pairs of watchful male eyes followed Deborah Cobb as she wound her way through the living room into the kitchen, her red hair dancing on her shoulders, hips rolling, beasts bobbing, voice sparkling with apparent happiness as she greeted friends. Cobb followed, his face wrenched into a poor, mooning grin. Inside the kitchen, behind the large roast, stood Santorini, chief prosecutor in a chef's *toque*. He put down his implements and put his arm around Deborah's lower back, gave her a quick cuddle and a gentle buss on the cheek. Santorini took Deborah by the waist and Cobb by the arm, bustling them to the bar.

"No time for cocktails," he said, pouring instead from a wine bottle into two crystal glasses. "The Bordeaux, alas, has disappeared. I offer in its place a nice St. Vincent, 1971, very full-bodied, very pleasant." He gave the bottle an expert half-turn as he raised it from each glass, and with a gallant flourish presented the glasses to the Cobbs.

Santorini was large in his gestures, especially when drinking. As a trial lawyer he was guilty of stentorian sermons. Robustly handsome and knowing it, he moved about the courtroom like a peacock. Cobb liked him, because behind the thin parchment of Santorini's blustering exterior was a generous and gallant ally. They counted each other as their respective best friends, and had grown to know each other over the years. Two years ago Santorini had been chosen over Cobb as senior city prosecutor, and openly stated he was unhappy with the choice, having considered his friend to be the better man, even saying so to the members of the police commission. Cobb's dark past was not discussed by the commission, of course, but hovered above their discussions like a fat balloon that everyone preferred to pretend was not there.

Deborah took her plate to the living room. Her husband stayed in the kitchen and listened to Santorini talk. The senior prosecutor complained as usual about the workload and heavy trial lists. He recounted to a distracted Cobb developments in a current fraud trial involving a lawyer who had tried to get too rich too quickly. Cobb was not helping the conversation out, and after a while Santorini said: "What's eating you, guy?"

Cobb shook his head. "I guess I'm feeling the strain — getting a practice going, a heavy trial coming up, Deborah and I are fighting. I'm bad company. I'll get it together."

Santorini put his arm around him. "Listen, Fos," he said, "once the trial is over, we'll all go up to Whistler, ski all day, and get pissed." He began to march him out to the living room. "Hey, how's that little chickie we sent over to help you?" he asked, leering. "Probably a nice little piece of ass if you're into trying something different."

Cobb flinched. Santorini enjoyed a locker-room reputation as a ladies' man, but Cobb doubted that he indulged in extramarital pursuits as frequently as he boasted of them.

Cobb paused before they entered the living room. "Eddie, do you know a Corporal Everit Cudlipp, RCMP narcotics? Smythe-Baldwin threatens to call him for alibi evidence. The guy won't return my calls. It makes me edgy."

Santorini shrugged. "I wonder what kind of game that old owl is playing now," he said. "Cudlipp is your standard-brand cop. Above average mind. Does heavy drug cases. The feds think he's fine. I've seen him in court — pretty solid on the stand. He'd be a tough nut to turn in cross. I suppose it's possible that the Surgeon didn't do this one — who knows? Maybe once in a while he's *not* guilty."

"He's guilty," Cobb said. "They don't come guiltier."

"That's the spirit," said Santorini, slapping Cobb on the back. "That's thinking like a prosecutor. That's what I like." And they passed into the living room, Santorini brandishing another bottle of St. Vincent '71, determined to see no glass remain unfilled.

Billy Sam had slept through the day, and by evening his head began pulsing brutally, and it woke him up like an alarm clock. Beside him, sleeping on her back, Millie Redfeather hoarsely snored. Both were clothed, but Redfeather's jeans were down, exposing her thick, mottled thighs and hips. Her pubic hair was matted where Billy Sam had attempted a clumsy, rubbery entrance about twelve hours earlier. He had encountered neither passion nor resistance from his common-law wife, who was already in drunken slumber as Sam exerted himself manfully atop her passive form, swearing at his limp and uncooperative member. A greater want than the need for sexual satisfaction had now overtaken his body: a fire had lit up his belly and spread to his throat, dry like tinder. No extinguisher could be found in their small room — the bottle of wine that he had husbanded through the previous night had fallen from the dresser and broken, leaving a sticky stain. So Billy Sam searched through the jungle of Millie Redfeather's purse, finding three dollars and some change — enough for a start. And more could be bummed on Hastings Street near the entrance to one or another of the nearby beer parlors.

Fastening his belt, Billy Sam woozily withdrew from the room — Suite D on the second floor of the Chungking Rooms — stepped gingerly down the dark stairwell and out into the dusk, groping his way to the Orient Hotel on skid row, where draft costs fifty cents a glass. He would wait for his woman to join him. They would drink together and would find happiness by midnight.

Skid row, squeezed into several blocks between Chinatown and the Burrard Inlet docks, comprises rows of poor rooming houses, junk shops, and barren square hotels and stores and coffee chops.

Chungking Alley was at the border of Chinatown and skid row, in an area of warehouses, tenements, and thirty-dollar-a-month hotels. It was a dead-end lane, narrow and forbidding. There were a few old rooming houses here, a small café, and one commercial building, which housed H-K Meats — a wholesale emporium catering to the Chinese restaurants — and, on the second floor, the Nationalist Benevolent Society. The only habitués of the area were drunks and bums and whores past their prime.

And because there was damn-all to do in this bleak outpost of old Vancouver, Police Constable Number 203 Terry Patrick had decided that he and his rookie partner, Number 416 Jake Moeller, could take half-hour coffee breaks — every two hours. What end was there for two men to be constantly standing guard on the Chungking Rooms?

Moeller, three months out of police academy, was concluding the first half-hour of his first coffee break. The last sip from his milkshake gurgled up his straw as he closed his book, a thin paperback entitled *Teen-Aged Nymphos — Their Case Histories*, by Arvid Schroff. Chapter Eight, the story of Miss Wendy K., the Teen-aged Orgy Queen, had left him flushed and hot. Moeller, a farm boy, had found an erotic fantasy world in the little news stands and confectioneries of skid road. He put the book in his inside jacket pocket, then rose from his seat in the little wooden booth at the Jo Wat Café, just half a block down from the Chungking Rooms, hunched into his coat, paid Mr. Jo Wat his sixty cents, and walked out.

There were stars out; it was crisp and cool and windy. He walked the street. After an hour of this, he would relieve Patrick up on the second floor, where his partner was sitting on a hard wooden chair, watching the doors to the rooms of an old man and a young boy. The hallway in the rooming house was drafty, but Moeller would keep himself warm with Chapter Nine: "The Strange Case of Marylou G. — Pigtails and Perversions."

A community within a community, the junkies lived among the rubbies, but were not close to them. In the heart of skid row, yet somehow not a part of it, there was the Corner, the addicts' Mecca, their prison, their Emerald City — where the junkies dance the junkie dance and score the magic powder that brings their dreams alive, and their nightmares. The Corner, as a corner, is quite an ordinary intersection, and tourists might walk by looking for the action and, not seeing it, shrug and pass on. They might have found it had they dared enter the dank bistros and beer parlors nearby, or the greasy coffee salons; and even then, their eyes untrained, they would not have seen the ritual of the Corner. The rhythms are there to be felt only by those attuned.

It is true that the Corner has a physical reality. It can be found on a street map as the intersection of Hastings and Columbia. The police, the social workers, and the other outsiders see it simply as that — an intersection. Where losers hang out. But the junkies do not see it in geographical terms. They see it as an abstraction, a style, a ceremony, a celebration. The Corner has its own liturgy; its heaven and hell do not await an afterlife. The sacrament of its ceremony is offered through a drugstore syringe. There are rites that are performed between the buyer and the pusher, and they are observed by custom: the language of the offer, the structuring of the exchange, the indications, the nods, the glances, the lethargic pirouettes of the dealers drifting among the tables.

The Corner is a community, tight, paranoid, persecuted like an ancient heretic sect; its membership is exclusive, the badge of entry being a long narrow tattoo of scar tissue inside the elbow. There is little trust in this community, and very little love, but its members, disgorged from the jails, always return, unable to leave forever its mystery.

Patrol cars cruise slowly up and down the streets, and the people of the Corner stand in the doorways, nodding, stoned, and distant, fearing the police, but knowing that the Corner does not happen without the police. The police must play a role, or the Corner has no meaning.

It is here, at the Corner, that the heroin marketplace completes its chain: from importer, to front end, to mixer, to middleman, to pusher, the final transaction being the sale of a single capsule from junkie dealer to junkie buyer. Everyone near the bottom of the chain is an addict, and the buyer one day will be the pusher the next, selling to earn a few hours of joy for himself.

Laszlo Plizit knew the Corner, but was not of it. He held the junkies in contempt. They were slaves, and Plizit was not about to become a slave to any thing or any person. Heroin was too down for him, and he preferred it mixed with Methedrine: speedballs. But usually he did straight speed, popping whites from about noon, when he got up, until midnight, when it was time to slow down, and when he would normally do a couple of downers to ease off. The ups kept him going and kept him sharp on the job for the various tasks assigned by Dr. Au. Plizit was a Hungarian who had escaped from an armed-robbery sentence in the old country when the jails were opened in 1956. He was now Au's bodyguard and odd-job man.

It was eight p.m., and Plizit was sitting alone in one of the stark drinking halls near the Corner. Two glasses of draft beer were in front of him on the terry-cloth table cover, and he was taking a mouthful every few minutes, once in a while washing down a pill. The combination of beer and speed made him feel free and brave.

The first task assigned by Au this night was straightforward: effect the sale of two ounces to a man from Spokane who was to meet him here. A Black who would be wearing a silver ring in his left ear. The man from Spokane would be looking for a face showing a five-inch scar running across the nose to a point under the right eye. The scar was a souvenir from a reluctant target who had slashed Plizit's face open with a knife, paralyzing the eye. Otherwise his kills had been clean.

The man came in on time and for a few moments peered about. Then he sat at a table next to Plizit, who studied him. Brown-skinned. Too short and emaciated for a cop. Besides, the bulls don't pierce their ears. He motioned for the man to join him and waited for the waiter to drop two more glasses on the table.

"You know Jimmy?" Plizit said. His accent was pronounced.

"I know Jimmy, and Lou and Lakey."

"What are their last names?"

"Jimmy Anderson, Lou Snider, Lakey Lakefield."

"Why did you come to Vancouver here?"

"We tried Seattle. It's dry, man. We'd be into something regular if this goes."

"Who do you know in Seattle?" Plizit was being doubly careful.

"Well, there's Rosie Jackson. Creaky. Link Jones."

"Who else, white?"

"Ianozzo. McKinnon."

Plizit nodded. "You want two?"

"Yeah, two complete. I'll pay forty-five per."

"You know the costs. Bottom is five thousand. Ten thousand for two units, no discount, do you see? I have thought it is all arranged." There was an edge of Plizit's voice. He did not want to horse around.

"Right. I dig it. What about a little tester? You got a safe place?"

It was arranged they would go upstairs to one of the rooms usually reserved for hookers. Plizit gave the man at the desk a few dollars for a key. Upstairs, the buyer cooked a little bit up from Plizit's bag, and cranked up, using his own outfit. He sat on the bed after that and looked up at the ceiling, breathing slowly and getting into it. "Yeah," he said after a pause. "Yeah."

Plizit took out a small bottle, tapped a pill from it into his hand, and popped it into his mouth. He watched the man, focussing his good eye to coordinate with the wayward one.

"It's been stepped on a few times," the man said.

"We get it this way," Plizit said, lying. "It comes this way, you see. It ain't your brown Mexican shit you used to. We have almost pure White Lady, no mix." But Plizit knew the man was getting off on it.

The customer hefted the two ounces, and Plizit knew the man

was experienced and could gauge weight accurately. He also knew the man or his people would step on the dope about eight times and make a killing from it.

"Eighty-seven American okay?" he asked. "That's less than fifteen per cent off your dollar."

"Okay," Plizit said after a little mental arithmetic. "Eighty-seven U.S." The man paid him in large bills.

The buyer took the ounces, threw his outfit in a wastebasket, and they left. "You the one they call the Hunkie?" he asked, smiling, just before they split up at the bottom of the sitars.

"Not to my face," said Plizit stonily, and walked back out through the beer parlor and onto the street, then south toward Chinatown.

His .45 was in his pocket, with a silencer. His second task was to kill an old man and a boy. He had heard there might be a policeman on the street outside the building, but risks were part of his work, and he had to admit to himself that they added spice to one's life.

After the other guests departed, Foster and Deborah Cobb stayed on, drinking cognac late into the night and listening to Santorini's new *Don Giovanni*.

At two a.m. there was a telephone call, and Martha Santorini told Cobb it was for him, and that it was important.

"It's me," Honcho Harrison said. "Sorry about this. I know it's late and all, but I've been trying to reach you every place I could think of. We got one of the Surgeon's punks in the cooler. Name of Laszlo Plizit. Picked him up at the Chungking Rooms. The little arsehole is in for it this time. You better get down here fast, because I'm just about to start talking to him. He pulled a good one."

Cobb thought his case against Dr. Au was blown.

Saturday, the Fourth Day of March, at a Quarter to One O'Clock in the Morning

There was no bull patrolling the street after all. That would make the task simpler. Plizit could see lights from second-floor windows of the Chungking Rooms, and that was a good sign, too. The old man and the kid were probably at home.

His best bet would be just to walk into the building, knock on the door, say hello, enter, kill them, and not fart around. Maybe it would not be necessary to use a chunk at all if these people could not move very fast. He would rather just use his hands, or hit them, causing as little noise as possible. But he had a silencer.

Before he entered the building, Plizit popped a couple of ups to make him sharp and alert. He was about to put the bottle away when he thought, what the hell, and swallowed six more for a big kick. May as well have a blast while I'm at it, he thought. Then he went through the doorway and up a flight of stairs. The stairs turned at a landing, half-way up, and he paused there, the speed starting to buzz him fast. He stepped carefully the rest of the way up, avoiding a creaky-looking step, and at the top he peeked down the corridor.

He saw a cop.

The uppers were popping and bubbling in his stomach now.

Holy Jesus, he thought — the heat! What a bitch.

The man was sitting on a hard wooden chair, reading a pocket book and kind of rubbing himself. His holster was clipped closed.

The ups were hitting him harder, jangling him. His plans for an easy hit were screwed. But this was what he got paid for. He knew he had to do the number, or deal with Dr. Au over it, and *that* could be even more dangerous.

He had never iced a pig before.

So. Think. Organize.

But suddenly the gears were spinning too fast, and his body was beginning to jerk and jump, adrenaline and amphetamine pouring explosively through his arteries.

Whoa, he thought. Slow down! Stop shaking!

Okay. Go up smiling and pop him close.

No, no. The silencer. Hit him while he's reading the book. Yeah, the silencer.

He fixed it to the gun.

Stop shaking, stop shaking. One clean shot, Laszlo. Please, God make it a good one. Please, God, make it just one good one.

His heart was thundering in his ears.

One shot. The bullets were blunted.

Please, God, don't let him get on me his gun.

He leaned forward. The cop was twenty feet away, still reading. Plizit held the gun in both hands to steady his fire.

Then he froze.

From behind him, coming up the stairwell, came the sound of drunken song — a dissonant choir it sounded to his erupting senses. In reality there were only two voices. He heard their steps now, moving up toward the landing mid-way between the floors.

The whites were giving him a full rush now. His mind raced and went nowhere.

"'My bonnie lies over the ocean,'" the voices sang. "'My bonnie lies over the sea . . .'" Then they were at the landing below him, staring at him, bleary and swollen with beer and wine.

"Who the hell?" Billy Sam asked, clutching a half-filled bottle of André's Cold Duck.

Millie Redfeather giggled. "Jus' in time for party," she cried. "Billy, give the man a drink. Have a party . . ."

Something snapped in Plizit, and he became unfrozen. He wheeled at them and fired, the bullet discharging with a soft thunk through the silencer, exploding the bottle of Cold Duck and sending a wash of wine against the wall.

Sam opened his eyes in disbelief, then charged, rushing up the steps, gripping the neck of the broken bottle like a dagger. Plizit moved sluggishly, as if in a dream, and when his right index finger found the strength to pull the trigger again, Sam was close enough to jar his arm. This bullet ripped a slab of plaster from the wall, leaving laths exposed.

Redfeather stood at the landing seven steps below them, her fingers pressed to her mouth. She was shrieking.

At the top of the staircase, with an erection, was Constable Moeller. He did not see the gun in Plizit's hand, because that hand was pinned beneath him. What the constable saw was a small man — Plizit — lying ungainly athwart the steps and heading down them on his ass, at the same time kicking a leg high into the air to fend of a bigger man — Billy Sam — who was bringing the cutting edges of the bottle down upon the smaller man's face, a grey rictus of fear.

The constable knew what he had to do. His training had been specific on the point. When a life is in danger, you do not fire in the air or in the ground. You do not try to disable or wound. Shooting at a man's gun is Hollywood stuff, and only John Wayne did it well.

You take your best aim at the most obvious vital target, and pump.

Moeller already had his revolver unholstered, and it was in his right hand, pointed down at a forty-five-degree angle, in line with the point which Billy Sam's forehead would reach in exactly one-quarter of a second, assuming the head's continued downward movement.

His left hand still clutched *Teen-Aged Nymphos*, his middle finger stuck between the pages to mark the point at which he had been interrupted.

As he pulled the trigger, his cock went limp.

The first bullet entered two centimetres above Billy Sam's right eye. The second went dead through the cornea, anterior chamber, and pupil of that right eye. The third shattered the cheekbone two centimetres below. The fourth went through the right cheek and exited through the back of the neck. The fifth caught the edge of the jawbone and ricocheted to the inside, splintering Billy Sam's face, causing flesh, teeth, and bone to explode outwards. As each bullet struck, Sam jerked back several inches until finally his corpse tripped backwards down the steps, moving like a headless chicken, slammed against the wall at the landing, and sagged slowly into its own puddle of blood.

Screaming and whooping, Millie Redfeather thundered like a moose up the stairs and piled on Moeller, a tackle atop a straying quarterback, her face livid with hatred — her weight, her breath, and his terror combining to render him helpless.

Plizit rolled over, freeing his gun arm and bring the .45 to bear upon the two people wrestling at the top of the stairs.

Moeller caught a glimpse of the gun, and with strength born of panic he rolled, getting on top of Redfeather, whose nails clawed gouges of flesh from his cheeks and neck.

Plizit's hand was wildly shaking and jumping when he fired and struck Moeller's left shoulder. Moeller shot without aiming, the bullet skewering the floor boards harmlessly.

He was still pumping, the empty chambers clicking hollowly, when Plizit pulled his trigger again, the bullet cutting through Moeller's neck and severing the carotid artery.

By this time Selwyn Loo, his eyes looming large behind the thickness of his spectacles, was peering through an open three inches of doorway in Suite B, watching Millie Redfeather scrambling from beneath Moeller's lifeless form.

The muscles and tendons of Plizit's knees were the consistency of Play Dough, and as he turned to descend the stairs they bent in different directions, and he stumbled down a step or two, momentarily reigning his balance on the landing. When he stepped on the pool that had drained from Billy Sam, his foot slid out from under him, and he landed hard on his back, his gun flying from his hand and spinning like a top on the between-floors landing. He started to crawl towards it, then stopped when his working eye made sense of a form at the bottom of the stairs.

It was Police Constable 203 Terry Patrick. The policeman's mouth was wide in wonderment, and his .38-calibre police special was in his hand.

The interview room in the homicide offices was small, spare, and cold. About ten feet square, it contained only a table and three hard chairs. Its entrance was a door with a small window. A naked bulb was set into the ceiling. Two of the chairs were now occupied, Laszlo Plizit sitting between the table and the wall, and Detective Lars Nordquist sitting across from him. Detective J.O. Harrison was leaning back against the door, his arms folded, his features grim.

Harrison had told himself to keep his cool.

Lars Nordquist, Harrison's partner, would be asking most of the questions. He would be calm and polite.

Plizit's eyes were red, and stared fixedly in different directions. His pupils were large because of the speed. He was jerking nervously.

"Now, we just want you to relax, Laszlo," Nordquist began. "No one's going to get difficult with you here. We just want to find out a few things, what happened in that building, what you were doing there, that sort of thing. Now, there's a tape recorder here, and we're going to leave it on, because I always like to have a complete and accurate record of what's said, so there can be no questions if this goes to court." His voice sounded flat in the small room.

"Give him the warning," said Harrison.

"Now, Laszlo," Nordquist said, "it's my duty to caution you that you need not say anything, but that anything you do or say may later be used in evidence. Do you understand?"

"Yeah," Plizit muttered.

"Could you just relate to us what was happening in that rooming house?" Nordquist said. "I mean, how you came to be there, et cetera."

"All right, here it is," Plizit said. "I am not doing nothing. Like I am in the wrong building. I came to visit friends, and I am in the wrong building, do you see?"

"Yes, the wrong building," said Nordquist, nodding. "Who were these friends? They lived down there someplace, I guess?"

Plizit's eyes were blinking rapidly. "Well, like only once before I meet them. John and Peter or something. We meet in beer parlor, and we get to talking, you see, and they ask me up, and I am in that part of town, and I go, do you see?"

"Yes, I see," said Nordquist. "And what address did they give you?"

"It's down someplace on Pender in that street. Someplace I have written note, maybe, I don't know. They describe the building, you see, and I am accidentally in the building where all the trouble is happening."

"Yes, two men got shot up there, Laszlo," Nordquist said. "I guess you know they're dead — an Indian fellow and a policeman. Now, I want you to tell me how that happened."

"I don't know really for sure, you see," said Plizit. His forehead was creased in concentration. His gaze was locked on the spool of virgin tape, smoothly unwinding. "Everything is mixed up. You guys think I do that? Like, I mean, shoot a police for no reason?"

"Well, Laszlo, we'll be honest with you," Nordquist said. "We've got nothing to hide, and I hope you'll treat us the same way. We'll be fair to you, and you be fair to us, okay?"

"Yeah, well . . . ?"

"Well, I guess you know about the gun that was found there. It's got your fingerprints on it, so I guess that bears some explanation, Laszlo."

Plizit sighed. "Yes, okay, I will be honest, like you say. So here's what happens. These guys, we get to talking in the beer parlor, you see, and so they want to buy a gun, and, uh, a silencer, and they have the bread. And I do not kid with you guys, because you have my record, and you know I deal a few pieces in my time, and I have this gun and will deliver it to these guys, do you see?"

"For how much?" said Harrison.

"Oh, three, four hundreds, just a little so's I get by from day to day, 'cause I ain't now working."

"You're broke, huh?" said Harrison.

"Well," said Plizit, attempting a smile, "there isn't too many jobs."

"Horsecock," said Harrison. He looked at Nordquist. "He was carrying nearly nine grand in U.S. dollars. Big bills, Plizit. Tell us how poor you are."

"Now, let's take it easy here," said Nordquist. "You want some coffee or something, Laszlo? I'm sure Detective Harrison will be happy to get us some coffee. I'd sure like a little myself. I'm in a bit of an overtime situation here." He chuckled.

Harrison left the room.

Nordquist smiled reassuringly at the Hungarian. "Now, Laszlo, I wanted Detective Harrison to take a bit of a breather because he's pretty upset about what happened at the Chungking Rooms. Maybe while he's out you can take this chance to level with me, because I don't think you've been telling me the whole truth here."

"I do my best, but I ain't had too much sleep. I am here as a circumstantial victim, do you see?"

"So now tell me about how those men got killed. We're just going to try to talk straight-forward like two men."

"It was an accident, you see." Plizit cleared his throat. "This guy is drunk Indian, and he smash his wine bottle and come at me, and there is shooting all around me all sudden, and I think there is his friend with gun, and I shoot blind. I don't mean to shoot, but actually this Indian's arm juggled me, and I guess I just hit this cop, this police."

Nordquist frowned. "Well, now, Laszlo, I'm a little disappointed here, because we have a statement from Miss Redfeather, and I want to be fair to you. She says you just turned around and shot at them from about eight feet away as they were coming up the stairs, and there was some kind of struggle, and you shot the policeman as he was lying on top of her. That's what she says, anyway."

"This old squaw is so piss she don't see nothing but a blur. . . . You guys don't hang no murder on me on some lies of some old drunken Indian."

"We did a breathalyzer on her, just like we did for you, Laszlo. She had a little bit, yes. How much did you have?"

"A lot, you know? Is why everything is fuzzy, you see."

Harrison returned and, glowering at Plizit, put a coffee in front of him.

"Well, your reading didn't seem to be that high," Nordquist continued. "We show you here as a point-oh-five. That's not too bad. Just a few beers will get you that."

Harrison snorted. "Didn't affect his aim any."

Nordquist shrugged. "Says it was accidental, J.O."

Plizit nodded eagerly. "It just sorts of just goes off, you know?"

Harrison bore down on the prisoner and slammed a hand on the table. "'*It just sorts of just goes off?*' You're holding a gun, pointing it at the man's head, and 'it just sorts of just goes off?' Listen, Plizit, we're not running no *Sesame Street* rehearsal here. Aw, Christ!"

"Now, let's just ease off here a bit," said Nordquist, holding up a cautionary hand. "Let's get back to the money. Now, where did that come from?"

Plizit scratched his head. "You guys is getting me so mixed up is hard to think back. Let's see. Actually, a guy gave . . . no . . . no, I sell some other guns . . . let's see . . . I am. . . . You know, I am asking here to make another phone call to my lawyer."

Nordquist looked at Harrison, who shrugged.

"You know we've been trying, Laszlo," Nordquist said. "We've left a message for Mr. Pomeroy, but I guess his answering service screens his calls at night. He needs his sleep like everyone else, you know."

"Let's talk about the money," Harrison said.

"I sooner not talk right now about that."

"Eight-seven hundred U.S," Harrison said. "That's over ten thousand Canadian, today's rates. The going rate for a hit is five G's, right? Two for ten. Why don't you cut out all this horsecock and lay it out for us, and we can all go home and get some rest."

"I want here to see my lawyer."

Nordquist persisted: "I think you know Dr. Au P'ang Wei."

"Don't believe I have the pleasure."

"I'm getting tired of this, Lars," Harrison said.

Nordquist sighed. "Look, Laszlo, I don't think you're doing your part. I think you're trying, but you're a little scared, right? I know — we're cops, and it's a kind of scary situation here, and to be honest, I think you're being used here, and I think you know it. I mean, you're looking at twenty-five years, no parole, and here's Dr. Au sitting around his swimming pool laughing. If I were you, I'd want to make sure the man behind this whole thing paid for his share, and maybe — you know I can't make any promises — but maybe the court will see you as the innocent victim of a man with a lot of power over you, specially if you help us out —"

Plizit interrupted sharply: "I want here to talk to my lawyer. I am not wanting to say a thousand times."

Harrison's voice was strangely muted. "Uh, Lars, Cobb's outside now wanting to get filled in. Why don't you do that while I have a chit-chat with Laszlo here about some personal details not related to the investigation. We'll fill out some of these here forms."

"Fine, I'll run along."

"Just a minute, Mr. Nordquist," Plizit said as Harrison's boot, with a sharp kick, neatly popped the tape-recorder plug from the wall socket. "I don't want to be alone here . . ." Plizit started to rise from his chair, but the door was already closed.

Harrison lumbered toward the little Hungarian. "It's all right, Hunkie, you ain't gonna be alone. I'm gonna look after you. Sit down!" He took the man's shoulders in his basketball-player hands and pushed him back onto the chair. Then he sat on the edge of the table, an arm's length from Plizit, who could feel heat radiating from the detective's body.

"Now, I'm just tired of farting around, Zsa-Zsa. You and me are going to have a little heart-to-heart, and if we don't get on friendly, I'm gonna be disappointed in you and lose control over my emotions, and I'm gonna dislodge some internal organs. Now, no more bullcock, Hunkie!" His words bounced heavily about the little room for several seconds.

"Okay," Harrison said, "you work for the Surgeon, right?"

Plizit's voice was a hollow whisper. "I think I maybe seen him around."

"I ain't interested in any more bullcock, Hunkie!" Harrison thundered in a voice that rattled down the corridor outside the interview room.

Plizit was jerking uncontrollably, and picking with his fingers at dope-bug scabs on his arms. "I seen him, yeah. I talk to him on street. Everybody knows him. No crime is to know someone."

Reaching out with one hand, Harrison grasped the lapels of Plizit's jacket and hefted him a few inches out of his chair. His fist was bunched against the man's neck, and Plizit's face turned red, his eyes cocking wildly in opposing directions.

Harrison lowered his voice and brought his face a few inches away from Plizit's and rasped: "I ain't in the mood to sit here all night and smell your lying little farts. We got enough on you to salt you, Hunkie. We've had a piece of tail on you since two months, and you drive for the Surgeon, you do little runs for him, and you brown your crooked nose off him, and you kill for him. Now, I'm gonna ask you just once nicely: did he send you up there to bump those witnesses?"

Plizit was choking and sputtering, and Harrison let go and dropped him into the chair.

"My lawyer . . . my lawyer . . . is get you busted all way down to bylaws —" Plizit began. Harrison drifted a chop to the chest that left Plizit gasping for air again.

"Now, Hunkie, you know I got a right to use a little force in self-defence, and it looked to me like you was gonna take a swing."

Plizit fixed a red eye on the detective, and hissed: "Pig, what you do here ain't a touch what I get if I open up. I know you ain't gonna cut me up. I know you ain't gonna kill me."

Harrison was shaking with fury, and roaring again: "Oh, yeah? *Oh, yeah?* Why, you filthy puny little lying yellow cocksucker! I'm gonna take you apart tooth and eye and nose in bite-size chunks!"

Then there was the sound of steps running toward them in the corridor, the sound of a knock on the door, and the face of Lars Nordquist peering in the window. He opened the door and leaned in. "Let's cool off here. His lawyer's outside. I got him talking to Cobb. It's a little loud, J.O."

Harrison groaned. "All right, take the useless little hemorrhoid back downstairs. Put him in a private cell. Clear everyone else out of the wing."

Saturday, the Fourth Day of March, at Ten Minutes Before Three O'Clock in the Morning

Cobb sat in the detective office shaking nervously and studying Nordquist's small pursed lips in their exquisite recitation of Laszlo Plizit's botched efforts. Lars Nordquist was tall and skeletal; his eyes seemed to crouch far back in their sockets, and he moved and talked in a precise and even manner.

Cobb was fuzzy, not drunk. He was down from his last fix of heroin taken many hours ago, and was suffering from the coming-down. Puffing furiously on his favorite Peterson bent, as if the fumes would clear the murk in his head, he collated Nordquist's facts and began to rework them into a usable schema.

"It is quite well known here that Plizit is one of Dr. Au's henchmen," Nordquist was saying. He liked the old words. "He is an ugly customer with a very sad criminal record. He is a gunner, a professional. He will not admit to working for Dr. Au tonight."

"He is close to Au?" Cobb asked.

"He is always with him. Dr. Au has many enemies."

"He was probably present when Jim Fat was killed? Probably one of the men in the car when Au went to pick Jim Fat up?"

"Yes, I am sure of that. We found a corner of Plizit's thumbprint on the carving block Not enough points for court, but enough to make it a probable."

A policeman came in to tell Nordquist that Brian Pomeroy, Plizit's lawyer, was downstairs at the duty sergeant's desk.

"You better tell Honcho," Cobb said. From the interview room down the hall Cobb could hear a muffled roar, and knew it was the sound of Honcho Harrison.

Cobb tried to steel himself, but his insides felt raw. The negotiations with Pomeroy would be protracted and complex. The young lawyer was a chess player, a shrewd negotiator in the courthouse corridors where bargains were struck. Plizit, who could now afford better, kept him on because of Pomeroy's ability to deal his client out of serious trouble.

But Cobb was not quite ready for him.

He went out the back door of the police station to his car, where he kept a bit of junk and an emergency kit. With the dope and his works he returned to the detective floor, bought a Coke from the soft-drink machine, opened it and took it to the men's room, where he dumped the drink in the toilet and used the bottle cap as his cooker. He cranked the hit into his leg and had a shit.

When Pomeroy walked into a detective office that Cobb had borrowed for the negotiations, he was dishevelled, sleepy-eyed, and grumpily complaining about a red-tape blockade keeping him from his client. Cobb greeted him expansively, arranged for coffee, and sat him down to outline the case against Plizit. When that was done, he stoked his pipe with fuel and leaned menacingly toward Pomeroy, who had backed up in his chair.

"Let's put it together," he said. "He works for Au. No issue. He handles guns, used to sell them, admits possession of the forty-five. No issue. He was out on an errand for Au. We can prove that. Not an errand of mercy. A bottle of pills. We have that old front-page favorite, the drug-crazed killer. Oh, yes, there's a silencer on the gun: trademark of the professional. Au has just found out the whereabouts of the only honest witnesses who could put him in the place and at the time of a particularly gruesome execution. The evidence of that killing goes in, relevant to prove a motive, to prove Plizit was up there with orders to bump a witness or two. You know I'm right about that, Brian." The smoke from Cobb's pipe settled around Pomeroy like a cloud of ill omen. "Now, I'm not saying the jury's minds would be inflamed by evidence about Laszlo standing around in all his cherubic innocence while some guy gets his balls cut off and his tongue sliced out and his throat slit ear to ear." He winked at Pomeroy through the haze. "You see, we can prove Laszlo was at least an attendant at Jim Fat's sacrifice. His prints are all over the carving block. So maybe we've got him as a party to *that* murder as well."

Cobb paused briefly. "Okay, the jury will draw the right conclusions. Laszlo is surprised by Millie and Billy while he's preparing to, what, drill the cop? Obviously. The silencer was fitted to the gun. Millie says he was standing there holding the gun as if he were going to shoot it at someone down the hall. Good evidence of intent to kill. Laszlo is caught in the act. He's cornered. He has to shoot his way out now. Fires at Bill, misses, hits the wine bottle. Fires a couple of times. They dug a piece of a slug out of the wall, and ballistics went on an overtime shift tonight. The machinery really revs around here when a cop gets hit. The slug came from your man's gun, so that little bit of evidence confirms Millie's story. Sure she's pissed, but she's an honest old sot who's going to tell the truth, the whole truth, and nothing but the truth, so help her God. So Billy, in self-defence, goes after Laszlo. He's going to make spaghetti out of his face with the end of a broken bottle, and Constable Moeller saves Laszlo's life. Moeller saved his own murderer's life! Oh, Jesus, Brian, they're going to run him up the courthouse flagpole by the neck. Jake Moeller. Teaches Sunday school. Wife and a baby and a mortgage. The courtroom will be chock full of dads and moms and grandpas and grandmas and Uncle Karl and Aunt Helga and pastor Schmidt."

"Do they supply gas masks in here?"

"Steady on. There's more. There's an exchange of shots between Moeller and Plizit. Moeller finally realizes that Laszlo is the man he's been posted there to watch out for. Laszlo gets him in the shoulder.

Moeller misses with his last bullet, and he's injured, on the floor, or on top of Millie, or somewhere. Down, anyway. Laszlo takes aim, right at his neck." Cobb pointed his pipe stem in the direction of Pomeroy's Adam's apple, and clicked his trigger finger. "Bang. Perfect aim. Almost cuts his head off. Not some blind, haphazard shot. Intent to kill. Murder in the first degree half a dozen ways: planned and deliberate, a cop's the victim. Murder in the commission of another offence, i.e., the attempted murder of two witnesses."

"What the hell is all this about, Fos?"

"Hang in there. Okay. Laszlo takes the stand with some hokey lie or other. So, hey, what do we have here? A criminal record! And it's all admissible — just to test his credibility, of course. We wouldn't want a jury to convict him just because he's an asshole with a dozen or I don't know how goddamn many convictions. Bunch of firearms charges. Attempted rape. Trafficking. Assaults. Looks to the jury like this guy is a professional criminal. Also a hit man. Which is what he is, isn't he, Brian?"

"Okay, Defences. Accident? We'll all have a good laugh. Self-defence? They'll send you both to jail. Provocation bringing it down to manslaughter? Good Lord, all Moeller did to provoke the man was save his life. Drunkenness? Point-zero-five reading, no way."

"Could be he was out of it, doing speed," Pomeroy said. "He pops pills for breakfast, lunch, dinner, and between-meal snacks. That and the booze could make it manslaughter." He did not sound convinced of his cause. "I'd better go down and hear his side of it."

"Just a second," Cobb said. Now for the kicker. "Just a second. There are all these u.s. dollars on him. Eighty-seven hundred, I think. That's the fee for the kill. That works out to about five thousand Canadian per hit — five for Selwyn and five for McTaggart. There'll be expert evidence put before the jury that that's the going reward in this town for a dead body. Why U.S. funds? God, I don't know. Maybe Plizit worries about the stability of the Canadian dollar. So here's our brave freedom-fighter with eight-point-seven big ones in a roll in his jeans."

"Now, hang on," Pomeroy said. "That's speculation and prejudicial to boot. You can't tie the money in, and you know it. He's got a right to have it released."

Cobb leaned back, pursing his lips, in apparent reflection. "Maybe something can be worked out about the money," he said. "I'd want to be fair."

Pomeroy smiled. "What all this bullshit means is you want Plizit to give state's evidence against the Surgeon."

"Yeah, Brian, I want Au. It's that simple. I'll recommend a murder-two against Plizit if he comes across for us."

"Aw, Jesus, you must have some shitty case against Au. Well, we'll just see what it's going to cost to buy up Plizit's contract. I'll talk to him. Maybe he didn't see Jim Fat get it. Maybe he won't be interested, being that life is a precious commodity. Mind you, he accepts my advice. I've done him a few good turns in his time." Smoke was still belching from Cobb's pipe, and Pomeroy glinted at him wet-eyed through the fog. "Now, is that old bugger Honcho Harrison in on this?" he asked. "You can get Santorini to okay something like this? Yeah, I know you can — you guys are thick as an old pot of honey."

"I'll soften Nordquist and Honcho up while you're down with your guy. It's not going to be easy, so the whole thing could fall through. What we would want to do is charge first-degree murder. It could be dropped to murder-two if he cooperates. He has to come across on the stand. That's the deal."

"And if Au gets off anyway?"

"The deal holds if Plizit takes the stand with a good eyewitness account or something close to it."

"Can't see a murder-one if he was blasted on speed," Pomeroy said. "Pretty hard for the crown to show some speed freak with his brain on fire knew what he was doing up there. I'd say we should be talking about a manslaughter. Sounds like a pretty weird killing."

"Talk to your man," Cobb said.

Cobb would take a good hard manslaughter. The murder-two was a bargaining lever.

Nordquist was not easy. As Cobb made his pitch to the two detectives, Nordquist just sat back impassively, his arms folded, staring at Cobb and shaking his head. He kept repeating: "He killed one of our men. He killed a police constable." Nordquist's eyes peered gloomily at Cobb from their caves. "A policeman, Foster. A young kid with his whole life in front of him."

Cobb exploded: "Goddamnit, Lars, he killed a cop — so what? I'm talking about a chance to make the Surgeon! Dr. Au, for God's sake! We have no fucking case against Dr. Au, and you goddamn well know it. We're down the tube, and he's out the front door whistling 'Dixie' down the street, off to hack some poor slob in the Jesus knackers." Nordquist set his lips in a prim, firm line. "Come on, Lars, you'll take a thousand Plizits for one Dr. Au. Plizit's five-and-dime. Let's go for the department store. Goddamnit, the day they send the Surgeon to the slam you'll be wetting your goddamn boxer shorts with the sweet piss of happiness, and you know it."

"But he . . ." Nordquist paused and glanced at Harrison. The old detective was sitting back, his eyes closed. Tired beads of sweat sat on his head.

James O. Harrison had lost many comrades during his thirty-six years on the force: policemen on duty cut down by gunfire from bandits like Laszlo Plizit. They had shared desks, shared patrols, shared danger. Off-duty, they had gathered for fishing trips, poker parties, evenings of just getting together for stories and laughs and beer.

But James O. Harrison had also, for the last ten years, been the self-appointed president of a one-man committee to end the career of Au P'ang Wei. He had followed Au's trail of carnage during that time, tracking bloody footprints that always seemed to fade and disappear. He had seen most of the victims, and on one occasion had seen a man die in a vacant lot, an old junkie who had cheated Au, and whose torso had been slit down the midline, gutted like a slaughtered hog. Another time he had watched patiently while men from the coroner's office pieced together a human jig-saw puzzle: fourteen pieces of flesh.

Harrison opened his eyes and looked directly into Cobb's.

"Yeah," he said. "Yeah. Okay."

But when Pomeroy came up, he was shaking his head.

"Nope, he won't buy it. Besides, on what he tells me, there's nothing better than a manslaughter here. Laszlo was drugged out. Not capable of the specific intent to kill. That vial of uppers was almost full when he started out yesterday. No, sorry. It can't be swung." He paused. "Too bad. He might have been of some help on the Dr. Au thing."

Cobb knew the hard bargaining was now about to begin.

"Well, let's find a drink somewhere," he said. "I don't want to let it go that easily." He called down the hall to Harrison, who was in another office. "Honch, I know you keep a mickey hidden in your locker. We'd like to borrow it for a few minutes."

Harrison brought the bottle in with a couple of paper cups. "Cooler's down the way," he said gruffly, then left, knowing he was not to be a part of the lawyers' manoeuverings.

"Okay, let's talk," Cobb said, pouring the drinks. "Maybe we can sweeten the pot."

Half an hour later they were still going.

"Manslaughter," Cobb was saying. "That's going to be *hard* to sell. These guys want Plizit by the jewels, Brian." He shook his head. "I don't know, I don't know. Santorini would want at least twenty years for your guy. Anything less than fifteen I can see being appealed. Mind you, that still gets him out on parole after about seven or eight. Jesus, Brian, you drive a pretty hard bargain. I don't know." He bit his lower lip, sat back, and started puffing again.

Pomeroy appeared to wilt under the smoke barrage. "We cop to a manslaughter, and you take your best shot. I don't care. You can throw everything in except the money. I still say that's irrelevant."

Cobb sat up suddenly. "Well, it's late," he said. "I'm tired. I'm not going to hassle. I'm against the wall. The trial starts a week Monday. Okay, manslaughter. The crown asks for a bundle. Plizit's whole record goes in — all the gun charges, the assault bodily harm, the trafficking in meth, the attempted rape ten years ago. *All* the facts go in — the gun pointing at the cop, the silencer, the motive. We'll have to tell the judge that we felt there was the barest reasonable doubt on the basis that Plizit was high on speed, incapable of forming an intent to kill at the specific time the shots were fired. Boy, we are going to look stupid in there."

Pomeroy smiled. "And the money?"

Cobb sighed. "Well, maybe we can do something about that. You go back down there and scribble out a statement for him to sign. Something short, enough to commit him to give evidence for us. On Monday we can get a full, typed statement for him. And then I think I can arrange for the release of the money to you, in trust, of course." After all, a criminal lawyer's fees had to be paid.

They shook hands to seal the deal. Despite himself, Pomeroy gloated a little: "You know, Fos, I think you're getting a little soft in your old age."

Cobb and Harrison were into their fifth hand of pinochle when Pomeroy came back upstairs. He was breathing hard, and his face was red and traced with rigid lines. His voice had the dry, cracked sound of a man who had been arguing hard.

"I can't believe it," he said. "He won't go for it. He just won't do it. Man, he is one scared son of a bitch. I told him I'm withdrawing. Aw, shit, what a night."

Cobb sagged. He was tired. It was five o'clock in the morning.

"Okay, boys, let's go home," Harrison said. "It's been a long hard night." He had the look of an old ox bowed from the yoke. He took them to the door. "I'll lock up here," he said. "Have a good sleep, you guys. Hope we get some decent weather this weekend. Thought I might get the boat out and investigate a few salmon."

For a while Plizit sat on the bed scratching at sores — from crank bugs; insects of delusion that bummed-out speed freaks commonly think they see crawling across their bodies. As the sores scabbed over, he picked them again, until he was bleeding in several places on his arms and legs. There was no noise in this wing of the police cells. Normally the cells were occupied by other prisoners — drunks singing, or crying, or talking to themselves. But the other cells in the wing were empty, and the only sound was an occasional creak, or a clank of distant metal on stone, or a dim shout from far down the way. Plizit had yelled to the night guard for water several times, but the man was too far away, or deaf, or just didn't care.

So he was alone with his amphetamine withdrawal, with his crank bugs, with his forty-watt bulb in a wire mesh, with his toilet that smelled of lye, with his cot and its mattress and its blanket made of a material that would not rip into strips. There were no windows to this cell — except for a small square in the door, with a view to the cell door across the hall.

And finally the ups relaxed their grip on Plizit, and he clawed his way into a kind of sleep. The dreams were of Billy Sam's face dissolving in front of him, pouring blood through orifices. Then an Oriental face, impassive, cold. A scream. Explosions. He rolled onto his side, and the black images passed away. Strangely, suddenly, it was a green spring day, and he was a boy beside his father, sitting on a hayrack. Then he was running through the fields, and his father was calling to him. "Laszlo," he said. "Laszlo . . ."

"Laszlo!" It was louder.

"Laszlo, you bag of slime, get up."

He felt something soft hit him in the face, and his left eye opened, and was not able to see. He realized then that some sort of garment had been thrown over his head. He groped weakly about and removed it. It was an overcoat, and as a matter of fact he recognized it as Detective Harrison's old rumpled coat. Its owner was standing a few feet from him, his arms folded, glinting down at him. The cell door was closed. Locked, he assumed.

The detective reached down toward the corner of the cot, grabbed the blanket, whipped it from Plizit's body, and tossed it into a corner. Plizit's clothes were stained with the blood of Billy Sam and the blood of his own crank bugs.

"You're the most disgusting piece of puke I've ever had to look at," Harrison said. "Stand up. Let's get this over with."

Plizit did not move.

"Get out of bed."

Plizit lay still, keeping his eye on the detective.

Harrison knelt and picked up the corner of the cot with one arm, turning it on its side, against the wall. Plizit felt himself sliding against the wall, slamming into it. Then he fell onto the floor.

Harrison grabbed him by the ankles and pulled him clear of the wreckage.

Plizit still did not get up. He looked up balefully at the policeman, who sighed, then kicked him lightly in the head above the hairline, where no mark would show. Plizit's head bounced against the wall, and he cried for help.

Harrison just shook his head, and a cold smile drifted across his face.

His coat was on the floor now, in a crumpled heap beside Plizit.

"Aw, Jeez, Laszlo, I don't know why we can't just be friends. Look, there's a deck of smokes in the right-hand pocket. Get me one. Take one of yourself. Let's try to get on sensibly."

Plizit gained a sitting position on the floor, then fumbled through one pocket of Harrison's coat, then the other. He did not draw out a pack of cigarettes. He pulled out Harrison's snub-nosed .38 instead.

So Harrison kicked his hand, hard this time, breaking a couple of fingers. The gun slid across the cell into a corner.

"Damn it, I was wondering where I left that thing," Harrison said. "Must of left my smokes in the office."

Plizit yelled a lot, but no one came. After a minute he quieted down and sat simpering and groaning, holding his injured hand.

Harrison took a sealed envelope from his back pocket, and a letter opener, and tossed them down to Plizit.

"Now, I want you to open that and see if I got it right."

Plizit was frozen.

"Open it." Harrison's voice was calm and deadly.

Plizit opened it, slipping the edge of the opener under the flap and slitting it lengthwise.

"Now, you read that. I think I got everything, but I might have missed one or two details." Waiting for Plizit to read it over, he lounged back against a wall, his arms again folded. He was wearing a white shirt stained with sweat. He also had a shoulder holster, but it was empty.

Plizit's shaking hands drew from the envelope five pages of lined paper bearing writing in Harrison's hand. It began: "This is the statement of Laszlo Plizit. I have been warned by Detective Harrison that I need not say anything and that anything I do say may be used as evidence. The events here described occurred on Saturday, December third . . ."

"Read it over, Laszlo," Harrison said. "If you think there's anything has to be changed, let's do it quick. I'm tired and I'm dirty and I want to go home and have a shower and a couple hours sleep." He yawned.

Plizit glanced over the pages, taking very little in.

"Okay?" Harrison said after a while. "Now sign it." He threw down a fountain pen. Plizit stared up at him dumbly. "Don't press too hard. It damages the nib."

When Plizit did not pick up the pen, Harrison picked Plizit up, wrapping his hands around the points of his shoulders, then throwing him hard against the wall, knocking his breath from him.

Plizit sank down slowly on his knees.

Harrison brought his right foot hard around in a circle, soccer-style, and embedded it in Plizit's stomach. The gunman doubled over gasping, too much in pain to scream. He did not quite pass out.

After a while Plizit untwined from his fetal position.

Harrison kicked him again in the same place.

"Please sign it, Laszlo. I still got the best corner kick in the police league."

Still Plizit made no move for the pen. He was huddled up in a ball, and was crying.

He looked up when he heard the sound of fabric tearing. Harrison was ripping his own shirt. Plizit thought the detective might be going crazy. He was actually ripping his shirt with his hands. He was tearing it in two long lines, from collar to shirttail, until it hung from him in loose fragments. Then Harrison rended his undershirt with two similar long slashes.

Even more strange, he then bent down and picked up the letter opener by its point, holding it between thumb and index finger. He drew two long superficial cuts down his chest, drawing blood, then wiped off the blade of the opener where his fingers had touched it. He placed it back on the floor beside Plizit.

Plizit just watched all this, not putting it together.

Harrison looked down at the man, smiling benignly.

"Now, Hunkie," he said, "see what you done? You've gone and got your dirty fingerprints all over my nice clean gun, and all over my letter opener." He took a step toward Plizit. "So I'm going to have to kill you."

On Monday the sixth day of March, Brian Pomeroy, back in the service of Laszlo Plizit, confirmed with Cobb that his client had had a change of heart. The deal was on. Two final terms were agreed upon: One, Plizit would be kept in protective custody while awaiting his plea to manslaughter and his sentence. The place of custody would be a country lock-up somewhere in the remote interior of the province, far from the reach of officers of the Vancouver city police, and far as well from the long tentacles of Au P'ang Wei. Two, after sentencing, Plizit would be transferred to a penitentiary in eastern Canada, several thousand miles from British Columbia.

At two o'clock in the afternoon of that day Pomeroy delivered to Cobb a neatly typed statement signed by Laszlo Plizit and attesting to the murder and mutilation of Jim Fat by Dr. Au. Cobb was glad to see it. The hand-written version given him earlier by Detective Harrison was garbled, vague, and generally unreadable.

Monday, the Thirteenth Day of March, at a Quarter to Ten O'Clock in the Morning

An electric tension swirls through the corridors. The many citizens summoned here for jury duty form a line. A sheriff's officer checks them off a list. Lawyers, wigless but wearing long black robes and vests, tabs, and wing collars, grandly weave their way through the crowd. Court workers drift through the hallways. Plaintiffs and defendants and witnesses slowly disperse in the direction of one or other of thirty courtrooms in the building.

Behind a pair of oak-and-stained-glass doors is the assize court — locked, empty, and still. The high, massive judge's bench dominates one end. To its left is the jury box with twelve chairs: simple, uncomfortable accommodation. To the right is the witness box; behind it, the press table. In front of the bench are the desks of the court clerk and official court reporter, and a step below these are the counsel tables where the lawyers will spread their books and make their notes. The defendant will sit in the prisoner's dock, an enclosed dais in the middle of the room, a centrepiece surrounded by high leaded-glass windows through which the cool March sun sends dancing filaments of light. For the spectators, there are rows of seats in the back of the courtroom, and a gallery above.

It is a theatre.

There is no curtain, and the lights do not dim. The players and the watchers filter in and take their places. First, the old-timers, the seasoned veterans of this show. They come in as soon as the brown-uniformed sheriffs unlock the doors, and they find the best seats, where the players can best be seen and heard. They are here in numbers because M. Cyrus Smythe-Baldwin will be working this house for a run of two weeks. Foster L. Cobb, who thinks fast on his feet and questions sharply and is a comer, gets second billing. A group of high-school students files noisily into the upper gallery, then is cowed into silence by the bulldog scowl of a tough old sheriff's officer.

Now three thin men file in quietly. Two of them are very young. The three sit together in the front row of the lower gallery. They are bony, emaciated-looking, and they seem nervous or ill. Their face muscles twitch. These men are junkies on big habits. Several policemen in the courthouse have seen them and know who they are. Their presence has been noted, and they will be watched. . . .

It is a few minutes before the hour, and Cobb comes in, striding hard, his books under his arm and his robes sailing behind him. He is exasperated because his collar stud broke, and he had to borrow another in the barristers' gowning room. He is, as well, anxious, and this shows in the set of his face. He has first-act jitters, an edginess fuelled by a fourth cup of coffee, tempered only lightly by opiates. His weekend has again been lonely, his bed empty, his dreams ravaging. He had filled the loneliness with work, and now his mind is crammed with submissions, precedents, and case references compiled in the law library. He has prepared arguments for a defence adjournment application, promised for this morning, together with a battery of arguments upon issues that might or might not be raised during the trial. His body and mind are running on caffeine and heroin. Over-prepared for this trial, he is exhausted before it is even to begin.

Following Cobb, cool, slender, graceful, and awed, comes Jennifer Tann, afraid of Cobb's mood, feeling vibrations from his tension, overpowered by the energies pulsing in this room.

Au steps calmly to the prisoner's dock. The gate is held open for him by a sheriff, and he sits. He will remain there while the trial proceeds, but will stay free on bail during the trial. He is serene. No flicker of emotion touches his handsome dark face. He wears a silk shirt, a grey light-patterned tie, and a grey suit, but he has accepted the advice of counsel and is without expensive jewellery.

As Au looks about him he sees the three edgy men in the front row, and for a second or two his eyes seem to speak words to them. They look at him too, but show no expression. Then Au looks ahead and folds his arms. For another man, guided less cerebrally, more emotionally, these last weeks might have been trying, but Au has mastered the art of self-control and through it the art of controlling others whose minds and wills are weaker. Charlie Ming is one of these, and Au takes pride in the knowledge that Ming will be loyal to him. He had expected more of Plizit, but also knows strength of character is not that disloyal man's great virtue. One day, of course, Au would make appropriate reward to the man for his failing. In the meantime, the trial is about to commence, and his mind will remain as clear as a mirror. He is a businessman and has wisely invested in the services of M. Cyrus Smythe-Baldwin, Q.C.

At thirty seconds before ten o'clock, Smythe-Baldwin walks into the courtroom and pauses. All eyes except those of Cobb — who will not play the old barrister's game, who knows that Smythe-Baldwin never enters a room until the stage is set — turn to the dignified don of the criminal bar: a magnet controlling fields of force. He revolves his head slowly, and offers a warm smile to Tann, who, recalling her earlier impudence, blushes and feels herself an intruder in this place where the old lawyer exercises his territorial prerogative.

Smythe-Baldwin now turns to the senior sheriff, taking his arm as if with a trusted friend, and speaks earnestly to him. The sheriff nods and turns to the spectators, and his voice rings out, temporarily silencing the buzz of quiet conversation. He demands to know if there are members of the jury panel in the courtroom, and if so, he asks, would they kindly leave. Three or four persons rise and depart to join others on the panel waiting outside the courtroom doors.

Another sheriff enters from the judge's door.

"Are you ready, gentlemen?" he said, addressing counsel.

They nod, and the sheriff ushers in Mr. Justice Selden Horowitz.

"Order in court!" the sheriff shouts.

There is a shuffling as everyone rises to his feet. Selden Horowitz, gowned in crimson-and-black robes, peering over his glasses at the full courtroom, mounts the steps, smiles and nods to counsel, and sits.

Then the sheriff, standing stiffly, speaks the words that for long centuries of the English common law have heralded the beginning of the criminal jury assize, the trial of citizen by citizens:

"Oyer, oyer, oyer. All persons having business at this Court of Oyer and Terminer and General Gaol Delivery holden here this day draw near and give your attention and answer to your names when called. God Save the Queen!"

Smythe-Baldwin rose to his full bearing. "My Lord," he began. "I apply to traverse this trial to a future assize."

Cobb had met with him last week, fought the issue in solitary combat, and had not relented. Smythe-Baldwin, professing anger and indignation, promised he would place the item first on the agenda before Mr. Justice Horowitz on the opening day of trial. The lawyer had been astounded by the events of the week before: Plizit's arrest in the course of an apparent attack on two witnesses, then the delivery by Cobb on Wednesday, five days ago, of a copy of Plizit's statement. Smythe-Baldwin's private urgings to Cobb for an adjournment had to do with his concern that the defence had insufficient time to prepare to meet the fresh evidence. He also complained that prospective jurors might be biased as a result of the excited newspaper accounts of the shoot-out in the Chungking Rooms. Cobb answered that the press had not uncovered a link between the shooting and the Au trial, and the jury would undertake their tasks in virginal innocence.

At ten-thirty, Smythe-Baldwin was still on his feet, punctuating his points with an index finger that sliced the air. The large courtroom was filled with his rich baritone. Cobb was anxious, and knew he would show nervousness until he had plunged himself into the thick of his submission. When Smythe-Baldwin sat down, Cobb stood up, almost knocking his chair over backwards, grabbing at it awkwardly with a hand still swathed in his robes. Then there were some moments of hesitation, a little stammer, some words repeated, an "uh" and an "er" as his engine coughed and warmed up. Slowly he drew himself into the current, and began not to think of the words he was speaking or of the phrases articulated, but of the sense and meaning of his argument.

"Certainly the man Plizit is a witness central to the crown's case," Cobb said. "But my learned friend has had his evidence for five days — ample time for a lawyer of his ability to prepare a cross-examination. A delay in the trial further threatens the lives of witnesses who have offered to come forward, responding to their duties as citizens."

Near the end of his submission, Cobb realized his words had connected with Horowitz. The judge said nothing, but there had been an almost imperceptible nod of the head, a pursing of the lips, a movement forward in his seat. As the judge tuned in more to Cobb's argument, he became a receptacle of a surge of persuasive energy that Cobb, encouraged, directed to him.

Jennifer Tann did not pick up the cues from the judge. But Smythe-Baldwin, after thirty thousand hours in courtrooms, knew instinctively his adjournment had been lost. His style, however, did not give countenance to surrender, and his reply to Cobb was an angry mocking attack upon the crown for its high-handed eleventh-hour deals of desperation in its insatiable hunger for conviction of his client at all costs. Smythe-Baldwin would lose this argument, but hoped to exact a price — the judge, needing to appear fair, might lean toward the defence upon a subsequent issue.

An hour had been consumed in the arguments. Horowitz thanked both counsel and said: "I am satisfied that the interest of justice require that the trial now proceed. The accused is represented by counsel of consummate ability and will suffer no prejudice to his right to fair answer and defence. Gentlemen, let us arraign the accused."

The clerk rose and asked Au to stand. Au stood up slowly, facing the judge, and Cobb saw that his face was still impassive. Although . . . there had been a look. Au's eyes had seemed for a flick of a second to meet Cobb's, and it seemed to Cobb that there had been a message, and not a kindly one.

The clerk, his voice rich with ceremony, read the charge: "Au P'ang Wei, you stand charged that in the City of Vancouver, County of Vancouver, Province of British Columbia, you did on the third day of December commit murder in the first degree of Jimmy Wai Fat Leung, contrary to the form of statute in such case made and provided and against the peace of Our Lady the Queen. How do you plead, guilty, or not guilty?"

Au's voice was cool and firm. "I am not guilty," he said.

Jennifer Tann turned to look at him, studying him with wonder at his composure and his elegance. She searched for some exposed mental warp, some damage of character, and saw only a chilling serenity. Whatever illness was in the man, she thought, was an illness well hidden beneath layers of ice. She knew somehow that some part of this man's soul had been gutted by fire, some fire of unknown origin.

And Au in turn had considered the young woman in front of him. Her eyes had searched him, and he knew that her look had tried to penetrate him. Many had tried to understand him, and failed. What beggar can fathom the soul of a kahn? The woman had eyes that spoke intelligently, but she too was blind, and all who tried to see into him were blind. Except one, perhaps. The prosecutor, Cobb. There was something about Cobb . . . But Au knew this: The prosecutor, Cobb, would fail because he was weak, and would become the victim of his own anger — being unable, in the manner of the Ch'ao-chou, to master such feelings.

The empanelling of the jury — a speedy process because prospective jurors are not asked questions — took half an hour. Smythe-Baldwin used all his allotted twelve peremptory challenges, attempting to avoid Asian-Canadians and women. After he had exhausted his challenges, three women next in line were consented to by Cobb, and the jury was completed.

It was an average mix. Smythe-Baldwin was content. No one swore the oath of a juror who had not returned his smile. The lawyer knew this jury would acquit if he could shake the evidence of the crown witnesses and if Cudlipp — a long-serving officer of the law — was strong on the stand. It would be difficult for twelve men and women to disbelieve unanimously a veteran policeman. But Cudlipp would be exposed to the whip of Cobb's cross-examination, and Cobb could injure. He hoped the man would prove honest — or a convincing liar.

The judge told the jury they would be sequestered. "I tell you that reluctantly, because it means that for the duration of the trial you will have no contact with your families, nor be exposed to media reports about the trial. You will be comfortably housed, I hope, in a good hotel. The decision to insulate you is made for your protection as well as the protection of the accused. It should never be suggested that your verdict was influenced by matters not before you as evidence."

While the jury recessed to make their arrangements, Cobb reviewed his notes for his opening address. It would be a summary of the evidence he hoped to call — evidence that would be heard by the jury during the first four days of trial. His witnesses would be taken by Cobb through their evidence, then be cross-examined by Smythe-Baldwin, who, in his turn, would call his witnesses in examination-in-chief, and cross-examination by Cobb. The defence knew generally what the crown witnesses would say; Cobb knew little about the defence. Smythe-Baldwin had disclosed to him only that the defence was an alibi — that during the time of the crime the accused was engaged in innocent pursuits, apparently in company with Corporal Cudlipp. More information than that, Smythe-Baldwin refused to give — despite Cobb's insistence that the crown was entitled to fair particulars of an alibi. "Talk to Cudlipp," Smythe-Baldwin had told him. "You have my blessing to do so." Cobb had tried, but Cudlipp had vanished. So Cobb resigned himself to the prosecutor's handicap: ignorance of the defence, and inability to prepare for it.

The jury, having selected a foreman, returned, and Cobb waited for the judge's nod, then approached them, leaving his notes on the table. He spoke slowly, carefully, reciting the details of the crime, touching briefly upon the evidence to be called from each of the witnesses.

"The detectives will tell you of the discovery of the body of the deceased," he said. "I warn you that the scene which assailed their eyes was sufficient to shock the most veteran of policemen, even policemen inured to the bloodiest and most awful scenes of violent attack by man upon man. I deeply regret that we cannot spare you from this, but to prepare you, I shall tell you now that the body of the dead man — known in life as Jim Fat — was naked, hanging from a hook. The throat had been slashed, his tongue and testicles removed."

Cobb saw eyes widen, and two or three faces appeared to blanch. One juror looked down and fumbled in her purse, and another closed his eyes.

When Cobb described the role of Laszlo Plizit, a juror in the back row frowned and shook his head. Perhaps, Cobb thought, this juror would find a man like Plizit too untrustworthy to be believed, would find that Plizit had made up his evidence to frame Au and buy a cheaper sentence for himself. Cobb realized he would have to defuse the attack that Smythe-Baldwin would surely launch against Plizit's character and veracity:

"Now, we shall not be offering this man to you as an exemplar, as a model for your children to follow. He is a man who has followed a criminal path, and he will say so. He is a man who has taken a life very recently. He is a man who was spurred to offer his assistance to the crown by the most basic of motives — self-interest. For it was agreed by representatives of Her Majesty, for whom I speak here, to allow him to plead guilty to a lesser offence than murder — it is manslaughter, a most serious offence still, I should caution you — in return for the favor of his evidence against the accused Au. I shall have cause to discuss with you later the unfortunate realities which make such distasteful contracts necessary in our imperfect world —"

Smythe-Baldwin interjected: "My lord, might counsel avoid gilding his wilted lily during the course of his opening, and be importuned to stick to the allegations of fact — if it is not too unbearable a strain on him."

"Yes, Mr. Cobb," Horowitz said, smiling, "you will have your chance after all the evidence is in."

Cobb held out his hands to the jury in a gesture of helplessness. "You will observe, ladies and gentlemen, that my learned friend Mr. Smythe-Baldwin dives like a hawk when he sights his helpless prey wandering unprotected in open fields." There was laughter from the gallery and from the jury box, and the tension created by the recounting of Jim Fat's bloody decease had now dissolved.

Nearing the hour of the twelve-thirty mid-day break — court would resume at two — Cobb quickly dealt with the technical evidence, then paused. He scanned the jury's faces, seeking eye contact, hoping he was reaching them, relating to them.

"Okay," he said, "that is all I have to say about the evidence you will hear from the crown. Please remember that what I have expressed to you is merely what I anticipate the witnesses will say. We may all be surprised — they may say nothing of the kind. If so, you will forget my words here, because what I say to you now is not evidence and may not be considered as such."

He was close to them, leaning against the counsel table, his arms folded. "You are strangers here, and it is proper that you are. You are drawn from all walks of life, and you serve here as the source and the fountain and the heart of our democratic system of justice. You come in here in innocence, with minds open, and you will be expected to give this accused man, Au P'ang Wei" — he swept his arm in the direction of Dr. Au — "a fair and impartial trial. He has a right to that. You should judge the man only after you have heard all the evidence, and you should not feel any enmity because you may think his manner of life, or his activities, or his associations are not those you would prefer to share. I hope you will be equally without bias when you consider the witnesses offered to you by the crown. All I can do is ask you to give them fair hearing. You will observe that I cannot attack my own witnesses — unless they prove adverse to the crown — nor can I help them by asking leading questions which suggest the answers I expect from them. I leave that to my friend Mr. Smythe-Baldwin, who can within certain bounds of fairness attack them or lead them or challenge their credibility. That part of his task is called cross-examination. If ultimately the defence calls witnesses, I shall have the opportunity to perform in like manner. You will come to understand that cross-examination is a tool whereby the truthfulness and reliability of a witness are tested. A decision as to whether a witness's words are to be trusted is solely for you to make, for you are the judges of truth in this court. And I pray that you will perform your duty as judges of truth — in accordance with the solemn oaths that you swore in entering upon the task that is before you."

He felt good about that. Many in the jury were nodding. And as he returned to the counsel table to take his seat, he saw Jennifer Tann looking at him with a shine in her eyes.

It dawned on him then that he had impressed her; perhaps, he thought, he had been trying to do so all along.

"Court will adjourn until two p.m.," the judge announced.

Monday, the Thirteenth Day of March, at Half-past Twelve O'Clock Noon

From the delicatessen: pastrami on rye. Milk. An apple. Cobb's digestive juices squirting into his stomach while the pathologist, in the interview room, recounts in a bloodless recitation the story of the autopsy. After about fifteen minutes of this, the milk is turning sour in Cobb's stomach. After Dr. Coombs, an interview with the police photographer, a man who takes pride. The pictures: stark, graphic, bloody. Finally, a hurried five-minute conference with Smythe-Baldwin, who beseeches Cobb to pull a couple of particularly candid photographs of the body. Constable Dickson balks at this, his artistic integrity insulted, but Cobb recalls the jurors whose faces whitened. So with Smythe-Baldwin complaining about underhanded efforts to inflame the passions of the jury, with the images of Dr. Coombs's autopsy still intruding ("the body is opened in the usual manner . . ."), with the pastrami and the milk rebelling with him, Cobb agrees that the jury need not witness the full aftermath of death. The pathologist and the photographer would be the first two witnesses, and would occupy the afternoon.

". . . extended from the left corner of the jaw, across the mid-line, over the thyroid cartilage of the neck, actually severing the larynx and running to the right side of the neck, three centimetres below the lobe of the ear." From the witness box, Dr. Coombs dryly and tonelessly finished his macabre portrait. "He died within seconds of receiving that injury."

"You are of course familiar with the surgical instruments commonly used in an operating room?" Cobb asked.

"Yes."

"The knife used in most operations is called what?"

"A scalpel."

"Can you say the injuries you observed on the cadaver could have been caused by an instrument such as a scalpel?"

"Very definitely," said Dr. Coombs. "The trauma is consistent with the use of a scalpel or any clean instrument with a keen edge. The cuts were very clean, no ragged edges."

Cobb hoped that Plizit, when he took the stand, would remember a scalpel was used. The last area of Dr. Coombs's evidence was time of death.

"I understand a series of anal temperatures was taken as the body cooled, to determine the time of death. Do you have them noted down?"

Smythe-Baldwin was on his feet, being magnanimous: "We *really* need not require the jury to suffer through all this detail, Mr. Cobb. The jury have more valuable things to do than sit about and laboriously work out anal temperatures The time of death was between eight-fifteen and eight-forty-five p.m. on December third last. I'll admit it, and we'll save the jury from all the medical bafflegab."

Cobb suspected Smythe-Baldwin would ultimately exact a price for this small gift. The old man was an expert at the we-have-nothing-to-hide strategy.

"Your witness," said Cobb.

Smythe-Baldwin had one question: "Any sharp instrument could have caused the injuries? Never mind a scalpel. Any sharp instrument?"

"Yes, any —"

Smythe-Baldwin cut him off. "Thank you. That is all."

Then the police photographer and an hour and a half of photographs. The last group was taken from Dugald McTaggart's window and showed the front window of H-K Meats across the street.

"The face in the window — who is that?" Cobb asked.

Smythe-Baldwin, perched over the witness's shoulder, smiled broadly. "I'd recognize that face anywhere. Well-known male model."

"It's Detective Harrison," the witness said. "He was instructing me what photographs he wanted taken. You can see his features can be made out clearly."

Smythe-Baldwin reached for the pictures before beginning his cross-examination.

"Let me see the last two photographs," he said, "the ones that show the sour and unsmiling face of Mr. Harrison. Yes, those two. Were they taken in full daylight, sir?"

"Yes," said the witness.

"How is that to help us? It's misleading, constable. During the night, that street is dark. There are no street lights, are there?"

"There would be lights reflected from the windows of the buildings."

"Oh, come now, officer. It's dark at night in that narrow little street. Let's be fair."

"Well, yes."

"And on last December third, the day was short. It was pitch-black. It was cloudy. You want to be fair to the jury, don't you, constable?"

"Of course."

"I suggest to you that in the dark of night an observer could not make out the features of a face looking through the opposite window. Looking from Suite C to the window of H-K Meats, you cannot make someone's face out. The light, if any, comes from behind. You see only a silhouette framed by light."

"Are you asking me a question, sir?" said the constable.

"Making a speech," Cobb muttered.

"I'm suggesting that had you taken those pictures at night, as properly you should have, you wouldn't be able to tell whether it was Detective Harrison or Inspector Clouseau. Do you agree, disagree, don't know, or simply fail to comprehend what I in my poor, clumsy fashion am trying to get at?"

"I don't know how to answer. I haven't tried to make out a face there at night."

"Let's not try to put anything over on the jury, then, officer. They're intelligent people and they can see through this. The fact is that at night a person looking from the window of Suite C could not make out the features of a person looking out the front window of H-K Meats."

"I don't know how well."

"You mean you don't know, period." Smythe-Baldwin's voice had become impatient.

"Well, I guess I don't."

"And if the viewer's eyesight were poor, as is sometimes the case with older persons, and always the case among those with eye defects, the task would be more difficult yet?"

"I suppose I would have to agree."

"Don't suppose, please. Do you agree?"

"Yes, I supp — yes."

"Thank you. That is all." Smythe-Baldwin sat down with a flourish, and with a grin hidden from the jury.

Court was adjourned for the day.

It was a fantasy, Jennifer Tann thought. An old English movie. She couldn't remember having bought the ticket, but she had a front seat. The pomp and ceremony: *medieval*. The old sheriff and his "Oyer! Oyer!" The lawyers swirling around the court like graceless ballet dancers in their black robes. (Hang on — she was *one* of them!

What was she *doing* there?) And now, what was she doing *here*? In a bar with this obscure, brooding Foster Cobb and this old raunchy-sounding cop with his rumpled old hat, and he's carrying on about these three wired guys sitting in the front row of the courtroom...

"These three guys are heavies, Fos. Well, kind of skinny for heavies, if you know what I mean, but heavies, you know. Hypes. Junkies. They're not hanging around here for the laughs. The book on them is they deal Dr. Au's dope. The young guys: Snider, the guy whose nose is always running — hate to look at the mess on his fucking sleeve, he don't have a hanky — and Klegg, the short guy. Tinpot gangsters. Records. The guy in the middle, though, Leclerc, watch him. Smart. A little daisy, you know, fruity. Au's back-end for a while, his mixer. Jean-Louis Leclerc. Ran with the Cotroni brothers, Little Joe Valentine in Montreal. Dubois gang. He's on parole for hitting a bank. Six, seven grand. Popped him in a gay bar a few years ago, and of course he's out already. Conned the system."

"So what are they doing here?" Cobb asked.

Harrison smiled. "I don't know, maybe shoot the prosecutors."

Her heart skipped. California-style courtroom shoot-out. Here's innocent Jennifer Tann in the middle of some bloody melee, guns blazing, people screaming. She's hit! And the career of the first great woman criminal lawyer nipped before the bud can blossom. . . .

"Seriously," Cobb said.

"I don't know. These cocksuckers — sorry, Miss Tann — aren't likely to do something stupid like take a pot shot at Laszlo. Here for show, probably. The Surgeon might have brought them in to throw a little scare into Charlie Ming, keep him honest, or whatever. Leclerc, he's been visiting Charlie in jail, giving him his lines, I'd guess. They're here to seal Charlie's lips, Plizit too if possible." Harrison took a gulp from his whiskey glass. "Well, I'm gonna have them assholes checked out, get the sheriffs to shake them down, see if they're holding, maybe catch them in the can fixing."

Tann watched Cobb as he fidgeted, staring down at his drink, puffing at his pipe.

Harrison continued: "They're junkies, you see. They'll do anything for the Surgeon's junk. Get all wired up on junk, they'll do *anything*. We'll sort of shake 'em up, let them know we're here." He drained his glass. "Gotta go."

Tann clutched at her glass of grapefruit juice. She was still and rigid.

Cobb looked up and took Harrison's arm to keep him there. "Just a minute," he said. "Where the hell are those wiretap transcripts? Three weeks ago you promised I'd have them before the trial. I can't wait until we all retire."

"Jeez, Fos, I haven't the faintest idea. They're being held up on orders from some brass upstairs. I got as far up as the deputy chief constable's office, and got some story about a continuing investigation, and nobody wants to blow it. Ottawa is somehow connected. I don't know what goes on. I'm just a homicide cop."

"Ottawa? I thought you told me the Mounties weren't involved. It was a city police thing."

All this stuff was just blowing past Tann. Ottawa? Mounties? Special investigation? What was she *doing* here? She *could* have specialized in estate planning.

"Yeah, well, I don't know what's going on," Harrison said. "They don't tell me bugger-all. All right. Apparently this clown Cudlipp's name comes up, and the surgeon's, and Jimmy Fat's, and they've been tapping some hang-out of Jimmy Fat's, maybe where he used to deal from — who tells me any of these things? Nobody tells nobody anything in a police department, Fos. I find from some poor bum in the street what the guy in the office next to *me* is doing, that's how tight things are. I'm in a very paranoid business, right? I mean, cops are paranoid, drugs don't trust homicide, homicide don't trust morality, morality don't trust community relations. Anyway. The guys upstairs say I'll get the transcripts before Dr. Au takes the stand, and that's not likely until next week, right? I'll get after it again tomorrow."

"Do it in the morning, Honch," Cobb said. "In the afternoon, I'm putting you on the stand."

"I'm ready," said Harrison. "I got my lines. 'I looked into the room, milord, and seen this chubby little guy on a hook, *de*-balled. Obviously, milord, only one man could have perpetrated the deed, and I identify that man sitting over there in the prisoner's dock. High and mighty, ready for a fall.'" Harrison showed his teeth in a jubilant smile. "And when the little Hunkie takes the stand, there's gonna be shit all over the Surgeon's sweet little three-piece suit." He glanced at Tann. "Aw, sorry, Miss Tann, about my language."

"It's okay." She thought she sounded like a mouse squeaking.

The whiskey at the bar and another when he got home were now mixed with the heroin and the day's adrenalin, and got him high. Deborah was in a strange mood, flashing, mysterious, expectant. She had been drinking, too, and came on to him in kittenish style, with a kiss from soft lips that tasted of sherry. She was grilling fat pork chops. Tossing a salad. Stirring a cheese sauce. Very domestic. Cobb had not seen her since Thursday night, because she had gone to Whistler on Friday and returned only this morning. The fight of ten days ago was out of her system now.

It took little to flush out the remnants of his love for her. The smile, the hug, the kiss — past bitterness was dissolved. She chatted about her weekend as they set the table, and she asked about the trial. Cobb, nervous and hopeful, poured himself another drink, sat down at the table, sipped whiskey, ate salad, and talked about it. It was almost like the old days, when he would talk about his cases to her, fulfilling the demands of her fantasies for stark dynamics of good versus evil.

At supper's end, she squeezed his hand, then got up to get coffee. "You're on the front page," she said, returning with the pot and coffee mugs. "'Prosecutor Says Murderer Hacked off Tongue,' or something like that. Jesus, let's go to bed early. You can help me get rid of my goose-bumps."

"You bet," Cobb said.

Cobb showered first, and was waiting for Deborah when the phone rang. He took it on the bedside extension.

"How about an autograph, headline grabber?" Santorini shouted at him. "Good start. Your country and your queen are proud of you."

"Tell her I'm doing my very best."

"I don't expect to be seeing much of her this weekend, unless she happens to be skiing the green chair at Whistler. Coming up this weekend, Fos? Boys' night out Friday *and* Saturday. The commanding officer is going to be visiting Auntie Minnie in Victoria this weekend, so I thought the two of us might get together up at Whistler for a little skiing and piss-up. It's time, you know. You'll need a break from that trial by then. We can throw a few snowballs and make out with a few snow bunnies."

Cobb could hear various sounds in the background. He formed an image of Santorini at his telephone, a glass of burgundy in his hand, feet propped up, kids jumping on his chair, a television set behind him loudly booming its wares.

"I'll meet you up there Saturday evening," Cobb said. "I want to get some work in during the day, but, yeah, I'll be ready for a few drinks by this weekend."

"That's my man."

Deborah walked into the bedroom then, wearing a towel, and smiling. She could hear the shouts from the receiver, held by Cobb a few inches from his ear.

"Give him my love," she said. "But not all of it, Mr. Cobb." She dropped the towel and moved close to him.

Santorni kept booming: "Until Saturday, Fossie, old friend, when we shall drink in celebration of justice, in celebration of the incarceration of evil men. I want you to give that jury hell, Cobb. Fire them up. Loose the hounds on that old fox Smythe-Baldwin. Let slip the dogs of war in there, Cobb. Passionate oratory, that's what it takes. There is too little passion in our courts. Win for Her Majesty."

Cobb hung up, smiling.

Deborah's lean, firm body was already pressed against his, and her hands and her tongue danced over him wildly. Cobb was astonished, and ecstatic. She threw the covers off, and ran her lips and tongue down his chest and stomach, and for a while teased his cock with her mouth, offering wet kisses down its length to the base. In an agony of pleasure, he arched his back, and her head dipped between his legs, then came up again, and she took his cock deeply and hungrily into her mouth. Her tongue found the thousand centres of pleasure that were there, bringing his spasms on early and against his will.

Afterwards, for several minutes he lay back weakly, his arm about her, her head on his shoulder, her russet hair damply covering his chest.

And he wondered.

He wondered from whom she had learned the technique so well. How often had she done it? How many men? He felt pain begin to pour into the empty places in his heart.

But he did not speak.

"Why have you started using again?" she asked softly. "You know I won't stand for it."

He closed his eyes, and waited until sleep overcame the pain.

Tuesday, the Fourteenth Day of March, at Ten O'Clock in the Morning

The first officer to arrive at the scene in answer to Dugald McTaggart's call about suspicious goings-on across the street was James Penn, a traffic cop. Cobb took him through his evidence quickly, hoping Smythe-Baldwin wouldn't notice the holes in it.

The defence lawyer was smiling as he stood to cross-examine.

"Okay, now you told Mr. Cobb you went across the street to H-K Meats, and there was a man there mopping the floor. Had you ever seen him before?"

"No, sir," said Penn. "At least, I didn't recall his face."

"And there was nothing at all extraordinary about a man — a janitor, you presumed — going about his chores, cleaning and mopping up a butcher store at around eight-thirty or nine o'clock at night? You did not take him into immediate custody and charge him with a murder?"

"I was not aware any murder had been committed."

"Of course you weren't. For the simple reason there was no sign of a murder having been committed, was there?"

"I didn't carry out a detailed search for clues."

"You saw no body?"

"No, not at the time."

"You saw no blood?"

"There might have been. It was a butcher store. I wasn't looking." The young officer was nervous and kept clearing his throat.

"Oh, come now, constable," Smythe-Baldwin said, his face expressing total disbelief, "do you wish us to understand that you have no eyes and no training in the art of detecting simple indicia of crime? If there was blood about the room, as some people want us to believe, you as a trained observer would have noticed it. Yes?"

"I would hope so."

"And you didn't, because there was not any there, and a trained observer like yourself would have seen it."

Cobb groaned. "Is he asking a question or giving his own evidence?" he said.

Smythe-Baldwin turned to the judge. "If my friend has an objection, I wish he would frame it as such, or stop sniping from the sidelines."

"Please continue," Horowitz said.

Smythe-Baldwin shook his head ruefully and returned to the witness.

"I put it to you, witness, that the circumstances at the time were such that you felt there was no problem in allowing this man, this janitor, to pick up his mop and pail and wander out of the office."

"I thought he would dump his dirty water, wring out his mop, come back and finish the job, and lock up," said the constable. "When he didn't come back, I got concerned and returned to Suite C to confer with my partner."

"And you didn't lock the office after you?"

"No, I didn't have a key."

"And you went to the Chungking Rooms and waited for the detectives, and then you stood about with them for fifteen or twenty minutes, and you were gone from H-K Meats altogether for an hour or so before you led the detectives back there."

"I don't think it was that long."

"Have you no memory of the time that passed while that office remained unlocked in your absence?"

"It could be half an hour to an hour."

"I suggest you were at H-K Meats just before eighty-thirty, and then you left and didn't return until at least nine-twenty-three p.m. with the detectives. I've seen their reports. That's the time. What do you say?"

"Well, it could be."

"And we also know, I should advise you, that the time of death was eight-fifteen p.m. to eight-forty-five p.m. So anyone could have entered that place during the lapse, committed some horrible crime, then wandered off?"

"That would be speculation."

Smythe-Baldwin had his eye on the jury. "Since speculation is the substance from which the crown has attempted to build its case, why should you feel awkward about engaging in it?"

Cobb could not help himself. "My learned friend knows the difference between cross-examination and self-serving rhetoric," he said.

"And my learned friend knows he should not interrupt when I am engaging in cross-examination. My lord, I seek a ruling enjoining my friend from his constant hen-pecking."

Horowitz said: "Well, my ruling is that it is now nearly eleven-thirty, and we should take our coffee break."

The old sailor Dugald McTaggart told his story well, although with too many words. On the key issue — identification of Au — he stood soldier-straight in the witness box and pointed a finger at the accused.

"That is the man whose face I saw in the window," he pronounced.

"Thank you," said Cobb, happily taking his seat.

Smythe-Baldwin rose grandly from his seat, turned to the witness, hooked his thumbs in his belt, and began:

"Sir, you were born in Glasgow in 1894, and you have seen

nearly a century come and go?"

"I was born on the fifteenth day of August, 1894, and I was a working man until a few years ago. I ha' a strong body, but I ha' a wee bit of arthritis now. I ha' spent my life on the sea."

"Ah, a sailor. A merchant seaman, were you?"

"I was, indeed, for fifty-five years," said McTaggart. "But in the great war I served in the trenches in France."

"And now you have earned your rest and are on a pension, is that so?"

"It is a poor wee pension."

"And you spend your time watching television in the evenings, perhaps, or reading books?"

"The eyes become tired at the end of the day, so I canna read much at all. I play a little chess with the boy, or listen to the radio, or watch television, like you say."

"And were you listening to the radio that night? December third, while you were playing chess?"

"Aye, I play it for the music."

"And loudly?"

"I dinna hear you."

Smythe-Baldwin raised his voice. "You play it loudly, because you are hard of hearing, are you not?"

"I wear a hearing aid."

"You talked to Selwyn Loo that night, and he told you what he heard?"

"I heard the poor man screaming, Mr. Smythe-Baldwin."

"And you say you also saw persons. You do not wear glasses."

"I see what I need to see."

"Do you see this calendar?" Smythe-Baldwin pointed to the calendar on the wall.

"Aye."

"Can you see these words on it?"

"My eyes are not perfect, if that is what you are asking."

"What are these words?"

"Ah, you ha' me there."

"I think we can all read these words, Mr. McTaggart. They say 'Royal Bank of Canada.' I see them. But then, I am wearing my glasses."

"Ah, well, my eyes get tired."

"Have you had your eyes checked recently?"

"Aye. In the last few seconds." Even Cobb laughed, but it wasn't easy.

"Well, it's no shame to wear glasses, sir. You'd still be the same handsome man with them, Mr. McTaggart. Still please the ladies."

"I've pleased a few, Mr. Smythe-Baldwin."

"In many ports, I daresay. Now, we are being candid here, Mr. McTaggart, and no doubt you saw a face in the window on the night in question, but not clearly, I suggest."

"Well, now, I'm afraid to answer, sir."

"You need not call me sir. I think you have seniority."

"Ah, but you have the rank. Rear admiral, were you not?"

"We are all simple sailors in this courtroom," Smythe-Baldwin said, beaming. Cobb thought the jury were enjoying this too much. "Now, it is true — you did not clearly see the man's face in the window?"

"I am pretty sure it was the accused, Mr. Smythe-Baldwin."

"Pretty sure? You had a glimpse for just a few seconds."

"Not long. He opened the curtains and peered out and made a signal with his hand —"

"Did you see what he was wearing?"

"I thought a suit. Very natty, I recall."

"It was an ordinary face, then?" said the lawyer. "Nothing unusual about it?"

"He was an Oriental, I am sure of that."

Smythe-Baldwin gave the witness a group of photographs and asked him to study them.

"Is the man you observed in the window pictured in those photographs, sir?" the lawyer said.

"Well, now," the witness said, "I am not so sure."

"There is no one you can pick out? *Please*, don't look at the accused."

McTaggart held out two pictures. "It may be this one," he said, "or it may be that one."

Smythe-Baldwin took the two photographs and held them up. "For the record," he said, "of the twenty photographs here, the witness has tentatively pointed to two. One is a photograph of one Gordon Yuen, and the other is a photograph of one Robert Wong. Neither man is on trial in this courtroom. A photograph of the accused is also in the group — number sixteen. I tender these as exhibits."

Selwyn Loo blinked nervously behind his thick glasses.

"Can you describe for the jury the sound you heard after the screams?" Cobb asked.

"It was a choking," said the boy. "A gasp, like. Or a gurgling in the throat. I don't know how to say it."

"Was that before or after you saw the face come to the window?"

"Before."

"Was your window open?"

"Yes, then."

"Did you hear any words before that?"

"He was pleading," said the witness. "I do not know his dialect. He called out a name."

"What name?"

"'Dr. Au P'ang Wei,' he said."

"Then you saw the face?"

"Yes."

"And whose face was it?"

"Dr. Au P'ang Wei."

"And do you see that man here in the courtroom?"

"Yes." The boy pointed. "There." Au shook his head sadly.

"The witness is indicating the accused, for the record," Cobb said, and faced the boy again. "And is that the same man you told us earlier you had frequently seen on your street, going up to the office of the Nationalist Benevolent Association above the butcher shop?"

"Yes," said Selwyn Loo.

"Now, Selwyn," said the lawyer, "did you go down to the police station later that night?"

"Yes."

"And were you shown any photographs?"

"Yes. One was Au P'ang Wei."

Cobb sat down.

"You suffer from astigmatism, don't you, Selwyn?" began Smythe-Baldwin. "Do you know what that is?"

"Yes."

"You have great difficulty seeing without your glasses?"

"Yes."

"Are your eyes getting worse?"

"The doctor says I will be blind when I am older."

"Oh, I am sorry," said the lawyer.

"It is all right."

"I am sorry, but I have to ask you these questions. Do you see that man over there in the sheriff's uniform, about fifty feet away?"

"Yes."

"Describe his face."

"It is round. He has brown hair. He has a big moustache. He is smiling. I think he has a bald spot."

"You can see that, eh?"

"I have to do eye exercises."

"And you say you have seen the accused several times in the neighborhood?"

"Yes."

"Has he ever talked to you?"

"No."

"But you know his name?"

"Yes."

"How is that? How did you find out his name?"

"My mother told me. He threatened to cut my mother up —"

"Now just a minute," said Smythe-Baldwin, "that isn't —"

"You asked," said Cobb. "If you don't know the answer, don't ask the question."

"I know what I am doing, Mr. Cobb," Smythe-Baldwin said haughtily. "Now, Selwyn, you say the accused once had harsh words with your mother, so you don't like him?"

"They were not harsh words," the boy said. "He threatened her."

"Well, I am sure there are two sides of that story. But you would be happy to see him convicted of this murder charge, is that so?"

"Yes. If he murdered a man he should be convicted."

"That's why you say you saw the accused in the window, because you do not like him? You want him to be convicted and go to jail for life, isn't that right?"

"I saw him. He was in the window."

"Describe the man you claim to have seen in the window."

"He had smooth skin, no beard, no glasses. Straight nose. Black hair, with some grey at the sides. He wore a grey suit with a tie and a vest."

"He looked like any ordinary well-groomed, well-dressed man you might see?"

"He looked like Au P'ang Wei," said Selwyn Loo.

"But others look like him."

"They don't think like him."

"You dislike him greatly, then?" said the lawyer.

"He sent a man to kill —"

"No, witness," Smythe-Baldwin said, interrupting, his composure leaving him for a second.

Now we're in trouble, Cobb thought. The whole trial could abort. Damn, he had warned Selwyn Loo not to mention the shooting. With the judge and jury looking on, Cobb had a quick, whispered conference with Smythe-Baldwin:

"Smitty, if you apply for a mistrial, I'm simply going to argue that the evidence of the Plizit shooting is admissible. We can show he was acting on Au's orders to do away with the two witnesses. That makes the whole area of the shooting relevant." Cobb prayed the bluff would work: Plizit had not been candid at all about having such orders from Au.

Smythe-Baldwin studied Cobb hard. If he were to apply to abort the trial, he had to seize the moment. But perhaps he could get Cobb's undertaking not to call evidence as to the shooting. Were that to go before the jury, his client could be sunk.

"There will be no mention by Plizit that he was acting on instructions from Dr. Au?"

"If you don't apply for a mistrial."

Smythe-Baldwin calmly turned to Horowitz. "My lord, I think it might be wise to caution the jury that the boy's last remark was careless and unintended, and that there is nothing remotely capable of proving any such suggestion."

Cobb stood up. "I agree with that, my lord."

"I don't think everyone heard it in any event," the judge said. "Please ignore that last reference if you heard it, ladies and gentlemen."

Smythe-Baldwin went back to work.

"Now, Selwyn, I put it to you," he said. "It was dark on the night of December third, and the face you saw in the window was a face in the shadows."

"There was light enough. There was light on his face. I could see him."

"There is very little light from those windows. Now, I'm asking you to be fair and tell us that the face could not be seen distinctly."

"It was Dr. Au," said the boy. "I know his face. . . ."

As a witness, J.O. Harrison could be cocky and bull-headed, too convinced of the rightness of his cause. Smythe-Baldwin knew that fact well:

". . . But Constable Penn tells us he saw no sign of a body, and no blood in the butcher store — on the floors, on the walls, under the table, anywhere. Does not that suggest that the murder occurred between the time he first visited the premises and the time you arrived, perhaps half an hour to an hour later?"

"All it suggests is that Constable Penn may not be very observant." Harrison was reacting as if answering questions was a distasteful part of his duties.

"You don't think Penn is a very good policeman?"

"He doesn't do murder investigations. Maybe he's better than me at seeing cars run red lights."

"He's not a very smart cop?"

"I haven't run an I.Q. test on him. He's young. He's learning."

"Let us move to something else. You say the accused had a small injury on his left hand when he turned himself in. I take it you wish us to draw some sinister inference from that fact? Have you ever injured your hand?"

"Of course."

"Perhaps you have suffered an injury to the area of your knuckles upon occasion?"

"What is that supposed to mean?" Harrison glowered at the defence counsel.

"I am suggesting that one can injure his hand in any vast number of ways — cut it, scrape it, scratch it, bang it."

"Oh, sure. It's even possible to bite your own hand, if you get the urge, Mr. Smythe-Baldwin."

"Oh, come. It is the suspicious police mind at work. Now, you say you recognized the body, had known the person as Jimmy Wai Fat Leung. His nickname was Jim Fat, is that right?"

"He was known as Jim Fat."

"And he was known in police circles?"

"He was known in *my* police circle."

"He was a criminal with a long record for everything from

pushing heroin to running a gaming house, is that so?"

Cobb stood up. "The deceased is not on trial," he said. "His character is irrelevant here."

"The crown would seek to suppress some sordid truths," said Smythe-Baldwin, pleased that Cobb had risen to the bait. "Very well, I can't do much about that kind of stone-walling. Now, I understand you engaged the, er, cooperation of one Laszlo Plizit. Or, should I say, purchased his evidence."

"Well, I resent the insinuation," Harrison said stuffily.

"So do I," said Cobb. "Put it correctly."

Smythe-Baldwin was grinning. "We have touched on some nerve endings. Let me put it this way: Mr. Plizit has agreed, as our American friends put it, to turn state's evidence in order to avoid a just and proper murder conviction for the first-degree murder of a Vancouver city policeman, is that so?" Smythe-Baldwin had Cobb's undertaking that Plizit would not mention his motive for being in the Chungking Rooms. He could now paint a sordid picture of Plizit without it coming back on him. "That is so — you did a deal with Plizit?"

"That is a way of putting it," Harrison said grumpily.

"Is that the way you operate? Trading off your own people like so many pounds of flesh? You're prepared to barter off a brave officer's memory for a promise of perjury?"

Cobb exploded from his chair. "Goddamnit, I'm not going to sit here and —"

"Mr. Cobb, please," Horowitz admonished. But Harrison held out his hand. "Let me answer . . . let me answer." Cobb slid back into his seat. "You see, Mr. Smythe-Baldwin, I've been doing this for nearly as long as you've been practising law, and at my level I'm not dealing with some spoiled momma's boy stealing chocolate bars. I have to make some hard decisions when I'm dealing with certain types of crime — and certain types of people. I won't say anything more about that end of it, it's a hell of a thing when a young kid just learning how to wear a uniform gets blown away. I'll tell you, it makes my heart ache. But there were unusual circumstances here. We're not hiding anything. It's open. His lawyer was involved in everything, and we got nothing to hide. He came forward. We took his statement. That's it."

"I commend you for your honesty," Smythe-Baldwin said. "I suppose we cannot expect equal candor from your good friend Mr. Plizit? You will agree he is the type of person who will say anything, make up any kind of fable to curry favor from the crown and save his skin."

"You have your opinions on that; I have mine."

"Well, what is your opinion?"

"Under the circumstances, I think he'll tell the truth. He had stuff in his statement he couldn't know unless he was there."

"Let's put it baldly, detective — the deal allows him to plead to a lesser charge if he puts the finger on Dr. Au."

"It could be put in fancier words, Mr. Smythe-Baldwin, but that don't mean he's lying."

"Perhaps some physical inducement was also tendered, Detective Harrison."

"You got me there. I took a statement. The lawyers did the rest." Harrison looked the soul of innocence.

"But I am given to understand he first expressed a reluctance to say anything about the December third matter."

"He made a statement after he spoke to his lawyer."

"Now, officer, we have known each other for thirty years, and I would not be mis-stating the matter if I suggested that you have a very persuasive way of dealing with people. Would that be fair?"

"I try to be a little fatherly and understanding sometimes."

Smythe-Baldwin snorted. "Oh, *come* on, detective. You're not suggesting you were treating Plizit like a father!"

"Well, no . . ."

"I think we would all be very much relieved if I were allowed to talk to Mr. Plizit before he gives evidence so that I might resolve some of these questions. But I understand you have hidden him away on us."

"He is in custody."

Cobb began to rise. Plizit's whereabouts had to be kept from Au at all costs.

"Well, where?" said Smythe-Baldwin. "Is it a great secret of state?"

"Yes," Cobb said.

"He's out of town, that's all I can say," said Harrison.

"I won't embarrass you by pressing the matter," Smythe-Baldwin said. "This gentleman Mr. Plizit had, to use your words, stuff in his statement he would not have known unless he was there when Jim Fat got killed. Now, there is a simple way to account for that fact, is there not? Laszlo Plizit killed Jim Fat."

"You got a right to your theories."

"Do you not think it a great tragedy that a killer like Plizit could be using the Vancouver police as pawns to shift blame for Jim Fat's murder from himself to an innocent man, while paying a penalty of only a few years in jail for the murder of a policeman? Perhaps that sort of business doesn't raise the hackles of a grizzled veteran like yourself."

That propelled Cobb to his feet again. "My friend engages in argument, supposition, rhetoric, and sarcasm," he said. "Everything but cross-examination."

"If there is an objection, please frame it as such," Smythe-Baldwin said.

"I think you are being argumentative, Mr. Smythe-Baldwin," the judge said.

"There seems a great deal about the crown's case to argue about, my lord, but I shall move on. Detective, you have also made the acquaintance of one Charlie Ming, whom all of us in this courtroom will have the pleasure to meet in a day or so. You arrested him in the early-morning hours of December the fourth?"

"About two o'clock in the morning. We found him hiding under a bed at his home."

"And you conveyed him to that sumptuous hostelry you operate on Main Street, and there proceeded to interview him?"

"Yes."

"In your own inimitable fashion?"

"Whatever that means."

"I think we know what it means. You have a reputation of possessing, I think it is put, a hard nose?"

"It's no harder than yours, counsellor." Harrison was impassive.

"I, however, have never engaged in the dubious thrill of dragging a manacled man to the police station in his pyjamas at two o'clock in the morning, then proceeding to extort a false statement from him."

"He was wearing a coat over his pyjamas. He resisted arrest. He wouldn't put his clothes on."

"And I suppose it was while he was resisting arrest that this otherwise perfectly healthy man developed an enormous pain in the abdomen area."

"He had to be subdued, but I don't think I would have hit him."

"Now, officer, we're all adults in this courtroom, and we can all handle a little honest admission. You threatened Charlie Ming, and badgered him, and beat him to elicit a lying statement in an effort to put the accused at the scene of the crime."

Harrison, looking uncomfortable, cleared his throat. "Well, I just disagree with all that, Mr. Smythe-Baldwin. If Charlie Ming says something like that, I feel sorry for the man."

"And he's being held in the cells of the city lock-up as a so-called material witness, is he not?"

"Yeah, he isn't going anywhere for the time being."

"And you know that he has repudiated his statement?"

"I heard something about that, yeah."

"And yet you plan to bring him into this courtroom in an

attempt to get him to lie again as part of your vendetta against the accused?"

"He'll say whatever he's going to say. I don't know what he's going to say. . . ."

Tuesday, the Fourteenth Day of March, at a Quarter Past Ten O'Clock at Night

The clouds that had clung all day to the snowy peaks above Vancouver spread softly over the city in the evening, drifting down from Hollyburn and Grouse and across the inlet and the city, across the great flood plain of the Fraser River. With the clouds came the tender coastal rain, given passage by westerly winds from the Pacific Ocean. These are the winds that soften this northern climate and bring an early spring.

Jennifer Tann allowed the slow flic-flac of the windshield wipers to lull her and blunt the strain of the day in court and the strain of the long hours later in the law library helping Foster Cobb track elusive precedent. Now Cobb was driving her home. The obtrusive, gaudy lights of Kingsway car lots gleamed at them through the rain, and colored the slick pavement with reds and yellows. There was warmth and comfort in the front seat of this man's practical old Volvo, and she felt a gentle, elusive energy flowing from him. She studied his face, staring, searching. His face glowed, then darkened as the light from the electric signs touched and colored him. She wanted to reach to him, to touch him. She had found herself starting to want this man — this had been happening for several days now — but she did not have the key to him. There was a hidden source of energy in him, and something closed and secret. . . . She wanted to rummage through him, to explore his strange fusion of knowledge and strength and sensitivity . . . and fear.

Preparing for the trial, they had often exchanged thoughts during breaks from their work, but he rarely spoke of himself. He seemed so outwardly cool, so detached, so . . . professional. Today he had talked easily about the ebb and flow of the trial — mostly ebb this day, because Smythe-Baldwin had disarmed McTaggart and brought out the rancor felt by Selwyn Loo toward the accused, an ill-will that might suggest to the jury the boy had wrong motives for identifying Dr. Au. Cobb spoke admiringly of Smythe-Baldwin, who had tempered so well the impact of the day's witnesses. And these, Cobb lamented, were honest witnesses. What would the old sharpshooter do to Ming and Plizit?

On the whole, Cobb complained to Tann, his efforts had been flimsy, and he felt himself a puerile beginner beside Smythe-Baldwin.

But Tann, although an inexperienced observer in the artistry of counsel, knew already from her two days in court that Cobb, a good trial lawyer — quick, with wit, finely tuned — was moving toward the apex of his career as obviously as Smythe-Baldwin was declining from his. She worried, though, that Cobb had not drawn himself apart sufficiently from the emotion to the trial, and his weakness might be his intense and undisguised hatred of Au, a hatred that flashed in his face each time he turned to look at the man in the prisoner's dock. She feared his anger might breed error.

That anger was the only emotion Cobb displayed openly — in court, in the library, over coffee. Otherwise, a crust hid his feelings. What routes might she follow to break trail to those regions lying hidden behind the facade of the coolly professional trial lawyer? What was real behind the crust? The old pipes he smoked? The funny little grin that worked so hard to break out into a smile? The gentle crinkles in the corners of his eyes? The gold wedding band on his finger? Yes, that was real, she feared. Too real.

A small, dark wave of guilt darted through her.

Goddamnit, Jennifer, the guy is capital M married . . . goes home to her every night (except weekends?) and seems to want to talk about her, seems to be searching for answers about her. Evilly, Jennifer Tann decided that she probably treated him unkindly, kept him somehow beaten and in servility. The woman was in his heart, but surely he was not in hers — and the territory was therefore open to minor trespass.

The guilt again. One does not furtively seek another's man.

Even if this Mrs. Cobb fucks him over, it could be she simply cannot help it. It's an imperfect world, and women learn their bourgeois roles, and sometimes are forced to be cruel to survive in the male world. Okay, there's all that, but . . . damn, there's that *need* in him, that longing for affection which his sadness sometimes speaks of.

Therefore: his lady does not answer his wants. There.

Tann had a picture of her, gained from reading liberally between the lines that Cobb had spoken. Over-indulged. Sexy, damn it. Sort of beautiful — if you like a big ass and big boobs. Flirts. Plays around? Yeah, sure, the sneak. Enjoys laying her trips on people. All sorts of Anglo control.

The woman had very few qualities that she admired, and therefore did not deserve to have this nice man, and therefore it was okay for her to like the guy a lot, to like the man's head, and to be fond of him, sort of . . . physically.

And maybe to invite him in tonight?

Guilt, guilt, guilt.

"Is this your street?" He speaks! Now, how is one to handle this little campaign?

"Uh-huh," she said. "I'm the little house behind the big cedar tree. It's small, but cozy." Yes, let him know it's cozy in there.

"Big yard, little house."

"Little, but friendly." She smiled. "Just one bedroom." With a big comfy old bed in it, Mr. Foster L. Cobb. In case you're interested.

Which you're probably not, you prune.

"What's that in the window?"

"A mandala. It helps keep me centred."

"Centred, hey?" He's probably too shy to ask what the hell that means. What does this ignorant straight lawyer know from mandalas?

The car is stopped at her curb. There is a long pause. And she is definitely feeling very uncentred.

Okay. Sink or swim. "Would you like to come in?" Now why did she have to clear her throat to get those words out?

He looked at her, and with a hand he brushed some unruly blond strands of hair from his forehead. And those little lines beside his eyes did their cute crinkling number, and he . . . actually *smiled* at her! "That's hard to resist, Jenn . . ." But? But what? ". . . but it's kind of late. Deb is away weekends, you know, and I don't get to spend much time with her during a trial. And we have some talking to do."

Ouch, ouch. The nail is driven straight to the centre of her conniving little heart.

"But if you're going to stay up a little late tonight," he said, "you might like to read these wiretap transcripts for me. Honcho finally got his hands on them." He passed her a file from his briefcase. "Cudlipp doesn't know about the tap. The local cops have decided to keep it away from the Mounties for a while. Interesting reading."

Fine. Great. A little homework to take to bed tonight. So romantic.

"Sure," she said faintly, "I'll read them, make some notes." (Sure you don't want to come in and look at my mandalas?) "What time tomorrow?"

"I'm having Charlie brought in early so I can take one more go at him before he gets on the stand. If Smitty's in form, he'll turn him right against us. So I've *got* to spend some time with Ming. Seven-thirty in the morning."

"I'll be there." So loyal, considering she was just kicked in the teeth. "Good night." May you develop a great boil on your bum.

"Sweet dreams."

Then, out of nowhere, his hand reached out . . . and touched her arm, her hand . . . and there was a little squeezing of hands together. And sparks went through her.

Then his hand was gone, and so was she: fumbling and bumbling her way out of the car, clutching the transcripts, then standing awkwardly on the sidewalk, crouching down to get a glimpse of him, waving at him, grinning there on the sidewalk like a simp. . . .

And he drove off.

Inside, she showered, washed her hair, rolled up a little joint, and crawled into a cold bed with the transcripts.

Tape #17 On: 4 Dec 77 17:10 Cst. Lesage
Off: 4 Dec 77 19:25

Conversation at 254' Mark

U/M	Archie's Steak House.
U/M	Joey?
U/M	No, just a sec.
Joey	Hello.
U/M	Hi, it's me.
Joey	Yeah?
U/M	Greek.
Joey	Oh, yeah, how are you? What's cooking?
Greek	Your bud got hit.
Joey	Who? What're you talking about?
Greek	Jimmy.
Joey	Fat got hit? How, what do you mean?
Greek	Think he got a little close to the man. Your phone safe?
Joey	Yeah, it's okay, it's a business phone. Let me take it in the office.
Greek	Call me back. I'm at a pay phone. Let's see, uh, 870-5513.

Joey	870-5513. Okay, in a few seconds.
Greek	Okay.
	. . .
Greek	Yep.
Joey	What went?
Greek	Listen to the news. They found him grinning from the throat.
Joey	Oh, fuck.
Greek	Cut out his tongue and his nuts. So you know.
Joey	Yeah. I thought something like that might be going down. I told him he was a heat-bag. I seen him down in the back, in the bar, sitting with the man.
Greek	I know.
Joey	You know?
Greek	There ain't gonna be no more fucking with civil servants. That's the word. Or you're long gone, John, and I'm telling you that because Jimmy used to hang around there, and the horsemen knew this, so your place could be in for a little steam, you know.
Joey	Fuck. What a pisser. Fucking dirty duty.
Greek	Yeah, one day you're doing easy fucking fast deals and wheels, up with the kingpin all the way from the pounds down to fucking single caps, next day you're cold and mould in the ground.
Joey	What a fucker. I can't believe it. Jimmy was down two, three days go buying the drinks, flush, laying cash sweetly all over.
	. . .
U/M	Hello, who's that?
Joey	Dino, get the fuck off the line, and don't let no one use the phone while I'm on it.

Dino	Oh, jeez, sorry.
Joey	Jesus.
Greek	Well, don't sweat it. Just cool it. Listen, I gotta go. There's half a unit here if you want. I got the mixer and the empty apcays if it's cool maybe later on in your kitchen.
Joey	No, no, been keeping it cool anyway, and I don't want no shmeck, you know, especially if the temperature around here starts to go up like you say. You can come by and take the grinder and maybe lay a couple of small ones on me, but I don't want nothing happening here for a while, hey?
Greek	Okay, I'll drop by.
Joey	What a bitch, hey?
Greek	Yeah. Look, sorry, I know you were buds and all. He just wasn't cool, you know?
Joey	Yeah, but fuck. God.
Greek	See you, Joey.
Joey	Yeah, bye.

Tann took a long, sweet toke and slowly blew the smoke out. Who was the "civil servant" Jim Fat was close to? A narc? *That* should be checked out, she thought.

Conversation at 281' Mark

U/F	Hello.
Joey	Hi, Babe.
U/F	Oh, wow, you sound far away.
Joey	Right here at the restaurant, Ginger.
Ginger	Wow. Everything is far away.
Joey	You just do up or something?
Ginger	How'd you guess?
Joey	How'd I guess, you spinny looney.

Ginger	Hey, I'm not, you know.
Joey	You're a fucking needle freak, you know that?
Ginger	I like it. Makes me feel all horny for you when you come home.
Joey	Bullshit, you dishrag.
Ginger	You gotta be nice to me, Joey, or I won't do it to you no more.
Joey	That don't do nothing for me if you're usin', babe.
Ginger	Aw, honey.
Joey	I know what I get when I come home. Fucking dishes all over. You don't even clean the spoon you cook it in. Fucking mess all over the place. Johnny Carson blaring at me from the TV, and you're nodding on the sofa with your clothes on, and I gotta clean your mess and put you to bed, and you're as horny as a lump of shit and smell like an old used armpit. Jesus, I get tired of it.
Ginger	Hey, honey, what's going down?
Joey	Aw, shit, I heard Jimmy Fat just got ex'd. I just phoned to tell you. Aw, fuck, you're in no condition. I'm gonna go out and get pissed tonight. Find myself some sweet juicy whore who's still got some fuck in her. Aw, shit, I'll see you.
Ginger	Hey, baby, hey.

What a crummy relationship *they* have, Tann thought. So far, not much useful in this stuff.

Tape #18	On: 4	Dec 77	19:19	Cst. Lesage
	Off: 4	Dec 77	21:03	

Conversation at 83' Mark

Joey	Archie's Steak House.

U/M	I guess you heard.
Joey	Hi, Jingo. Yeah, what a bum.
Jingo	You and him was pretty tight, so I'm sorry, but the word is he was rapping with one of the finest, and setting up the White Lady for a lifer in the slam.
Joey	Well, I don't know about the last part, but a few weeks ago I seen him here sitting with the heat, and a few times before that. I thought the man was pumping him for stuff, but I keep my ears open and my mouth closed, you know, a little. The narc, Cuddles Cudlipp, he's been nosing around here a lot, comes in for a drink, looking for Jimmy, stays, chats up the girls, and you know, they're fucking busy, Cindy just quit, and we're short-staffed, and they don't need his hands pawing at their pussies all the time, and he knows me, knows I'm on parole for that beef they made me on in '75, you know, and he's watching me to see if I'm using, you know, looks at my eyes, squints at me, like, but he can see I got no marks, and if it wasn't for Ginnie, I wouldn't have any smack around, but this cop comes on all friendly, just keeping tabs, looking for Jimmy, and the house buys him a few, and he likes to knock a few back, this cop, a real juicehead.
Jingo	Yeah, I'm hearing some stories about him, but you know, you hear stories about narcs all the time, and you don't know what to believe.
Joey	Yeah, well, I'm gonna get hammered tonight. Come on down after closing, we'll go out, hit the booze can, nothing else will be open tonight. You gotta little blow with you? I can use a little snort or two to buoy me up.
Jingo	I got.

Joey	You always got, you're the snowman.
Jingo	Sure, let's get blasted. You know who did the trip on Jimmy?
Joey	Yeah, I know. I think you know, too.
Jingo	They'll never make him. They never make him on anything.
Joey	No, he just wipes off the blood and slime and laughs at them.
Jingo	I heard he don't laugh much. You ever met him?
Joey	No. Jimmy talked about him. Thought he was the Lord High Muckey-Muck. Cold. Cold, man. Cold as the end of an Eskimo's dink. He don't fuck chicks. He don't eat cock. Don't do dope. He don't boogie. Only one thing turns him on.
Jingo	What?
Joey	Cutting people's nuts off, then watchin' them die.
Jingo	Jeez.
Joey	Yeah. Make sure you bring the after-burner.
Jingo	Right on. See you.
Joey	See you.

So: The civil servant was Cudlipp, Smythe-Baldwin's witness. Why had he been hanging around with Jim Fat? What was the connection?

Tape #28 On: 17 Dec 77 20:43 Cst. Orville
Off: 18 Dec 77 11:25

Conversation at 28' Mark

U/M	Archie's Steak House.
U/M	Can I speak to Alice.
U/M	She's with a customer. Can you hold on?
U/M	Yeah, sure.
	. . .

Alice	Hello.
U/M	Hi, do you know who this is?
Alice	Voice sounds familiar.
U/M	I like it well-done.
Alice	I'm sure you do.
U/M	With fries, onion rings.
Alice	Uh-huh.
U/M	Drink Heinies.
Alice	I know you. You're the twelve-ounce T-bone.
U/M	Hey, that's pretty good.
Alice	Well, I noticed you.
U/M	Well, I've been looking at you, too.
Alice	You were down here last weekend, just after I started here.
U/M	I guess that's why I never seen you around before. I eat down there a lot. I said to myself, hey, they finally hired something good-looking down here.
Alice	Gee, flattery will get you everything. So, what are you up to?
U/M	Oh, nothing much, for a Saturday night. Sitting in front of the old TV watching a crummy movie. Not too exciting for a single man on a Saturday night, I guess.
Alice	So what's a good-looking old stud like you doing being single on a Saturday night?
U/M	I wish I knew. I figure maybe later on I'll go out for a few drinks.
Alice	Uh-huh.
U/M	Wouldn't mind a little company. I don't know what your situation is. Maybe you got something happening, I don't know, but if you're not doing anything after you get off shift, how would you

	like to get together?
Alice	Well, now, Mr. T-bone, I might just be able to manage that. I'm off at eleven.
U/M	You told me you sometimes like to down a couple after work.
Alice	Did I say that? I must of been hinting or something.
U/M	Should I meet you outside there?
Alice	Sure. About ten after.
U/M	You know what I do?
Alice	Seems to me I heard something about you around here. Doesn't bother me at all. I like a little pork once in a while.
U/M	Well-done?
Alice	Raw.
U/M	I'll pick you up just after eleven.
Alice	Bye.
U/M	Bye.

Tape #33   On: 21   Dec 77   22:12   Cst. Orville
          Off: 22   Dec 77   16:00

Conversation at 132' Mark

U/F	Good evening, Archie's Steak House.
U/M	Hi, who's this?
U/F	It's Alice, who's this?
U/M	Why, it's Robert Redford, looking for a new co-star, but I need to do a little screen test first for the bedroom scene.
Alice	Hi, there, Jingo. Afraid you ain't got a bed big enough to hold me?
Jingo	What I got is big enough for you.

Alice	Don't flash it around. Somebody might think it's a match and try to light it. You want to speak to Joey? He's in the kitchen, I'll get him.
	. . .

Joey	Jingo Balls, Jingo Balls.
Jingo	Jingo all the way. Hey, man, you called.
Joey	Weird. You know who was here tonight?
Jingo	Margaret Trudeau.
Joey	Close enough. That narc, Cudlipp. He's been in here a few times since, you know, Jimmy met his. Still poking around, looking for something. But this time he brought a friend, a lady, a White Lady.
Jingo	Oh, yeah?
Joey	They wandered in together, looked around, sort of. He's looking very dapper and spiffy, and he turns on the charm. Alice is just swimming. She gets them, the dick takes a Heineken, the top man has a Courvoisier, you know, in a snifter, wants it warmed. I don't know, Alice probably puts it between her legs. He gives her a twenty, tells her, you know, don't bother to break it. Thank God the house keeps half. Alice is just purring around them, Cudlipp takes a pinch of her ass like he always does, I don't know, he's probably fucking her. She'd be rolling in it if she sold it, the way she puts out, but she's just dripping for the Lady, he's so swav-ay, you dig?
Jingo	All right!
Joey	They're sitting in the back, not in the bar, in the dining room, way at the back, deep in conversation, I don't know what about, but this has become the copper's, like, bailwick, and he knows people around here keep their mouths shut, like I never

said nothing when he used to meet Jimmy here. It's a safe place, you know, whatever your scam is, but I get the impression the cop is on the take, somehow, they're too friendly.

Jingo   Out of sight.

Joey   Archie, you know, my old man, he's down tonight checking out the till, and he sees these dudes talking very cozy in the back and comes up to me and says, he says, Joey, I told you we don't want no fucking fruits in here.

Jingo   All right! Outrageous.

Joey   I lay this trip on him about it's a fucking narc and somebody important, I don't tell him who, and he says I don't want no fucking narcs hanging around either, upsets the regular clientele, if you can dig it.

Jingo   All right!

Joey   So they have their drinks, and just saunter out. The top man gives me this winning smile and a nice-to-see-you-again like we're good old buds, and Cudlipp takes me aside. Says, Joey, he says, this place is cool. No hassles. Like, man, he promises nobody's gonna bring any heat down on Archie's friendly little neighborhood steak house.

Jingo   Sounds weird.

Joey   So there he was, sitting right in my dad's place, this spiffy sucker, so cool butter wouldn't melt, and I'm thinking, you know, here's the guy who sliced up poor old Jim Fat, and just cold as anything, cuts out his tongue, and he's smiling at me, and I don't have the jam to say anything, of course, and I'm sort of wondering, hey, what's going on here, what's going down, I mean, here's this guy, kills, tortures, I guess, my friend, and he's out on bail like he owns the fucking city, which he probably does, half of, anyway, and fuck, I need to go out and get a little zingo, Jingo, I mean, you want to do a little blow, a little snow, a little ho-ho-ho, have a little Christmas party, because shit, Ginnie's a little pissed off, threatening to split, 'cause I ain't providing, you know, I closed it down, too much hassle with the steam in here damn near every night, Cudlipp hanging around all the time. I don't think I trust the sucker.

Jingo Hey, I'm your man.

Joey I'd like to call somebody about this weird biz with the narc and the White Lady, but who do you call, the cops? They got their man in here, and I'm gonna end up pushing posies with my nuts hanging beside the mistletoe. Jeez.

Jingo Okay, let's dance.

Joey I'm ready to fold the tent.

Jingo Right over.

Joey Good man. See you.

The plot thickens, Tann thought, growing excited. Sounds suspiciously like an alibi in the making. How did the cops get these tapes?

Tape #124 On: 17 Feb 78 16:13 Cst. Lesage
      Off: 18 Feb 78 23:36

Conversation at 258' Mark

U/M Hello.

U/F Okay?

U/M Yeah, it went just right.

U/F The whole thing?

U/M Hey, baby, I told you not to call me from work. You

	never know when somebody might be listening.
U/F	Pa-ra-noi-a.
U/M	Listen, I know. No phone is safe.
U/F	Sorry, baby.
U/M	Anyway, we sold the property. Down payment of fifty, and the balance when the deal is sealed.
U/F	How much?
U/M	Can't you wait until you get here?
U/F	I'm just heading out.
U/M	Two-oh-oh.
U/F	What?
U/M	Five-oh plus two-oh-oh.
U/F	Five . . . Far. Fucking. Out. You are my baby. You are my baby.
U/M	Includes your half of the property, sweetheart.
U/F	You just got yourself a great big juicy piece of ass coming your way in about half an hour.
U/M	I wouldn't have done it if it weren't for you, baby.
U/F	See you.
U/M	I'll be waiting.

Tann wasn't sure what all *that* was about. She carefully put the transcripts in a folder, turned off the light, wiggled the blankets into a comfortable mould around her, and began to sleep, her mind drifting out the front door of Archie's into a more peaceful and secure place. The soft, mocking eyes of Foster Cobb gently haunted her dreams.

In his Vancouver place, the penthouse he shared with Prince Kwan, Au P'ang Wei sat in his robes while his bath was being prepared. He enjoyed these few minutes at the end of the day, enjoyed a communion each evening with Prince Kwan, and gave him a form of love.

Au contemplated the price of innocence. It was high, indeed.

Poor Cudlipp was obviously being led by the nose by a grasping woman, and the result of this greed would be an unfortunate business loss coming at the end of the current fiscal year. But one should not lament these things — the deal had been struck: The rice, as it was said, had been boiled. Au had insisted, however, that final payment be deferred until Cudlipp had begun his evidence. This condition would ensure that Cudlipp would be committed to Au's defence. (One could never be too sure about policemen, however friendly they may appear on surface. They tended to be unreliable.) And was there not something particularly dangerous about a man who so easily worked both sides? The two-headed snake, the Ch'ao-chou say, hurts or pleases one of two contending parties to suit his purpose.

A sharp pain entered the acupuncturist's heart as he thought about these things, and he knew there was no point upon his body which a needle could penetrate to sufficient degree to ease it. And suddenly, abruptly, a searing flash of memory . . . of coarse faces . . . black with anger . . . hands tearing . . . blood . . . a deep and primal anguish . . .

In the flat and fertile delta of the Fraser Valley, south of the city, in a farmhouse hidden from the road and fields by rows of tall poplars, on the second floor, in a bedroom, lay Jean-Louis Leclerc, in the arms of his compliant teen-aged lover, who, weakened more by heroin than lust, surrendered to Leclerc's languid efforts to achieve connection. The heroin dampened Leclerc's ardor, and the night dragged slowly for his companion.

In the morning, awakened by the alarm, Leclerc sprang from bed and dressed to meet Klegg and Snider for court. He had worked hard and long with Charlie Ming, and today he would observe the fruits of his labors.

Byron Jones lay weakly in bed, happy that soon he would be alone, free of Leclerc. But he was not entirely free.

"Can you fix me before you go?" he asked.

"*Oui, ma chérie.*" And Leclerc gave the boy a fix from a fat little bag of heroin.

"Please leave me some."

"No way," Leclerc said. "I have special use for this." There was enough heroin to kill a team of horses in Leclerc's little bag.

"Fuck you," said Byron Jones.

"And fuck you, too," said Leclerc sweetly, throwing him a kiss as he walked down the stairs to the front door.

Wednesday, the Fifteenth Day of March, at Eight O'Clock in the Morning

"Damn it, Charlie, you said Dr. Au was at the H-K Meats." Cobb was shouting inside the small interview room.

"Don't remember."

"Come on, Charlie, you know you are lying. You *do* remember, and you signed a statement saying he was there when Jimmy was killed."

"Uh, don't think so."

"Who was with you when you went to pick up Jim Fat? Was Laszlo Plizit with you?"

"Uh, yeah, think so."

"Well, I *know* he was there. He *told* me he was there, and you were there, too. There was someone else, too, wasn't there? There were you, Dr. Au, Plizit, some other guy standing guard outside." Plizit had been close-mouthed about the identify of the fourth person. "Come *on*, Charlie, who all went up there to pick Jimmy up?"

"Don't know."

"Did Dr. Au say what he was going to do to Jimmy? You understand Chinese, Charlie, what was he saying?"

Charlie Ming looked dumbly up at Cobb. His mouth came open, but no words came out. His hairless scalp glistened with wet beads of effort.

Ming was attempting to summon great resources from within him in an effort to power the ponderous cognitive gears in his mind. That mind was a struggling steam engine, and it seemed forever to be grunting up a hill. Did the prosecutor not understand that he spoke too quickly, and asked too many questions all at once? It was especially hard for Ming to remember whether a particular question called for a truthful answer or one of Leclerc's.

Leclerc was a patient and persistent teacher who had tutored the slow-thinking Ming in his evidence with dedication — and with a certain feeling of affection. Leclerc liked this blunt ox, a man so inefficient in the arts of deception that he developed headaches while mastering simple untruths. But the script did slowly penetrate the mind of Charlie Ming, and Leclerc had been pleased at his work. Charlie Ming would testify, on oath, that after Jim Fat had been picked up, they had driven to a restaurant on Kingsway, where Au had alighted. According to this version, Ming, Plizit, and Jim Fat then proceeded to Chinatown, where Ming dropped Plizit and Jim Fat off in front of H-K Meats. Ming would testify that later that evening he returned to the building, went inside, saw some blood, and was cleaning it when the police arrived. The evidence was attractive in its simplicity.

For Ming, the task of memorizing all this evidence had been exhausting, raising sweat under his arms and red welts on his scarred face.

As an aide-de-camp to the general in Au's army, Ming had proved himself a faithful retainer, a fearless enforcer.

But fearless as he was in battle, he was as fearful in tasks of the intellect, and cowed easily by those with quicker minds. He was afraid of the prosecutor, Cobb, and wished the man would stop asking questions, would let him rest and save his strength for court. He had been told not to say much to the prosecutor.

"Charlie, listen to me carefully," Cobb was saying. "In a couple of hours you are going to be brought into the courtroom, and you are going to have to take an oath on the Holy Bible, an oath before God that you will tell the truth. I am going to ask you in that court whether Dr. Au was in the meat store with you on December third."

"Uh, don't know nothing about that," Ming said.

"You were supposed to clean the place up and get rid of the body, weren't you, Charlie?"

"No, uh, don't know."

There was a knock then on the door of the interview room. A sheriff who had been posted outside waiting to return Ming to the cells looked in. "Miss Tann is here," he said, and let her in.

"Sorry, I'm late," she said, smiling and sitting beside Ming. He had met her during previous interviews and considered her a beautiful but untouchable lady, too perfect to be a prosecutor or a lawyer. Being with her, Charlie felt shy and nervous.

"Hello, Charlie," she said. "How do you feel today?"

"Not too good. Feel better maybe later, when, uh, go home."

"I told Charlie he can go home after his evidence is finished," Cobb said. "If there is no perjury charge, he can go home. Do you know what perjury is, Charlie?"

"I guess, maybe."

"That's when you lie in court. The Criminal Code says you can go to jail for fourteen years if you lie in court. Do you understand that?"

"Uh, yeah."

"Now, Charlie, we know you were in that building with Dr. Au and Jimmy Fat, right?"

"No, no, that not, uh, true."

The lady was smiling and shaking her head.

"Help us, Charlie," she said. "You should do the right thing." Her voice was the sound of bells, and he cleared his throat and swallowed, casting his eyes downward. He said nothing.

"Charlie," said Cobb, "who told you to say these untrue things? Did Dr. Au visit you?"

"No, no, Dr. Au not come." He was still looking down.

"We know another man came to se you. Leclerc. You know Leclerc, right?"

"Uh, no, no."

"Jim Fat was a friend, wasn't he, Charlie?" said Cobb. "You are not being fair to Jim Fat."

Ming shook his head truculently.

Cobb could not have known of the battle raging within his witness's trembling heart, where two contending terrors engaged in unyielding combat. The first was a fear of the Surgeon's knife, but the second fear, more abstract yet as deadly, was a fear that clutched at his bowels — it was a fear of the witness box. Blunt Charlie Ming, lacking too much in wit to be capable of devious speech, was oppressed by the image of himself on the witness stand under the solemn eyes of a hundred people and the stern and forbidding countenance of a powerful judge. There had not been such terror even during the great pitched knife battles of the gang wars of his youth. Charlie Ming had been in court before, for things like assault, drugs, and theft, but his lawyers had considered him to be too dull to make a good witness, and since they could not put him on the stand, they made him plead guilty, and let him go to jail.

The elaborate trappings of the justice system, its ceremony and observances, moved Ming not just in fear, but in awe too. The great assize court was a palace of a higher civilization; the judge's bench, a throne.

Perhaps Jennifer Tann knew something of his fears. Her mind was more finely tuned to the awareness of others, and at one point during a pause in Cobb's insistent cajoling, she said:

"Charlie, when you come before the judge, you must speak the truth. He is a great and powerful man." Then, with Cobb giving her a strange look she spoke a sentence in Cantonese dialect: "In the court he is an emperor, and his net stretches wide, and nothing escapes its meshes."

Ming looked up at her, and his lips trembled. For Charlie Ming, this was a day of despair.

The judge looked over his glasses at Cobb and nodded for him to begin. Cobb turned to the sheriff.

"Please bring in Mr. Ming."

As Ming walked through the door, the first person his eyes fell upon was Au P'ang Wei, sitting alone, high in the centre of the room. Their eyes met hard, and Ming felt a burst of electricity run up his spinal cord. He then dropped his eyes, seeking to hide them from the forces churning in this great echoing space. Someone took him by the elbow and led him in a slow march to a wooden stand with railings. He heard voices speaking to him, but fog billowed through his head, and the words were unclear. Finally someone thrust a book into his hand and said something, to which Ming mumbled a response. Then other words: "You may put the Bible down." He heard that, and obeyed, and dared look up. To his left and above him, in robes of dark black and brilliant red, was the man he knew was his judge. He heard him speak in calm and even tones: "You may be seated if you wish, Mr. Ming." He understood the words as a command, and sat.

Across from him sat the wise men and women of the jury. From his right eye he could see Dr. Au, and seeing him, he felt a pulling in that direction, a force that could tear his eyes out if he refused to look full at him, to obey his silent commands. He now saw the prosecutor, standing near the jury, who was saying, to Ming's relief: "Now, look straight over here, at me and the jury. Don't look around the courtroom. I want you to listen to my questions and answer carefully." The prosecutor paused, and keeping his gaze steadily on Ming, began:

"You are Charlie Ming."

"Uh, yeah."

"And you know the accused, Au P'ang Wei."

The prosecutor had ordered him to look only at him and the jury, but there was a need to look at Dr. Au, and he looked that way and saw his eyes piercing like daggers. Ming was held by the eyes, frozen.

The prosecutor must have understood, because he said: "Just look over here, Mr. Ming, and concentrate on my questions. You know him?"

"Yeah."

"Now, I want you to remember back to December third last year. Were you with Dr. Au that evening?"

Ming looked at the prosecutor helplessly, and he looked at the judge, and knew that the judge, the man they called a lord, would know when an answer was false.

"Yeah," he said.

"And did you know the deceased man, Jimmy Wai Fat Leung?"

"Yeah."

"And were you with him on that day, too?"

"Yeah."

"And do you know a man called Laszlo Plizit?"

"Yeah."

"And was he with you, too?"

"Yeah."

"And did you go in a car somewhere with Au and Plizit?"

"Yeah."

"Where did you go?"

Ming studied his answer, breathing heavily. "We, uh, go pick up Jim Fat." He could hear whispers from behind him, where some people were writing notes of his words. It was hard to concentrate.

"Where did you pick him up?"

"At his house."

"Did the three of you pick him up?"

"Uh, yeah."

"In whose car?"

"Dr. Au."

"And where did you go?"

"We go, uh . . ." Ming looked quickly at Au, and the voice of Au in his head was powerful in its exhortations. "We, uh . . ."

The man sitting high above him spoke again, calmly giving an order that sounded in Ming's ears like a pronouncement from the heavens: "You must answer the question, witness."

"We go, uh, to National Society office, then, uh, H-K Meats."

"And what happened at that place?"

Ming could see the other lawyer, Smythe-Baldwin, looking at him from below, his face angry. He was the man who had warned Ming that his words in this court could help convict his benefactor of murder. The man was powerful, Ming knew, but seemed not to have the ultimate power to stop these answers.

Again the judge issued his command: "Please answer the question."

"What happened there?" the prosecutor repeated. "What happened to Jim Fat there?"

"We, uh, make Jim Fat take off, uh, clothes, and tie him, uh, tie him on table."

"Why did you do that?"

"I . . . take orders from Dr. Au."

"Did you know what was going to happen to Jim Fat?"

"No, no, no, I never know. I only help." His tongue was thick, his head aching.

"What did Au do to Jim Fat?"

"He, uh, talk. They talk. I, uh, not understand. I, uh, I, uh, need water." He clutched the wooden railing for support.

"Miss Tann," the prosecutor said. She rose and went to a pitcher on the counsel table. "What happened after they talked?"

"I, uh, not know, not know what." The beautiful lady brought a glass of water, and she smiled at him, and she must have known the great trouble. The lawyer, Smythe-Baldwin, was shaking his head and whispering something to the young man beside him.

"Did you go somewhere?" the prosecutor asked.

"Yeah, I go, uh, look for pail and mop. Go to basement."

"Why did you go for a pail and mop?"

"Uh, uh . . ." The answer would not come, but he knew it must, or it would be ordered. "Dr. Au tell me. Get mop to clean up. Jimmy, uh, sick."

"How long were you gone?"

"Uh, long time. Have to, uh, go to basement."

"And what did you see when you got back?"

"Nothing."

"Now, tell us what you saw, Mr. Ming."

"Uh, see, uh, blood, some blood. I, uh, clean up."

"And who was in the room?"

Ming stared ahead of him, his mouth open, caught on words which would not come. If he looked at Dr. Au, he would see in his eyes the warrant of death. Yet Au still had the power to make him look, and Ming did look, and saw the message of his own execution. Then he looked behind Au to the front row, where the watchers sat, and he saw the messengers, Leclerc, Klegg, Snider.

"Mr. Ming, please answer," the judge said.

"Who in the room?" Ming repeated. "Uh, me, uh, Laszlo . . . Dr. Au."

"Anyone else?"

"Jim Fat, uh, not there. Laszlo and Dr Au P'ang Wei, they go. I clean up." Words that he knew he must not say had now been said, drawn from him by forces beyond his control.

"Thank you, Mr. Ming," the prosecutor said. "Answer Mr. Smythe-Baldwin's questions, please."

The old lawyer, still shaking his head, stood up, holding in his hand a piece of paper. What was he now to do? Here was another man of great importance.

"Mr. Ming," said Smythe-Baldwin, "is this your mark?"

"Yeah, I sign it."

"You signed it a week ago Saturday, isn't that so?"

"Yeah."

"I want you to read it."

"I, uh, not read too good."

"Then let me read it for you. 'This statement has been read over to me by Mr. Smythe-Baldwin, and it is true. On Saturday, December third, Dr. Au and I drove to the home of Jimmy Wai Fat Leung, and he came with us. We drove to a place on Kingsway where Dr. Au left the car because he wished to meet with a man about business. I drove the car to H-K Meats, and Jimmy Wai Fat Leung left the car and went into the building. This was about seven o'clock at night. I returned to the building an hour later to meet Jimmy Wai Fat Leung. He was not there, but there was blood on the floor, which I cleaned with a mop. After a while a policeman came, and because there was blood, I was scared, and I ran away. Dr. Au was a good friend and employer of Jimmy Wai Fat Leung in the mortgage business, and I have no reason to believe he was responsible for his death. I have made a statement to the police in which I said that Dr. Au was at the H-K Meats on the night of December third. I said that to the police because I was scared of Detective Harrison, who had dragged me from my bed in my pyjamas later that night and who struck me in the stomach to make me come. He also placed handcuffs on my wrists, which caused bruises and shouted at me, telling me I must say Dr. Au was at H-K Meats or I would be charged with murder. The statement I gave to the police is untrue, and I would not have made it if I had been allowed to see a lawyer. Dated this twenty-four day of March at 312 Main Street.'"

Smythe-Baldwin paused. All those words were a great confusion in Ming's mind.

"Now, Mr. Ming," Smythe-Baldwin continued, "that is the statement you gave me, and you gave it to me without my putting any words into your mouth, and you gave it honestly, isn't that so?"

Now the prosecutor spoke again. "He is being asked to answer three questions at once."

The defence lawyer then spoke: "Is this your statement, Mr. Ming?"

"Yes."

"Is it true? You are under oath. I warn you that if you lie you can be charged with perjury."

Fear was compounded by fear now. The man's voice was very strong, and he was angry. How could it be answered?

"I think it, uh, true. I don't know."

"What I read to you was true, was it not?"

"I, uh, don't remember. Maybe. Maybe Dr. Au not there."

"He wasn't there, was he?"

"I, uh, maybe, uh, don't know."

The judge spoke then. "Mr. Ming, I don't quite follow. Was the accused at H-K Meats on that night, or not?"

"My lord," said Smythe-Baldwin, "I am in cross-examination."

"Yes," said the judge. "I am sorry, but it requires to be made absolutely clear. Was the accused there, witness?"

Ming looked up at the judge, and felt himself turning cold. After pause, he said in a quiet voice: "Yeah, he there."

Smythe-Baldwin's words now came at him from another part of the courtroom, and Ming, turning to his right, saw him standing beside the prisoner's dock, only two feet from Au P'ang Wei. "Mr. Ming," the lawyer said in a calm, steady voice, "you are mistaken. I put it to you that my client was not there that evening. This is important, Mr. Ming. The future of this man is at stake. Whether he goes to jail for his life is up to you. You must be very careful. Now, I ask you again — he was not there, was he?"

Au's hard eyes bore into Ming's head like drill bits of tempered steel. From the right side of his vision, Ming saw the executioners sitting in the front row, and he felt a shadow pass in front of him.

"Dr. Au there," Ming said. "Dr. Au there."

Au then looked away from him, to the left, toward the three addicts, and Ming saw Leclerc nod slightly, and smile. For the remainder of Smythe-Baldwin's cross-examination, which lasted to the end of the day, Au did not look upon Ming again.

At the end, Smythe-Baldwin sat, and Cobb arose.

"May the material-witness warrant be cancelled, my lord?" the prosecutor said. "There is nothing to hold Mr. Ming here further."

"Yes," said Mr. Justice Horowitz. "You are free to go now, Mr. Ming."

"I would simply ask that the witness make himself available should an occasion arise requiring his further attendance," Cobb said.

"Please give the sheriff your address as you go," said the judge. "I would suggest you not leave the city for a while."

For some reason, Ming thought that was funny, and he chuckled to himself as he walked out of the courtroom and down the street. He was feeling well, all things considered. The day was warm and pleasant, and he did not expect to see another one, so he enjoyed it.

And the plainclothesman whom Harrison had assigned to watch over Ming was enjoying the day, too. He was watching the girls on the courthouse lawn as Ming strolled down the street behind him, disappearing around the corner.

Wednesday, the Fifteenth Day of March, at Five O'Clock in the Afternoon

For the addict, death comes in many ways: from dirty needles that carry bugs, or contaminants in the mix that do not dissolve and are carried to the lungs and damage them, poisons that are added to the buffing agent — by accident or design. (Rat poison has been found to be cheap and effective.) But a simple overdose of pure heroin — even a single capsuleful — will do in a user whose tolerance is low after a long stay in hospital or jail. A junkie who has built a high tolerance will just get high with ten times the amount.

The heroin way is held in high regard by the aficionados of death. They will urge upon you that for your final passage, for a blissful rendering of your soul to worlds that lie beyond, you should spoil yourself with a rich preparation of diacetylmorphine. It is a way of death that gently eases you into arms.

By the time your lungs give in, their tissues swollen, their air sacs filled with fluid, and by the time breathing struggles and stops, you will already have drifted from trance to coma to shock, and you will have had no sense of the end that is arriving. Before the trance, there will have been dreams of many colors and textures, and your fantasies will have given you diamonds to pluck from the sky and golden palaces to rule. You will have soared and swooped like an eagle. You are neither awake nor asleep, and if your eyes are open and your ears tuned, they will create beauty where before there was degradation, fear, and loneliness. The dreams will have followed the opiate rush, a sweet orgiastic feast for all your senses.

All it will take to go this way — for those whose bodies are not trained in the processes of addiction — will be one or two capsules of Dr. Au P'ang Wei's 97-per-cent pure White Lady. If you are uncomfortable about poking needles into your flesh, then you can eat the heroin, but death will demand it in much larger quantity. (However, by eating it, you will get off for a longer time before checking out.)

A concluding word: do not fight it. Flop with it. Let it carry you. Because otherwise your fantasies become nightmares, and pleasure gives way to an awful terror.

Charlie Ming, although a non-user, was aware of the fact last stated, and when, while looking up at the two dark holes of the barrels of Leclerc's loaded, cocked, twelve-gauge sawed-off shotgun, he washed down a quarter ounce of the acrid powder with a half-pint of chocolate milk, he decided to lie back and let the narcotic waft him across the Styx.

He was not pleased to know death so early, but content at least in the manner chosen for it.

In the late afternoon, Ming had enjoyed the last taste of a sunny day in March, walking the three or so miles to his home from the courthouse. He had refused Leclerc's offer of a ride, and Leclerc understood, and directed his men to follow on foot while he circled slowly about here and there in his car. Everyone joined in a quiet group at the entrance to Ming's small duplex, and Ming invited them in. He was glad that the place was tidy — his sister had a key, and must have cleaned it.

He was allowed to go to the bathroom and shower and brush his teeth and change into his pyjamas, ironed crisply by his sister and folded at the bottom of his bed. No doubt she would visit tonight, after her dinner, and he wanted her to find him cleanly attired, not unpleasant in smell or in sight. Beyond requesting the privilege of cleaning himself for his decease, he expressed no final wishes. One, however, was asked of him, and he found no reason to refuse; and so in a poor choppy scrawl, with Leclerc directing his hand, he write in English upon a scrap of paper these words: "I am not able forgive myself for my errors of the past and I give my soul to God." He was allowed to add some words for his sister: "To Mary, my sister, I give all stuff here, and thank you for frais pigamass." No one could spell pyjamas, although the issue was hotly debated, and Leclerc believed "fresh" might be spelled somewhat like the French word.

The glutinous mix of white powder and chocolate milk in Ming's mouth slid down like syrup. Leclerc kept a little stuff for himself and his two companions, and the three of them fixed, and sat back to watch Ming die. Leclerc had seen the effects of overdoses before, but John Klegg and Easy Snider — junkie dealers from the Corner — were interested in the process, and joked in a good-natured way with each other as Ming nodded off. When his breathing finally became labored and hoarse, they got up to go. Leclerc wondered what it would feel like to ball a dying man, but decided against it.

Mary Ming, looking forward to seeing her brother after his absence of more than three months, came by after dinner and found him in his bed in smiling permanent repose, a bubbly red froth upon his lips and nose.

Cobb's sleep that night was far less pleasant than Ming's, and the only thing that could be said for it in preference was that it was concluded by an alarm clock. The news of his witness's death had struck him hard, and late at night he had cranked up a good hit — despite his best intentions to keep his use down to a two-cap straightener in the morning and a couple more in the late afternoon. After Ming's sister had called the police Wednesday night, there had been a hurried conference at Ming's duplex, at which Harrison lacerated the ashen-faced plainclothesman who had let Ming slip away. Finally, at three a.m., Cobb had dragged himself into bed beside his fitfully sleeping wife.

Harrison, on the other hand, had slept not at all, but angrily stalked the junkie bars and gay clubs in dogged but futile search for Leclerc.

Cobb was heading for the shower at eight a.m. when Harrison phoned.

"Nothing," the policeman said.

"Where was Au?"

"You got to be kidding."

"Well, where was he?" Cobb said.

"Very conspicuous until the call came in at six-thirty. Then we lost him."

"Well, where was he until six-thirty?"

"In a Chinese restaurant surrounded by a couple of dozen witnesses."

"The mayor, city council, and seven or eight members of Parliament."

"Something like that. Well, what's going to happen, Fos?"

"What do you mean?"

"The Hunkie."

"Oh, shit, I'll just keep my fingers crossed, Honch."

"If he's heard something? Jugs have ears. Cops who don't think talk a lot, and prisoners pick up what's going on. They flew him in last night. If the word's out, he knows."

"Aw, fuck!" The word exploded from Cobb's rank morning mouth, and he hung up.

Cobb checked into his office before going to the courthouse. The news from his answering service added a decidedly unattractive complication to Cobb's already disordered world: Bennie Bones had been picked up during the night in an RCMP sweep. He was in the city bucket waiting for bail to be fixed. Cobb hurriedly made arrangements with the federal drug prosecutor to put the case near the bottom of the first-appearance list so Cobb could run down to remand court during his noon break.

Then, his door locked from the prying eyes of his secretary, he cooked up a rich shot, popped a virgin vein in his leg, and lay back for several minutes, blinking, floating, swept away in the rush.

Then he went to the courthouse to meet Plizit. Flown in from his interior hideaway jail, Plizit had been kept locked up overnight in isolation, and Cobb kept his fingers crossed against a leak. Plizit, looking sour and depressed, was brought by the sheriff to Cobb's courthouse office.

"How long is this take?" he asked.

"It will take half an hour to go over your evidence, Laszlo. I want you to read your statement so it's fresh in your memory." Cobb fished a duplicate copy from his briefcase and gave it to him. "Let me tell you the questions I will be asking you, and you can tell me your answers."

"I am dead man this country."

"What?"

"I am dead man this country. They kill me any way I go."

"You'll be okay, for Christ's sake. But you'll be safer if you help us put Dr. Au away. When he is in jail, he will have no power."

Plizit snorted. "Who you kid, Mr. Cobb? Nobody is put Dr. Au away. Not me, not you. He kill us all."

"Let's go over your evidence."

"I know what I am saying in court. You help me get out of this country, don't worry, I tell you truth."

"Get out of the country?"

"You ask parole board, maybe they deport me. In Hungary they give me time for rob a store I did not do, plus I get some time for run away. Maybe deuce more. Is goulash all week, or I am dead man this country other ways. But goulash tastes better in throat than knife." Plizit broke into a hollow chuckle. "Maybe they educate me, make me good socialist citizen."

"If you give up your claim to refugee status, the parole board will send you out on deportation parole," Cobb said, more optimistic than sure.

"I take my chances communists not put me against wall. I hate Hungary jail. It is teach, teach, teach, work, work, work. But I am dead man here."

"I will help you," Cobb said. "In Hungary, there is no Dr. Au."

"In Hungary, they shoot Dr. Au." Plizit picked up the copy of his statement and looked at it without interest for a while. Then he put it down and looked hard at Cobb.

"How is Charlie?" he asked.

"Charlie Ming was a good witness."

"How is Charlie *now*?"

"He's a free man, Laszlo. We let him out last night. He went off, had a good night's sleep. We're looking after him."

"I hear is reward out for him."

"A contract? Well, I saw him just this morning. Safe and smiling. He's somewhere no one can get at him."

"I think we should wrap it up," Superintendent Charrington said. He was out from Ottawa and had read Flaherty's detailed reports. "Before it goes too far. I should think it would be well to fill in Detective Harrison."

"Give me another couple days," Flaherty said. "I can really nail this cocksucker in a day or two. By the weekend, you'll be able to use his balls for Easter eggs."

Charrington blanched.

Cudlipp, in the old days, had worked in small towns with Constable

Bob Klosterman, an easy-going Mountie who did not like the city and whose only ambition was to remain right where he was: head of a two-man detachment in a little cowboy town called Tlakish Lake. Cudlipp figured he might take Alice up there for a little fishing holiday after the trial, before moving to Australia.

On the phone, they talked about this and that, and Cudlipp learned that Klosterman was keeping a special guest in his cells.

Thursday, the Sixteenth Day of March, at Ten O'Clock in the Morning

Cobb took a deep breath, glanced over at the jury, and began.

"Your name is Laszlo Plizit?" said Cobb.

"Yeah."

"And you know Dr. Au P'ang Wei?"

"Yeah."

"Point him out, please."

Plizit pointed to the accused without looking at him.

"Were you with him on the evening of December third last?"

"Yeah."

"Did you go somewhere with him?"

"We gone first to Jimmy Fat Leung's home."

"What happened there?"

"Well, me and Dr. Au and Charlie Ming, we have pick up Jim Fat and went to office of Nationalist Association, where Dr. Au paralyze Jimmy with needle." His words came in a great rush. "I know nothing about what will happen, believe me. We go to Jim Fat home, you see, and Dr. Au say there is important job for him in business. That is what Dr. Au say for us to say, do you see, and —"

"Not so fast," Cobb said. The jury were losing this. Plizit was barrelling along too fast in his thick accent.

". . . Jimmy Fat is paralyze with needle, can't move, and Dr. Au, he ask Charlie Ming to take him downstairs to butchering shop, and they tie up Jim Fat. I seen all this, but don't do nothing, don't touch. Just stood, not helped. Dr. Au, he makes Charlie Ming takes all Jimmy's clothes off first, let's see, that is in butcher office. Then ties his hands and feet to butcher block. And he cut two, three times, and I see Dr. Au cut Jim Fat's throat with some knife, and that's all."

"A little too fast, Mr. Plizit . . ." Somehow, Cobb was going to have to retrace the ground. Some jurors looked puzzled.

"I done nothing but help, and too scared to call police."

"Let's go back a bit," said Cobb. "Who was driving the car when you left Jim Fat's home?"

"Me . . . Charlie . . . I can't remember."

"What conversation was there in the car?"

"I don't know," said Plizit. "All in Chinese, do you see? There was nothing I understand, just that we go to office to talk about business."

"What business are you referring to?" said Cobb.

"What business I don't know. Just business."

"What business did you do with him?"

"I quit now."

"Mr. Plizit, what business?"

"Um, I have serve as personal secretary, property management, charge of collections."

"And did Jim Fat work for him too?" said Cobb. "What was his job?"

"He was also personal secretary, handled some accounts."

"And Charlie Ming?"

"He also has handle property-management stuff, adviser for mortgages."

"The National Benevolent Society — what kind of business is that?" said Cobb.

"I think Dr. Au has charity for refugees from China. He is sending money to Hong Kong for refugee stuff."

"How did you get into the building?"

"Dr. Au have key," said Plizit. "Charlie have key too, I think."

"Describe those offices."

"Two rooms, nothing. Tables, chair. Usual stuff, you see."

"Tell us what happened in those offices."

"Dr. Au is talking to Jimmy in Chinese, and after a while he goes, gets a needle and, like, jabs Jimmy in the back, you see, and Jimmy falls down, can't move. Then Dr. Au says something to Charlie, and Charlie picks up Jimmy. We got downstairs to H-K Meat Store . . ."

Smythe-Baldwin climbed wearily to his feet. Cobb knew this would happen. "He has already given this account, my lord," the defence lawyer said. "Perhaps my friend could move off onto a less travelled road."

Cobb would have to make a stand. Plizit's evidence was too important, and Smythe-Baldwin, he knew, would dig deeply into his bag for means to cut the detail down. The problem would be with the judge, who was squinting narrowly at Plizit from behind his spectacles. Cobb could see that Horowitz was making an effort to disguise his distaste.

"My lord," said Cobb, "I am trying to elicit some detail."

Smythe-Baldwin huffed: "He is attempting to bolster his witness's credibility — if one can grace his testimony with such an unsatisfactory word — by having it repeated. My friend no doubt works upon the assumption that lies that are repeated often enough gain credence, and that there may be somebody in this courtroom so gullible as to believe some of them." The lawyer was shaking his finger to emphasize his points.

"My friend might save his arm-waving histrionics for his final address," said Cobb.

Smythe-Baldwin went at it full throttle. "Now, I have had quite enough. I have sat here patiently through my friend's case, watching amazed while his noble Roman soldiers parade through this court and do their vicious worst to crucify my client. I can no longer remain silent. It becomes a mockery of our great judicial system that the representatives of Her Majesty may in their avaricious hunger for conviction flaunt murderers and scoundrels before a jury of twelve honest men and women." The courtroom was reverberating. "My friend has discovered he cannot make a case out of speculative evidence, and now glibly tries to rebuild it with a witness whose lips drip with deceit, who has falsely answered every question since he falsely swore an oath, a witness —"

"I wish my friend," Cobb began, trying to halt the deluge, "would resume his seat."

The old lawyer talked right through Cobb's words: "No, I will not remain silent and submit to this."

"Please, gentlemen," the judge said.

Even this did not stem the flow: "Never in my career have I encountered such . . . In all my forty years of practice at the bars of six provinces of this dominion, I have never before encountered such brazen attempts to found a conviction on the words of society's worst riff-raff, the worst . . . the worst, the worst, a witness who . . ." Smythe-Baldwin seemed to clutch at the edge of the table, as if overcome. "I am sorry, my lord, I have let my concern carry me away. It must be the strain. I must apologize, I have gone too far. I tender my sincerest apologies."

Horowitz looked down with an expression of concern. "Would you like a short break, Mr. Smythe-Baldwin?" he said.

"No, no . . . please let us proceed. There is much work to be done in this court. I will carry on." He delivered himself of a long, weary sigh and shook his head as if to clear it.

"Quite an actor," Cobb said *sotto voce*.

"What did you say, Mr. Cobb?" The judge looked at him threateningly.

"The strain is quite a factor, my lord," Cobb said brightly. "These trials can be very difficult. Perhaps we should take a short break."

"No, the trial must carry on," Smythe-Baldwin said, breathing heavily, as if recovering from a stroke. "I should not have interrupted. I was concerned about repetition of evidence. Please pour me a glass of water, Wellington." One of his juniors hurried over to the water pitcher.

Cobb, knowing much damage had been done, knowing the jury was now concerned more with Smythe-Baldwin's health than with Plizit's evidence, took one more crack at his witness.

"All right, Mr. Plizit, now, look this way. I want you to describe everything that happened in the meat store as you observed it."

But Plizit, too, had been distracted. "I . . . would you repeat the question?"

"What happened in the meat store?"

"They have just talk in Chinese, you see. Jimmy is yelling, and Dr. Au just cutted out his tongue, and Jimmy is yelling, you see, yet, and spitting, and Dr. Au he takes knife and go between Jim Fat's legs, and cuts, like so, and cuts open throat after some time —"

"Please," interrupted Smythe-Baldwin. "It is offensive. Must we be steeped in it?"

He had won Horowitz. The judge spoke sternly to Cobb: "I think you have adequately pursued this line. Get on to something else."

Cobb knew the going would now get sluggish.

"I show you a scalpel." He had the instrument in his hand. "Did you see anything like this?"

Smythe-Baldwin would press home his edge. "There is no evidence of a scalpel."

"Yes, Mr. Cobb," Horowitz said, "it would not be fair to show it to the witness."

"Very well," said Cobb. "Mr. Plizit, did you see the accused look out the window at any time?"

"Leading question, my lord," said Smythe-Baldwin.

"*Please* don't lead the witness counsel," the judge said sharply.

"Well, did you see Dr. Au do anything in the area of the window?"

Smythe-Baldwin: "Same objection."

"That is right," the judge said. "Just ask him what he did or what he saw."

"What did you see the accused do?" Cobb said wearily.

"What else?" said Plizit, now confused. "I don't understand."

"Describe Dr. Au's movements about the room."

"I don't understand."

Cobb turned to the bench. "My lord, I should be able to point the witness in certain directions."

"No," said Horowitz, "not with *this* particular witness."

Cobb tried once more: "What can you say about the accused in relation to the window?"

"Don't understand."

Cobb swore under his breath. "This is impossible, my lord. I am hamstrung. I say that *with* deference, of course." He underlined his last words heavily with sarcasm.

"Counsel," Horowitz said, his expression icy, "I want to hear nothing that even remotely hints to the witness the answers that are expected from him. And I think you know why."

Jesus, thought Cobb, the judge might just as well have told the jury the witness was paid by the crown to lie.

"Please go on to something else, Mr. Cobb," the judge said.

Cobb turned back to his witness. "When did you leave the H-K Meats building?"

"I don't know the time."

"Where did you go?"

"I have walk out and gone home. I tried to forget."

"What did the accused do after you left?"

"He has gone too, I guess."

"What did Charlie Ming do?"

"He has stayed, I think."

"Did Ming do anything while you were there?"

"He cleaned up." Plizit's answers had all become clipped and sharp, without body.

"What did he clean?"

"The blood. Jimmy Fat also throwed up."

"Where was the blood?"

"On the floor."

"How much?"

"I don't know."

"What did he clean it up with?"

"Mop."

"Okay, now, Mr. Plizit, are you currently under any charge?"

"Murder."

"How did that come about?"

"A drunk Indian has attack me, and a policeman shoot at me by mistake, and I have shoot back in self-defence."

"Had you taken any drugs?"

"Uppers."

"Methedrine?" asked Cobb.

"Yeah."

"Did you know what you were doing"

"Ah . . . no."

"Did you sign a statement for the police giving an account of what you know about the murder of Jim Fat?"

"Yeah."

"And why did you do that?"

"Because you promise not to charge me with murder since I have been overcome by effects of drug."

"That is all."

It was time for the noon break.

Cobb wrestled out of his gown, bolted down the courthouse steps, and caught a cab to the Main Street court, hoping to get to the remand courtroom before it broke for lunch. The federal prosecutor nodded to him as he entered, and called the case of Regina versus Benjamin Bowness.

A sheriff brought Bennie Bones from the cells, and when Cobb looked at his friend his stomach tightened into a ball of hard muscle. Bones had always looked wasted and anemic, and today he was a white and shivering skeleton.

Bones looked up at Cobb, shook his head sadly, then dropped his eyes. A wash of pain went up Cobb's back and down again as he listened to the prosecutor read the police report. Apparently the RCMP drug squad had had a tail on Bones for the last few weeks, and finally one of their street undercover men made contact with him, befriended him, and prevailed upon him to sell him a bundle for seven hundred dollars. The facts made Bones look like a middleman, when in fact he was only a street dealer, selling single caps to stay alive and keep his habit fed. Bones's record was put before the judge — three heroin-possession convictions, two for trafficking, and the service-station robbery of twenty years ago. Cobb pleaded with the judge to set low bail, hoping to spring his friend for at least a few months before his trial.

The judge looked down at Bones, who looked nauseated.

"No, Mr. Cobb," he said, "I think we should let the man dry out. He has roots here, of course, but I am of the view that his continued detention is necessary for the protection and safety of the public, as well as himself. You and I both know that fellows like this, if they're let back on the street, will only continue to push their wares. Menace to our young people. Strong case alleged. There'll be a detention order."

Bones leaned over to Cobb and whispered: "It's okay, Fos. It's the end, anyway."

"No, it's not okay," Cobb whispered back. "I'll appeal that."

But Cobb knew a bail review could not be brought on until the following week, and in the meantime, Cobb would suffer with his friend — because Cobb had only five caps left in his stash, and there were no other dealers he knew well enough to trust. By tomorrow he would be without. He was already beginning to feel nervous and shaky.

Back at the crown counsel office in the courthouse, he fell heavily into a chair and smiled wanly at Jennifer Tann.

"You look like a homeless puppy," she said. "What's the matter?"

"Nothing. Tired. You listen to the one-o'clock news?"

"No mention of Charlie Ming's death. It still hasn't broken."

"Plizit was awful," he said.

"Kind of, I guess. But he got most of it out."

"He was an asshole up there," Cobb said. "Smitty will cut him into tiny little rancid bits of meat. Anyway, we got enough in there now to force them to call a defence. I guess we'll hear from Mr. Cudlipp tomorrow, maybe Au on Monday. Addresses Tuesday, and we'll probably go to the jury by Wednesday."

"You got a cold?" Tann asked. Cobb had started to sniff and blow his nose.

"Spring cold."

Tann searched his face. There was something odd; Cobb was shivering, but the room was really very warm. There was something very odd, indeed, about Mr. Cobb.

Court resumed and Smythe-Baldwin lumbered to his feet with a show of great effort.

"How old are you?" he asked.

"Forty-three," replied Plizit.

"And when did you come to this country?"

"Nineteen-fifty-seven."

"And you came here as our guest?"

"What?"

"Your way was paid over?"

"Yeah."

"No doubt since your arrival here you have been a good tax-paying citizen?"

"Yeah."

"And when did you last file an income tax return?"

"Well, not yet."

The lawyer smiled benignly. "How long have you worked for Dr. Au?"

"One year."

"And did you receive a salary?"

"Yes."

"You were destitute, without a job, and you came to Dr. Au and he found you a job because he felt sorry for you, isn't that so?"

"I don't know."

"And that is the only honest job you have ever held down since you came to this country, is it not true?"

"Honest job? I have lots honest jobs."

"Let's hear about them," said the lawyer. "When was the first?"

"Well, I have work dishwasher in restaurant in Toronto."

"And when was that?"

"Nineteen-sixty, sixty-one, around there."

"And for how long did you work in that restaurant?"

"Maybe two months."

"My!" said Smythe-Baldwin. "Two months. What was your next job?"

"I work carnival, Tilt-a-Whirl."

"When was that?'

"Maybe 1967."

"For how long?"

"Maybe two months, maybe six weeks."

"And what were you doing between 1961 and 1967?"

"Doing time, I guess."

"You mean you were in prison?"

"Most of time."

"I see," said the lawyer, pausing to let the answer sink home. "When did you work next?"

"Maybe 1973."

"And what did you do then?"

"Loan business."

"What — you were lending money?"

"No, I collect."

"And what great Canadian financial institution was your employer?"

"No insti . . . no big business, just a guy."

"He was a loan shark, yes?"

"What you mean? I don't know."

"Loans to gamblers at ten per cent a month," said Smythe-Baldwin. "Something like that. You carried a gun to collect the loans, isn't that so?"

"I don't know what you mean."

"Oh, *come*, now, witness," the voice boomed. "You beat people up and threatened to shoot them if they didn't make payments. That was your business. The police knew that. Everybody knows that. Don't play games with us here."

"Whatever you say," said Plizit. His voice in comparison to Smythe-Baldwin's was squeaky, rat-like. "I collect loans. Was dangerous."

"I'm sure," the lawyer said. "What was your next regular job?"

"Dr. Au."

"You had other jobs perhaps, and you are a little bashful about describing them?"

"I don't know what you mean."

"Let's be frank here. You were a gun runner, bringing guns up from the States. Hand guns."

"I don't know what you mean."

"Perhaps we can refresh your memory," said Smythe-Baldwin, pulling out several sheets of paper.

"You were convicted in New Westminster, British Columbia, in January 1959, of seventeen counts of possession of unregistered firearms, and sentenced to two years' imprisonment concurrently in a federal penitentiary on each of those counts?"

"Yeah," said Plizit.

"You were transporting illegal firearms, is that so?"

"They were not registered, is all."

"And at the same time you were also convicted of assault with a deadly weapon and sentenced to three years, also concurrent?"

"Yeah."

"You threatened somebody with a gun?"

"Had to defend myself," Plizit said. "Didn't shoot him, just hit him a bit."

"And there was a common assault before that, in September 1958, in Winnipeg, two hundred dollars fine or thirty days in jail?"

"Yeah, maybe."

"And another one in Calgary, January 1959, five hundred dollars or two months?"

"Yeah."

"It sounds as if you were a violent man, Mr. Plizit, or was all that just youthful exuberance?"

"I don't understand."

"Never mind. Now, again in 1961, in July, you were convicted of possession of a weapon for a purpose dangerous to the public peace and sentenced to two years less a day in Sudbury, Ontario?"

"Yeah, I guess. I don't know date. You have all the dates on that paper, I guess."

"Oh, yes, it's all here, Mr. Plizit. All except the things no one ever caught you at."

Cobb stood up. "There is a proper way of putting a record to a witness."

"I won't interfere," the judge said. "This is cross-examination."

"You say you were working with a carnival in 1967," continued Smythe-Baldwin.

"Around there," replied the witness.

"Is that when you were caught attacking a little teen-aged girl?"

"I don't know."

"Behind your Tilt-a-Whatever, no doubt. You were convicted in September 1967, in Toronto, of attempted rape and sentenced to three years in the penitentiary?"

"Yeah, I guess."

"And in July 1968, in Halifax, Nova Scotia — you get around, don't you? — you were convicted of a breach of parole and a common assault, and your parole was revoked and you were sentenced to an additional three months' imprisonment?"

"Yeah, maybe."

"What else do we have here? Let's see, July 1972, common assault, two months. January 1973, common assault, four months. I won't bother with all these minor things. Let's see, I'll go down the list here. Here's a good one, October 1975, in Vancouver, possession of stolen bonds, six months, is that right?"

"If you say."

"Witness, is that right?" Smythe-Baldwin shouted.

"Yeah, sure."

"Then in February 1976, for trafficking in methamphetamine, you were given nine months. You must have hit the judge on a good morning. What's this methamphetamine? Is that what you call speed?"

"Meth, speed, yeah."

"You were doing that for a living?"

"I had to sell, to be honest."

"Yes, *please* be honest. You were selling speed in large quantities?"

"A little, yeah."

"I guess you know a little about this drug," said the lawyer. "You told us you were high on it a couple of weeks ago when you shot somebody, is that so?"

"Yeah, I was stoned."

"'Speed kills,' you've heard that?"

"Yeah, I heard."

"Gets you all confused and mixed up, doesn't it?"

"Yeah, you can't think straight."

"Are you an addict?"

"Not now."

"What about two weeks ago."

"I used a lot, yeah."

"It makes you all dopey, does it? Makes everything fuzzy?" Smythe-Baldwin's eyes glinted. Cobb had an idea of what was coming.

"Makes everything pretty clear sometimes. You just don't have control, is all."

"Everything looks distorted?"

"Yeah, I guess."

"You see things that aren't there?"

"Well, maybe."

"Just as on December third in H-K Meats you saw Dr. Au and he wasn't there?"

"I ain't so high I see Dr. Au if he isn't there. I was just feeling good, is all."

"You were feeling good?" Smythe-Baldwin's tufted eyebrows were raised in shock.

"Yeah."

"Jim Fat was having his throat slit, you say, and you were feeling good?" The lawyer appeared goggled-eyed in amazement.

"I think you is twisting what I say."

"I am not twisting anything at all, Mr. Plizit. The only twisting being done here is being done by a lying, twisted mind."

Cobb stood up to object, but Horowitz looked down at him coldly, without sympathy, and Cobb flopped back into his chair.

"Let's get down to simple realities, Mr. Plizit," said Smythe-Baldwin. "You'll say just about anything to protect your own skin, won't you, even if it means sending an innocent man away for life?"

"Why would I do that?"

"Don't play the innocent here!" he barked. "You cooked up a story about Dr. Au killing Jimmy Fat in order to beat a murder charge."

"No."

"You have falsely sold the accused to the police, who are always ambitious to convict a prominent citizen, in order to purchase your own freedom."

"I do not think so. I think maybe they export me to Hungary to do my time there."

"Ah!" Smythe-Baldwin affected surprise. "So there was some other conviction in Hungary. What was that for?"

"They accuse me of anti-socialist activity, and want to put me in communist jail for ten years, you see?"

"And what was this so-called anti-socialist activity, Mr. Plizit?"

"They have frame me, call me enemy of the people."

"And what were you jailed for, trying to cause a revolution?"

Plizit shrugged. "The secret police claim I rob a store, but they lie."

"Robbery, was it? I suppose those poor misguided communists think robbery is some sort of revisionist crime, when of course we all know that you were just engaging in an innocent act of free enterprise." Jurors were chuckling. Smythe-Baldwin had most of them in his corner. "Let us seek some information about this murder charge you face. It was a week ago Friday, I believe, that you shot Constable Jake Moeller through the neck with a pistol equipped with a silencer, am I correct?"

"No, I have shoot blind," Plizit said. "Indian was very drunk and come at me, and I have defend myself, and police shoot at us and I shoot back, was all mistake. I am not guilty of murder. I have made statement to police, yes, because my lawyer have said it will help me. I am not a fool."

"I have no doubt," said the lawyer. "A fool will turn down such an offer while a dishonorable man might not. There is another motive for accusing Dr. Au of being a murderer, is there not?"

"I don't understand."

"Oh, come. Why do we play such games? The accused was miles from the scene, and you know it. You dropped him off somewhere on Kingsway, before the three of you proceeded to Chinatown, isn't that so?"

"No. Dr. Au, he came with us."

"You and Charlie Ming were alone with Jim Fat in the office, yes?"

"No."

"Where did you go after you killed him?"

"I went . . . That is a lie."

"You were going to say you went somewhere?" Smythe-Baldwin wore an innocent smile.

"You try to make me say I killed him. No, I deny."

"You and Charlie Ming killed this man, and the both of you have tried to cover up by blaming the accused. Now, that is true, is it not? Be honest now!" Smythe-Baldwin stood in front of Plizit like a bull, nostrils flaring.

"I know what you try to do," Plizit shot back.

"I put it to you that you took the life of Jimmy Wai Fat Leung!" Smythe-Baldwin roared.

"I put it to you I don't." Plizit tried a wan, fake smile, but his voice was cracking.

"I am accusing you of the murder!"

"This is lie, lie, lie."

"You have come before this court and you have sworn an oath before God to tell the truth. Do you swear now that you and Charlie Ming did not take this man's life?"

"I do."

"And you remember taking that oath?"

"Yeah."

"And is your conscience bound by that oath?"

"What do you mean, conscience?"

"Do you *have* none, witness?"

"What is it?"

"Do you understand what an oath means?"

"To tell truth."

"Did you swear before God?"

"I guess, yeah."

"Does the Deity mean anything to you? Are you bound by an oath before God?"

"It makes no difference. I tell truth anyway."

"It makes no difference that you have sworn an oath on the Bible to tell the truth?"

"It makes no difference."

"An *oath* on the *Bible* means nothing to you?" There was horror on Smythe-Baldwin's face.

"No, I —"

Smythe-Baldwin cut him off sharply. "That is all, thank you. Thank you very much. I am satisfied." He sat down, looking over at the jury with a sad smile and shaking his head.

Cobb, rising, sensed he had few friends in the jury box.

"Any re-examination, Mr. Cobb?" Horowitz asked.

"No," Cobb said cheerlessly. "That is the case for the crown. I have concluded my evidence."

Court was adjourned until Friday morning.

"Goddamnit, Cobb, it's putrid, and I can't stand it!" Deborah had gone on a hunt while he was in court, and found an outfit in his library, behind *The History of the Industrial Revolution*. She had drunk sherry until he walked into the apartment, then made great ceremony of dropping the syringe on the kitchen tile floor and smashing it with her heel. "I won't have any goddamn needles in this place!" The book came whistling through the air at Cobb, and he dodged it and it struck the wall behind him and fell to the floor, old newspaper and magazine clippings fluttering out from between its pages.

Deborah sat on a chair, livid, with tears coming. "That's all I need in my life, a goddamn dope fiend! You bastard! You promised!" This time the half-empty bottle struck the wall and sent a sticky splash of sherry over the spice rack.

Cobb put his coat back on and headed for the door.

"I don't want to see you!" she yelled. "I'm going to Whistler tonight. I don't want to see you this weekend. Get your shit together."

Before going to the courthouse library, Cobb stopped in at a White Spot for a hamburger and read the newspaper accounts of Ming's suicide. He then went up to his office and did up two caps of junk to get him through the evening. He had only two left.

Friday, the Seventeenth Day of March, at Five Minutes Past Ten O'Clock in the Morning

"Do you swear to tell the truth, the whole truth, and nothing but the truth, so help you God?" the clerk asked solemnly.

"Yes, sir, I do," said Corporal Everit Cudlipp, his hungover head and body neatly composed for the defence's opening round. He was dressed in a bright red dress uniform and stood tall, feet apart, hands behind his back. At ease, in the military.

"You may be seated, corporal," said the judge.

"Thank you, my lord, I prefer to stand."

"You are wearing a uniform," said Smythe-Baldwin, "but for the record, would you state your occupation?"

"I am a corporal in the Royal Canadian Mounted Police, stationed here in Vancouver. I have been a member of the drug squad for the last ten years and a police officer for going on seventeen years."

"And your duties now include what?"

"Investigation of major heroin-trafficking operations, conspiracies to traffic and to import heroin, on-the-spot surveillance, telephone wiretap operations. I specialize in fairly big transactions, particularly amounts coming from Southeast Asia, Hong Kong."

"And you have served in an undercover capacity?"

"Yes, sir. I was undercover for six months."

"And you received a commendation from the force for your efforts in that regard?"

"Yes, sir."

Smythe-Baldwin asked for his credentials. Cudlipp, in his best poker-faced police-witness style, listed them: he had taken specialized courses in Ottawa and Regina in drugs and organized crime, headed up RCMP tactical squads in major investigations, worked with the FBI, the DEA, Interpol, the Royal Hong Kong Constabulary, and he had given expert evidence on drugs at least a hundred times in court.

Cudlipp spoke precisely and with practised ease. He had gone through a package of Clorets this morning, because Dr. Au's down payment had arrived the previous night, and a little of it had bought a lot of Heinekein beer. He and Alice Carson had celebrated wildly.

"You say you specialize in Far Eastern heroin exports," said Smythe-Baldwin. "Where does most of the heroin come from that is the subject of your work?"

"Hong Kong is the major Eastern embarkation port," Cudlipp replied. "It is refined there or in Thailand. Most of it comes from Thailand or Burma originally. It used to come from Laos as well, and Vietnam."

"How dangerous is the work?"

"It is a deadly serious business to those who traffic in large amounts. There is gunplay, and people do get killed. I have had to defend myself on more than one occasion."

"Do you use your informants as an investigative tool?"

"Yes, sir. I have private sources of information. I make it a policy not to reveal their names, of course."

"Are these informants known to other members of the drug squad, or other police officers?"

"Some. I have used a few who trust me and I have not given away their names to anyone, even to officers I work with."

"I am going to ask you to name one of them here. Will that be all right?"

"I understand it will be necessary for this trial," Cudlipp said. He looked straight ahead of him, his eyes unwavering.

"His name?"

"Dr. Au P'ang Wei. The accused, sitting in the dock."

"How long have you known the accused?"

"Seven or eight years, sir."

"And when did you begin to use him as an informer?"

"It was a year ago at least that he first became an informer. He came to me."

"Explain the circumstances of that."

"I had been in his office one or two times during investigations of some of his business associates, and I guess at first I thought Dr. Au, because he was close to these fellows, might also have something to do with the narcotics trade."

"What office had you been visiting?"

"Well, I know Dr. Au has several businesses, mortgage and land, that sort of thing. I had met with him a few times in a place on Cambie, the Inter-Pacific Loan and Mortgage Corporation, I think it is, and I got to asking him about the movements of some of his employees, and he told me he was suspicious about them, and thought maybe they were using his name to gain respectability."

"What employees are you referring to?"

"There was one fellow in particular, Jimmy Wai Fat Leung, and we were watching him because we had reason to believe he was bringing in large quantities of heroin from the Far East. Jim Fat."

"Tell us about this Jim Fat, officer. What had he been doing?"

"We weren't sure about the extent of his operations." The witness appeared to clear his throat again. Cobb thought he was covering up a belch. "He was bringing stuff in under cover of Dr. Au's business, I knew that. We got a tip last year, and I'll be honest with you, it was Dr. Au who steered me onto this, that Jim Fat would be receiving a large shipment of contraband, and we did in fact find him with a big supply, about thirty thousand dollars' worth, uncut. Now, we decided not to arrest him then because we were interested in infiltrating his organization. We had no idea how big it was. So Jim Fat gave us information on the understanding we would not charge him, and it was through him ultimately that we made several major arrests, major importers from Hong Kong, and we broke the back of the Asia connection through Vancouver. I have to credit Dr. Au with the initial breakthrough here. He helped us stop, oh, I don't know, fifteen, twenty million dollars' worth of heroin from reaching the streets."

"Yes." Smythe-Baldwin looked at the jury. Some were nodding their heads. Others merely looked curious. No one looked as if he disbelieved the witness.

"Dr. Au told us he also suspected two other men who were working with him," Cudlipp continued. "And through my contacts with Jim Fat I confirmed that these two men were fairly high up in the syndicate."

"Who were they?"

"Charlie Ming, Laszlo Plizit. We placed these men under surveillance. We were hoping ultimately to catch them moving a large amount of narcotics."

"Yes?"

"I would meet secretly with Dr. Au several times a month, and he agreed to keep track of the movements of these two men. I gave my word to him that no one, absolutely no one, including men I worked with, would be told that he was a secret informer. I gave him my word, and it is important to me in my business that my word be trusted."

"I'm sure we can all understand why that has to be," said Smythe-Baldwin. "Why was Dr. Au so adamant that you not tell even your brother officers that he was working with you?"

"Because if there had been any leak, he would have been killed, just like that. These people don't fool around."

Smythe-Baldwin paused to let this sink in. Cobb was bothered by two of the jurors particularly. They were leaning forward, concentrating hard.

"I want to take you to the month of December last year," Smythe-Baldwin said. "I understand you met with Dr. Au then."

"Yes, sir, the third of December, a Saturday, I received an urgent call from Dr. Au asking me to meet him. He sounded very excited."

"What did he say?"

"He told me some lives were in danger, and he said he wanted to meet me at a convenient place late that afternoon or early evening. I recall it was about three o'clock that he phoned. Thereabouts. I was at home. I told him to meet me at a place on Kingsway, Archie's Steak House, which was fairly near my home. It was a place I used for meeting people, and it had booths there that are fairly private. In fact, I was also in the habit of meeting Jim Fat there, and I had also been there once or twice with Dr. Au."

"Yes."

"So anyway, we arranged to meet at six p.m. Actually, I was half an hour late. I remember I had been watching an NFL game on TV, and it took me a while to clean up, and it was about six-thirty that I arrived."

"Go on."

"We both ordered a meal, and I would say we were there together for three hours, what with a drink or two, and the meal, coffee afterwards, and we spent a lot of time talking. When we finally got up to go, it was after nine." He paused, struck a pose of intense thought, and said: "No, gosh, I remember it was almost exactly nine-thirty, because I remember correcting my watch with one of the waitresses there, and it was nine-thirty on the dot. That stuck in my mind because it was the first time I had talked to that particular waitress, and she was kind of pretty. As a matter of fact, I got to know her really good after that."

Cobb's writing hand was aching. He wished he had more time to study the witness.

"Please relate the conversation," Smythe-Baldwin said.

"Dr. Au was scared. He knew by this time that Jimmy Fat was

also giving us information, and he was afraid that the Plizit gang were on to both him and Jim Fat. Laszlo Plizit apparently found out that Dr. Au and I had been seen together a couple of days earlier in a restaurant in Chinatown. All this was at a time when I felt we were close to moving in and breaking up a huge ring involving Plizit, Ming, and a number of other known traffickers in Vancouver, and their connections in the U.S. and Hong Kong."

"Yes."

"And he was certain that Plizit had sort of fingered Jim Fat, and they were going to do away with him. What he said specifically is that he overheard a conversation between Plizit and Ming which suggested that they were going to torture Jim Fat —"

Cobb jumped to his feet. "My friend and his amazing witness are taking too much licence. This last evidence is a salad of hearsay and self-serving testimony, and in my respectful submission it should not be allowed."

Horowitz was still not buying Cobb's arguments: "The defence is entitled to some leniency in matters of this kind. These conversations go to state of mind, not truth of fact. The evidence is allowed. I think we should take the morning break now, gentlemen."

The judge, Cobb thought, seemed to be in a temper this morning. Cobb filed out of the courtroom with Tann, and they had coffee together in one of the small interview rooms.

"Wow," she said. "Ouch. He is *good*. I mean, he seems bloody *honest* up there." She looked stunned. "Do you think the jury are *believing* this guy?"

"He's a pro," Cobb said.

"He's so proper, and polite. And earnest! I mean, talk about your over-age boy scout."

"Don't let it fool you." Cobb was holding a wavering flame to his pipe, and he was shaking.

"I'm not worried about him fooling *me*. It's the jury. I mean, they are listening *hard*, Foster."

"I'll tell you something. He's at the edge of nervous exhaustion. There's a little catch in his voice. Just a little. Watch him shift his feet. I think he knows he's in too deep. He's been drinking, too. I got close to him when he left the stand. Watch how he holds onto the railing so you can't see his hands shake. Always watch a man's hands to see if he's on the bottle. Smitty's done him up with coffee, talc, mouthwash, and deodorant, but the fumes are still coming through the camouflage. He's shaky."

"Yeah, well, he doesn't look any shakier than you, Mr. Prosecutor. I've been watching *you*. You're either going to have to relax or relapse. Bad night?"

Cobb let that slide past him. "Also," he said, "watch his eyes when I have him in cross. When cops give false evidence, they don't look you in the eyes."

"How *are* you feeling, Mr. Fossil Cobb? That cold getting the best of you? Nurse Tann wants to know." She was sitting on the edge of her chair, perky and nervous, nibbling at the end of a pencil.

"Feeling fine," he mumbled.

"Look me in the eye, witness, and tell me the truth."

His eyes were red. Hers were dark and discerning, and seemed to see inside his paltering soul. "Sort of shitty, actually," he said with a grim, tight smile. He shifted the conversation to an easier track. "The judge wants to recess for the weekend at half-past twelve today. I might get started on him before then. I think the strategy will be to pin him down, and save the cannon fire for Monday."

Tann put the pencil down, then started fidgeting with the tassel of her barrister's gown. Finally she cleared a slightly husky throat.

"Are we working tonight?" she said.

"It's Friday. Don't you want a break?"

"I'm sort of free tonight. If you need any help. With the law, or anything else." He looked at her for a long moment, with a frown of puzzlement. "Hello," she said. "Are you there? Is anyone home? Can Fossil come out and play?"

Finally he shook his head, as if freeing it from cobwebs. He said: "Maybe I *am* a little old-fashioned. Are you asking this stodgy old married guy out for a date?"

"Yes, goddamnit. Jesus, what does a lonely spinster have to do — kidnap the man at gunpoint? I'm beautiful, sincere, and lots of fun, and from everything I can see, your marriage is hung up — if it's not already breaking up on the rocks. I *tried* playing hard-to-get. I now quit that. You're too slow on your feet." She was blushing prettily, and he had to smile. "I make a great Moo Goo Gai Pan, just like the Chinese," she said.

"I'll bring the wine."

"Seven o'clock? *Je-sus*, what a hassle!"

"Witness," said the clerk, "you are still under oath." Cudlipp nodded.

"Now, corporal," Smythe-Baldwin said, "you were about to relate a conversation which the accused had overheard between Plizit and Ming."

"He said he feared for his life, and even more for the life of Jim Fat. He said Plizit was talking about torturing Jim Fat to make him talk. That's what he overheard. Then, what happened later that afternoon, after he phoned me and before we met in the steak house, was that Plizit and Ming came by Dr. Au's house, and then they went to Jimmy's house to pick him up, too. Apparently they wanted Dr. Au to go along with them and discuss some sort of business they weren't clear about. Dr. Au figured the worst, that they were going to take him and Jim Fat for a ride, and you know what that expression means. Somehow, Dr. Au persuaded them to drop him off at Kingsway, at the steak house, Archie's, where he would be meeting me."

"What was your reaction to all of this?" asked the lawyer.

"Well, to be honest, and here maybe I wasn't thinking too clearly, but I guess I didn't take all this too seriously, or I would have taken more decisive action. But I guess by now we all know that I should have been much more concerned about it all." He looked sorrowful.

"Now, corporal," said the lawyer, "we heard evidence earlier this week from Dr. Coombs, the pathologist, that the deceased died almost instantly after the wounds were inflicted upon him. His best estimate of the time of death was between eight-fifteen p.m. and eight-forty-five p.m. on December the third. Where were you at that time?"

"In Archie's Steak House, having dinner," the witness replied. "Maybe coffee by that time, and a brandy."

"Where was the accused, Dr. Au?"

"With me, sir."

"There is no mistaking that?"

"There could not be, sir."

"And why are you giving evidence here today in court?"

Cudlipp's chest puffed an inch or two larger, and he sucked his paunch in.

"I have been a police officer for seventeen years, but I have never and could never be a party to the conviction of an innocent man. I could not live with myself if I were to remain silent and allow Dr. Au to be convicted of a crime I know he did not commit."

"Thank you, corporal," Smythe-Baldwin said solemnly. "Please answer my learned friend's questions." As he sat, he scanned the jury and was satisfied.

"Do you wish to start now?" Horowitz asked. "It's nearly a quarter to the half-hour."

"I would like to start." He would have to give the jury something to keep their minds open over the weekend, some hint that there was much more to come.

He stood up and strolled to a point beside the jury box where he could watch Cudlipp's eyes, and he leaned against the railing. He held no notes. His cross-examination was in his head.

"Why did you not come forward until now?"

Cudlipp frowned. "I spoke to Mr. Smythe-Baldwin several weeks ago," he said.

"Why did you not speak to the Vancouver police? Do you not trust them?"

"My word to Dr. Au was my bond," Cudlipp said, his voice earnest. "A police officer must never reveal his informants. I think *you* know that, Mr. Cobb. You're a pretty experienced prosecutor." Ingratiating.

"And if the accused had not released you from that bond, you would ultimately have gone to your grave carrying the secret of his innocence, while the accused spent his remaining years in a jail cell. Is that what you are suggesting?"

"The problem never arose. I wouldn't want to deal in hypothetical situations."

"I suggest to you that you deal very well in hypothetical situations," Cobb said sharply. "It is true, is it not, that the whole of your evidence about meeting with Au on December third is a pure, imaginary hypothesis?"

Smythe-Baldwin called to him: "That is argumentative."

"We shall see," said Cobb. "What do you earn, corporal?"

"About twenty-seven, twenty-eight thousand a year."

"That is your sole source of income?"

"Yes, sir. RCMP pay."

"And you have received no money from other sources?"

"You mean, have I won a lottery?" He smiled. "No, sir. I wish I had."

"But you have met the accused socially from time to time?"

"No, sir, only for business."

"You have met in restaurants and cocktail bars?"

"Sure, but only in the line of duty."

"You have paid your own bills, then?"

"Sometimes. Sometimes Dr. Au would pick up a bill. I don't sell myself for a cup of coffee, Mr. Cobb." Again, a smile.

"Well, how much *do* you sell yourself for?" Cobb's face was bland.

"Don't answer that," Smythe-Baldwin ordered. "Most unfair."

"I agree," Horowitz said, glaring at Cobb.

"Where do you claim you were before you went to the restaurant to meet the accused?" Cobb asked.

"I was at home."

"Alone?"

"Yes, sir. I live by myself."

"And you cannot tell us the name of anyone who saw you there with the accused?"

"I have no idea. The waitress, Alice, for sure. Maybe the manager, Giulente."

"You went there a lot?"

"I used to meet Jim Fat there. He was a friend of Joey Giulente."

"Tell us what you ordered."

"A steak, a T-bone. Maybe a beer before salad. A coffee and brandy."

"Who served you?" said Cobb.

"The waitress. Alice was working that night. Why don't you ask her? She might remember. I didn't make a note of it."

"What did the accused eat?"

"I don't know, sir. I was more interested in what he had to say."

"Come. You are a trained police officer."

"It was a few months ago, Mr. Cobb." Cudlipp's expression suggested the questions were silly.

"You considered his information that night to be important?"

"Certainly," said Cudlipp. "Although I see now I should have acted on it." A theme repeated.

"Yes," Cobb said. "Dr. Au thought Jim Fat was in danger, and Jim Fat was an informer at the time, is that so?"

"Yes, sir."

"And as a trained, experienced police officer, you recognized the importance of the information?"

"I never thought Jim Fat was going to be killed." The witness shook his head, as if blaming himself. "But I intended later on to follow the matter up and determine whether there had been a leak, whether it had been discovered that he was an informer."

"And as a trained, experienced police officer, you make notes of important matters?"

"Often. Yes, sir."

"No doubt you made a note afterwards in your police notebook about this conversation with Au?"

"I can't recall. Sometimes I made notes."

"Where are your notes for December third last year?"

"I haven't got them with me. I didn't think they would be necessary."

"Well, I want to see your notes for the week ending December third. You have them somewhere?"

"At home, I guess."

"Please bring them on Monday. Please bring any notes you have referring to conversations with Jim Fat or the accused."

Cudlipp turned to the bench. "My lord, am I required to do so?" He sounded hurt, unsure why all the bother was necessary.

"Under the circumstances," said Horowitz, "I think Mr. Cobb has a right to examine any matters relevant to your evidence."

"We will meet here again Monday, corporal," said Cobb.

"We will adjourn until then," the judge said. "Corporal Cudlipp, you are a trained witness, and you know you must not speak to anyone about your evidence until you resume the stand."

"Of course, my lord."

Packing papers into Smythe-Baldwin's briefcase, one of his juniors whispered to him: "Thank God. Looks like the guy is going to hold up."

But Smythe-Baldwin sadly shook his head. "He is lying, my young friend. Watch his eyes."

Friday, the Seventeenth Day of March, at Half-past Six O'Clock in the Evening

Detective Harrison found Archie's out on south Kingsway on the motel strip. It was a brassy place, finished inside with new brick intended to look old and with plastic intended to look like wood. In the front: a quick-food dining area, brightly lit, with blown-up photographs of an earlier Vancouver. In the back: a dim and quiet place with candles and better service, with booths along the walls. There was also a bar, where most of the customers were. Harrison recognized some of them: small-time bookies and cheap fiddlers. No one big.

He found a book in the back and waited for a waitress, hopefully this Alice Carson girl. He also wanted to speak to the manager, Giulente, an ex-con.

Harrison was tired. He had spent two sleepless nights on the track of Jean-Louis Leclerc. Harrison knew Leclerc was an habitué of two or three gay bars and discos, but it was as if the man had never existed. Prowling through those swish jungles, he felt absurdly straight, a heavy old draft horse under the scrutiny of many eyes. Some guessed he was a cop — not hard to tell — and there had been a lot of giggling and whispering. ("Look at the buns on that baby," he had heard someone say.) Nobody had heard of Leclerc, of course, not even the managers of the gay bars, who knew all their customers. Trusted sources of information had dried up: it was dangerous business to get involved in a manhunt that featured Honcho Harrison on the one side and, on the other, a lieutenant of Dr. Au's loyal corps of irregulars.

Tonight there was other business to do, an alibi to be checked out. He wondered just how cozy Cudlipp and Alice Carson were.

He sat watching as two or three waitresses bustled about, chatting up the customers, selling a little come-on with the food and drinks. They wore frilly skirts that left exposed generous expanses of soft white thigh. Unbuttoned blouses offered a small thrill to a customer if the angle of vision were just right.

One of them came his way. "Hello, I'm Donna. I'm your waitress tonight. Can I get you something from the —"

"Get me Alice Carson."

"Alice? Hey, what's she got I don't?"

"Just send her over. Please."

Donna gave him a look, then a weary shrug, and went away to fetch Carson. When she came to his booth, Harrison gave her a quick scan. Good-looking, but hard-looking. High, sharp cheekbones. Mouth full and red. Eyes wide-set, heavy with mascara. Low-keeled. Bouncy. It didn't take Harrison long to learn that the woman used sex appeal like a weapon.

"Am I supposed to know you?" she asked.

"You're about to." Harrison showed his badge.

"Darling, I'm innocent. I didn't do it."

"Sit down."

"Look, I'm busy. My other customers will get jealous, and the boss will get on my case. So unless I'm under arrest, I got to work. Also, fella, I'm tired, a little hung, and very grumpy. If you want to talk business, why don't you come back at quitting time? It's about the Au trial, I suppose." She gave him a little pouty smile.

"It will take five minutes. Where's the manager? Giulente."

"Joey!" she called. Giulente, a slight and nervous person, dressed very disco-hip, came treading up to them on shoes with three-inch heels.

"Joey Giulente? My name is Harrison, city police." He fished out a sheet of blue-colored paper. "It's a subpoena. You're going to appear Monday in Supreme Court assize, ten o'clock. Now, I want you to give this lady her coffee break, and I want to talk to you later."

Giulente squinted at the subpoena. "I don't know nothing about it, Mr. Harrison. Jimmy Fat used to come in here, is all. What do you drink?"

"Rye. Whatever you got. Bar rye, water on the side. Sit down, Alice."

She did, and Giulente went for the drink. Carson leaned on her elbows, her face in her hands, and gave the policeman her big, winning, number-one smile. "You wear that ugly scowl just for work, or does it sit there on your face all the time?"

"What's the story?"

"Gee, well, you know, I was told by Mr. Smythe-Baldwin that I don't have to say a goddamn thing to you." But she was still smiling.

"You're going to be a witness, hey?"

"Yep. I got me one of them things you gave to Joey." Giulente brought the drink and quickly edged off. "But I like to be open," she said. "I got nothing to hide."

"So I noticed."

"Yeah, it gets cold if you don't move around a lot." She winked. "Well, okay, December third, a Saturday night. The place was pretty full, like it is tonight. Dr. Au was here until about nine-thirty, had steak and lobster. Nice man, big tipper, sharp dresser, very dis-tang-way and charming. You should try it sometime, detective. He sat with Ev Cudlipp back here in one of these booths. Let's see — other side of the room, about third down. Ev had a steak. Always a big T-bone. They were here three hours. Ev checked the time with me when they left. Woops."

Carson had knocked over the water-on-the-side, and it slopped off the table onto Harrison's lap.

"My, I'm careless. Dear, dear." She leaned over with a serviette and rubbed his legs near the crotch. Smoldering, Harrison pushed her hand away hard.

"Get off, lady, get . . . God *damn!*" His head was red from neck to pate with anger and embarrassment. She shrugged, gave him a teasing sad look, and walked away. Harrison rose to go to the washroom and clean up. He would talk to Giulente, then go home to bed. The hell with it.

A hand took him by the shoulder, and he wheeled about, ready to plow the trespasser.

"Detective Harrison? I'm Superintendent Charrington, RCMP. I was told I could find you here. I want to introduce you to Jess Flaherty, from Washington."

Before going to Tann's house, Cobb had cooked up a big shot with the last of his dope, deciding to defer until the morrow the problem of how to handle going without. If he could handle it at all. It would be a very damn cold turkey in the morning. But tonight he wanted to be straight enough to relax and enjoy the friendly company of Ms. Jennifer Tann. And so far, he had done just that. She really could cook Moo Goo Gai Pan, as advertised. There had also been almond cookies from her oven that crumbled lightly in the mouth. The talk tonight had been warm and lively. With unspoken suggestions of intimacy. Okay. But what came after? Was he to seduce — or, in more liberated fashion, allow himself to be seduced?

He rummaged through his musty old library of sexual prowess, failed to find an appropriate source of material, and decided to sit back in a stuffed chair — Tann was perched like a swallow on a large, inviting chesterfield — filled his pipe with pungent tobacco, and tried to centre himself, whatever that involved, by studying the outlines of the large mandala on her window.

Tann looked balefully at his pipe and the creased leather pouch from which he was pulling pinches of shredded tobacco. "Why don't we try putting something in your pipe that smells a little sweeter?" she asked.

"I *beg* your pardon. This is a *fine* blend of old Virginia inner tube."

Tann went to her bedroom and returned with a silver jewellery box. "Now we'll get rid of all this goat dung in here," she said, plucking the unlit pipe from his mouth, dumping the tobacco, and fitting a copper screen into the bowl. She removed a cube of hashish from the silver box, warmed it with a match, and crumbled a bit into the pipe. "Afghani black. Super stone."

Cobb looked at her evenly, without a trace of a smile. "Won't this lead to harder stuff?"

"You're too much. Just relax and don't get uptight. You may not get stoned the first time. I didn't the first time I smoked dope. Or at least I *thought* I didn't. Getting stoned is a sort of learned response."

"I won't lose control and start attacking you like some wild animal?"

"I should be so lucky." She lit up, then puffed hard for a few seconds to get a good burn, then passed the pipe to Cobb. He took a draw on it, then blew the smoke out.

"Aw, Jesus," she said, "don't you go to the movies?"

"I guess I blew it."

She snorted. "Take it in your lungs and hold it."

Cobb did it straight the next time, sucking the sweet smoke into his lungs.

They passed the pipe until it burned out. Cannabis always made Cobb garrulous. "Well, here I am," he said, "a fusty old conservative lawyer sitting in a hippie pad consuming illicit narcotics with a young lady who obviously subscribes to all sorts of kinky radical ideas." Tann by now was stretched lengthwise on the chesterfield, her bare feet on its arm, her skirt hem somewhere above her knees — and inching, it seemed, gradually higher — her hands behind her head. She was smiling, glowing. Cobb kept on. "What work of Satan has so corrupted my stern soul that I indulge in such evil practice? Sitting here in a drug-maddened state. A beautiful woman — with a pair of *amazing* legs — lying near me, close enough to touch."

"Yeah, but I notice you haven't." True enough. He didn't quite know why.

They looked hard at each other, then suddenly Tann blinked, shook her head, smoothed her skirt down, and rose from the chesterfield.

"Don't leave," Cobb said. "I get suicidal on drugs."

"Well, I'll just have to bury you in the back yard with the others." Her voice came from behind him, where her stereo was set up. She was giggling lightly. Cobb loved the sound. It reminded him of temple bells.

"Your smiling hostess even bought a record for the occasion. You're into Mozart, right?" From the speakers there was suddenly pouring the opening bars of the clarinet concerto. "I didn't have the faintest idea. If you can't dance to it, I don't know it."

"Groovy," Cobb said, deadpan. The music was swirling magically in his head.

"Did you get off?" she asked, returning to her chesterfield.

"Can't feel a thing. I was hoping I'd be able to start acting weird. So now what do we do?"

She curled her legs under her and sat like a nesting swan. She gave him an innocent leer. "You know, I like you, Mr. Cobb."

"That's one of us. A tie isn't bad."

"Ego needs a little tune-up. Come on. Give. What's with you?"

"Usual criminal-lawyer mix of drive, bullshit, and childhood trauma. None of it can be changed now. Too late. I'm thirty-eight years old."

"Built-in excuse."

"I lack ambition."

"Good."

"So my wife doesn't love me."

"Her problem."

Cobb studied her. There seemed to be a gentle kind of aura surrounding her person. He wanted to touch her, but felt strapped to his seat. "I won't shatter your simple-hearted illusions by throwing my history up all over your rug."

"Let's hear about it."

"You really don't know, do you?"

"I've been prying. Nobody talks. An enigma. I love enigmas. I want to get inside you, Foster."

"What?"

"Your head. Your head."

"No trespassing. I've got it mined."

"Come on."

Uncharacteristically, he found his tongue starting to ramble. "My father died in the bush when I was six. He was a high faller, and went down with the top fifty feet of a Douglas fir. He died with his spurs on, as the story goes. I have no memory of him save as a tall man, dirty with sawdust, forever in a bathtub. He made up fairy stories and sat by my bed and enthralled me with them. I was alone. No brothers or sisters. My mother was a teacher, and encouraged me to read a lot. She's dead now, too. I think I caused her heart attack."

"So he's left holding a big bag of guilt. How did you kill your mother?"

He shrugged. "I had some trouble. Anyway, I'll skip a couple of chapters. I worked nights to go to school and get my degrees. I ran a pool hall."

"A *pool* hall? A *pool* hall? You?"

"If my office goes broke, I can hustle a living. Anyway, it turned out I was smart, won scholarships, got a law degree, got to be good at what I do."

"Aw, you're not telling me anything. What do you like? What do you dislike?"

"I don't like bad manners, loud mouths, plastic, television. Except the odd hockey or football game. Let's see. This is hard . . ."

With Tann prodding him, he carried on, offering scattered clues, but steering clear of things he felt ashamed of: the robbery, his jail term, junk. His marriage.

After a while there was a silence, and Cobb found himself studying her. She was an Oriental Mona Lisa, her expression quietly asking the important questions. He suddenly felt uncomfortable.

"I feel guilty about this," he said.

"About what? The wife?"

"That's part. Other things."

"Why don't you take all that smelly guilt out and bury it? It makes great fertilizer." She reached over and touched his arm, and the unburied guilt churned within him.

They smoked some more hashish.

"And what," he asked, "should I know about you?"

"Well, I, in contrast to the simpering, guilt-ridden lump who sits here beside me, am fascinating. I am twenty-four years old, charming, self-reliant, smart, keen of eye, sharp of tongue, very snoopy, kind of pleasant to look at, if you dig the slant eyes. I've been through the whole radical trip. I like honesty, and I like being high. I'm capable of a *lot* of affection and love. If you lack that sort of thing. Which I suspect you do. Goddamnit, Foster." And she stood up, went to him, and kissed him on the mouth.

She held herself to him for a long time. He was filled with the smell and touch of her, and there was a hunger for her that enveloped him. But he withdrew from her and stood up, breathing heavily.

"I'm sorry," he said.

"Something bite you?"

"Yeah, yeah. Something bit me. I can't deal with you now. Yet. I feel like a hypocrite." He felt edgy, prickly inside, and he knew a narcotic hunger had begun working at him. And somehow he could not face Jennifer Tann with that fact.

She stood up and touched his arm. "Are you all right?"

There was perspiration on his forehead. "Yeah." Then: "No. Oh, God, I don't know what to do. I'm fucked."

"What?"

He spread his hands in front of him as if groping for words. "I . . . I have a problem."

"A what?"

"Jenn, I'm . . ."

"For God's sake, Foster."

"I'm *wired*."

"Wh–a–a–t?"

"I'm wired. Wired on junk." A panic had begun to seize him. "I've been doing four, five caps a day, and I've got no more fucking junk, and I don't know what to do or where to go. I don't know how to get any more, and I don't know how to quit." He had gone to the closet and was putting on his coat. His face was white. "And I'm going to blow this trial." He went to the door. "I'm sorry, you don't need this."

"Oh, God, Foster." She had a hand on her mouth, and her eyes were wide.

"I'm sorry, I'll make the evening up to you. If I can." Stoned on hashish and suffering heroin withdrawal, he felt as if everything was rolling around him.

"Oh, please stay," she whispered.

"I can't." And he went out the door.

Jennifer Tann stood at the doorway biting her lip while tears came.

For a long while he drove without direction, haphazardly, through the streets of the East End, then into the old city, into Gastown, and parked. He sat for several minutes, trying to settle the flutters of panic that radiated through him. Then he got out and walked to the harbor and stared across the inlet. A pale yellow moon had risen and was climbing over the North Shore mountains, and it lit the snow fields on top of them. A few tugs and small boats were working their way across the inlet, and their lights glistened on the water. Cobb looked down, over the edge of the dock, and the water below him was black and littered with flotsam.

He closed his eyes and hunched his body tightly together. Then quickly turned about and walked some more.

He found himself drifting toward the Corner.

And after several minutes he was there, among the other junkies, looking into their sad and frightened eyes as they drifted from doorway to doorway or sat huddled on steps. He walked, looking for faces . . . for whom? Who could he find here?

Then there was a dark figure beside him. "Hey, Mr. Cobb, this isn't your part of town. Doing some slumming?" He was a young policeman.

Cobb managed a smile. "No," he said, "I'm just passing through."

"Not so safe around here. Never know when some junkie will come at you with a knife." The policeman insisted on walking with Cobb a ways, and Cobb found himself back in his car.

He pressed his hand to his head. He knew he should not go to Deborah. He had used her as a crutch when he wasn't using smack. But he needed a crutch now. Badly. Some help to get through the weekend. If he could just hang on for a few days . . . Maybe. With her help . . .

He began to drive.

He found the Lions Gate Bridge and followed the Upper Levels Highway toward Horseshoe Bay, then north to Squamish, toward Garibaldi Park and the Whistler ski complex. Highway 99 branched from the freeway and clove to the mountain cliffs along Howe Sound into the Squamish Valley. The moon sent a dancing bar of light across the saltchuck, and Cobb felt the sadness and the pull of the moon. Headlights of approaching vehicles loomed and floated past him. It would be nearly three a.m. when he arrived at the condominium, but Deborah would wake up for him. He would prepare a plate of cheese and wheat thins — one of their traditional bedtime snacks — and would talk to her, unburden himself, tell her the heroin thing was over, and tell her . . . what? What about the marriage? He had struggled with that since his visit to the psychiatrist. It *had* to be worked out. Or the needle would kill him.

The road now turned away from the ocean and climbed slowly up the valley of the Cheakamus River. Patches of snow glowed in the moonlight alongside the road. In the Whistler Valley, the air was crisp, and the moon was a pale lamp that showed white secrets to fields and trees and snow-capped cabins.

Cobb's Volvo crunched into the driveway leading to a cluster of skiers' condominiums. The owners' parking lot was in the back, but he left his car near the front door in the visitors' area. When he turned his engine off he was drawn into the pervading silence of a still, windless night. The mountain air was not suffused with dampness, like the air near the ocean, but was crisp and allowed the stars to sparkle. He was wearing shoes with leather soles, and walked gently to keep his footing.

When he got to the door, he found it unlocked, and he felt an icy prickling. Deborah was cautious when alone, afraid of intruders — her practice was always to lock the door before retiring.

As Cobb stepped into the front hallway, he saw that there was soft light coming from the living room. There was a murmuring. Then he realized it was the shadowy light from the black-and-white television, and the voices were speaking lines in a late movie. (If she had been watching the late show, she should have been sitting there, on the sofa which faced the set. But no one was there.) To Cobb's right was the kitchen area, and he could see that it was in good order.

Cobb stepped quietly into the living room to turn the television set off. He noticed some clothing on the sofa. A blouse. Hers.

There was light from a small wall lamp set outside the bedroom door. That door was ajar.

He looked inside. He could see the heavy quilt bunched about her on the bed.

He relaxed. She was snoring loudly. Cobb thought that unusual, but charming.

Maybe the edginess he had felt was just the withdrawal. There was nothing out of place.

He moved to the head of the bed and reached down and pulled the quilt from over her head, which was buried. It was the head of Ed Santorini he first saw. With Deborah's head somewhat lower on his shoulder. Her red hair spilled softly over Santorini's chest.

A bottle of Veuve Clicquot stood beside the bedside table, with two empty glasses, some cheese and wheat thins. He saw Santorini's clothing then, on a chair, piled there with her slacks and underclothes.

The snoring stopped, and there was a shock of silence. Santorini's eyes opened. Those eyes fastened on the form of Foster Cobb standing above him, and they fixed hard on Cobb's face, not moving from it. Santorini's face was blank, without expression, although his lips slowly parted.

There was a taut electrical energy in the room, and the power of it must have awakened Deborah. Her eyes did not quickly focus, and the first messages that went to her brain spoke of a dark figure hovering above her in the dimness.

"Burglar!" she screamed. "Eddie, a burglar!"

Santorini still did not move.

Recognizing her husband, Deborah bolted up, pulling up the quilt to hide her nakedness.

"Oh, God, you scared me," she said, breathing heavily. Her face was a wild mix of feeling.

Cobb felt the pain coming hard, in great surging waves. "If I had known you were fucking tonight, I would have knocked," he said. Then he turned around.

As he went to the front door, he heard her call: "I'm sorry. I'm sorry." And he heard the sounds of her crying.

He was a ghost in the moonlight. The stars were cold and brittle and lonely.

The sweats were coming hard, and his joints had begun to ache.

Saturday, the Eighteenth Day of March, at Two O'Clock in the Afternoon

After another fruitless day of hunting Leclerc, Harrison visited Cobb's apartment. Cobb received him in a kind of frenzy. He seemed as jumpy as an ant on a hot pan. The apartment had suffered ruin: glass was broken here and there, and clothing was piled in heaps near the door.

"God, it's cold in here," Cobb said.

Harrison narrowed his eyes and studied the apparition. "Are you sick?"

"Got a fever. Must have caught a bug. Working too hard. Got to slow down. Got to work on my cross. Jesus, it's cold in here. Jesus."

"You're sweating."

"Yeah, yeah. What is it, Honcho?"

"Got some people I want you to meet. RCMP Superintendent. Cop from the States. About Cudlipp. Stole some heroin from the RCMP. I told them we'd meet here tomorrow at ten a.m. But, Jesus, what a mess. Are you okay?"

"Dying, dying."

"What's wrong with your back?"

"Must have got into my bones. Bones ache. Back aches. Aw, fuck. Just don't know if I can do it." Cobb's voice was like a croak.

Harrison was aghast. "The trial? You *gotta* do it. You gotta do Cudlipp. Hey, Fos, you gotta finish him."

"Yeah, yeah, I know. I know. I don't know, though. Don't know if I can handle it. Ran out of aspirins."

The old detective's face began to show panic. "Jesus, we're talking about Dr. Au's trial! You seen a doctor?"

"Yeah. No. I don't know. Doctor's no good. Got to get some pills. Got to go out."

"Better see a doctor, Fos."

"Yeah. No. It's Saturday. Shit. Broke some glass here." Cobb was staring foggy-eyed at a shattered wine glass.

"A bomb go off in here?"

"No, no, I'll clean up." He gave Harrison an imploring look. "Adjourn the trial. Put it off. Tell the judge I'm sick."

"Goddamnit, we can't! We've got to get the Surgeon *now*, Fos. Look, I've got some written reports I want to bring up so you'll be ready for these guys." What the fuck! he thought.

"Aw. I don't know. I can't see anybody. I don't know. I'm going to be sick."

Harrison listened to the dry gasping sounds coming from the bathroom. Then he left.

The tourniquet, held tight by a flawed set of moulding teeth, went slack as the blood rushed up the tube. The junkie eyes of the man called Pogo were pinned and sharp by the time he pulled the point from the solid callus at his inner left elbow. The swollen vein that he had popped submerged like a retreating earthworm. An ooze of blood seeped out, and he wiped it off with the back of his hand.

Then he tied a tight knot at the end of the condom and stuffed it and its contents into the toe of a boot, which he shoved back under his bed.

The heroin that was in the capsules in the condom in the toe of Pogo's boot had come from his middleman, by way of Dr. Au's back end. Originally, it had come from Burmese poppy fields half-way around the world, through jungle trails by elephant and mule train, by trawlers and junks, and finally by body pack on a Ch'ao-chou seaman across the Pacific to Vancouver.

It had been cut only six times, and the hit that Pogo took had a stiff bite to it. The street and the junkie lifestyle had taken their toll by now, and Warren Leonard Possit — Pogo to his friends — was on a fifteen-cap-a-day habit, strung out half the time and dozing the rest. He was a skinny shrivelled little man with a grey pallor and the reek of death. He was waiting to go to jail. The next arrest would save his life, because although another trafficking beef would put him away forever, he would have a bed and food.

Pogo Possit's beat was downtown south Granville. He looked after the hotels there around Davie and Drake. He had twelve caps left for sale tonight and he wanted to get rid of them fast so he could cash out with his dealer, who then would cuff him another bundle. That would ensure that Possit would have a few caps in the morning to get straight with. Unless he got popped in the meantime.

He was heading for the Alberta Hotel, and if he could find ten or so hypes there with bread, that should do it.

A Pacific low had moved in during the day, and chilling rain penetrated through the cloth coat he had boosted earlier that week from the racks of the Army and Navy. A hustler stared at him with drawn eyes as he went toward the door.

"You got, Pogo?" she said.

"Yeah, you ready?"

"Aw, man, ain't no tricks happening tonight. Too cold. You got a spare, maybe, for an old friend?"

"No, nothing. I ain't got nothing to donate."

"Come on, Pog. Get your rocks off. Free for a cap."

"Hey, Cheryl, you kiddin'?" When you're doing fifteen caps a day, you don't exactly burn with unrequited desire.

He walked in and waved to one of the waiters, who dropped a

beer on the table for him. You don't buy a beer, you don't sell dope — that's the rule. Possit sat down and had a little sip, and looked over the tables. Two or three persons nodded to him, giving him the sign. After a while he got up and began to cruise.

"You want?"

"Yeah, one, Pog."

"You?"

"Couple."

"You want?"

"Yeah. Yeah, okay."

"You lookin'?"

"Take a sawbuck? I'm short five."

"You owe me already. A fin from this afternoon."

"Please, Pogo."

"Split one with Jerry. . . . You want? Yeah, I got you. You want?"

"Strapped kinda shitty right now. Front me on, I'll catch you tomorrow."

"Need the cash, Sandy. You okay?"

"Yeah."

"Take a cassette deck? Came out undamaged, radio, too, it's like new."

"Let's see it. All right; if I can deal it, I have you down for a cap. Fritz okay? . . . "

"See Pat. He'll get you ten or fifteen for it new."

"Fritz okay? Wake him up. You okay? Hey, you okay?"

"Yeah, yeah."

"Phyllis?"

"Yeah, a couple. Arlene's up in the room sick. One for her."

"Hey, Pogo."

"Yeah?"

"Man's in the corner."

"Uh-huh."

"The big Fosdick reading the paper."

"Know him?"

"Homicide dick."

"He ain't interested in me, then. You guys okay?"

"Fuck off, heatbag."

"Awful bright and cheery, ain't you? How about you, Glen?"

"How long you be?"

"Few minutes."

"Okay, a single."

That was eight, maybe nine if the car radio sold. Good enough. A fair tour. Possit went back to his table, took a couple of sips, and left the glass half-empty. He went out toward his hotel, for his stash.

In the corner, Honcho Harrison put his newspaper down, drained his glass, left fifty cents on the table, and strolled out the door, too. Cheryl was still standing outside, shivering in a short skirt that showed thin legs and knobby knees. "Sure wet out," she said. "Would you like to warm up a bit?"

"Get outta here or I'm gonna run you in."

"Let's see your badge, asshole."

Harrison took her by the wrist, twisted it, and pushed her out, away from the hotel doorway and onto the sidewalk. She cursed at him, and he returned to the beer-parlor doorway, then edged off a few feet to a point near the steam-bath sign where it was dark. He waited for Pogo to return.

He waited for about ten minutes. It was nearly ten o'clock. Then, from the alley, the pusher came in view.

There were eleven caps of heroin in the condom in Pogo Possit's mouth. He had done the twelfth up in his room. Possit saw the burly man standing in the shadows near the door, and wondered if the bust were finally, at long last, about to happen. When he saw the man start to walk toward him, his old dope-dealer instinct told him to swallow the stuff, but he saw his chance to get back to the safety and order of the B.C. Penitentiary. The condom was tucked between his tongue and palate when Harrison grabbed him by the throat.

"Vancouver police. Spit." Harrison's hand had choked off Possit's gullet. "Spit."

With his tongue, Possit pushed the bag from between his lips, and it fell to the pavement. Harrison picked it up and let the man go.

"There's only eleven."

"What's your name?"

"Possit. Len Possit."

"Dealer, huh?"

"Uh, no." The lie was instinctive.

"For your own use, hey?"

"Yeah, that's right. I'm an addict. I'll show you my tracks. Fresh marks." He rolled up his sleeve to show the needle marks.

"Yeah, well, eleven ain't much. I'll let you go this time."

"What?"

"You got me in a relaxed mood this evening, Mr. Possit. Go home."

"You're not taking me in?"

"No. This good stuff?"

"Dynamite. White Lady. I don't deal garbage."

"You don't deal at all, do you, Possit?"

"Er, no."

"Okay, then beat it."

"Yeah? Just go?"

"Yeah, beat it."

Fifteen minutes later Harrison was at Cobb's apartment with copies of Special Officer Flaherty's reports. Cobb was still jerking about. He could hardly talk.

"Read these," Harrison said. "We'll see you tomorrow, ten sharp, here."

Cobb just hugged himself with his arms crossed over his chest. He stuttered some words: "C-c-can't, d-damn it."

"You'll be okay in the morning. Here, somebody must've left this on your doorstep." Harrison handed over an unmarked manila envelope, the kind police use to place exhibits in. Then he quickly left.

The envelope contained a condom and eleven number-five gelatin capsules filled with good white heroin donated to Cobb by Pogo Possit pursuant to the merciful sponsorship of Honcho Harrison — by way of Dr. Au P'ang Wei's shipping lanes.

Monday, the Twentieth Day of March, at Ten O'Clock in the Morning

Cobb started out bluntly.

"The whole of your evidence has been purchased, Corporal Cudlipp."

"What?"

"I am suggesting that to you."

"You can suggest anything you want, sir."

"Very well," said Cobb. "I suggest you are a bought liar." He let the words hang out heavy and hard. He knew the accusation would bring Smythe-Baldwin to his feet, and he was right.

"That is infamous and high-handed," shouted the defence lawyer, an expression of hurt on his face. Cobb did not mind a brief display of injured innocence. It would be useful.

Horowitz, of course, agreed that Cobb had gone too far. Such accusations are required to be more subtly put in a courtroom. "Please avoid epithets, Mr. Cobb," the judge said.

Tann looked up at Cobb as he glared at Horowitz. She knew Cobb was angry and she worried that he would tangle with the judge. She wondered at the reason for the anger.

Tann had not seen him since Friday night. She had called a half-dozen times on Saturday, but he did not answer. Finally she went to his apartment and buzzed him from the loudspeaker panel at the front door. He excoriated her, warned her to leave him alone, refused to release the automatic lock. Then, late on Saturday night, he phoned her, and he was calm and gentle on the phone, remorseful and apologetic. He gave her instructions to research the law of rebuttal evidence. And this morning, when he met her near the courthouse for breakfast, she studied him hard, saw the anger and tension in his face. But that dissolved for a moment or two as he came up to her and put his hands on her shoulders and kissed her on the cheek. He put up a warning hand and said: "Don't ask. We'll have time later."

Cobb, staring hard at the witness, now changed direction.

"Corporal Cudlipp, I think you have told us that you are well qualified to give us information about the world of heroin trafficking," Cobb said. "That is true: you *are* an expert in that field?" It was usually easy to play to a witness's sense of his own small majesty.

"Some consider me an expert," Cudlipp said. "I have been accepted as such in court many times by many different judges."

"Yes. You know as much about heroin dealing as any policeman in this country." Cobb was standing beside the jury, not moving about the courtroom, disciplining himself to stay put and concentrate the jury's attention on the exchange between him and the witness. He had funnelled all his sorrow and anger into this cross-examination.

"Heroin trafficking is my field, Mr. Cobb," the witness said. Cudlipp was standing soldier-straight and unblinking.

"There are great sums of money to be made from heroin. Fortunes can be earned, is that not so?" Cobb knew that Cudlipp would now be alert to the direction Cobb was headed in, but the witness had frequently given such evidence and would be consistent.

"Yes, sir. A pound of heroin worth fifteen thousand dollars in Hong Kong can be broken down here into thousands of capsules and be worth maybe a million or two million by the time it all reaches the street. An importer or a top man in the business can get a pretty big chunk of all that money."

"And there are certain persons in Vancouver who have amassed great wealth in that business?" Cobb turned and let the jury see he was looking at Au. The accused returned the look, cold, without expression.

"Some people live very well," Cudlipp said. "Until we catch up with them. They are always caught in the end."

"The big criminals always end up getting caught, is that so? That is reassuring, corporal."

"I think we have a good record in that regard." The pride of the force was in Cudlipp's voice.

"And sometimes there are . . . smaller criminals who attach themselves to these big criminals?"

"Of course."

"And do *these* fellows get found out all the time as well?"

"You can't remain for long in the business of crime and not get caught out." There was a distant note of strain in Cudlipp's voice.

"And the big operators, the organizers of crime, the men on top of the heroin syndicates, do not these men have the financial resources to avoid conviction in the courts?"

"I don't know what you mean."

"They can pay for very expensive defences, employ the best lawyers that money can buy, that sort of thing." Cobb knew Smythe-Baldwin was smoldering, but would have to sit still.

"I suppose that's true."

"And they can bestow largesse upon those easily corrupted, and purchase the lies of witnesses for alibis in court?" Cobb was close to the line, but still on the safe side of it.

"I suppose that can happen," Cudlipp said. "There are people who would stoop that low."

Both witness and lawyer were masking pain. Cudlipp's pain was of a milder form, and he had received a quarter of a million dollars' worth of relief for it. Cobb's pain was not physical now, just emotional

— he would have preferred Ed Santorini to be at the receiving end of this cross-examination, but Cudlipp would have to do. And the task he had embarked on this morning had one goal: the ruin of Cudlipp beyond repair or healing. Cobb had the power to achieve that goal, and the resources. They had been delivered to him on the weekend, at his apartment.

"That is so, is it?" he said. "There are actually persons who will accept money to give perjured evidence?"

"I believe it happens."

"Has it happened in your experience?" Cobb hoped to taunt Smythe-Baldwin into a further objection, but the defence lawyer would sit through this, knowing it would not look good to protect his witness.

Cudlipp said: "I have known of cases in which I believe a man has been paid to give false evidence." He paused, glanced at Cobb, then away. He plunged ahead. "If you are inferring something of that kind about me, I just feel badly for you, Mr. Cobb. For someone with your experience as a prosecutor, I think it is cheap."

Smythe-Baldwin smiled at the jury and said: "Well, the witness said it, not me." Cobb knew that it was Smythe-Baldwin's act, however, and that the old lawyer smelled something bad.

Anger and strong heroin were carrying Cobb through this day.

For a moment Cobb allowed himself to be distracted, and an image, almost hallucinational, intruded. He saw Deborah on the bed, sleeping, her head on Santorini's shoulder . . .

He switched channels quickly, returning to Cudlipp. "Corporal," he said, "I *am* accusing you of selling your evidence. If it turns out that I have slandered you, it will be my solemn obligation to apologize and beg your forgiveness." Cudlipp said nothing to that and looked stonily ahead into space, looking not at his questioner, or the judge, or the jury. Cobb continued. "Are they ruthless?"

"What do you mean, exactly?"

"It is a dangerous business, is it not?" said Cobb. "Big-time traffickers can go to jail for a long time — twenty years, even life imprisonment is not uncommon. That is so, isn't it?"

"Yes, sir, it is a very serious crime."

"So although the money is good, the risks are high, yes?"

"Yes, sir."

"One is always in danger of discovery, and one is always wary that there may be informers close to him, am I correct?"

Cudlipp had no alternative but to follow the prosecutor's lead. "Yes, I have already said I deal with informers."

"An informer can put a big dealer behind bars for life, I suppose," Cobb said.

"He can be very instrumental in that, yes."

"So if a man is an informer, and is found out, his life is not worth very much."

"Jim Fat's life was not worth very much, that is for sure."

"No. He was an informer, wasn't he?"

"I am afraid that is so."

"Instead of arresting him, you used him, is that so?" Cobb said.

"In our business we have to make certain decisions like that from time to time. We were looking for bigger game. He was bait."

"And he was killed because he had informed on someone very big, is that right?"

"He was giving me information on Ming and Plizit. I have already said that. Somehow they found out. I don't know how. I believe they killed him."

"And he was killed in a pretty bloodthirsty way, you know that."

"So I have heard." Cudlipp shook his head sadly.

"And whoever informed on the informer was as much responsible for this death as the man who wielded the knife, would you agree?"

There was a hesitation. "I am not competent to judge that sort of issue," Cudlipp said.

Cobb was through skirting the point and honed in: "Did you ever tell any person that Jim Fat was your informer?"

"No, not even my superior officer. I maintain a trust with my informers." There was a muffled laugh from somewhere in the gallery. The sheriffs looked stern.

"Come, corporal, did you not tell the accused, Au, that Jim Fat was an informer?"

"Of course not." Cudlipp, blustering, sounded indignant.

"You met with the accused a couple of days before Jim Fat's death?"

"I may have. We met often. He was giving me information, too. I have already said that."

"It was at a time when you were carrying out an investigation as to Au's activities as a drug trafficker, that is what I am suggesting. Did you not tell fellow officers you were expecting to arrest Au in his car with a large quantity of heroin?" Charrington had learned of the December first stake-out of Au's car during interviews with junior drug-squad officers.

There was a delay before Cudlipp said anything, and when he spoke, he repeated the question: "You are asking whether we expected to arrest the accused with some heroin." Cudlipp looked down at Smythe-Baldwin, who simply stared at his notes, unable to help. "Well, there was an investigation. We have to follow all leads. I had information there might be some heroin in Dr. Au's car, but it was probably Plizit's. He had access."

"Where did that information come from?"

Smythe-Baldwin was on his feet before Cobb finished the last word. "My friend knows that the rules of evidence do not require a police officer to name informants in these courts. We have just heard an exposition of the dangers that exist to their lives if their names become known, and I am sure my friend would not wish to find himself in the position of being a party to endangering someone's life. How did he put it? 'Whoever informs on the informer is as responsible as the man who wields the knife.'"

"I am sure fraud is an exception to the rule," Cobb replied.

The judge ruled against Cobb, reserving a right to change his mind if Cobb could offer proof of fraud. Then they took the regular morning adjournment. Jennifer Tann brought him a coffee, and they went to the crown-counsel room.

"Very briefly," she said, "evidence can be called by the crown to rebut only issues raised which are not collateral. You can call evidence to disprove alibi, but the cases say credibility is collateral, and you cannot call evidence to prove a witness has lied about some unrelated issues. For instance . . . hey, are you all right?"

Cobb had a far-away look. He had not heard her essay on law. His anger gripped him and his muscles became rigid.

"Foster," Tann said. "Hey."

"Right," he said. "That's good. That's excellent."

"*Where* did you migrate to?"

"When — Friday night?"

"No, just now."

"I don't think I can tell you."

Tann put her hand over his and held it there for a moment.

On the way back to the courtroom, Cobb stopped by the witness room. Special Agent Flaherty seemed composed, ready, and was reading over the Cudlipp notes. Giulente was tense, and gave Cobb a tight smile.

Outside the courtroom, Cudlipp was finishing a cigarette, talking bravely and earnestly with the sheriffs. He was still one of the boys.

Inside, Au calmly looked around. He saw Charrington sitting in the front row beside Harrison, near the seat Leclerc had occupied. Au assumed correctly that the man was of high rank and had business here, and that the business had to do with Cudlipp. The slightest fringe of a headache was making passage from behind his optic nerve to the base of his right ear. He touched a place in his lower back and the pain ceased. But he knew it would return, travelling different routes. The prognosis was uncertain, and because the illness was novel to him, and seemed to centre somewhere in the brain, no diagnosis could be accurate. But there was serenity in his expression. He did not betray the subtle erosion of his inner tranquillity. His mind, he believed, was still as clear as a mirror.

Cudlipp was unhappy. He had spent Saturday with Alice Carson, and she had puffed him up to full confidence, but on Sunday, alone, he had sagged, feeling the confidence hissing out through small leaks. This morning he had picked Carson up and they had gone to the courtroom together, and again she had given him courage — but that had ebbed as Cobb seemed to guess too closely at the truth.

But perhaps Cobb had nothing, and the whole of the cross-examination would be bait and bluff. The money was safe in Carson's sock. Two hundred and fifty thousand dollars would be sufficient recompense for whatever humiliation he might suffer here.

Alice Carson was quite relaxed. She was dressed tastefully in a new suit which showed only a little leg. It was an expensive outfit, but Cudlipp had insisted she buy it. Appearance mattered in court, he said.

M.C. Smythe-Baldwin leaned back on his chair at the counsel table, trading quips with reporters who hovered about him practising cynical lines upon him. When Cobb re-entered the court, he caught his eye, and raised his eyebrows, as if to ask: How do you plan to do this man in? What do you have in your pocket?

When court resumed, Cobb switched the topic. "Did you bring your notes relating conversations with the accused?"

"You mean notes of my conversation with him last December third? I know you are going to make something of this, but I lost them."

"You lost them." Cobb said it as a well-predicted truth.

"Yes. I'll be honest with you. I didn't think they would be important, so I just mislaid them someplace. I spent the whole weekend hunting high and low for them, Mr. Cobb, and I know the first thing you're going to think is I destroyed them or something."

"Your notes for December third are missing."

"Yes."

"And your notes containing other references to the accused, recounting other meetings with him — where are they?"

"To be quite honest, the only notes I have are with respect to on-going investigations, or matters that are coming before the courts. I don't usually keep my notes unless I know they will be used."

"So you destroyed them?"

"No, I lost them. Or just threw them away, I don't know."

"You lost them. Or you threw them away."

"I can't find them, anyway. I looked high and low."

"And where did you look high and low?"

"All over my house. I never keep them at the detachment."

"And when did you look high and low?"

"All weekend."

"Oh," said Cobb. "You have decided to return home. I think I may have called you there a few dozen times in the last few weeks, and the phone kept ringing. Were you on holidays?"

"I took some holiday leave, yes."

"You were not hiding from me?"

"Oh, no."

"And where did you take these holidays? Some sumptuous tropical resort?"

Cobb regretted that. Sarcasm was a poor weapon.

"Where did I spend my holidays?" Cudlipp gave a grunting, forced laugh. "Well, it wasn't a pleasure holiday, believe me. I was asked by Mr. Smythe-Baldwin to help with the defence, so I stayed close to the courthouse, where I would be handy to him."

"And where was that?"

"Hotel Vancouver."

"Hotel Vancouver? You had a room there all this time?"

"A room, a suite."

"A suite? That's larger than a room, then? It would cost about sixty, seventy-five dollars a day?"

"I don't know. Mr. Smythe-Baldwin paid the bill."

"How generous. And you were all alone in this hotel room? I take it you are not married?"

"I am separated from my wife. I don't mind you knowing that. I have a girlfriend and she visits me, and I don't mind you knowing that, either. We love each other very much, and you may as well know that, too, if you are interested in my personal life."

"Since you are not shy about such matters, perhaps you can tell me something about your current relationship with Mrs. Cudlipp. I take it you may be paying her some form of financial support."

"I have three children. I pay seven hundred and fifty a month."

Smythe-Baldwin rose wearily from his seat to complain. "Is my friend interested in these details, or is he hoping to try to toss a little dirt around? The witness has nothing to hide, and is he not entitled to keep the facts of his personal life to himself."

"I will show the relevance, my lord," Cobb said.

"If you can, I will let you proceed, but you should exercise care, Mr. Cobb," said the judge.

Cobb, flaring a bit, said: "I try always to exercise care, my lord. I do not enjoy rummaging for scandal."

"Proceed, Mr. Cobb," Horowitz said. "When you have gone too far, I will let you know." Judges do not like to be upbraided, even mildly.

"Are you up-to-date in the payments to your wife and family?" Cobb asked.

"I am, sir."

"Have you always been?"

"I have paid every last cent I owe, or that family court claims that I owe."

"Were you always up-to-date, corporal?"

"There have been disputes about how much I owe, but I am paid up fully to date."

"Were you always up-to-date on these payments, corporal?"

"I suppose I was behind for a while."

"In fact, in early December you were behind to the tune of seven thousand dollars, isn't that so? Seven thousand dollars?"

"If you've been talking to my wife, I suppose that's what she might have said. She and I don't get along well, and I'm not afraid to tell you that."

"Seven thousand dollars. I put it to you."

"I don't know. December? No, it couldn't have been that much." Cudlipp gave the air of carefully trying to reconstruct his marital financial history. He looked at the ceiling, then closed his eyes, frowning.

"This will help," said Cobb, flashing from his file a court document. "This is a family court order for payment of arrears of maintenance, and it is dated November twenty-eight. Do you see any names on it you recognize?" He walked to the witness box and placed it in front of Cudlipp.

"Yes, I am shown here. And you're right. Well, it says seven thousand dollars. I honestly couldn't remember. I ask you to believe that."

Again Smythe-Baldwin rose, and Cobb heard tension in his voice. "In the name of decency, my lord, my friend should now stop this invasion of a man's private life."

"I will tell him when he must stop, Mr. Smythe-Baldwin." The judge had caught the scent.

"Tell us when you paid out this debt, witness," Cobb ordered.

"The middle of December, or thereabouts." Cudlipp's voice was slightly ragged now, and he cleared his throat.

"And where did you get the money? Tell us that, please."

"I had some money in the bank, and I got a loan."

"How much money was in the bank, and how much did you borrow from it?"

"I didn't borrow from the bank. Well, I had a few hundred in the bank, and the rest I got from a friend."

"A friend?"

"Yes, sir."

"A very good friend."

"I suppose."

"Will you tell us who the friend is?"

"He is a man who I know from back east. I wrote to him and he sent me some money, that is all."

"What is his name?"

"Franklin. John Franklin." Cobb wondered whether that name had just now been obtained from the air, or whether Cudlipp had prepared for this area of questioning.

"His address."

"It's a Toronto address. I don't have it here. Probably at home, somewhere."

"What does he do?"

"He has a . . . he is a businessman. Tools and implements, I believe."

"And he sent you a cheque?"

Cudlipp hesitated for a moment. "Well, now, gosh, I can't remember whether it was a cheque or money order, or what, to be honest."

"Well, if it were a cheque or money order, we could easily trace that, couldn't we?"

"I suppose. No, wait. It was cash. I remember. He was in town. He travels a lot. And he must have gone to his bank and withdrawn the cash for me."

Cobb let all of that sink home for a while while he looked at the jury. One man was smiling.

"Witness, the money was given to you by Au P'ang Wei, the accused. Please tell us if that isn't so."

"I deny that," Cudlipp said. "I know what you are trying to do."

"I am merely trying to seek the truth, witness."

"I think you are trying to discredit me."

"Yes, indeed," Cobb said. Cudlipp was a very big fish, but he was on the line now. "You didn't consider that it was curious of Mr. Frank Johnson — is that his name?"

"Yes. No. I said John Franklin."

"That Mr. Franklin would pay you this whole sum in cash?"

"He deals in large sums of money all the time."

"And did you sign a promissory note or some document?"

"No. We work on trust."

"Yes, and you deposited all of that in your bank account?"

"I believe so, yes. Yes, I sent a cheque to family court. You probably have that, too."

"Well, I have a record of it, as a matter of fact. The cheque was issued from your current account, number 4578403, Bank of Nova Scotia on East Broadway. Is it not true, as well, witness, that you had lost a large sum in stock-market speculation last year? Some penny stocks that didn't turn out?"

"I invest a little, win a little, lose a little. A lot of people do that." He cleared his throat again.

"Your bank covered you to the tune of about fifteen thousand dollars, is that right? You borrowed to cover these losses?"

"You seem to have done a fair bit of poking around. Yes, I'm not going to lie about it. I borrowed money, and I paid that off, too, and that money came from my friend as well."

"What — he gave you twenty-two thousand dollars? Cash? No receipt? No note? No record?"

"I am a policeman, Mr. Cobb. People trust my word."

"People trust your word. And you put all this money in your bank?"

"Yes, to pay off the loan and to pay off Stella and the kids."

"And you received this cash in the middle of December."

"Thereabouts."

"I suggest that you deposited it on Friday, December second."

"Oh, you probably have something to prove that, too. I'm not sure of the dates."

"Well, now, there is someone here who perhaps can help us with all of this. You know your bank manager, Mr. Jessup?"

"Yes, I know him."

"Mr. Sheriff," said Cobb, "please go to the witness room and ask Mr. Jessup to step inside for a moment." The bank manager came through the door and looked about, lost.

"Do you know this man?" Cobb asked Cudlipp.

"Yes, that's Mr. Jessup."

"Now, unfortunately, he can't release any of your documents without a court order, but I am sure he has brought them with him. For the time being, will you agree that you made the deposit on December the second last and it was in the amount of twenty-two thousand dollars?"

"I won't dispute it."

"Send him back for now, Mr. Sheriff. Now, December second was the day before Jim Fat was murdered, yes?"

"Yes."

"And it would appear that someone must have advised his murderer that Jim Fat was an informant — that is a kind of information that can be bought, is it not? In your wide experience?"

"If you say."

"Don't play with me." Cobb bit each word off and spat it. "Do you say it?"

"It happens."

"And it happened in this case a day or two before Jim Fat's death."

"How would I know?"

"How would you know? Because, witness, I suggest to you that you sold his name to his murderer."

"I gave no information." Cudlipp's voice seemed duller now, the modulation gone.

"You were in debt, and family court was hounding you, and you were not able to hold everything together on a salary of twenty-seven thousand dollars a year, and you sold Jim Fat to the accused as a butcher would sell a side of beef." Cobb was shaking; his voice was ringing. He was aware that Smythe-Baldwin was speaking, and the judge was speaking. Cobb waited until the judge finished admonishing him, then continued.

"Witness, there was a bonus, was there not, a further thirty thousand dollars that you received a few days later?"

"Oh, God." That was the only response from Cudlipp. "Yes, there was more from Franklin." The voice was wooden. "I needed more to invest to earn enough to pay back the debt to him. I told him I had a good bet on some investments."

The lies were becoming palpable. Cobb turned to look at Au. There was no emotion that could be read, no bead of sweat, no tremor of the hand. Cobb saw a man in apparent control of himself.

There was little point of playing about further with the apparition John Franklin. It was time to lay waste the December third alibi.

"Witness, you claim to have been with the accused during the time that Jim Fat was killed. You claim to have been in Archie's Steak House during that time."

"Ask Alice Carson, she was the waitress. As a matter of fact, it's her I am going out with."

"And of course she will say anything you ask her to, will she not?" Cobb asked.

"She will not lie."

"The fact is that she was not even hired there until a few days later, on December sixth. The fact is that she was not there at all, and I suggest that you have tried to use her to falsely corroborate your evidence."

"She was there, I swear it."

Cobb turned again to the sheriff. "Bring in Mr. Giulente." Timorous Joey Giulente came in and stood by the door. "Do you know this man?"

"Yes, that is Joey, the manager of Archie's."

"And there is no question in your mind that Joey Giulente possesses the records to prove that Alice Carson was or was not employed there as of December third?"

"I suppose you looked at them," said Cudlipp. "I haven't. I just recall Alice being there and seeing me and Dr. Au. I could be wrong. I am trying to do my best here. Maybe it was another waitress. I am not trying to play any games here. I am just trying to tell the truth as I remember it. People can make honest mistakes. You're just trying to make me seem a liar." But Cudlipp had lost spunk. He was becoming exhausted from the chase.

Cobb dismissed Giulente, who would be prepared to testify, in rebuttal, that neither Cudlipp nor Au had been in the restaurant on December third. His memory was aided by the wiretap transcripts shown to him and by his desire to help avenge the killing of Jim Fat, a close friend. Cobb knew he would also confirm that Alice Carson had responded to his "Help Wanted" window card on Monday, December fifth, and started work the following day.

"Can I say something else?" Cudlipp said.

"You should just answer Mr. Cobb's questions," Horowitz said.

"No," said Cobb. "I'm interested in anything he has to say." He was not, but the jury might resent the fact that a witness was not allowed to make a comment.

"I happen to believe there is drug trafficking emanating from that restaurant. That's one of the reasons I go there, as part of my job. And if I can add something else, I wouldn't trust anything Joey Giulente says because he has a record of trafficking in heroin and he uses cocaine." It was a wild roundhouse swing.

"But you would trust anything Alice Carson says? Did she not tell you she was once a prostitute?"

Cudlipp flared. "Where did you hear that? That is a cheap shot just because you know she has been subpoenaed to give evidence. I didn't believe you would stoop to that."

"How do you know she was subpoenaed?" Cobb was unfazed.

"She told me on the weekend."

"Were you with her?"

"We spent some time together. We went off to Harrison Hot Springs on Saturday for a little break."

"And of course you discussed the evidence with her on Saturday, with this woman whom you say you love?"

"I don't *say* I love her. We both do. We care for each other very deeply. And no, I did not discuss the evidence. I know my duty as a police officer and a witness, and I do not disobey orders from a judge."

"Let's go back to Archie's Steak House. You took the accused there on Wednesday, December twenty-first, am I correct?"

"I don't know where you get your information from."

"Just answer the question."

"I can't remember."

"Try harder."

"I don't think so."

"You were there that day trying to set up the alibi. That was the evening you had a meal with the accused and were served by your friend Alice Carson."

"I don't know who's telling you these things. I'm sure it was December third."

Cobb had in his hand the steak house telephone transcripts, opened to the conversation of December twenty-first between Joey Giulente and his friend Jingo, the cocaine dealer.

"Refresh your memory from this," Cobb said, placing the transcripts in front of the witness. "You may as well know that the telephone at Archie's restaurant was being tapped —"

That was all he got out before Smythe-Baldwin, slower than usual, scrambled to his feet. "Let me see those," he demanded.

"Order the jury out," Horowitz said. Then, less brusquely, he turned to the jurors and said: "I'm sorry, ladies and gentlemen, but something has arisen which might require discussion in your absence. You may as well retire to your hotel for lunch, and you will be returned here at two p.m. Mr. Sheriff." The sheriff's officer led them out, and Tann arranged about a dozen case books on the counsel table.

"Ms. Tann will make the argument," Cobb said, and sat down.

"The crown's position rests upon the combined effect of Section 178 decimal sixteen, Invasion of Privacy part of the Code, and Section Eleven of the Canada Evidence Act."

"Just a minute," said the judge. "Let me get those. All right. Yes."

"The crown also relies upon a line of authority going back to 1853 in England for the proposition that a witness may have his memory refreshed by writings not necessarily of his own making. I have passed to the clerk for your lordship a list of such authorities commencing with Rex and Isaacs in the Court of Common Pleas and concluding with Jamieson versus Marquette in the Ontario Court of Appeal, in 1972. There are citations in the Dominion Law Reports, and Ontario Reports. I should say, before dealing individually with the cases that your lordship will be asked to make an analogy between written documents and electronically taped recordings of human voices."

The argument was put with earnest precision. It had been worked over many times between Tann and Cobb. She had it nearly put to memory. Cobb saw Smythe-Baldwin eyeing her warily, but with respect.

For the time, there was no work to occupy Cobb's mind, and it slipped unreined and ran loose among thoughts of the perfidy of those too well loved, of the shame he had felt in his own betrayal.

At some point during the long hours of the past weekend Cobb had decided that there were no more tears to be shed. He felt he had been tested, in the cruellest biblical sense. There was the heroin, and it eased the suffering, but it could palliate suffering in only the most fleeting and transitory way. Somehow, he must begin to survive without it. Somehow. Seven more capsules to go. By then, hopefully, at least the trial would be over.

A revolution, still inchoate, was simmering now within the recesses of the soul of Au P'ang Wei. Even the closest observer, however keen to his perception, would not detect outward clues, so delicate was the subtlety of the change that was beginning. The grey stone eyes were hard set but had lost a glint, and perhaps a slight glaze now dimmed the sharpness. His composure was still serene and settled, but in the muscles near the lumbar vertebrae there existed a faint degree of tension now, a tension that despite the extraordinary resources of his will Au was unable to still — except momentarily by pressure of his fingers. There was a spot of phlegm in his throat which he was disinclined to clear, and thereby give evidence of its existence. The pain recurred in the centre of his head at regular intervals, and was more insistent upon each return.

Dr. Au, since he had left medical school in England, had never allowed himself to hate, but felt hatred breaking free within him as he watched Cudlipp's poor efforts, watched the man's credibility slowly erode under fire. The hatred was not felt toward the person of the helpless policeman — for him Au felt nothing, or if anything, contempt — but toward the prosecutor, whom Au now understood was effectively working to destroy him. As the danger to his freedom became more easily perceived, a dark mist began to discolor the clarity of the mirror of Au's mind.

The awesome fact was this: Au was at the edge of sanity, peering into the abyss. He had never been far from it, since those months of torment many years ago in England, and now he had been led to the precipice by Foster Cobb.

Despite his show of outward composure, Au was growing ill inside with the hatred, and with a fear of a confrontation between prosecutor and accused, a confrontation that Cudlipp's dissembling answers seemed now to make inevitable.

Perhaps it was in response to the power of the massed, malignant energy that Au was focussing on the person of Foster Cobb that the lawyer suddenly felt a primal shudder rush up his spine. The spasm began at the lower end and ballooned in intensity as it climbed the cord, sending dark shivers through his synapses. Instinctively Cobb turned around, and his eyes met the eyes of Dr. Au, and they clashed and locked. There seemed to pour from Au a powerful thought transference, and although no lips moved, Cobb heard a message distinctly enunciated.

It said: You will die at my hand.

Monday, the Twentieth Day of March, at Twenty Minutes Past One O'Clock in the Afternoon

Cobb spent the lunch break pacing the halls of the main floor of the courthouse. The silent words of Dr. Au rang hollowly, echoing still, whispering in his mind the curse of death. A delusion induced by drugs and pain? A kind of madness? He had known auditory hallucinations. . . . But the voice had been flat and toneless, and it *was* the voice of Au.

He was too on edge to feel hunger. Tann had been unable to take his tension and had gone off somewhere for a sandwich.

In all his years of prosecuting, Cobb had rarely failed to display the impersonality that is proper in an advocate of the crown, but he felt deeply and personally involved now — it was the first time that he had felt his own life might be put in danger by a failure to win conviction. Never before in his life had Cobb felt such a flow of energy or such intensity of malevolence from another being as that felt from the force of Au's eyes when court adjourned. . . .

It was the worst of times for Ed Santorini to attempt a rapprochement.

"I hear you got the lying asshole on the run, Fos," he said, catching up to Cobb near the annex hallway, and keeping quick step with him. Cobb did not look at him, and merely uttered a foul imprecation.

"Fos, I'm sorry about the thing that happened. I want to clear the decks. I'll be honest, it happened a couple of times, but it wasn't Deborah's fault." Cobb quickened his step in an effort to escape. "I'm the original Lothario, man, and each time it happened, there was a lot of booze, and we just sort of fell into it."

"I could have given you some helpful hints, Eddie. She likes to watch you wet your finger and wiggle it up your ass."

"Come on, Fos."

"Did you use a safe? I'm sterile, so she doesn't bother with contraceptives. Maybe she does now, I don't know."

"Fos, the three of us can get together and talk like human beings."

"Suck off, Eddie. 'Fellatio,' from the Latin root *felare*, 'to suck.'"

"Goddamnit!"

"You still bucking for judge, Eddie? Wait until those nervous Nellies in Ottawa find out you're named as adulterer in a divorce action. Good luck, judge."

"Damn, you're my best friend." Santorini stalked off.

Horowitz had worked on his ruling over the noon hour, and by the time court resumed at two o'clock, he had it ready: Cobb would be allowed to put the wiretap transcript to the witness to refresh his memory. Horowitz would defer until his charge to the jury any instructions as to what parts they might consider in evidence. It was a crown victory, and Cobb felt pleased for Tann.

When Cobb approached Cudlipp to put the transcript again in front of him, he detected the rankness of alcohol on the man's breath. It had been a lonely, wet lunch for Cudlipp.

Cobb addressed the court: "My instructions are, and I will undertake to prove this, my lord, that certain conversations were taped on the restaurant's telephone by the Vancouver city drug squad." He then turned to the witness: "I gather you were unaware of any wiretap surveillance at the time by the city police?"

"I didn't know about it, but I'm not surprised. The place is a hotbed for drugs. The Vancouver police, for reasons of their own, don't always let us know what's going on."

"Now, you've read this conversation recorded on December twenty-first, and you will agree that it refers to your visit to the restaurant that evening with the accused?"

"I take your word the transcript is accurate. So it looks like we were in there."

"The accused apparently gave Alice a twenty-dollar tip, is that right?'

"Yes, I think so."

"You pinched Alice on the behind?" A laugh escaped from the gallery.

"We were very friendly already by then. It was a joke."

"Now, does this transcript help you to recall that December twenty-first was the first date you ever went with the accused to the restaurant?"

"No," Cudlipp said, "it doesn't. There's nothing in there to say that. We were there the night Jimmy Fat died, and I'm sure of it." The drink had given Cudlipp fight.

"Because you had checked your watch that night with a waitress who wasn't even working there at the time?"

"I checked my watch with a waitress. Maybe it wasn't Alice."

"Witness, I want you to admit now that you were never present with the accused on December third at Archie's Steak House."

"I was there."

"If I am forced to embarrass you, I will. I shall put it to you one time more: you were not with Au that evening at the time of Jim Fat's death."

"Well, by God, I was."

"Okay." The rest Cobb would do in good conscience. "You told Alice Carson on December thirty-first, at her apartment, that you were prepared to lie for the accused in court."

"I deny it."

"At that time and place you told her you would lie about being at Archie's restaurant with the accused that evening."

"I deny that." Cudlipp's face had reddened.

"You told her you received twenty-five thousand dollars from Au for letting him know that there was heroin in his automobile."

"That is not true."

"You told her you received a further thirty thousand for telling Au that Jim Fat was a police informer."

"No. I didn't."

"You said you were negotiating for a large sum from Au for the favor of giving perjured testimony on his behalf."

"No." He croaked the word.

"You urged her to give false evidence that she, too, was in the restaurant on the night Jimmy got killed, and she agreed to it."

"No."

"To give you some small measure of credit, you told her that you wished you had never gotten into the situation and regretted your responsibility in the death of Jim Fat."

"No."

"On subsequent occasions you reiterated each of the statements I have put to you."

"I deny it all."

"On February seventeenth last, you discussed the amount of the bribe with her, and you settled on an asking price of two hundred and fifty thousand dollars."

"No."

"She agreed also to give perjured evidence as an inducement to the accused to pay that amount."

"That is not true."

"On March twelfth, just over a week ago, you were again in her apartment and you said Au had agreed to pay the whole amount, a quarter of a million dollars. All cash."

"That is a damn lie."

"You told her you would get fifty thousand dollars on the day you showed up to give evidence, and the balance before or after you concluded your evidence."

"It's a lie."

The courtroom was still, almost in shock. The reporters were huddled over their notepads, writing furiously. Cobb could see Charrington leaning forward on his chair.

"You said you would quit the force after the trial and take her to Australia and buy a business."

"No." Cudlipp was standing forward in the box, leaning hard on his hands, looking down.

"Oh, yes, somewhere along the way you admitted stealing four ounces of heroin from the RCMP exhibit locker. That was the heroin which you had Jim Fat plant in Au's car."

"No, no, no."

"Let me go back. In a conversation with Alice Carson on February twelfth, you said you would try to implicate Ming and Plizit as the murders of Jim Fat."

"All lies. You are trying to trick me. Her apartment wasn't bugged. . . ."

"How do you know?"

"I . . . I just know."

"You mean to tell us you searched for bugs?"

"No, you're putting words in my mouth. You're trying to trip me up and admit something that's not true."

"You are only hurting yourself. Last Thursday you received fifty thousand dollars in bills from Au."

"I deny it."

"He delivered the money to you in Carson's apartment that evening."

"Lies."

"And on Saturday, two days ago, you received a further two hundred thousand dollars from the accused."

"No . . . this is incredible." Cudlipp was staring at Cobb wildly.

"Mr. Sheriff," Cobb said, "please bring Special Officer Flaherty into the courtroom."

There was quiet.

In a moment Flaherty stepped casually through the doorway.

Cudlipp's face went the color of old stained ivory.

"You know her as Alice Carson," Cobb said.

Special Officer Jessica Flaherty smiled prettily as she looked about the courtroom, enjoying the attention.

One of Smythe-Baldwin's juniors rolled his eyes to the ceiling and dropped his pencil.

Judge Horowitz peered at her over his spectacles.

M. Cyrus Smythe-Baldwin's was suddenly wishing he were in his garden planting tulip bulbs.

For Au P'ang Wei, the edge of the precipice was crumbling, and he was falling, falling.

Cobb paused a long time, looking sad and solemn. Then he said: "You gave the money to her to hold for safe-keeping. You will be pleased to know that the two hundred and fifty thousand dollars remains safely in her custody. You can count it if you wish."

Flaherty gaily held up a thick wad of bills.

Cudlipp's starched face went totally blank. He stood for a moment in the witness box, swaying like a buoy in the wind upon the sea. He moved back a step, and his heel caught on the single stair that led to the witness box, and he swivelled on his heel artfully, as if the movement had been choreographed. With a ballet-like movement, he stepped gingerly down and away from the box and took three short precise paces in the direction of Jess Flaherty, who stood motionless in her demure three-hundred dollar suit. Cudlipp shook his head slowly, then moved ghost-like to face Au P'ang Wei above him in the prisoner's dock.

There was expression now on the acupuncturist's face. However, it was expression that could not be read by Westerners familiar with only their specific forms of facial aspect. It involved a tightening of all the muscles of Au's face. It was a look known to Oriental experts in psychosis.

Cudlipp was tranced. Slowly his knees gave way, and he sank to them on the carpet, his eyes remaining fixed upon the man in the dock. For several moments he knelt, a petitioner at the shrine of a god. He stretched his arms before him in urgent pleading prayer. Then he fell forward onto his face and began to shudder and cry.

Court was adjourned until the following morning.

Monday, the Twentieth Day of March, at a Quarter Past Seven O'Clock in the Evening

Even the hum and static of five thousand miles of telephone cable did not drown the tremor that Ma Wo-chien, the ancient overlord of his Ch'ao-chou family, detected within the gently undulating speech of Au P'ang Wei, his third grandson. The subtly discordant notes, the disharmony of Au's words, were a cause of great anxiety to the old man, who lacked much of the calmness of spirit that he sought from his descendants and followers. Ma Wo-chin, in fact, could be irascible, and in his frailty would often scream at his retainers, sending them scurrying in fear from his presence.

Seated now in the great decorated hall of his Victorian mansion atop Pottinger Peak, where he could look down over his fleet of trawlers and junks moored in Tai Tam bay, he felt anger and bitterness toward the man on the other end of the line, a man whom he had taught, a student in whom Ma had observed a brilliance of mind in earlier years. The third grandson had excellent qualities — a firm business sense, a strong hand, an ability to effect difficult decisions and enforce them. But (Ma had of late begun to realize) Au P'ang Wei was not a truly well person. Ma had been displeased at reports of certain unnecessary cruelties, and now entertained a grave concern about a deepening rift in Au's mind that foretold unhappy difficulties in the maintenance of the Vancouver link, a link that the elders had hoped would ultimately complete a circuit to Montreal and New York, perhaps thence to Amsterdam and Paris, where there were many Ch'ao-chou.

Au had been brought into the inner folds of the family as a child when his parents died, and the patriarch Ma Wo-chien had taught him personally, and paid for his training in schools of acupuncture, and later, in medical school in England — which Au, for reasons unclear, had quit despite high grades.

"You do yourself and our people a great disservice, Au P'ang Wei," the old man shouted. "You shall return. You shall return. Arrangements will be made tonight."

"In time," Au said calmly. "In time."

"I am most displeased," said Ma, spitting his words out. "You have put everything in danger. Yourself as well. Uselessly. You expose everyone to destruction. You have under-valued the skill of this man Cobb and over-valued the obviously poor quality of the policeman. Ai, you have been a great failure! A great failure, Au P'ang Wei."

"The matter of Cobb is in hand. The arrow is already fitted to the string." Au spoke calmly, but the strain in his words did not escape Ma's ears, still keen. "And I will return when I am ready to return, venerable grandfather. You will understand that I mean no disrespect: but I am master here, and there has been no vote of the elders. I will stay until full accounting is complete."

"And what do you mean by that?"

"The old mind is slow and soggy," Au said. Ma burned. "One does not stop the digging of the well until water is reached," Au continued. "There are tasks yet to perform. There is a man who would destroy me, who dares test my power."

What garbage was he speaking? Ma wondered. What sickness was this? "Yours is the voice of a man whose mind is fouled by illness, Au P'ang Wei. What tasks? I am sending Jin Feng. He is well-trained. Leave him the tasks."

"There are two tasks," said Au. "The duty of performing these shall be mine. I am honored by your expressions of concern." Au spoke icily. "And I do not need the assistance of Jin Feng." Feng was Au's cousin of the fourth generation, and was close to the inner circle.

"You will hear me," Ma said. "The vicissitudes of fortune are such that you have lost your use to us in Canada. Things change and stars move, Au P'ang Wei. Ai, there will be a great reckoning!" Ma flung an empty teapot at one of his prize chow dogs, and sent it scampering out of the room. A manservant came quickly in, picked up the broken pieces and vanished. Ma stared angrily out the window, seething, trying to bring himself under control.

Au's voice remained even. "The custom is settled by ancient agreement. It will take weeks to collect the elders. I learned the customs in your house, Ma Wo-chien. Do you forget? Is your mind grown dim? Is the sun so near the west mountains, old man?"

With great effort Ma summoned all his resources of reason. "To endanger yourself is one thing," he said. "To endanger the whole of the great plan is another thing, scandalous and unnecessary. Rigidity in matters such as this, where my counsel is urgently given, may be investigated by the elders, with possibly direful consequences to yourself. I need say nothing more." He swore, with a guttural exclamation.

"The elders will know that my purpose is to make our business safe here and to improve the line to America and the Atlantic," Au paused. "You see," he continued in a hushed tone, "they are plotting to destroy me, and they must be taught that this cannot be done, that such conspiracies only injure their makers. You cannot understand how persistent these men are: Cobb and these others." He paused again, and his voice continued on an even lower, darker note. "Cobb is behind it. They purchased his services at great cost to bring destruction to me. The man Cobb." His voice shook, and Ma knew now that his grandson was very ill. "Cobb," he repeated. "Cobb. he is the sting in my eye. I must pull it out."

"And what," Ma said coldly, "will his death bring us? What

advantage, Au P'ang Wei? You are merely hurling eggs against stone."

"Ah, Grandfather, at your feet I also learned the principles of deterrence that have so successfully guided our efforts in this country. Cobb is the symbol and the heart of all the forces arrayed against us here. Upon his death, I will be strong. We will be strong. Our family will prosper."

Ma recalled now that there had been an episode like this when Au had returned from England twenty-five years ago. Jin Feng would have to act quickly and cleanly.

"I will not sanction it," he said.

"In your house, Ma Wo-chien, one command draws a thousand answers. But it is not so here. It is my choice in this place, and our people here take my direction."

"Pah! I will convene the elders. You will be sent to a clinic for your health."

Au laughed. "My health! I have the health of a tiger."

"The health of mind, Au P'ang Wei."

"The edges of *your* mind are no longer sharp, Grandfather. Mine is as clear as a mirror."

"Stained with the glaze of self-deception. Jin Feng arrives Friday by plane. Eight a.m. by CP Air. Hong Kong, Honolulu, Vancouver. You will meet him."

"No," said Au. "It will not be safe. The trial is over for me and I shall be in hiding." Au was starting to speak quickly now, his voice a high sing-song. "And by the time he arrives, the work will be done. The traitor Plizit and the destroyer Cobb. Ah, of Cobb you know nothing — he has followed me secretly for ten years, seeking my destruction."

Ma tried reason again. "Can these tasks be of such supreme necessity? Must they be done immediately, in any event?"

"The Westerners have a saying: strike the iron on the anvil when it is hot."

"Perhaps," Ma continued in his reasoning tone, "the tasks seem important merely for the time."

"The tasks are important. The traitor and the destroyer cannot live, or their passing years will be proof to the world of the weakness of Ch'ao-chou."

"Perhaps you will consider the wisdom of many decades," said Ma Wo-chien. "Consider my advice that you should take rest until the elders have met and discussed this."

"It is as a mirror, old man."

Ai, Ma thought. A mirror distorted, that returns a twisted reflection of the man.

"The informer, yes," Ma said. "That is clear. The man Plizit is anathema to good order and profit . . . Plizit, yes. The elders will accept it. Cobb: you must realize he is merely a mechanic, a worker for and within the system of his country. There was no betrayal. The test is betrayal. The elimination of those who enforce the laws is wrong and without precedent." Ma Wo-chin argued his case carefully.

But Au had learned the laws of the Ch'ao-chou. "There is precedent. The officer Sung, in the early years. It was sanctioned. You performed it personally. The year 1905 on the Western calendar. How the memory has faded, Ma Wo-chien."

"He was corrupt, and took our money, and effected arrests."

"Convene the elders. By then it will be done, and you will be seen as a fool."

"Au P'ang Wei!" the elderly man's thin voice cracked. "You will have Jin Feng met at the airport!"

"Yes. I will do that. He will be needed here to help carry on."

Thank the stars for that, Ma Wo-chien thought. Otherwise, it would be difficult for Feng to track Au down. The elders would later ratify the action.

"Good-bye," Au continued. "I seek no blessing. I trust you will give to all our people the words that I hold them in my thoughts." Au hung up. The old man, he thought, had finally succumbed to the decrepitude of age, and had begun to babble like a weak fool. Jin Feng

. . . Yes, he would be needed. It was time to spawn new organizations in the family. It was time to bring to fruition great plans, to destroy the enemy and gain strength thereby, to destroy a great foe — and doing so, make a brother of him, and become strong through this brotherhood. . . .

And the pain came. He touched the point for it, and it relented. Then he closed his eyes. The pain came back.

Prince Kwan, his brother, came to him, and began to purr. Au stroked him gently behind the ears and along the spine, and along the myriad points of pleasure.

And the pain was on him strongly, and was deep within, and it carried him back to a time of young manhood . . .

> . . . When the older man saw Au, standing before them in plain view in the deepening twilight, brazenly almost, he called to his son, who had dallied behind. "The bleedin' louse wants another taste of it, 'arry. Let's kill the cruel bastard." This time Au, limping and bearing unhealed wounds, was ready for them, his bowels on fire with the need for vengeance. Harry moved first, and Au deftly slid the needle into the Archway of the Gods needle point, along the spine meridian between hip and pelvis. A clean penetration. Harry's body immediately went numb and his autonomic system began to misfire, and this caused spasms. His breathing became hesitant and irregular, and soon stopped. The father, burly and red-faced and smelling from the numerous pints of half-and-half consumed that evening, wore a look of disbelief, and began to back up slowly. Au walked toward him with the other needle, and when the man turned and started to run, Au leaped and stabbed twice before finding the heart meridian on the right side of the buttocks, at the Hill of the Two Rivers point. The muscles of the man's heart froze and he stopped in his tracks and fell. . . .

Au had collected his first trophies that night, in the mews behind the Raven Arms public house, the local where Harry and his father gathered with friends each night. When the bodies were found next morning in the brome grass beside the lane, Au was in quarters on a freighter at the Mersey docks, waiting to be returned to Hong Kong. The acts of vengeance had removed the pain that had gripped him, a pain of that same force and quality as that which now demanded the removal of Foster Cobb from this earth.

Tuesday, the Twenty-first Day of March, at Two O'Clock in the Afternoon

Set by the frozen southern shore of Tlakish Lake in the small community to which it gave its name (Village of Tlakish Lake, pop. 342, elev. 417 metres), the lake and town sit quietly in the valley, contemplating each other's navels, bored with their marriage. There is little to do at this time of year in the Tlakish Valley, and the boredom settles like a dull fog on the group of bungalows and cabins that cluster aimlessly about a grocery store, a service station, and two or three shops by the lakeshore dock. Tlakish Lake waits for the summer — when the town is full of yelling bow-legged men on the rodeo circuit; when the tourist campers arrive, jammed with fishing gear; when the streams and lakes of the Chilcotin Hills churn with rainbow, Dolly Varden, and kokanee; when the summer grasslands are home to wandering herds of Herefords which loaf about as carefree as the grizzlies and bighorn sheep.

Spring has touched British Columbia elsewhere, but in the Chilcotin rangelands east of the Coast Mountains, a barrier to the soft Pacific winds, the air is cold and sharp, and snow is still banked high along the lee of the hills. The lake provides a landing strip, and chartered planes are often seen to land here to pick up and carry away the bodies of men so overcome by ennui that they must flee south to Vancouver to recharge their spirits.

At two p.m. on this, the first day of spring, the telephone rang and reserve officer Joe Bigelow, happy at playing cop, eagerly took the details. Then he called Bob Klosterman at Lasko's Groceteria and Coffee Palace, where the constable usually stopped off for a mid-day milkshake break with whoever was hanging around. Klosterman and Gary Sedyk were the only two regular RCMP members of the Tlakish Lake detachment.

"There's a guy phoned," Bigelow said. "There's a car in the snow-bank, slid down the road. Guy said someone is wedged in there, kinda hurt. Guess you might want to pick up the van and the winch."

"Where is this? Who called?" Klosterman spoke excitedly. He had pictures of pulling someone's mangled body from a wrecked car.

"On the Kwahalee Creek Road, he said, about forty or fifty miles from town. . . "

"Damn! That road is *closed*."

"Not sure who it was phoned. Said a man on a logging road survey crew up there radioed down to him, and he phoned in. Kinda roundabout."

"What survey crew? That's all closed up there. Aw, damn. Is that it? What else he say?"

"Well, that's it. That's all he told me."

"Joe, you know, try to get people's names and where they are."

"Sorry."

"No time for sorry. Call Gary at home. He better go with me. Tell him to meet me down there, rig up the van with chains. You'll have to run the ship for five or six hours. And call Doc Fairweather and have him ready, just in case, for when we get back. I'll be right there."

For the rest of the afternoon and for the early evening, Joe Bigelow, RCMP reserve officer, a man who all his life — forty-three years — had hungered to be a policeman, would keep the peace alone in the valley of Tlakish Lake. In real life, Joe Bigelow and his wife ran a motel in Prince George. His service to his country as a volunteer reservist in the RCMP was poor compensation for his more subservient role at home, where he was a subaltern to a stern commanding officer. Mrs. Bigelow shot from the lip first and asked questions later, if at all, and she ran a strict house.

Two weeks ago, Bigelow had been assigned the job of guarding Laszlo Plizit, and it was a chance gladly accepted to escape the rigors of his life at home.

This afternoon, after Klosterman and Sedyk departed in the van east to the Kwahalee Creek Road, Bigelow, alone in the detachment except for Plizit in the back, settled easily into the routine — which involved propping his feet on the desk, folding his arms, and falling into dream-riddled sleep. There was nothing else to do except, at meal time, to fetch some hot food for Plizit from Lasko's café. As Bigelow dozed off he could hear pop music from Plizit's radio.

Somehow Bigelow had suppressed his qualms about the prospect of having to deal with professional gunmen from Vancouver, but they came out at night, and twice last week his loud nightmares had awakened the Klosterman family, in whose home he was staying. As days and nights passed, however, Bigelow's dreams, fuelled by cheeseburgers and chips, settled into brave but uncertain reveries of Gary Cooper, strapping on his gun to await alone the arrival of the noon train, while the cowardly townspeople scurried for shelter.

Bigelow never had a chance. The noon train arrived and somehow the sheriff never got up to meet it. The thing that awakened him was a sudden sharp twinge in his left arm, near the elbow. That sharpness, that pain, was the last physical sensation Joe Bigelow ever knew. He did not lose consciousness after awakening with that little jolt of pain — he merely lost all ability to feel, all sense of touch. Every muscle was paralyzed. Every nerve cell numb. The thin gold needle of Dr. Au had penetrated the Song of Sorrows meridian at a paralysis point near the elbow. Bigelow opened his eyes at the touch of the needle, and they remained frozen open, unable even to blink back the tears that formed and slowly found pathways down his cheeks and jaws.

Bigelow's range of vision allowed him to see the two men in the room. Easy Snider stood watch at the door. Au P'ang Wei wandered in and out of Bigelow's view, going through desk drawers and filing cabinets, apparently searching. Bigelow was still uncertain whether this was nightmare or reality. He was certain, though, it was indeed no dream, that he would rather be home helping Mrs. Bigelow run the motel and enduring her savageries. He was not aware that piss had discolored his pants at the crotch and was running down his legs.

Bigelow observed the Oriental man, dressed warmly in an expensive fur-collared coat, disappear into the back room. Then he heard Laszlo Plizit's voice: loud, broken, with calls for help.

Bigelow heard the sound of a key scraping against the lock, and the screaming was almost ear-splitting for a second or two after that. Finally there was a resigned grunt, and the two men came back, the Oriental gentleman wiping the end of the needle with a cloth and placing it in a carrying case.

"Very well," Au said.

"What about him?" Snider asked.

"Put him in the cell, Mr. Snider."

"What if someone comes? It's about ten minutes' walk to where the plane is."

"We shall take our chances. There is always risk."

The thin man approached Bigelow, who, although he did not feel it, was aware that he was being pulled off his chair, dumped to the floor, and dragged to the back, into the cell beside Plizit's body.

The man left. There was a brief silence. And then the strangely soothing vice of the Oriental man: "Perhaps the occasion should not be wasted. A simple ceremony is in order."

Bigelow, who was lying twisted on the floor like a Raggedy Andy, saw the man approach, open his case, and pull out what looked like a long straight razor. Then the man disappeared from his view, moving somewhere down toward the direction of his legs. When the man straightened up, Bigelow could see red smears on the razor and on the gloved hands of the man.

When Klosterman and Sedyk arrived back, at about seven p.m., Bigelow, from the cell, could hear them cursing and complaining about what Klosterman referred to as "a wild-goose chase that ass-hole sent us on."

"No wonder he wasn't answering the radio," he heard Sedyk say. "He ain't here."

"His car's outside."

"Where is the useless little tit, then?"

I'm in here, thought Bigelow, in the cell.

Bigelow, despite his blood loss, was still conscious and staring.

"Check to see if they fell asleep playing crib," Klosterman said.

Then Bigelow heard steps, and then he saw standing above him the figure of Constable Gary Sedyk, his face white and contorted with shock.

"Oh, Jesus," Sedyk said softly. "Oh, Jesus." He kept repeating it, louder each time. "Oh, Jesus. Oh, Jesus! Oh, Jesus!"

Klosterman, who had been pulling off his jacket in the office, heard Sedyk's voice, and felt something thump him hard deep in the bowels.

He ran to the back, where an ashen Gary Sedyk was clutching the bars of the cell. There was the body of Laszlo Plizit. And there was Joe Bigelow, his pants down around his knees, recently emascu-lated, staring at him — grinning, in fact. Grinning vacuously from a pale and empty face.

Tuesday, the Twenty-first Day of March, at Half-past Two O'Clock in the Afternoon

There were currently two Supreme Court judgeships open in the province, and Santorini suspected his name was high on the justice minister's list of prospects. There was to be a reception for the deputy minister at the Bayshore Inn this evening, and Santorni had been cordially invited. That affair was central in his mind. But other matters kept intruding this day.

The day had already been a crazy-quilt of confused activity. Dr. Au had skipped bail. The word from the courthouse this morning was that Mr. Justice Horowitz had waited until the noon hour, and when finally Au did not appear, and no reason for this failure could be advanced by Smythe-Baldwin, the judge had issued a bench warrant for Au's arrest, ordered his bail marked for estreatment, and discharged the jury panel.

So Santorini had been bouncing about in a hectic run of meetings and telephone conversations about the disappearance of Au and about the manhunt into which Detective Harrison demanded that every spare resource of the police department be poured.

Santorini knew that politically, for the attorney-general, there would be hell to pay. Mile-long line-ups, because of border checks at the main U.S. crossing near Blaine, Washington, had already caused a flood of angry phone calls to police offices, to the provincial government, and to the media. Respected members of Vancouver's powerful Chinese community were complaining about door-to-door searches in Chinatown, and they were on the mayor's back, and on the attorney-general's back. Everybody seemed to be on Santorini's back. And Santorini, appearing for the crown at Cudlipp's bail hearing, was tired and bitchy.

Cudlipp was standing in the prisoner's box, his eyes rimmed with red lines, listening to the clerk read the charges: count one, perjury; count two, obstructing justice; count three, accepting a bribe; count four, theft of a quantity of narcotics. A further charge alleging a conspiracy between Cudlipp and Au to obstruct justice would be held until Au's arrest.

Bail was set by the provincial court judge at thirty thousand dollars.

Then Santorini returned to his office to return two calls his secretary had marked as urgent. The first was from Harrison.

"Jesus, Eddie, I've been trying for the last hour to reach somebody in the Tlakish Lake RCMP. No answer."

"Oh, *no.*"

"Maybe I'm worried for nothing. The Mounties like their lunch breaks."

"Yeah, maybe we're all seeing ghosts. Keep after it."

The other call was from a Dr. Jack Broussaud:

"Santorini, I think you have to do something to protect Foster Cobb."

"Who the hell are you?"

"I'm his headshrinker. Cobb's."

Santorini remembered. Broussaud had helped Cobb beat heroin years ago, and had become his friend.

"He came to see me this morning after the trial aborted. He told me Au threatened to kill him. He thought he might have been hallucinating, but I don't know. I'm not sure it's so simple."

"What?" Santorini asked. He did not need more heavy news today.

"Au didn't use words, he just gave Cobb a look, a message, drilled it right through his middle eye into the centre of his head. Maybe Cobb's crazy, too, but he said he heard Au's voice in his head."

"Aw, come on!" What kind of bullshit is this? Santorini wondered.

"Okay, okay. You can't go to the police chief for a twenty-four-hour guard because of some kind of ESP threat. But I've been following the trial, and I've talked to Cobb a lot. I want you to listen to this: First, Au's a psychopath. He's got some sexual dysfunction I can't put a handle on. Goes for the nuts. Who knows why. But he's got an obsessive thing about reproductive organs. So you've got in this Au what's-his-face some unholy kind of combination of obsessive-neurotic psychopath who has probably been undergoing a psychotic breakdown."

"I'm listening." Santorini was doodling little arrows.

"This type of guy is prone to a reactive kind of psychosis. Shows up under stress. Like maybe he sees his defence fall apart in a murder trial, and he starts crumbling, and he starts looking for the most apparent enemy out there. Like the poor bugger prosecuting him."

"Yeah, well, who can say?"

"Look, I know the field; I know the literature. Just take my word. Call him an obsessive-paranoid psychopathic personality. These guys all centre on some figure of reference, an enemy, a nemesis. I think that's Cobb — the guy you hired to prosecute this crazy — if you don't mind my laying a guilt trip. I mean — would you want to be responsible for Cobb's death, Santorini?"

There was a pause at Santorini's end.

"Think about it," Broussaud said, "because I'm telling you he's a dead man unless you do something."

"Yeah, well, we'll catch up to Dr. Au. He can't do much from a cell."

"Are you *nuts*, Santorini?" Broussaud yelled. "Au's got more contacts than the pope."

"Maybe we can send Cobb into hiding for a few weeks."

"Santorini." Broussaud began to speak in careful, measured words, as if lecturing a student in the slow class. "I *could* be wrong. But if I'm *not* wrong, you've been warned. Dr. Au is the kind of guy, he'll wait for three weeks. Three weeks? Three *years*. *Thirty* years. Now, I'm going to tell you this, and listen carefully: Catching Au may not be good enough. He can reach outside. He will engineer Cobb's death. Some way."

Broussaud paused, then said: "He'll kill Cobb. Unless someone kills him first."

Santorini closed his eyes and seemed to meditate.

"I think you're getting carried away with this, doctor." Psychiatrists, in his experience, tended to be hysterical. "But I'll get him some protection."

Protection for the s.o.b. who's threatening to ruin me? Santorini thought. Well, he hadn't time to work on that right now. He had to get out of the office fast, have a shower, and meet the deputy minister for cocktails. He did not want to be late.

After returning from Dr. Broussaud's office, Cobb went to his own. His secretary asked him if he would take a call from his wife.

"Hello."

"Cobb, it's lonely up here on the hill."

"Uh-huh."

"Can I come down and talk to you?"

"I don't want to talk. You can come down and get your clothes. I've packed them. They're by the door."

"I think we should talk."

"I'm busy."

"Let's be civilized, Cobb, goddamnit."

"You've got a key. Come down and get what you want."

"I think we should straighten things out."

"Come down when you want. I may not be home. I may be tied

up." There was a heavy pause. "It's through, you know."

"I know."

He hung up. In those last few words they had spoken the unspeakable, and it was necessary to kill the pain. He locked the door, brought out his heroin and his outfit, and did up. After a few minutes he began to feel warm and secure, and a little braver, and he called the prosecutor's office.

"Jennifer? Hi. How about joining me for a few drinks tonight? Let's celebrate."

"You are on, Mr. Cobb. You are *right* on."

"Meet you somewhere?"

"Why don't we just start up at your apartment, and see where we want to go from there." Her voice was light and lilting.

"We may not get very far."

"Who knows."

It was eight p.m. Foster Cobb was in his shower. Jennifer Tann was in his bed, waiting for him, nervously sipping from a glass. She was exultant and frightened and high: It was finally happening. The phone on the bedtable was off the hook, and a bottle of champagne was beside it.

Deborah Cobb, suffering intermittent showers of tears, was packing her skis on the rack of her TR-7, preparing to drive into Vancouver and make her arrangements with Cobb.

Julius Katsknywch was washing down the day's dirt from the front steps of the Cobbs' apartment building.

Winnifred Fenwick, on the twenty-fourth floor of the building, just below the Cobb apartment, was in her nightie and curlers, settling down to watch *Kojak*.

Jean-Louis Leclerc, holding a sawed-off shotgun, was in the front seat of an old Chevrolet, borrowed for the night from a downtown parking garage. Beside him, at the wheel, was John Klegg. He had a handgun in his jacket pocket.

Honcho Harrison and Lars Nordquist were in the homicide office speaking excitedly to Constable Bob Klosterman by telephone.

Everit Cudlipp was in a city jail cell asleep, waiting for relatives to post bail.

Special Agent Jess Flaherty was on a 747 en route to the eastern U.S., getting drunk with a long-hair in the adjoining seat, laughing at his heroic tales of beating the system dealing weed.

Julius C. Katsknywch was the building manager, a handyman who liked tinkering with residents' broken appliances. It was dark now. Katsknywch turned off the hose for a while to tease one of the young women tenants who was coming up the walk with groceries. He was too engrossed to notice the old Chevrolet that rolled slowly past the building and down to underground parking.

Harrison and Nordquist began making frantic arrangements for roadblocks on roads in the Chilcotin in the unlikely event that Au was fleeing by car. They also began phoning air charter operators to inquire about flights that day into Tlakish Lake. They were anxious to put Cobb into the picture, but his phone kept ringing busy. That made Harrison uneasy.

Cobb had just taken a cold shower, then a hot one, and after towelling himself, he came to the bedroom. He was about to switch off the light.

"Don't," Tann said. "Not yet."

The bedroom was warm and Tann was naked. She had kicked off the covers and was under a single sheet, her hands over it, folded.

Cobb sat on the edge of the bed, his champagne glass raised in his hand. "I toast you — you were great working with," he said. "Good job."

They smiled and clinked glasses.

Cobb hoped the small hit of junk he had taken before Tann's

arrival would not slow him up. Then he looked down at Tann and saw her gentle smile, and felt a surge of desire.

And there was a sound at the lock.

He jolted back to a sitting position. Oh, God, it wouldn't be Deborah. It would be like her to select intuitively the wrong occasion to collect her things. Well, he thought, it would be a form of just vengeance if she walked in now.

Then it slowly dawned on him that the sound at the lock was a scraping noise. It did not seem to be the sound of a key. It continued for a strangely long time — twenty, thirty seconds. A little nut of fear stuck in Cobb's throat. He felt his body stiffen and his prick soften, and he felt tension coming from Tann as she pulled the blankets back over her.

"Who is it?" she whispered.

"I'm not sure." But in fact he felt danger.

"Listen," she said, "I think someone is picking your lock."

She was lifting herself from the bed when they heard the click of the lock releasing. This is crazy, Cobb thought. It's just Deborah. She was having trouble with the key.

Then they heard footsteps and voices. Tann, in the midst of rising, sat back, grabbed a sheet, and wrapped it around herself. Cobb's reaction was to reach for his pants on the chair beside the bed, and then suddenly he was frozen in time and space as the bedroom door, slightly ajar, crashed open.

Through the doorway protruded the two short barrels of Jean-Louis Leclerc's twelve-gauge shotgun. The butt was braced against his shoulder. His feet were splayed wide apart. His face was in the shadows, but Cobb could see his mouth open wide in a chilling smile that displayed small and malformed teeth.

Leclerc uttered a high-pitched laugh. "Look at dis here," he called to Klegg. Behind Leclerc, another face wandered into view. Cobb vaguely remembered Klegg from his visits to the courtroom with Leclerc.

Cobb was gripped by a kind of fear that kept each muscle rigid. He was still part way off the bed, and slowly, as his muscles released, he sat back down. He wondered whether he had the courage to die well. He knew he would find out.

Leclerc gestured at Klegg with his head. "The telephone," he said. Klegg opened a jack-knife and cut the cord. He was young, thick-set, and bearded, and his eyes were ablaze from a heavy addiction. Leclerc was badly wired too, and both men knew they had to do Au's bidding without question.

"All right," Leclerc said, "get the little lady prosecutor out of here."

"No," she whispered.

"Leave her, Leclerc," Cobb said.

"We're not gonna do nothing to her," Leclerc said, turning his head away from Cobb to wink at Klegg. "It's you Dr. Au wants us to do business with, Mr. Cobb."

Klegg reached down to the bed and tried to remove the sheet from Tann. She jerked it back from him and held it tightly to her chest. Her face was white. Cobb felt an immense caring for her, and wanted to hold her.

"You better tell her to go to the other room with my friend," Leclerc said. "My orders are only for you, but if I get trouble, I got a license to do what I figure I have to do."

"Leave me alone with him, Jennifer," Cobb said. It would be just as well, he thought, to remove her as far as possible from the sights of Leclerc's shotgun. But he suspected Leclerc, whatever Au's orders, would not wish to leave any witnesses.

Tann looked wide-eyed and imploringly at Cobb. "Oh, my God, what do they want?"

"It's probably for hostages, Jenn. To get Au safe conduct out of the country." Cobb had no remote hope for that as a real possibility. "Go to the living room and let me talk with Leclerc."

Tann looked once more at him, took a deep breath of air, let it go; then, with the sheet clutched around her, climbed from the bed.

Klegg tried to take her arm, and she shrugged it off. Klegg, grinning, tried to pull the sheet from her, and she gave him a wild look. "Get your hands off, you bastard," she said.

Klegg's eyes narrowed.

"Don't fuck around," Leclerc said. "Just take her out of here."

"Just go, Jenn," Cobb said.

She strode into the living room, followed by Klegg, who whispered huskily: "Hey, lady, don't try to be tough. You can save yourself a lot of hurt if you just try to get along with me."

She sat on the sofa. He sat beside her. She got up to move to a hard-backed chair, but Klegg grabbed a corner of the sheet and pulled her sprawling back to him.

She nearly convulsed with the gamy smell of the man and her fear of him. He pressed her to him, and she felt a hard bulge in his pants and a harder bulge in his jacket pocket.

She did not call out, but tried to still her terror by centring on it, in the yogic way. . . .

Cobb was still on the bed, naked, immobile, breathing in short puffs.

He desperately wanted a terrific hit of junk.

Never in his life had he needed one so badly.

Leclerc stood with his feet splayed, the shotgun held in both hands and pointed at Cobb's chest. He was leaning against the locked sliding door which led from the bedroom to the balcony outside. He kept blinking his eyes, and he wore a thin smile.

Move! Cobb told himself. Move against Leclerc.

Instead: "Well, what are you doing here?" It sounded like a pleasant pass-the-time opening in a gentlemanly conversation.

Leclerc shrugged. "You was just about to get it on with the lady prosecutor, huh? I been fucked *over* by lawyers, but that's as close as I ever come." His smile opened up over crooked dark teeth. "She hot for you?"

"Why did Au send you?"

Again Leclerc shrugged. "He says you are brothers, him and you.

I don't understand it, but I don't ask. *Yin* and *yang*, or something like that, he says. One's gotta die so's the other can live." Again the black smile. "And guess who gets to die?"

Cobb felt his guts contract. Could he save Tann? Leclerc and his friend would not risk staying long after the sound of a shotgun being fired in the building. If he jumped Leclerc now, and the man had to pull both triggers . . . if there were a struggle, a diversion, she would have time to get out the door. . . .

Leclerc took a few steps and glanced out the bedroom door to the living room. He laughed. "Looks like you gave your girlfriend too much hots, Mr. Cobb. She ain't saving any for you, that's for —"

Cobb was moving.

There was not much chance. He had seven feet to travel before he could reach Leclerc, and by the time he had scrambled off the bed, Leclerc had swung around. He brought the shotgun around in a wide arc, and the barrel crashed into the side of Cobb's head. Cobb went reeling back onto the bed, dazed, barely conscious, blood trickling from a gash near his right ear.

"You didn't think I plan to shoot you, did you?" Leclerc said. Balancing his shotgun in the crook of his elbow, Leclerc extracted from his sweater pocket a syringe and a packet of white powder. The sound of his voice came distantly to Cobb: "Well, what I'm gonna do is shoot you *up*. Dr. Au figured you should eat it like Charlie did. But I say that's a waste of good stuff. I figure I can fix you in the mainline with about half a gram, keep the rest. Don't think you'll tell on me. Half a gram of pure, it'll have you out of it in ten minutes, *alors, tout fini. Mort avec un sourire*, Monsieur Prosecutor."

Cobb was trying to to struggle into wakefulness. He was aware that Leclerc had slipped briefly into the adjoining washroom and now had a tumbler of water and was mixing a heroin solution to the bowl of a bent spoon.

"I always get a t'rill when I turn some guy on first time. I got a friend, there, Bryon, I turned on. Now he uses all the time. But don't worry, Mr. Cobb, this won't get you addicted."

As he chattered on, he held a lighter to the bottom of the spoon and cooked the dope. Then he pulled it into the syringe.

He took Cobb's belt from his pants and tightened it around Cobb's right bicep. Cobb was still weak, unresisting.

"You got the nice big veins, Mr. Cobb."

Cobb started to jerk away from the needle, and winced from the pain in his head, nearly blacking out again. Then there was the sharp prick of the needle in his arm, and he felt the heroin rushing into him.

"You just O.D.'d, Mr. Cobb," Leclerc said, and he began cooking up a smaller shot for himself. He yelled to Klegg in the living room: "Hey, you wanna do up, John? Mr. Cobb and me is having a party."

"Having a party myself, man," Klegg called back.

Leclerc smiled at Cobb. "He's getting his rocks off wit' your chick. You don't mind?"

Cobb was into a hard, banging rush, struggling to breathe, his lungs on fire, his body convulsing in a wild narcotic orgasm.

Tuesday, the Twenty-first Day of March, at Nine O'Clock in the Evening

"You want it, lady, I know you want it." Klegg was breathing hard, his hands groping at Tann under the sheet.

She was on her back on the sofa, trying to jam her body in behind the cushions. He was on top of her, hot and foul of breath. She felt his hands go down to her thighs and felt the strength of his arms as he tried to pull her legs apart. His pants were down around his knees.

"Yeah, you want it," he said.

Her right hand was pinned to her side. If she could free it, she would be able to reach into his left jacket pocket.

"Please, I can't breathe," she said.

He grunted and shifted his body, and her hand came free.

Klegg felt her hands caress his body.

"Yeah, you *do* want it. Just hard-to-get, ain't ya, counsellor?"

Her legs were apart now, his knees between them, and his hands were sliding up her thighs.

"Making out with a lady lawyer. I'm *really* gonna get off on this."

Klegg heard a muffled roar from underneath him and felt a biting flash of pain as a bullet tore through his groin.

His scream was shrill and long, wild and piercing, and it brought Leclerc to the bedroom door. His pinned eyes danced about the room; Cobb's belt was tied about his arm, and he was holding his outfit in one hand, the barrel of his shotgun in the other. His mouth was open, and for a few seconds he was immobile.

Klegg was yelping like a stricken dog, grabbing at his groin as blood seeped through his fingers and ran down his legs. He rolled off the sofa, scrambled to his feet, and, crouching and skipping and clutching his pants, made it to the front door and outside the apartment to the elevator.

Tann was now standing, her sheet wound about her like a sari. The gun in her hand was hidden from Leclerc's view, the sheet bunched around it.

Leclerc, stoned now, slowly raised the barrel of the sawed-off shotgun. Then he saw a little hole pop open where the sheet was bunched around Tann's hand, and he heard the crack of her gun as it fired, and a framed Cézanne print beside the bedroom door — three feet from his head — crashed to the floor, glass splintering. There was another shot, and the bullet sliced through the door frame. Leclerc went to his hands and knees and crawled backwards into the bedroom to get behind cover.

Winnifred Fenwick was seventy-two and hardly ever left her apartment, except to buy a few things or take some air on a nice day. She lived on tea and toast and salads, and pills for her nerves. Tonight she had a full two-hour *Kojak* special to enjoy before tucking herself into bed. During a commercial break she went to the front door — for the fourth time that evening — to reassure herself again that the lock button was pushed in and the chain hooked in place. Earlier she had checked the sliding glass doors in the living room and bedroom, which entered onto balconies.

Suddenly she sat bolt upright. The building was not soundproof, and the explosions of gunfire on the floor above so loudly assaulted her frail ears that she had to fight strongly to clench the muscles of her urinary tract.

And about fifteen seconds later outside her balcony came the blast of a shotgun, and a man flew onto her balcony — a tall blond man whose mouth was agape and whose eyes were wild, and whose buttocks were streaming blood. This person, she observed, arrived with a crash on her flowerpots.

The fearsome event that Winnifred Fenwick had long awaited was now giving life to her terrible fantasies.

The gunfire was a distant echo in Cobb's ears. He was hallucinating now. His roaring chariot bore him wildly, mercilessly through billowing crimson clouds and surging crimson rivers, across fields and seas of red-brown and red-purple and crimson.

More distant sound of guns. Ringing like gongs in his ears now, sending frenzied vibrations into the protoplasm of every quivering cell. He was unable to organize rational processes in his mind, and acted with instincts, not thought. His instincts, in fact, comprised the only working structure of his central nervous system. The mightiest of them was toward self-preservation, and these instincts directed the muscles of his arms and legs to carry him off the bed and onto the floor and to the sliding glass balcony door, and they directed his hands to unlatch and open it. He stepped foggily across the outdoor carpet on the balcony. All this happened in seconds, but aeons passed in his mind. (He was transformed in his mind into a giant fuzzy caterpillar inching across the deserts of infinity. He was a man trapped lethargically in a nightmare.) He moved far faster than he knew, driven by a powerful surge of adrenalin that pumped through his system, hoisting him to the top of the railing.

As Tann's gun fired again, Cobb was looking twenty-five stories down, watching Julius Katsknywch, like an ant below him, spraying wildly with his hose, shouting and gesturing, and running about. Cobb leaned over the railing, unevenly balanced, like a drunk on a tightrope, swaying, concentrating woozily upon the balcony below — the balcony of Winnifred Fenwick's living room.

And then he saw Leclerc was behind him, and Cobb leaped, and heard the thunder of the shotgun, and felt a searing pain . . .

. . . and descended with a crash upon Winnifred Fenwick's flowerpots, bouncing from them loosely and drunkenly onto the carpet of her balcony. The left cheek of his buttocks was lacerated where the shot from the shells grazed his body.

Winnifred Fenwick, in her fortress, stared at him through the glass, her mouth an oval of fear.

Cobb saw on the balcony above, through shimmering patterns of light and color, his intended assassin. Leclerc stood for a time, motionless, uncertain, the shotgun dangling from his arm. Then he rushed away.

Winnifred Fenwick opened her mouth. She could not shout, could not scream. Lieutenant Kojak shouted orders to Stavros. The nude and bloodied man on her balcony stared at her with bright, pointed eyes, and crawled to the glass door, and banged on it, and clawed at the lock.

She unfroze. She screamed. She ran to the front door, fumbled with the chain a long time, then disappeared howling into the corridor.

Cobb, his instincts still acting on his brain's behalf while the overdose insisted that he sleep and die, lifted one of the earth-filled pots above his head and hurled it at the door, shattering the glass. He crawled into the apartment, cutting himself on broken shards, and clutching at the carpet with his fingers he crawled toward the front door, his adrenalin slowly dissipating, a lethargy taking over. He was creeping toward the front door with the strength of an infant. The God of Dreams whispered sleep to his ears. . . . Kojak, on the tube, snarled snide accusations at him. . . .

Julius Katsknywch finally let the secretary depart with her beer and groceries. "Now, if there's anything your boyfriend can't fix, you give me a call. I'm a handyman." She gave him a teasing wave, and wiggled up the stairs and into the lobby. Katsknywch, whose lust for some small romance had once again been satisfied in the foreyard of his majestic high-rise, turned on his hose again, went down to the public sidewalk, and began to wash it, watching passers-by, when he heard from above him some . . . what? A banging. Thunder. Or a series of explosions.

Was it coming from his building? Yes. It *was* coming from his building. He strained his eyes to see if there was fire or smoke. Nothing, or . . . what? A man — he was naked — was hanging over a balcony! Katsknywch's hose danced crazily, sending wiggling fountains over the street and boulevard. Then there was another man up there! A shotgun rang out . . . the naked man fell to the balcony below, and the other man disappeared. Katsknywch did not know what his responsibility was in such a situation.

He yelled: "Hey!" To no one in particular.

He was about to run in, to his ground-floor suite and telephone the police, when a car came screeching to a halt on the street and a man who looked like a long-retired football tackle emerged and came thundering past him.

"What apartment is that?" the man yelled, gesturing upward.

"Uh, twenty-fifth floor. Oh, God, that's Mr. and Mrs. Cobb's."

"Jesus fucking Christ," the man said, drawing a gun from his inside jacket pocket.

The front door was locked.

"Open it!" the man yelled.

"What?"

"Open it! I'm Harrison, city police. *Police*, you asshole!"

The building manager fumbled with his keys for what Harrison felt was an infinity before they got inside. The policeman roared to the elevator and pounded on the button.

"Anybody comes down while I'm up there, you hold onto them," Harrison said. "And call homicide and get some men down here. Fast!"

Katsknywch made his call from a pay phone in the lobby while Harrison fumed and snarled at the elevator.

The elevator door finally opened.

"Help!" Out came Winnifred Fenwick, screeching in a tinny little voice.

In went Harrison. And huddled in the corner of the elevator, in pain, looking balefully up at the big detective, was John Klegg. The door closed on the two men.

Julius Katsknywch, dredging a few pints of courage from a nearly dried reservoir, clenched his fists and stood guard.

Tann ran from the apartment and down the hall. She pounded first on one door, screaming: "Help! Oh, God, help! They're killing him!" From inside came a plaintive voice: "I can't help you." She ran to the next door and banged on it and screamed.

Then Leclerc came out, stuffing two more shells into his gun. He saw Tann.

She screamed again. Then she fainted.

Leclerc levelled the shotgun at her prostrate form.

The elevator door opened.

The first person Leclerc saw in it was John Klegg. His face was red and he was gasping for air. Behind him, his burly arm about Klegg's throat, holding a snub-nosed .38 to his back, was Honcho Harrison.

Leclerc whirled, started to go one way, then another.

"Freeze, you little cocksucker!" Harrison barked.

Leclerc backed up slowly, then rushed into Cobb's apartment, slamming the door shut and bolting it.

Harrison, still holding Klegg by the neck, dragged him out of the elevator and dropped him in front of Cobb's door. With one perfect kick he splintered the door at the lock and it crashed open.

He picked up Klegg, and carrying him as a shield, walked inside, gun levelled.

Leclerc was not in view.

"You got ten seconds to throw the gun down and get your hands up and come out where I can see you, Leclerc." Nothing happened. "You rotten puke. If Cobb's dead, I'm gonna make ground meat outta you."

There was nothing. Harrison noticed the door to the balcony was open. He carried Klegg toward it. Klegg was choking and sputtering.

"Five seconds," Harrison said.

"Four seconds.

"Three."

"Two."

"One. You're dead."

And Leclerc, as if answering the bell, emerged from behind the balcony door, low and fast, firing off one barrel at Harrison and Klegg.

But Harrison was a moving target by the time Leclerc pulled the trigger. He had thrown Klegg, wild-eyed and screaming raggedly, onto the floor. Harrison dived to his right, moving like an athlete, hitting the floor with a whump, and rolling, while Leclerc's shot ripped the back off a leather chair.

Leclerc wheeled the shotgun around for his second shot, trying to get a bead on the big target.

But Harrison was a marksman from a standing or moving position. As he bounced up from his roll, he fired three times.

Three soft bullets from his Smith & Wesson exploded in Leclerc's heart, lifting him in the air, sending him reeling backwards onto the balcony railing and down over it, a scream dying on his lips as he plummeted toward the bed of azaleas in the foreyard of Cobb's apartment building.

Tann gained consciousness to the sound of Harrison's gun being fired. She rose woozily to her feet, seeking to escape from the floor, found the fire exit, and stumbled down the stairs to the twenty-fourth floor, and out into the corridor, toward the elevator.

She stopped, put her hands to her mouth, and gasped.

There was a body in the corridor, several feet from the elevator, beside the open door of an apartment.

She ran to him, stumbling as the sheet tangled beneath her feet, and knelt over him.

Foster Cobb was sprawled face down on the corridor floor, his fingers curled into the carpeting as if he had been trying to dig. There were superficial wounds on his buttocks, and the blood was drying. Tann could not tell if he was breathing.

She took off the sheet, placed it over Cobb's back, and rolled him over onto it.

"Foster . . ." she whispered.

There was no response. She put her ear to his chest and could not be sure if there was a heartbeat. Her own heart was panicking. She arched Cobb's head back to open his airway, pinched his nostrils, placed her mouth over his, and blew softly, watching his chest rise. He smelled dankly of perspiration. She took her mouth from his and he expelled her air. Again she placed her lips over his, and blew, and watched his lungs fill. His mouth tasted rich and warm. Her lips tingled with the feel of his. Again his chest fell as he let the air out. Again she pressed her lips to his mouth and gave him her air. His lips seemed, almost, to move within the inner rim of hers, and a shiver wiggled up her spine. Again she blew. And again. Every five seconds. With her hand she searched his chest for a heartbeat, and was not sure.

With her mouth pressed over his, she did not see his eyes snap open. But he did give her a clue — a vital clue — to the fact that he was still in this world: his tongue went into her mouth, and his arms went around her and pulled her to him.

Tann did not raise her lips from his for a long time. Seconds accumulated and became a minute. Two minutes. They kissed with a passion that to Cobb, drugged, seemed timeless; that to Tann, stoned only with her desire for this man to live, seemed eternal. Finally she withdrew a few inches from him and looked down at his pin-pointed eyes. "Damn you, Foster. Damn you. What are we doing?"

To that, Cobb made no direct reply. All he said — and he kept repeating such words until men came to carry him away on a stretcher — was this: "Outrageous junk, Jennie. Outrageous junk. God damn! What a *mother!*"

Wednesday, the Twenty-second Day of March, at Twenty Minutes Past Ten O'Clock in the Morning

Deborah Cobb fought panic as she entered the hospital. She wished she had rehearsed something for Cobb. What does one say to an estranged husband who had been seconds from death? She drew close to Honcho Harrison, who put his arm about her and helped her into the elevator. A uniformed policeman was stationed outside the elevator and nodded to Harrison as they entered.

On the floor of Cobb's private suite, there were other policemen, one standing by the elevator, another at the door of his room, others at the stair and fire-escape entrances to the floor.

Her mind was in a turmoil. She felt a duty to be affectionate, but wondered if she could express affection. She cared for him deeply, and had finally broken into tears last night when told he had suffered only minor injury. But caring for him deeply was not loving him, and although she wished her feelings were still those of love, she knew in her sorrow that she had grown away from him, or he from her. Her concern was now that Cobb not hate her; her hope was that he might forgive.

She stopped at the entrance to the private ward, took a long shaky breath, and stepped inside.

Ed Santorini was there, seated, edgy, lacking his strutting confidence.

Cobb greeted her with: "Hello, dear. Sorry about the mess in the apartment."

That sort of thing was the reason Deborah had to let him go. She managed a wan smile. "Cobb," she said, "you're okay." She leaned down and kissed his cheek, and felt no response, no warmth. Her eyes filled, and she took a handkerchief from her purse.

Santorini cleared his throat but said nothing.

"You already know Mr. Ed. Santorini, I believe," Cobb said. "Eddie, you remember my wife? You have known her, I believe, in the biblical sense. Perhaps a couple of times, anyway."

"Cobb, don't," Deborah said.

She tried to control herself so she would not break down. There was a long silence.

"Hello Honch," Cobb said, at last recognizing the man beside the door, looking like a sour uncomfortable kid waiting to be excused from class. "Here. I wrote out a statement this morning." Cobb passed up some pages of paper and handed them to the detective.

"Thanks," Harrison said. "We'll find Au, Fos."

Santorini cleared his throat again, but no other sound issued from it.

"So," Cobb finally said, "we're here to decide what to do with the body. Eddie and the cops want to parcel-post me off to some desolate island on the coast." He shrugged. "Fine. But they also want to surround me with SWAT-squad sharp-shooters. I told Eddie I can't think of a better way to attract attention: guys with rifles and bullet-proof jackets wandering all over the place coming and going for supplies. The whole Vancouver police department and half the provincial RCMP knowing where I am. Boasting in some bar about knowing where this poor exiled lawyer is hidden away on his Isle of Elba. Jesus."

Santorini finally spoke to Deborah: "Judge Hugo Land — he's a County Court judge, a friend of mine and Foster's — he has a place, a summer place, really, a little island, ten acres or around there. Just off Long Beach. Well, Barclay Sound, off the west coast of Vancouver

Island, out in the ocean. I made arrangements with the judge this morning. There's a big cabin there, a log cabin. Big, rambling place, actually." Santorini spoke in a quick, clipped way, without animation. "There's no phone. But there's water, toilet, and bath. There's a generator for power, and lots of fuel. Wood heat. Lots of wood stacked up. There's a little bay on the east side, away from the breakers, and there's a dock there, and a little runabout, so Fos can do some fishing. The generator will run radio and lights and a toaster, that sort of thing." He stopped. Deborah noticed dark circles underneath his eyes. She had never seen Santorini under strain. He had always been so free, easy, ebullient. "I don't know about no cops. Fos says no cops. I don't know."

"Give me a gun," Cobb said. "I'll practise with it. I won't shoot my toes off."

"I don't know if he should go alone," Santorini said. "What do you think, Honch?"

"Yeah, I don't think he should go alone."

"Okay," Cobb said. "I'll take a bodyguard." He twisted around and looked at Deborah. "I'll take Jennifer. She's pretty good with a gun. Eddie can spare her from the sweat shop for a couple of weeks." He turned back to Santorini. "Can't you, Eddie? You can spare Jennifer for a while. You wouldn't deny your old friend a little female companionship."

Deborah found herself breaking down.

"Don't be cruel, Foster," she said.

"Cruel?" Cobb said. His voice was rasping, sharp. "Who knows from cruel around here? Eddie knows from cruel, don't you, Eddie?"

Deborah was weeping now, and the mascara was running. Santorini touched her on the shoulder, delicately.

"I gotta go," said Harrison. "I got work."

"What's the matter?" Cobb asked him. "You don't like soap operas?"

"I don't think it's my place to be here."

"Well, just a second, Honch," Cobb said. "Let's get a few things straightened out. Who knows about this deal? I take it nobody's issuing any press releases that Foster Cobb is going off to Judge Land's island retreat? Who knows about it — the judge? Who else?"

"Judge Land won't speak about it, even to his wife," Santorini said. "Nobody else knows."

"Judge Land, me, and the three other persons in this room," Cobb said. "All of whom I trust with every ounce of my being." He glared at Santorini. "So why do I need an armed guard?"

"Au found Plizit," Harrison said.

"I discovered the leak," Santorini muttered. "Some shit-for-brains cop in Tlakish Lake. Klosterman. Old buddy of Cudlipp."

"The fuck . . . the stupid yahoo," Harrison said.

"Okay, okay," Cobb said. "Well, let's all agree not to tell Cudlipp, okay? Everybody promise not to tell. Cross your hearts and hope to die."

Santorini started to say something, but nothing came out.

"Eddie, old buddy," said Cobb, "I've been on the needle. It's been going on for a few weeks."

"I heard."

"Jesus, does she share *everything* with you?"

"Fos, don't be . . . Aw, forget it."

"Honcho knows. My sweet and innocent junior now knows. I'm kicking, Eddie. I bought the ultimate cure last night. I almost creamed the nurse when she tried to give me a shot. Thanks to Dr. Pavlov's half-gram of pure smack, I had the world's heaviest conditioned response laid on me. I no longer salivate at the sight of a hypodermic needle. But I'm going to be sniffing and aching and suffering a lot for a few days, and I don't want some fucking cops hanging around watching me perform. I could use some kindly ministrations, though. That's where Jennifer comes in. And that's another reason I want no cops hanging around. All right, folks, everybody clear out. I'm going to try to roll over on my stomach and sleep some of it off. Before they kick me out of here."

"There'll be a plane going from the harbor first thing in the morning," Santorini said. "You stay here in the meantime. We'll post somebody at the door. Somebody will get your clothes and stuff. Make a list of what you need."

"Yeah. Good-bye. Maybe I'll see you in court someday, Eddie." He looked coldly at him. "Divorce court."

"C'mon, Fos," Santorini said. "I'm sorry."

The three visitors went to the door. Deborah was last. She stood at the door for a moment, looking at Cobb with hurt. She had wanted to end it, but in a gentler way. Cobb would not look at her, and she went through the doorway.

Then she heard him call her.

"Deb, come here for a second."

The others looked at her. "Excuse me," she said. "I'll meet you." She went back in.

"I'm sorry, baby," he said.

"It's okay." She was fighting her emotions hard.

"Let it go," he said.

Deborah poured tears.

"I've been a bastard, I'm sorry."

"I said it's okay."

"I guess it stopped for you a long time ago, Deb." He took one of her hands. "It was pretty hard for me. It's the way junkies are, baby. But, hey, if I can kick one habit, I can kick another. Junk may be a little easier — I can get around the turn in a few days. Deborah Cobb will be harder — it will take a little longer. But you don't owe me anything, and don't take any guilt trips home with you."

"Cobb, Cobb . . ." Her face was a ruin.

"Some kinds of juices don't mix well. I was just hanging on, hoping and hoping. Being a fool for you, making it kind of tight for you, making you unhappy. You'll find some sweet prince out there. There's lots of them."

"Yes," she said. "Yes, I guess. Well, I haven't been as lonely as you.

You figured that out."

"Sure. I knew it. I didn't believe it, but I knew it."

There was a pause.

"Is there much skiing left this year?" Cobb asked.

"Oh, I guess another couple of months. We'll close down about the May twenty-fourth weekend. I may quit before that. It's been a long season."

"You'll stay with your folks?"

"I think I should."

"Tell your dad he should retire from the bench. He's earned a few years."

"I know. He won't."

"Yeah."

"Well."

"You don't need any money?"

"No, I'm fine."

"We'll work out the details when I get back."

"Sure."

"I just want my books and record albums, that's all."

"Yes, whatever . . . Cobb?"

"Uh-huh?"

"Don't hate Eddie. He's sick with worry about a scandal. A messy divorce will ruin his chances."

"Too bad. Tell him I'm going to ruin him if I can. Man, I cannot forgive him. Guy who cheats on his best friend shouldn't be a judge."

"It was my fault."

"I said don't blame yourself."

"No, not. It's my fault. I arranged to get the trial for you."

"What?"

"I asked . . . I asked Eddie to give you a big case to start you off with. I knew you didn't have anything. I knew you were sitting in that office hating yourself because nothing was happening. I knew you wouldn't call him. I asked for a big case for you. For the money, reputation. He . . . he told me he had just the right kind of trial."

"God damn. Ed Santorini did all this just for me?"

Santorini waited for Deborah Cobb downstairs at the hospital entrance, then led her out and helped her into his car. Neither spoke for a while. Finally she said: "He's going to do it. A divorce. Naming you. I think he wants to sue you."

Santorini said nothing. She put her head on his shoulder and shook. She was empty of tears. Santorini drove her to her parents' home in the Kerrisdale district, where they were waiting for her. Before she left his car, he kissed her tenderly on the forehead, promised her that everything would be all right, and said he would pick up her things from her apartment that evening and visit with her for a while.

His next stop was his office. He was grim-faced.

Everit Cudlipp had finally been released on bail, and Santorini had his telephone number. He dialled it.

"Cudlipp," he said, "this is Santorini, and I want you to listen very goddamn carefully. Your ass is in a sling."

"Talk to my lawyer."

"Look, you bag of snot, listen very, very carefully. If this thing goes to trial, I'm going to stick a ramrod up your ass and through your nose, and if you don't get twenty years to life, I'm going to take the sentence to appeal."

"What do you want?"

"I want you down here in half an hour in my office. We're going to make a deal."

At noon Cudlipp walked alone from the crown counsel office onto Main Street and into a mournful day. The sun was hidden by a grey blanket which stretched everywhere to the horizon and enfolded the mountain peaks. It was not too early in the day for Cudlipp to start drinking, but he avoided the nearest bars and beer parlors and headed for Gastown, Vancouver's old section, refurbished for the tourists but populated by a curious blending of derelicts, freaks, long-haired lawyers, and proprietors of fashionable restaurants and shops. His route was taking him to a bar on Water Street, where better-class pushers sometimes congregated and talked business over drinks.

The place was full. He went to the bar, ordered a beer, and adjusted his sight to the darkness.

The first beer went down quickly, and he was paying for another when he finally caught the eye of one of the brokers, Big Benson. Cudlipp gave him a sign, a slight inclination of the head, and after a few minutes Benson waddled up to the bar and grinned at Cudlipp.

"Got yourself in a bit of a fuck, didn't you?" Big Benson said. "Hope you got some friends in the joint, buddy. You're gonna need a little love in there."

"You still working for Ernie?" Cudlipp asked.

"This some kind of business, Cudlipp?"

"Yeah, it's some kind of business."

"What?" Benson asked.

"Get ahold of him for me."

"You still giving orders? Don't seem to me you got the jam to order folks about no more."

Cudlipp gave him three twenties. "All right? Just call him. I'll be here. I need him to make a connection, that's all."

"Well, you're a pretty hot property, Cudlipp. I'll try." He went away to a pay phone.

An hour had gone when Ernie Cantone showed up. He stood in the doorway, blinking for a few seconds, and gave the nod to Cudlipp, who followed him outside to his car. Cudlipp got into the passenger side and Cantone drove off. There was another man in the back seat, whom Cudlipp did not know. They stopped near Ferguson Point in Stanley Park.

"I'm gonna search you for bugs and barrels," Cantone said. He ran a detector over Cudlipp's body, went through his pockets, and patted him down. Then he turned to the man in the back. "Okay," he said. The man nodded.

Cantone spat out the window of the moving car, then turned again to Cudlipp. "Last time you and me did a number, seems I got me six bits in the box," he said. "Now you're looking for favors. I should tell you to blow it up your snout."

There was a time Cudlipp would have knocked teeth out for that sort of thing. He said: "I want to connect with the top man. I got a real nice fat score for him. He'll thank you."

"Yeah, well, maybe he figures you done him enough favors. Maybe he'd like to make supper on you with a couple of butcher knives."

"I didn't cop out on him. He knows that."

"He won't talk to you. You're hot. I guarantee he won't talk to you, man."

Cudlipp took four hundred-dollar bills from his wallet and tore them in half. He gave a set of halves to Cantone.

"Just get me two minutes on the phone." He checked his watch. "It's thirteen past one o'clock now. You pick the phone booth. I'll be there exactly thirteen minutes past two o'clock."

Cantone looked at the other man, who shrugged.

"Okay, give him a number," the man said.

Cudlipp was at the phone booth a couple of minutes before two-thirteen. He knew he had to show himself. A car cruised by a couple of times and a man was across the street, watching him through a drug-store window. He took the phone off the hook, but held the hook down and pretended to be talking into the receiver. The car drove past the phone booth one more time, then stopped at the curb nearby.

The phone rang thirty seconds after the appointed minute.

"Yeah," Cudlipp said.

"What do you want?" Cudlipp was disappointed. It was not Dr. Au's voice.

"I want to speak to him."

"What can you do?"

"You on a pay phone?" Cudlipp asked.

"Of course."

"I don't know you."

"I'm doing the talking."

"I want to earn some money. I can tell him where he can find a guy."

"I see."

"I know where they're going to put him. I'll take payment when it's over. Say, five down, and I'll take twenty-five on the balance. Less isn't worth the risk. But no deal unless I hear his voice. That's my guarantee. I got other terms."

"Okay. The guy in the drug-store will give you another phone booth. The call will be at six minutes to four."

At exactly the appointed time Cudlipp received his call.

"Yes," he said.

"Yes, my friend."

"Uh, can you say something else?"

"It is a pleasure to hear an old friend's voice."

"Okay, thanks. I have to stick to the five and twenty-five."

"It is fair, if you deliver."

"Well, I wasn't sure. The guy —"

"Let us not waste time. There were other conditions?"

"I get to kill him," Cudlipp said.

"No. That is reserved."

"Well, I want a part."

"I understand that. It would be cruel of me to refuse."

"And payment of the balance when we meet."

"Yes. When we have him. How certain are you of this?"

"I have . . . a friend."

"Yes. It will be appropriate if you join us. In the event that the information you provide is false, we would want you there. Do you understand that?"

"Yeah, well . . . yeah, I understand."

"That would be our guarantee of your honesty in this dealing. I will not accept further failure. That is understood?"

"I know what you mean. But trust works both ways."

"I think you have found me honorable."

"You will need a boat."

"Yes."

"A cabin cruiser, lots of horses."

"Yes."

"On the west coast of Vancouver Island, there is a town. Glenda Bay. G-l-e-n-d-a Bay. There is a café. Only one. Nine a.m. Friday? The day after tomorrow?"

"Do I understand that is all you care to divulge at this time?"

"I would prefer to do it that way."

"Friday. It is the day Jim Feng arrives."

"What?"

"Perhaps you will perform a small service. It would be stupid of me to go to the airport. And my people are being watched."

"Uh, I'm sorry?"

"My dear cousin of the fourth generation will arrive at the airport on the overnight flight from Hong Kong. He shall be taking over my duties here until the various problems have been resolved. I must speak with him before I leave this country."

"Yeah."

"Perhaps you will be good enough to escort him to Glenda Bay, so that we might have a reunion, however short."

"All right, I guess."

"My contact is to meet him at the CP Air information counter. You will be my contact. You are not being followed?"

"Naw."

"Very well. You do not wish to divulge the specific whereabouts of our friend near Glenda Bay?"

"I just want to make sure I'm there when it happens."

"You have lost much trust in humanity, my friend. But you have suffered."

"Yeah."

"The rest waits until Friday. He is a cancer."

"What?"

"He is a cancer, a scourge that must be eradicated before our bodies are fouled with disease."

"Well, yeah, sure."

"Do you understand?"

"I think so."

"Even now he is eating at our brains."

"Yeah. Well. The down payment?"

"Reach under the telephone. You will find an envelope taped there. In the envelope you will find fifty bills, each of one-hundred-dollar denomination."

Thursday, the Twenty-third day of March, at Half-past Two O'Clock in the Afternoon

The lowering mass of morning clouds had passed overhead and retreated to the east, carrying its burden of rain to Vancouver Island and the mainland, and the afternoon was sunny and majestic, splendid and rare. There were still stragglers in the sky, scurrying puffs of cloud which scudded eastward, then atrophied and faded before reaching the low mountains of Vancouver Island, where they built again and clung like wisps of wool to the cliffs and tops of trees. Spring's sun sent warm messages. Steam rose from the silver shakes upon the roof of the rambling house, and about the clearing the hot rays pried open the buds of daffodils and crocus, and the flowers radiated flashes of color — yellow, and yellow edged with red, and mauve and violet and orange.

The house was set in a ten-acre island in the coastal rain forest, and its clearing of flowers and untamed grass was surrounded by looming giants — red cedar, Douglas fir, and hemlock — beneath which grew sword fern and vanilla leaf and trillium, and great tangles of salal, the evergreen shrub that finds refuge everywhere in the North Pacific woods, and grows seven feet tall, a thicket of leaf, branch, and bush that rivals in density the jungles of the wet tropics.

The clearing extended from a curving beach on the westerly

windward side of the island to a small bay on the leeward side. The island was narrow here — four hundred feet across a slight rise — and on the rise was the house, commanding a view from the front porch westward to the beach and the long horizon. The view eastward, from the back of the house, was over the bay to the shredded coast of Vancouver Island, a few hundred yards away across a channel. The inlet at the back provided sheltered mooring, and a pier led to a floating wharf to which a small outboard was tied. Across the channel were sand and rock beaches strung along the shores of Vancouver Island, and above them were cliffs, and beyond the cliffs, mountains.

The island of Judge Hugo Land was narrow, running parallel to the opposite shore, and a path ran around it, leading from the wharf to rock points at the north and south ends, and back to the western side to the beach. Another path led across the isthmus from the dock across the clearing to the house and the nearby outbuildings. The path then continued west and disappeared in the soft grey sand of the crescent beach, which today was being gently slapped by the waves in slow, unceasing beat. The beach was guarded on either end by high rock promontories — granite columns seventy feet high. Upon their crests, shore pines grew, grotesque and knobby-limbed, groping landward as if in sluggish flight from the battering westerly winds.

Although the breezes had slackened by mid-day, and now only softly buffeted the waves, the ocean rollers still carried the energy of old Pacific blows, and they lashed the rocks at the feet of the promontories, pounding with the sound of artillery. But the waves that licked up the beach had spent their strength getting there, and were now subdued.

A flock of wintering plovers scurried along the sand, picking food at the tide-line. Offshore, on rocks, a pair of cormorants sat, while grebes and Arctic loons dipped and rolled nearby. Farther at sea, a family of guillemots scuttered about the waves.

Foster Cobb stood barefoot on the beach, waves rolling up his feet and ankles, then falling back, running to the ocean.

On this glorious day, he was regurgitating clam chowder, returning it to the sea.

Clam chowder had been his lunch, tenderly and lovingly prepared by Nurse Tann.

Tann watched him from the front doorway of the house. She hollered: "Once again, the chef is insulted."

Earlier, Cobb's angry stomach had similarly rejected breakfast.

They had arrived at nine a.m. The police Cessna had stopped only long enough to unload them and their supplies. For the first hour Tann had followed her jittery friend as he prowled about the house, examining its great stone fireplace, its well-larded pantry, its driftwood ornaments, and its collection of Japanese fishing balls, arrayed on shelves and counters. In the spacious den he had discovered (unexpected treasure) an eight-foot slate pool table.

After breakfast, and Cobb's subsequent apologies, they had strolled around the island, dug razorback clams on the beach, collected shells and sand dollars, and exchanged greetings with a pair of foraging seals. The seals, full of wonderment, poked their noses and eyes above the water and for a time solemnly squinted at the two land creatures: the slim, dark-haired woman and the tall blond man — shivering, quaking, flailing his chest with his arms. Then the seals submerged and went fishing.

Inside the house again, he paced and fought withdrawal. Back outside, he vomited once more, and paced again along the margin of the water.

For a while, for a change, he tried potting shots with his borrowed police revolver at a tin can on a stump. The can remained inviolate throughout, and the noise made his head jangle, so he quit, returning the gun to the table in his bedroom.

Inside, he paced again, his hot pipe clenched between his teeth, which left gouges on the pipestem. The airtight woodstove crackled and spit, the ocean thundered, the generator added a soft and constant putt-putt, and the Fourth Brandenburg Concerto sang from the stereo speakers. Cobb paced to rhythms of his own. He clutched his chest with folded arms, then banged them on his sides, trying to beat back the waves of nausea that sent ripples of gooseflesh across his skin. He had had no sleep on the previous night, and was wan and grey from lack of it and from the warfare in his body.

It would take another two days to get over the hump. After that, the descent would still be hard, and it would be a ragged march down, with jumps and jitters all the way. About three or four weeks of gritty pain before his habit was finally beaten into submission.

Tann watched him warily, chatting and flitting about like a wren, observing his every move, assessing every complaint, smiling when she could.

She told him of the yoga method of dealing with pain.

"Concentrate upon it," she said. "Focus every part of yourself upon the pain. Don't run away from it. Search out the worst of it, and centre on it. It will go away."

"Yeah, yeah," said Cobb. "Centre on the pain."

He focussed all his energy, and the pain dulled for a while. When he relaxed and tried to enjoy his pipe, it caught up to him again.

He paced, jumpy as a sand flea.

He concentrated on the pain. It went, came back. He paced.

He paced into the recreation den and studied the pool table. He wondered if he could do it, if he could control his line and make a clean shot. He picked up the cue ball and threw it with others onto the table, chalked a stick, took quick aim, and, to his astonishment, sank a ball dead into a corner pocket. He tried the different spins and banged a few more in. A better shot with cue stick than handgun, he found he could play with old instinct, running off series of up to a dozen balls, somehow mastering his shakes at each shot.

"I'll play you," Tann said, smiling at the door.

"Ever held a pool stick?"

"Um, sort of. I mean, well . . . no."

"Great," he snorted. "You can't do anything I like to do."

"Well, Mr. Cobb, if we keep working at it, we'll find something. I could learn to like Mozart."

Cobb put his arms around her, directed her hands into place around the cue, and demonstrated the stroke and follow-through. She tried it for a while, and did not do very well. Then he felt her relaxing against him, leaning back into his body. He took his hands from the cue and put them around her middle and held her close to him for a few minutes. He kissed her hair around her neck and ears. Then the shakes got bad again, and he let her go. And paced.

Outside, for a while he chopped wood, splitting cedar from dry butts piled in the woodshed.

Back inside, he paced.

"All right," Tann said, looking at her watch. "I'll make you some strong peppermint tea. It will either cure you or kill you."

Cobb watched her fuss about with her herbal potions in this new attempt to establish a beach-head at his stomach. A pot of hot water sat heating on the stove. When it boiled, she poured it into a teapot, and after it steeped for a while, she poured some in a mug and gave it to him. Sweet with wild honey, it went hot down his throat, tasting strangely bitter. He sat gingerly on an old stuffed couch, praying the tea might stay inside him. Another thirty-five or forty hours of this.

The thing was to keep his mind together.

He centred on the pain, trying to keep the tea down. He centred on the pain. . . .

Need. Need. The need throbbed in his brain, beating to a slow drum.

Need. Need. Need.

Prickling, biting, sticking, jabbing.

Needles on the table, needles on the rug, needles on the walls.

When had his withdrawal taken on this new, strange form? The bottle on the windowsill was a syringe; its neck, its point. The coal-oil lamp: a bulbous needle. The candle: a long, slim needle. His pipe on the table: Could it enter his arm?

When had this begun? Needles of sunlight stabbed through the window and ricocheted off glasses and seashells and the colored glass fishing balls, and these coruscated richly, sending shafts of color through the room. When had the colors become so lustrous, so dazzling? And the sound: each note of the guitar was a single singing, liquid quaver suspended in the silence around it.

And he was shaking, and sweating, and needing.

And he was in fear. Why? Something foreboding. . . . Where was Jennifer Tann? No, don't look. Because there is something . . .

Was that the sound of his heart? The generator outside? No. No. Something else. It was harsher. An engine noise. A boat engine? A boat?

He tried to sit up. What was it? There were psychotropic colors, sounds, rhythms.

Something hallucinogenic?

Waves of pure color from different parts of the room. . . . The notes of the classical guitar up and down his spine, pricking at his arms.

The engine sound. Louder. Filling his ears. Approaching.

Outside, through the window: clouds and trees, caricatures of demonic faces. Faces in the fir needles. Needles. . . .

Something terrible and lonely. His mind splitting into many parts, debating the many theories. Was she near? Behind him? He sensed it. Mushrooms in the soup? No, there had been tea. A peppermint tea. LSD in the tea? Acid herbal tea?

What?

He could stand by grasping the fireplace mantel and leaning heavily against it, woozy, wobbling. He knew she was behind him.

Outside, the engine coughed, sputtered, died. If he moved to the window, he would see the boat. And the men in it.

"What is it?" he asked. His voice came from a far place.

"Five thousand micrograms." Her voice was matter-of-fact. Too calm.

"What?" He revolved slowly toward her, his hands grasping the fireplace stone for support.

"Orange sunshine," she said. "Blotter acid."

She was smiling. Serenely. Her eyes were ice. She had the eyes. They sent thin needles to his heart. There was no birdlike shrug. No laughter. Her face was composed, without expression, without feeling.

His police handgun was in her hand, its barrel drawing a line to his abdomen.

He took a step to the window. Men walking up the path. Then Dr. Au. Yes, Dr. Au. Strolling leisurely. Dr. Au. Of course. It seemed natural. He had known they would come. The men were laughing, chatting, gesturing.

Sunshine flashed from the water of the ocean, blinding Cobb. Orange sunshine.

The forest green was black-green, the forest recesses were cold caves.

Dr. Au smiled at him from the dock and waved cheerfully. Compelled, Cobb waved back. And smiled, a death-like smile.

He turned back to Tann and tried to move toward her. Better a bullet. He moved lumpishly, dreamily, and fell against a chair, then against the wall, and was on his hands and knees, a dog on the floor.

"What else?" he said.

"I cannot betray my people. There are laws."

Cobb nodded. He understood. There was a sudden cataclysm of meaning, of insight. Those closest to him would cause most pain. Those closest would destroy him. Those to whom he had given himself.

Centre on the pain.

There had been failures of friendship and love. Paul Quade, who had given him his wings. Bennie Bones, who had given him crutches. Ed Santorini, who had given him horns. Deborah, who had given him pain that only a needle could dull. Jennifer, the last . . . Jennifer Tann.

Centre on the pain.

"Do it quickly," Tann said as the men entered.

Dr. Au nodded. "Yes, it is your right," he said.

Someone nudged him with a boot and he fell on his side, then rolled onto his stomach, crawling again. Crawling. Crawling. He would return as a slug or worm. He felt someone turn him over.

The faces were strange, distorted, cruel, laughing.

Tann was looking down at him, shaking her head slowly. "How little you understand," she said. Her eyes hard, mocking. "You tried to destroy him," she said.

The laughter of Dr. Au.

Hands touched him, moved him, stripped him. The quickness and the dexterity of the Surgeon. Deft and sure. Time collapses inward. The needles. Penetrating, sticking. Needles in his veins, his arms, his thighs, his feet. Needles. (Centre on the pain. There is no pain.) The clean scalpel slitting across his skin. The high, slow glissando of the guitar. A thin strip across his abdomen, glowing red. The heavy, dull explosions of the surf, pounding pulsing. The stylized dance of bodies swirling through the room. A red line from throat to pelvis, artistic, clean, immaculate. The blood: rich, blinding, hot, and pumping from naked red orifices. Dr. Au, triumphant, displaying between thumb and forefinger the sticky trophy of a long hunt . . . applause . . . laughter . . . his own tears . . . no pain . . . no pain. . . .

There was pain. And with the pain, a joyous flooding of release: a rush, a blast, an orgasmic, atomic, screaming kick, as Cobb awoke from his long withdrawal sleep, driven awake by pain and by the terrors of the subconscious.

The wetness was his tears and sweat.

It was dark. A lamp glowed. The largo, the final movement of the guitar sonata, was slow and moving.

Jennifer Tann's slender arms enfolded him. Her face was touching his, her mouth upon his tears, upon his eyes, his lips. She whispered words of love and peace.

After a while they made love, hard, driving to the slow beat of the surf.

Good Friday, the Twenty-fourth Day of March, at Half-past Eight O'Clock in the Morning

There were cheerful shouts of children in the yard outside. But Santorini's living room was filled with the sombre sounds of *Tosca*, an opera of brooding torture and treachery. At one point he felt the edge of nausea, and he suddenly jumped to his feet and glared morosely out the window of his living room over the vista of English Bay and Vancouver and the Fraser delta beyond. Glints of hard sunshine sparkled off the waters of the bay and caused his eyes to water.

For the rest of the morning he would remain near his telephone, waiting for a call he feared. The call should come around noon.

Santorini might have been happy today. He had much reason to rejoice. Yesterday he had received another, important call, from Ottawa, a call that would shape his future. It meant that in a few weeks, barring some untoward event, he would be known to the world as Mr. Justice Edward Antonio Santorini (a fair and equable man on the bench, respected by all). The call had confirmed that investigators from the justice ministry had completed their search into his past and had given him passing grades.

There was no scandal in the background of Eddie Santorini.

Now his house was silent, except for the playful cries of his children in the yard outside. He sat by the telephone, waiting.

His palms were sweating. His eyes were raw.

Jin Feng had brought only a small satchel, and he sat immobile in the passenger seat of Cudlipp's Buick. He was dressed in a black turtleneck and trousers, and was ascetic in appearance, and sinewy. His eyes, like Au's, had the quality of metal — a trait of the family. Ma Wo-chien selected for higher duty only those who had inherited that quality of the eyes.

Beside him, at the wheel, raw-faced and cheerless, Cudlipp cursed and seethed as he piloted his car along a gravel logging road which led to Glenda Bay, an outpost of humanity on the wild west coast of Vancouver Island.

Despite nearly a day of sunshine, the road was muddy, and Cudlipp's windshield was coated with a thick brown film which his windshield wipers had fanned dry. The washer had clogged. Cudlipp was furious at his Buick, and even more furious at the pick-up truck in front of him, which obstinately kept to the centre of the road, denying passing room.

The terrain through which he was driving had once been beautiful, a virginal wood. But the forests of Vancouver Island had been cut back and down, victims of the giant scythe of the logging companies: strong reapers, poor sowers. The road wound through twists and hairpins among the slash and wreckage left by the loggers, descending at times to blue lakes — pretty once, but now filled with a tangle of limbs and bodies of dead trees.

Cudlipp's face was etched with lines of anger. His features seemed to implode toward the centre of his face — eyes, nose, and mouth coming together in rigidly set formation, with lines of strain radiating outward. He cursed everyone connected with his plight: Cobb, Au, Santorini, Harrison, his lawyers. And Flaherty. His dreams shattered, he sought revenge.

There was no conversation in the car. In fact, the only words spoken by Jin Feng — on the car ferry from the mainland — were an inquiry as to whether Cudlipp was armed.

"You bet I am," Cudlipp had said. He was carrying a police .38.

"I would like you to give it to me," Feng had said.

"The hell I'll give you my gun."

Feng had shrugged.

They were late. The meeting was set for nine, and Au and friends would have waited for an hour by the time they got there. Well, Cudlipp did not give a shit. He was no lackey to the Surgeon. When they got together, there would be the usual slow coquettish dance of distrustful men. But Cudlipp would prove his worth and loyalty, and he would join them, if not in friendship, at least by means of the mortar of hard currency.

Soon, Australia. Finally.

A few grey shacks announced the entry into the village of Glenda Bay, a community of fishing people, a town of weathered cedar where residents travelled back and forth over ocean channels by rowboats and outboards. Cudlipp parked and found a boy with a boat and gave him three dollars to take them to the restaurant. Feng waited outside; Cudlipp strode in. He first saw a young waitress, working there alone; and at a table near the wall were her only customers: Easy Snider (whom Cudlipp knew from old dealings) and Ng Soon, a young Ch'ao-chou gunman who had been chosen for this job because he could handle boats.

Cudlipp sat down across from Snider. "Wipe your nose," he told him. "No wonder they call you Sleazy."

"They call me Easy, man. And you can call me Easy too, if you don't mind."

"Wipe your fucking nose, Sleazy," Cudlipp said. He was used to talking that way to addicts. He regarded them as beneath contempt and felt insulted now to be allied with one.

"Took your time," Snider said.

Cudlipp did not explain or apologize. "Who's this bright light?" he asked, arching his head in the direction of Ng Soon. "He do the brain work for you guys now that Charlie Ming got himself retired?" Ng Soon looked blankly at Cudlipp.

"He doesn't speak English," Snider said. "Actually, he don't speak at all, far as I ever heard. He got an M16 rifle does all his talking, corporal."

"Where does the Surgeon get these pukes from?" he said.

"You're lucky he don't understand you," Snider said. "Dr. Au snaps his fingers, you get your ass blown off before you say you're sorry."

Cudlipp hollered to the waitress: "Bacon and eggs. Easy over. Extra toast, and jam. Got any beer?"

"Man, we got to be going," Snider said.

"I'm buying you a beer, Sleazy." he turned back to the waitress. "Old Style, Blue, Lucky — whatever's cold." He glanced at Ng Soon. "Does the dummy drink?" he asked.

"Don't call me Sleazy, corporal. Maybe was a time you could do that."

"Hey," Cudlipp said to Ng Soon, almost shouting. "You drink? Beer? Drink?" He made a motion as if tipping a bottle to his lips. Ng Soon shook his head.

"Jesus," said Cudlipp, "they forgot to wind him up today."

Easy Snider waited sourly while Cudlipp finished his breakfast. Then he said: "Let's go."

Cudlipp gave the waitress a wink and a dollar tip, and followed Easy Snider and Ng Soon out the front door, where they joined Feng. They walked down a broad sidewalk along the docks. It was obvious which was Au's boat — the only yacht there — a diesel-powered sixty-foot cabin cruiser. "What do you think of her?" Snider asked, waving his arm at the boat. "Five hundred bucks a day. Does fifty knots easy, flat out."

"Where's Dr. Au?" Cudlipp asked.

Snider smiled. "He's being careful. Wanted to make sure you weren't being followed." The engine started, rumbled, then purred. The boat backed slowly into the channel, turned about, and headed toward open water.

After a few minutes they reached a deserted stretch of beach where the sandstone shelf was cut by a narrow channel through which a river flowed into the ocean. Ng Soon put the controls into neutral, and they waited.

After a few minutes, a small outboard emerged from the channel. Cudlipp could see a lone figure in it: Dr. Au, huddled in a cape. The boat came closer, and Cudlipp saw that Au's eyes seemed glazed, tranced. After Snider helped him aboard the cruiser, the small boat was winched out of the water, onto its place at the stern. Au did not seem to notice Cudlipp, but walked past him gloomily, nodding to Jin Feng, who followed him into the cabin. "Your satchel is heavy," Au said, taking it from Feng.

"Books. Toilet articles." Feng watched as Au rummaged through his bag with his hands. Finding nothing, Au looked up sharply at his cousin.

"Is it on your person?"

"I am sorry, Au P'ang Wei, I do not know —"

"The weapon! You have come with a firearm! You are here with orders from Ma Wo-chien!" Au shrieked the words.

"My orders are to replace you here, Au P'ang Wei. I am not armed." He calmly extended his arms and allowed Au to search him.

Au dropped his voice. "No. I will stay here, and you will work with me at my direction. You will assist in the Cobb matter today, and after that I will run over the routines with you, and the financial records." His voice became lower still, almost a mumble. "Cobb is not alone. . . . There are others. . . ." He opened his needle case and with a clean cloth began to polish the needles and a scalpel that were in it. After a while he looked up at Feng. "Send Corporal Cudlipp in and leave us."

Feng, who had remained expressionless throughout, left the cabin and nodded to Cudlipp to go in.

"You have kept us waiting," Au said, not looking at him, still polishing. Cudlipp said nothing at first. He watched Au, fascinated. The man looked skeletal and drawn.

"You have kept us waiting!" It was a shout, high-pitched, vibrant.

"I'm sorry," Cudlipp said. "The road was bad."

After a while Au turned his eyes to the policeman, and they seemed to slowly focus on him, and suddenly they began to sharpen and glisten coldly. It was as if Au had returned from a place far away. Then he stood up, before Cudlipp could react, and reached into Cudlipp's bulging jacket pocket, pulling out his revolver.

"Corporal Cudlipp," Au said, "trust is best maintained if the serpent's tooth is blunted. That does not suggest that I regard you as unfaithful to my cause." He smiled weakly. "I apologize. I am being hot-tongued and most inhospitable. We will have a warm cognac and relive more pleasant days."

Au drew a bottle of Remy Martin from a cabinet above the bar and poured from it into two snifters. He set each glass in turn upon a brandy warmer, which he lit, twirling the glasses slowly.

"Let us drink," he said, "to ultimate victory. To Cobb, whose spirit will join mine in brotherhood." As he raised his glass, he turned his eyes toward Cudlipp. They had become hollow again. He touched his glass to Cudlipp's. "He haunts me. . . Do you feel his power, too?"

"Well, I guess so, yeah."

"*You* will be rewarded. Oh, yes *you* above all will be rewarded. It would have been ungenerous of me to refuse your terms. They will be respected, and you will be given a place . . . of honor." He laughed. "Oh, it will be an excellent entertainment for you!" Au held up his glass again for Cudlipp, who again touched it with his. They both drank.

"I have always shown integrity in dealings with you, corporal, have I not? This will seal our trust." He reached inside his cape, into a pocket, and withdrew an envelope. "It is merely a token, Mr. Cudlipp, a token in payment for praiseworthy service, for the delivery of merchandise that is beyond value." Again he smiled, passing the envelope to Cudlipp, who opened it, riffled through the bills without counting them, and pocketed it. "The life of this prosecutor might seem to many unnecessarily dear, but luxuries are dear, Mr. Cudlipp, and that man is priceless to me."

Au finished his cognac, and Cudlipp gulped back his. "The matter about the gun, I regret," Au said. He squeezed Cudlipp's arm with such intensity that he almost cried out. "You are trusted, my friend, but we have found such disloyalty . . ." His voice trailed off, and he looked at Cudlipp through eyes now masked again by film. "Yes? You, as well?" The fingers of Dr. Au dug deep into Cudlipp's biceps. "You, as well? Are we not brothers in suffering? Are we not brothers of vengeance?"

Cudlipp felt a cold cloud settle upon him and a shiver wiggle up his spine.

"Please take us to him." Au released his hand from Cudlipp's arm, leaving welts.

"Foster, wake up."

"Why?"

"Oh, God, I thought you were having another nightmare."

"No."

"You were groaning and moaning."

"Yes. I do that a lot."

"Oh. Well, I'm sorry I woke you up."

"You didn't. I wasn't sleeping. I haven't slept."

"Does it still hurt?"

"Only when I laugh."

There was a pause.

"Foster."

"Yes."

"Are you still awake?"

"Yes."

"I want to talk to you."

"You *are* talking to me."

"Do you mind?"

"No." Squirming and gritting his teeth, Cobb lay in his own rancid sweat, studying the undulating wall patterns created by the notched cedar logs. It was morning, and hazy rays of sun filtered between the trees outside, entered through the windows, and dappled the walls.

Tann said nothing for a while. Then: "I had an incredible flash. I was just lying here asleep, and something hit me, and I awoke and you were groaning. Are you listening?"

"Yes."

"You don't care."

Cobb took his red-rimmed eyes from the wall, wrenched his body into a half-sitting position, and peered at Tann. She was lying on her back, looking at the ceiling. She flicked a glance at him, then fixed again upon the ceiling.

"You don't care," she repeated.

"My whole being is inflamed with an irresistible urge to hear all about your incredible flash."

"Well, that's just it. You don't really care, do you? Who needs your patronizing attitude?"

Cobb sighed and lay back again.

She continued. "You're going to think I'm dumb, of course. You think I'm pretty naive anyway. Don't you? You think I'm silly and naive, right? Why don't you answer? I know you're listening. Are you all right?" This time she half-raised her body, leaning on her elbows and looking down at Cobb, whose face muscles were painfully taut. "*Are* you all right, Foster? Are you getting better? Maybe you're not ready for this."

Cobb looked into her eyes, which were liquid and dark. He worked mightily to assemble a grimace that he hoped would pass for a smile. She shook her head sadly, leaned down, and put her lips softly to his. Then she put her head on his shoulder, slipped her hand beneath the sheets, and stroked him with sensitive fingers that read his body.

"Do you want to hear this, Foster?" she said. "Maybe you're going to hate me." She paused again. "Do you think people should always tell the truth about what they feel?"

"No."

"Well, *I* think so. Here it comes. Are you ready?"

"Jennifer, I am dying here. The only thing that is keeping me alive is a profound curiosity about what in God's name you are talking about."

"You don't want to hear. You're scared of it. Here comes Jennifer Tann with another heavy load of worry. Another monkey for him to carry. Does he need it? No way. I'll just shut up."

Cobb turned his head to look at her. Her lips were pursed, little lines of effort radiating from them. Despite everything, he began to laugh.

Her face melted. He kissed her eyes, which were wet.

"I think I'm falling in love," she whispered. "I can't help it. That's the flash."

Cobb stopped laughing. He closed his eyes and drew her tight to him. She bit her lip and clung to him, sticking to his sweat, warming her naked body in it. She waited for a long while. Cobb said nothing. She waited, eyes squeezed shut, heart exposed. She waited for a response. Anything. A snort of derision, some false words of comfort, some patent easy lie, some caustic Cobbian dagger. Anything. She felt her heart pounding, through her chest, her skin, into him, deeply into him.

After five minutes — or was it ten? or an hour? — Cobb spoke.

"I take it," he said, "that this piece of wreckage beside you is the object of your regard?"

"Oh, yes."

"Generally speaking, I am complimented —"

She cut him off, and found herself babbling wildly. "Shut up. You are going to be sarcastic. You are going to make fun of me. You think I'm weak. Don't you? Well, it's okay, I can handle it. I can handle rejection. Just be honest. Don't play games. Don't try to let me down easy. God!" She almost screamed. "Why am I such a *rattlemouth* around you? You give me a bad case of nervous tongue." For a while, neither spoke. "You don't want to deal with this, do you?" she said finally. "I told you: I can handle rejection." There was another pause. Then she whispered: "Just say you like me. That will do. Nothing heavy. You can pretend. You don't have to mean it."

She raised her head again and dared look at his eyes. "Lie to me," she said. "I'll believe anything."

"Jennifer . . ." he began.

She clapped her hands to her ears. "No, don't say it, don't. Change the subject. Talk about the weather. Hey, it's sunny outside. What a nice day! Let's have fun, go for walks, gather clams, have a boat ride."

"Hey, Jennifer," he called. She pressed the flats of her hands more tightly, shutting out all sound.

"Don't talk," she said. "Don't even think about it. Forget I said anything."

As Cobb opened his mouth to call to her, she brought her mouth down over his, and did not withdraw her hands from her ears until he could no longer speak, his lips and mouth caught up in the heat of her kiss. Her tongue was a wild dancer; her lips swirled hungrily over his. Her long fingers curled about his cock and testicles and pumped him full with a driving passion.

He made love to her, desperate and ravenous.

She made love to him, shy and giving and joyful, and at the end, she came with a long, shuddering orgasm.

She was smiling as she fell asleep.

Cobb waited until her breathing became soft and regular, then quietly withdrew from her, rose from the bed, and showered. He dressed in blue jeans, denim shirt, a pair of old tennis shoes and a cap, put a jacket on, and went outside.

Twenty-four hours to go, and he would be around the bend, on the homestretch. Twenty-four hours to go. A day and a night of this. He had not slept during the night, partly because of his pain and partly because of his fear of the horrors sleep brought. He felt ragged, charred, burned out. He was still enduring alternating chills and flushes, and the ache in his limbs was powerful. His bowels were still the slaves of some intractable and unforgiving tyrant.

Outside, long arms of mist reached toward the beach, where the breezes shredded them. The sky was vapid, aqueous, and behind the house the sun inched gingerly above the trees. A chocolate-colored song sparrow, testing the spring, sat on an alder branch and sang with lilting grace.

Cobb was bitter that he could not enjoy the beauty of this place and time, and grumbled to himself as he walked toward the beach, onto the wet sand. A group of beachcombing crows flapped into the air and shrieked displeasure at his intrusion.

Cobb walked the length of the beach, then back. And forth. And back. He walked with a quickening pace, then began to jog, then to run. He ran over the sand, back and forth between the giant granite pillars that guarded the beach, and startled a pair of oyster-catchers, which peeped and squeaked at him, then flew to the rocks and rested there, tilting their heads at him inquiringly. He ran until his breath came in gasps, until the pain in his lungs was greater than the pain in his limbs. Then he stopped and sat for a while panting on the sand, a huddled lonely form.

Above him, high atop one of the rock pinnacles, seventy feet above him, a bald eagle sat on a pine branch surveying its wide kingdom, casting an evil eye upon the strange conformation on the sand, its knees clasped between arms, rocking, swallowing deep lungfuls of air.

Cobb stared back.

The climb to the top of the rock would be ardous, but Cobb, tracing a possible route, thought it could be managed without a rope. Managed easily, perhaps, if he were in health. The rock was the highest point on the little island, and from the top of it he would be able to see the eagle's world, the sea around the island, the desolate shores of Vancouver Island.

Tentatively at first, he began to climb, using handholds in the rock, or grabbing at roots from shrubs growing in its niches. The pain was there, but it did not control him. His efforts were focussed on climbing, not suffering.

In twenty minutes, surprising himself, he was at the top, beside the eagle's contorted roost. The eagle frowned; then its great wings lifted it from its perch and slowly carried it into a warm updraft, and it soared away.

Cobb, triumphant upon his conquered peak, scanned the west horizon where the sea and sky merged in mist. A distant seiner bobbed in the ocean, struggling north to the good herring waters. Cobb swivelled in a half-circle and saw below him the house and its outbuildings. Smoke drifted from the chimney. His eyes followed the path which led behind the house to the dock, where the small boat rocked and dipped in the gentle waves.

Cobb looked beyond the bay to the shore of Vancouver Island and its beaches and sandstone ledges stretching endlessly south and north. His eyes followed the shoreline north until it melted into the mists.

And in those mists, in the amorphous merging of land, sky, and ocean, his eyes caught something.

Something moving. Passing in and out of the swatches of grey that hung over the ocean. It emerged from the mist. A boat. A long wake behind it.

A high-powered launch that was making turbulent passage. A rich man's plaything, he could see now. An unlikely presence in the open North Pacific in March. It definitely was not a police boat.

Cobb knew.

Good Friday, the Twenty-fourth Day of March, at Eleven O'Clock in the Morning

Cobb went through changes. Standing frozen, immobile, at the top of the rock pinnacle, he underwent an explosive head trip.

The first reaction was not at all complex. He felt jolted by a pulsing high-energy current.

Then slowly, from some secret spring within him, came a strength flowing and rushing into his organs and limbs and his heart and head.

The withdrawal sickness seemed to shrink into some far compartment of his brain. The tremors in his hands stilled. It was a calming, deep and serene.

Partly, he just willed his strength, and partly, he got outside himself and excised fear, confusion, and sickness. To break an addiction, it is ultimately necessary to find that kind of strength, and Cobb had found it once before, in jail at the age of eighteen, when he made a decision about the path of his life. A similar strength came to him now. But it came rushing.

He took three deep breaths to still himself. He felt his heartbeat slacken and his mind begin to click, to gear up.

He started to climb down, weighing and assessing the factors as he did. It was unlikely that they had seen him. It was also unlikely that he could get to the house before Au and his men arrived there. And his gun was in the bedroom. Where Jennifer Tann was sleeping. He took another deep breath.

The boat was looming swiftly closer, and Cobb could see figures in it now. His route down the rock would have to be out of sight of the bay, or they would see him. A possibility: if no one remained to guard the boats, he might make his way to them before being sighted from the house. The ignition key was in the runabout. But Jennifer? Some way would have to be devised . . .

Jumping to reach a narrow ledge that would take him out of view from the house and the bay, he slipped as a loose rock crumbled beneath his foot. He grabbed the rock face for holds, and found none, and slid six feet to a grassy outcropping, tearing skin from his palms and twisting an ankle.

He took another deep breath, and kept descending. Time seemed to rush past him as he moved with aching slowness.

Then he heard the engine cut. They were at the dock.

The yacht drew into the dock at the bow of the outboard, and Snider and Ng Soon scrambled off and tied her up. Cudlipp followed, then Au in his long cape, and Feng, whose eyes rarely left his cousin.

"Please look to the small boat," Au said to Feng. "Then join us at the house." Feng was pleased at that. He would have a chance to be alone for a few minutes.

The four other men began walking toward the house; then Au looked at Ng Soon and spoke to him harshly in Ch'ao-chou. "You are not prepared." Ng Soon trotted back to the launch and returned from it with an American war-surplus M16. "It was stupid and dangerous to leave that aboard," he said, glancing quickly at Jin Feng. Feng remained expressionless, his eyes half-lidded.

Ducking behind a growth of salal and Oregon grape, Cobb found his way to the path that headed north to the top of the island. A few hundred feet to the south were the clearing and the house.

Were they already there?

His answer was a single gun shot, which rang out from the direction of the house. As the shot echoed, he heard a human voice crying out. A scream. And it was Jennifer's voice. . . .

His heart seemed for a moment or two to bounce wildly in his chest cavity. He stilled it with a surge of effort. And he took another deep breath. And somehow he was again his own master, under the control of his own will.

Again he ticked off the factors. One: the men were inside the house. Two: Jennifer Tann was . . . shot? He made his calculation coldly: if she were dead, there was no reason to go directly to the house. Three: he was unarmed, helpless. Four: the men did not know where he was. Five: the boats provided the only escape route. Perhaps the ignition key had been left in the launch. Perhaps a weapon.

It would take him ten minutes to circle the island, along the path from the beach to the north point, then to the cove and the wharf. He went at a trot, limping slightly.

He rounded the point, breathing heavily, and finally slowed where the trees began to thin near the clearing. The salal was high here, and he crouched behind it and scanned the clearing.

And there: Dr. Au. Standing by the side of the house. Now turning to walk. Now a young man joined him, carrying an automatic weapon. Then they disappeared around the corner toward the front of the house, and Cobb, running and stumbling, sprinted across the clearing to the water, toward the barnacle-encrusted rocks that were grouped along the shoreline. The tide was low, so the rocks afforded cover, and he was out of sight here from both the house and the wharf. Craning his neck, Cobb could see the boats, and suddenly he saw a man dressed in black step lithely into the outboard boat.

To reach the wharf from the rocks would be a wet but not impossible feat. It was possible to stay between the rocks and the boats, yet remaining out of view of the house, and one could crawl under the wharf and slip into the water then swim to the point at which the boats were tied. Once there, Cobb would have to dive below the yacht and come up on its starboard side, away from the wharf and out of view of Au's man.

Cobb was a strong enough swimmer, and the cold of the water could somehow be borne. He waded in, and finally plunged, keeping only his head above water. The cold of it was numbing, but Cobb knew he could handle it for the short time he would be in. He swam to the floating dock and crawled along beneath it, raising his head every several feet for air. Looking up between the cracks of the decking, he saw no sign of Au's man. He prayed he was still in the outboard.

Cobb rested for a minute, then took a deep swallow of air and dived beneath the cabinet cruiser. The keel was deep and he was struggling as he reached it, and then suddenly he was beneath it, coming up the other side with a gasp and a splash — sounds which he prayed had been drowned by the steady slap of waves around him.

There was no ladder, but he found a rope hanging loosely over the side, near the cabin. Using it, he pulled himself over the bulwarks and hoisted himself over the rail and onto the deck. As he went over, he spotted the man in black, still on the small boat, working at something. His back was to Cobb.

Cobb lay quietly for a while on the deck, gaining his strength. Then he crawled on his stomach to the cabin door, which was open, and entered.

He scrabbled about hurriedly in quick search for weapons, and found none. The key was not in the ignition. But with time, barring any interruptions, he could wire it (certain skills had been learned in the Youthful Offenders Unit). He would need a knife, and something like tweezers. He rummaged through drawers for tools, and finally found a large tool kit beneath the steering panel.

Then suddenly the boat lurched a little, as if someone had just boarded it. Grabbing an eighteen-inch crescent wrench, Cobb scrambled to the top of a high bunk beside the cabin door, just as Jin

Feng, lowering his head to clear the portal, stepped inside. Peering over the edge of the bunk, Cobb watched Feng, below him.

Feng opened his satchel swiftly, turning it upside down and dumping out clothing and books. Then, crouching, he pried loose with his fingernails a wooden false bottom. Beneath was a two-shot derringer pistol and a few .32-calibre bullets wrapped in tissue paper. Feng clicked two bullets into the chambers.

As he stood up, Feng sensed movement above him. He turned his eyes upward and suddenly opened them wide in surprise at the sight of the crescent wrench accelerating downwards toward his forehead. It connected with a crack, the sound of hard metal on bone. Feng's pupils rolled up and he collapsed in a limp tangle of arms and legs.

Cobb jumped down and retrieved the derringer, which was spinning slowly on the cabin deck. He went through Feng's pockets, finding no other weapons. He did find the keys for the outboard.

He put the gun to Feng's head and slapped him hard three times.

"Is she alive?" he asked in a heavy, angry voice.

The man did not stir. Cobb pulled off his soaking jacket and wrung water from it onto the man's face. Feng groaned. He slapped him again. Feng rolled over and slowly opened his eyes.

"Is she alive?"

Feng slowly focussed on Cobb standing over him, leaning against a table, water streaming from him, breathing heavily, clenching the derringer, which was pointed at his heart. Feng eyed the gun and wet his lips.

"Is she alive?"

"What?" Feng groaned.

"I said: Is she alive? If she has been killed, nobody will leave this island. Nobody. I will bust up the engine, and then I will kill as many as I can."

"The woman," Feng mumbled. "I don't know." He started to get up.

"Don't move," said Cobb. "I will shoot you."

Feng eased himself back to the floor, propping himself up with his elbows. A purple welt was emerging slowly on his forehead.

Feng shook his head as if to clear it. Then he looked hard into Cobb's eyes. "Mr. Cobb. You are making a mistake."

Cobb cut him off. "Shut up. Put your hands on top of your head and walk out in front of me." His speech was clipped and sharp.

"Mr. Cobb —"

"Get out the door. Or I will kill you. You can bank on it."

Feng grimaced, and joined his hands over his head. He went outside the cabin, and Cobb followed, the gun inches from Feng's back.

Ng Soon, standing by the back door of the house, saw them emerge and began running toward the dock, his rifle held in firing position. When he saw the gun in Cobb's hand he stopped cold, then backed up a step or two. He was fifty feet from them. Cobb moved Feng between them as a shield.

Now Au came from the back door of the house and stopped there, leaning against the doorpost, watching. After half a minute he pushed himself away from the doorway and slowly walked down the path toward the dock, stopping beside Ng Soon.

Cobb and Feng stayed on the boat dock. A minute passed. Then Au spoke. "May I suggest an arrangement?" he said.

Through the doorway of the house Cobb saw a frightened, quick movement. Was it Jennifer? Was she alive?

As if he had heard the questions that had been spoken in Cobb's mind, Au provided the answers.

"No, she has *not* been hurt," he said. Au turned to the house and called to someone. "Send her out."

An arm appeared, pushing Tann through the door. She stumbled at the threshold, falling to her knees. Slowly she got to her feet. She was barefoot, wearing jeans and a blouse torn down the middle. A red welt and a trickle of blood showed on her left cheek. Otherwise her face was ghost white. Her eyes were the eyes of a dazed and frightened fawn. Cobb held off an impulse to run to her. He calmed himself again, breathing slowly.

His eyes went from Tann to the figure now standing beside her. Everit Cudlipp . . . Cobb was shocked. The man had sunk to the ultimate depth.

Cudlipp was holding Cobb's police .38 in his hand. There was blood trickling from above his left knee. A flesh wound. So. The shot that Cobb had heard from the house had apparently been fired by Tann.

Au called to him again: "Mr. Cobb, I am suggesting an arrangement. A deal. Lawyers are always partial to a little plea bargaining."

Cobb waited for him to continue.

"An out-of-court settlement, as it were," Au said. He and Ng Soon began slowly walking toward Cobb. "All I want is your life. I will give you the woman's in exchange. She means nothing to me. You will give our Jin Feng the gun, and she will be allowed to leave in your boat. She can land anywhere on shore. There are many places to hide. When the authorities come, they will find her." They were within thirty feet of Cobb now, and he stopped them.

"Don't come closer. I can kill this man and one other."

Au smiled. His mind was in a functioning phase, and his eyes were sharp and alert. "Unfortunately," he said, "the young lady did not demonstrate much dexterity in the use of your firearm. The reflexes of my good and proven friend Mr. Cudlipp were equal to the task of disarming her."

Cobb made no response.

"Mr. Cobb, we will let her go to the boat if you will render the gun to Mr. Feng."

"Please give me the gun," Feng whispered. "It will save your life."

"Jennifer," Cobb called. "Come down to the wharf."

"Mr. Cobb," said Au, "your part of the bargain involves the surrender of the gun. I promise you that she will be safe. She will be allowed to depart before you are killed. I will go this far: I will kill you quickly, without pain."

Tann stepped woodenly down the path toward the wharf, clutching the torn blouse about her. She stepped off the path to get around Au and Ng Soon, and kept coming.

"Yours is not a position of strength, Mr. Cobb," Au said. "You might have time to shoot once, and then you will fall under our fire. After that, I assure you, Miss Tann will die. And I can promise you that her death under the circumstances will be a long and arduous and artistic piece of work. She will remain conscious throughout."

Tann seemed to hesitate.

"Keep coming," Cobb told her. She walked a few more steps forward, and Ng Soon, on a word from Au, quickly went forward and grabbed her arm. She did not struggle.

Cobb studied the situation for a minute, and finally said: "Give her a head start. When she has gone, I will give your man the gun."

"Mr. Cobb, I prefer it otherwise," said Au. "I had rather you give Jin Feng the gun now, and then Miss Tann will be allowed to go. I promise that your ordeal will be a short one, because in any event we cannot tarry here. Does it not seem fair?"

"Tell your goon to let her go or I will blow this man's head off."

"It is a sad commentary upon the human condition that you are so lacking in trust, Mr. Cobb. How am I to know that when she has left us, you will not do that very thing? How am I to know that you will not then blow his head off, as you so articulately put it?"

"I am a man of my word, Dr. Au. As you are."

Au smiled. "We shall all learn a lesson in trust, Mr. Cobb." He spoke to Ng Soon, who let Tann's arm go.

"Keep coming, Jennifer," Cobb said. "I have the key. Head straight across the channel and ditch it and run for the bush."

"Very well," said Au. "But if you try to go with her, Ng Soon will disable you both." He spoke in Chinese dialect to the gunman. "He now has instructions to take your legs off should you act unwisely. He will not kill you, and he will not kill her. I shall perform those services. I did promise Mr. Cudlipp that he could watch, and I am a man of my word."

"Get on the dock," Cobb ordered Feng. "Untie the outboard."

Cobb followed Feng over the railing, keeping him between himself and Ng Soon's gun. Au and Ng Soon walked toward the wharf.

Tann reached Cobb. She seemed in shock.

Cobb gave her the keys to the outboard; then in a low voice, out of Feng's hearing, he said: "Never mind the shore. It's twenty minutes from here to Glenda Bay. Go flat out. There should be a cop in Glenda Bay, and there will be radios. I'll hold them as long as I can here. If they kill me, they will come after you, and they will catch up in a few minutes. If you see them coming, head for the beach. They won't be able to beach the big boat without wrecking it on the rocks and stranding themselves. Just run for cover and hide in the bush. If I can get way with it, I'll take their boat. Do you understand all this?"

She nodded weakly.

Cobb gestured at Feng with the gun. "This guy's my insurance. Now, get in the boat. Go fast!" He kept his eyes on Au, who was at the dock now and moving closer.

"Get back!" Cobb shouted.

Au hesitated.

"They will kill you," Tann whispered.

"Just do it, Jennie. Just go."

She got behind the wheel of the small boat and started the engine. It coughed and caught, then sputtered and died.

"A little throttle," Cobb said.

This time it caught and held.

"Put it in gear, swing it around, and fly!"

The boat inched away from the dock, and as it did, Cobb released his eyes from Au for two seconds, turned his head, and called to her: "Look: I love you, okay? Now, get the hell out of here!"

The boat turned about and she gave it full throttle.

When Cobb turned back to Au, it was too late. He was lunging already. Before Cobb could squeeze the trigger the needle had stuck him and his four limbs were without feeling. He lost his balance and fell hands forward, and he heard the snap of cracking bone in his wrist as his arm hit the planks. The derringer bounced from the wharf into the water.

He heard the sound of the engine of the small boat coughing again. Then the engine died.

Feng, solemnly shaking his head, said: "I was asked to remove the fuel tanks, Mr. Cobb." Au, smiling, kicked Cobb in the head, snapping it hard sideways and sending him sprawling across the boards.

The reverberations in his head dimmed and became distant echoes.

There was a stillness in the room, and Foster Cobb awoke into it in pain. The familiar sounds were gone: the generator was off; the fire in the wood heater had died; there was no music. The only sound was the pounding of waves, which came to him distantly. The only feeling was the pounding in his head. Soon he became aware of sharp pain as well from his right wrist where it had been broken. He could not move the arm to relieve this pain, because his wrists were tightly bound. As he slowly became conscious, he became aware that the side of his face felt swollen and tight as if caked with clotting blood. There were splotches of blood on his shirt.

He could hear the men speaking now.

"Hey, he's coming to."

"Yes, and the paralysis is gone. He is moving his hands."

"Do you think he can hear us?"

"Mr. Cobb." It was the voice of Dr. Au. "There is a matter of some importance. And since I will elicit it from you in one manner or another, please help yourself by telling me now. It is about the small gun. Where did you get it?"

"The gun . . ." Cobb groaned. As his eyes focussed, he saw Au standing in front of him, Snider and Ng Soon at either side, and Cudlipp at the far end of the room.

"Yes, the gun," said Au.

"The man . . . in black."

Au's eyes glinted. He turned to Snider. "My devoted young

cousin. He is in truth, then, an emissary with an unsavoury message. We will ship him in parts to Hong Kong, and that will be Ma Wochien's answer. He has been told to remain guarding the boat?"

"Yeah," said Snider. "He's sitting on the dock staring at the barnacles."

Cobb had only dimly been taking this is. As he became more alert, he began to see around him. And he saw Tann.

"Let her go, damn you!" he shouted in a cracked voice. "You gave me your word."

She was on the floor, bound and gagged, her eyes open and staring at him.

"It was, after all, an excellent lesson in trust, Mr. Cobb," Au said. "You are a wiser man for it." He withdrew from his leather case a series of needles and laid them gently on top of a table. They were variously gold, silver, platinum, and stainless steel. He began polishing them. Then he paused, and Cobb saw that his eyes had dulled. He spoke to Cobb in a low and knowing tone: "You knew I would come, Mr. Cobb. I think you understand the nature of this visit. One must die that the other be free. Do you understand? Thus it had to be. Our destinies have become intertwined."

Cobb had no words for the occasion. He wondered if ultimately he would plead for his life. Could he master his fear? Would he find some dignity in all of this? As he searched himself for strength, he felt a tight knot form in his stomach and felt it grow and begin to take him over. Dizzily he looked at Au's face. The man had moved outside reality.

"You are not well, Dr. Au," Cobb heard himself saying.

"Oh, I have had that tried on me," Au said. "Please don't be banal at this most momentous occasion of the meeting of two great spirits. Two great spirits which now come together in majestic climax."

Cobb wondered whether he would beg for his life. He had never begged for anything. Would he grovel?

Perhaps there was some level of the man's head that he could reach into, some level of communication.

"Do you understand why you are doing this?" he asked.

"Of course, Mr. Cobb. For a brotherhood, a union of the opposite forces of *yin* and *yang*, a conjoining of your spirit with mine. We should have been brothers, Mr. Cobb, except for unfortunate circumstances of place and heritage. In spirit we have always been brothers. In flesh, we soon shall be brothers in fact."

Snider returned to the cabin, and took a seat beside Ng Soon, who cradled his M16 on his lap. Both were hoping for a good show. Cudlipp was further back, standing against a wall, holding Cobb's gun.

Au's eyes blinked, and Cobb saw life return to them.

"What I built, you destroyed, Mr. Cobb. I had grown fond of this country. Now I must hide in the shadows." He picked up a silver needle about seven inches long, and wiped it with a sterile cloth.

"It is better that you lie still, Mr. Cobb. It is not easy to find the points on a moving man. If you cause me to err and strike a pain point, the process will take much longer. Although, in all modesty, I must proudly own to an almost unerring ability to work with moving targets. My hands are very quick, very sure. I am wonderfully agile. I might have been an excellent surgeon, and of great fame. Do you not think it is false modesty to disclaim one's greatness? Do you not regard yourself as a lawyer of exceptionally quick mind? We do each other honor."

Cobb, fighting nausea, heard Au's words vaguely in his ears.

"The old practitioners fuss about for many minutes before finding the point of the meridian they seek, and are often unsure of the proper angle of inclination. The operations — I have seen many — can be tedious indeed." Au tested the point of the needle by touching his finger to it. "It is an ancient art, yet there are so many secrets yet to be learned, and which, foolishly, I believe, we turn from. For instance, there are seven hundred and thirty points upon the body which we recognize as healing points. There are as many from which *ch'i* is released, points of destruction, points of pain. Is it not a waste to the world of science that such matters are ignored? Why should man be denied the benefit of wider knowledge?"

"You slimy fuck," Cobb snarled. He felt it didn't matter now.

Au showed him the needle. "The analgesic power of these simple devices has long been known. It is possible to anesthetize individual organs, or limbs, or combinations of organs and limbs, or the whole body. Thus, as you were standing on the dock, I found one of the points upon your body that temporarily removes sensation from the four limbs. Likewise, it is possible through acupuncture to heighten sensitivity in certain areas of the body. The point I am now seeking is the Point of the Gentle Fragrance, as it is called in the old language." He inserted the needle at a point near the first knuckle of the fourth toe, jabbing it in and out by the sparrow-peck method.

"It will make all parts of the body, particular the groin and pelvis areas, extremely sensitive to pain, lowering the pain threshold."

"God damn, Au, let her go. And get this over with."

"Oh, there will be such a rich feeling in the area of your groin." Au was radiant in his enjoyment of this. "Perhaps it will not be the same delightful feeling you enjoyed while in the company of the lovely young lady." He chuckled. "Oh, in many ways, we are brothers in spirit."

Cobb glanced at Tann, whose eyes were wide and filled with tears. He could not take it, and had to look away.

"Just get it over with. I am ready." Cobb surprised himself.

"I suppose, Mr. Cobb, that you are hiding your sorrow. You need not feel that you must do so. I understand your pain. I, too, have felt pain." Au closed his eyes as if to shut out the pain he now himself was enduring. Suddenly he felt it wash over him, and when he opened his eyes, Cobb could see they were glazed again. "We shall be brothers soon. I am honored to have you share the very feelings I once endured. There is a destiny which we share. The prosecutor and his victim. The doctor and his victim. Coming together . . . coming together . . ."

For several seconds Au said nothing, and slowly, awareness came back into his eyes.

"During the process of slow dismemberment, one may enjoy release from pain through entering an unconscious state. If that event occurs, I will seek certain points in the ear." He brandished a pair of long platinum needles. "Platinum for the ears, Mr. Cobb. It will keep you awake, although it will be a feeling of flames devouring you." A pause. "Snider," he said, turning to the young addict, "the gown, please."

Snider wiped his runny nose on the back of his hand.

"That will not do, Mr. Snider," said Au. "You will wash your hands. I will not have your dirt about me." Snider went to the bathroom, and returned. Cobb was trying to shut his world off, but his body was alive with feeling. "Now the gown, please," said Au. Snider held it, and Au slipped his arms into it. Snider tied it at the back.

"Gloves," said Dr. Au. He held out his hands and Snider tugged the gloves onto each hand by turn.

"Yes, Mr. Cobb, I, too, was in the process of enjoying a woman once, and paid dearly for it afterwards. In a sense, I have said, we are brothers." He turned to Snider.

"Scalpel."

Au's pain came back, eating at his back brain and wounding him as Snider slipped the handle of the scalpel into his outstretched hand. And with the pain came a searing memory . . .

Janice's screaming enhanced the excitement for him, and he had intercourse a third time. But still, tantalizingly, his loins withheld from him that final rich burst of joy that was his due and right. The girl, naive and pretty and eighteen years old, had thought the handsome young medical student was playing a silly game of seduction when he asked to tie her ankles and wrists to the corner posts of the bed. ("May I suggest a complete medical examination?" he had said. "Oh, you!" she had replied, and coyly let him take her clothes off and tie her.)

Au P'ang Wei, twenty-five years old, a second-year medical student and already an accredited acupuncturist, was discovering a great truth: The true pleasure of sex comes from pain. What a world had opened to him this night! There were so many exciting ideas, so many means of inducing the ecstasy of pain, so many secret keys to the dark chambers of forbidden sexuality. But why had he not thought to bring his medical kit? Or his needles? There were the usual utensils in the kitchen — but the knives were dull. Au groped through the medicine cabinet for something sharp — her father and brother were well-shaven, and must keep razors. Unless they took them with them to the inter-city rugby match.

Ah! There! A straight razor. And a shaving mug. What intriguing ideas suggest themselves! But it is past midnight, and there may not be much time for lengthy surgical foreplay. Perhaps it could end quickly, perhaps the feel of sharp metal might induce the terror in her that would build for him that final agony of pleasure-pain, that seminal explosion, that wrenching climax of which he had always dreamed, yet which teased and tormented, and evaded him.

He went to the girl, who was whimpering, her eyes closed. The bruises on her chest and legs were dainty, sweet, and sensuous. The voice whimpering softly. The flesh soft. The woman timidly delicious.

When she opened her eyes to see the razor and mug in his hands, she screamed again. "Soap before dissection," he said. "You must be clean."

Her scream was wild and extravagant, and her evocations of terror so filled the room that Au P'ang Wei did not hear the creak of the door as it opened. Then he saw her brother, Harry, back early. Harry was at the bedroom door, still in his playing togs, gaping. . . .

Au stood still, the mug in one hand, the razor held high in the other.

Harry called: "Jan! Jan! What has this bugger . . . ? Dad, come quick!" The two men leaped at Au P'ang Wei, who now knew fear himself. That fear caused him, when striking at the young man's neck with the razor, to miss the neck and bury the point harmlessly in the forearm. A hard and expert tackle brought him to the floor, and his breath rushed from his lungs as Harry's head struck the pit of his stomach with a crunching thud. A boot from Janice's father, a boot studded with metal cleats, arrived with ringing impact at the side of Au's head, and split his right ear open, tearing it nearly off.

When the young medical student awoke in the breaking dawn, he found he was lying in a green hay field. The straight razor was between his legs. . . .

"I am a eunuch, Mr. Cobb. A castrato. Now we shall truly be brothers."

The knowledge that again he would not be alone caused the pain in Au's head to ebb, and for a few seconds he balanced the scalpel in his hand, getting the weight of it for the delicate cutting touch of which he was justly proud.

"Ah, Mr. Cobb, I could have been a great surgeon."

Cobb opened his eyes and stared hard into the blazing eyes of Dr. Au.

"Please let Jennifer free," he pleaded. "Please don't harm her."

"It cannot be allowed. Mr. Cudlipp deserves some say in these matters, and he has expressed a wish that there be no witnesses."

Cobb could see Cudlipp standing against the wall, behind everyone else, smiling, his arms folded. His leg was now bandaged.

"You must understand the matter of loyalties, Mr. Cobb," Au said. "Mr. Cudlipp has rendered service. I owe him a debt of gratitude. It was through his good work that we all came to be here today."

"You're slime," Cobb called to Cudlipp, who returned a large grin and said:

"Your good old buddy Eddie Santorini must want you dead very bad."

Santorini . . . Cobb gasped.

"Who *can* you trust?" Au said. "Now, Mr. Snider, will you lower his trousers?" Snider did, tugging them down to Cobb's knees.

Au paused. "Where is Jin Feng?" he asked.

Snider looked through the window. "Still down at the beach."

Au nodded, and returned to Cobb.

"God damn, let her go, let her go." Cobb kept mumbling this, and as he did, he closed his eyes and tried to shut his world off, to shrink back deeply within himself.

The words he next heard were Cudlipp's and seemed to come from a distance away, and at first they registered only dimly:

"Cobb, you bastard, I'm finally getting mine back. I've been living for this time all week, since you did me in, in court." A guttural laugh, a series of short grunts. "Don't feel too good, hey?"

Cobb found himself returning to the room, and his eyes reopened. "You're asswipe, Cudlipp. You got what was coming."

Cudlipp's face flushed as he raised his gun and with a grimace fired two shots in rapid succession.

As he fired, Cobb rejoiced with the thought that he had taunted Cudlipp into taking his life, into cheating Dr. Au of his slow kill.

Good Friday, the Twenty-fourth Day of March, at Twelve O'Clock Noon

The contortions of pain and disbelief that expressed themselves upon the face of Au P'ang Wei seemed to Cobb awesome and terrible. He got the merest glimpse of Au's face as the man leaped toward him like some ungainly panther, his limbs flailing. He sprawled across the table, coming to rest on his face and stomach a foot or two from Cobb. The scalpel and two platinum needles were clutched tightly in his hand.

Blood boiled from two ragged holes in the middle of his back.

He was still alive, screaming.

"Freeze! Both of you!" Cudlipp snapped at Snider and Ng Soon.

Snider had half-risen from his chair, but stopped on the command, motionless, suspended, his mouth hanging wide, his nose flowing.

Ng Soon, who did not understand English, just kept getting up, picking the M16 rifle from his lap as he rose.

Cudlipp calmly fired a bullet directly into his head.

Zombie-like, Ng Soon dropped the carbine and, like a drunk doing the white line, deliberately and carefully walked to the open back door and down the step outside. He took three or four paces in the direction of the dock; then he crumpled like a stuffed doll on the ground outside.

Cudlipp reached inside Snider's jacket pocket, pulled out a gun, and threw the man on the floor.

"Face-down, Sleazy, and spread-eagle," Cudlipp ordered. *"Do it!"*

Snider did it.

Cudlipp tore a lamp cord from a wall plug and cut it with a knife, then bound Snider's wrists behind his back.

He called to Cobb: "I need some more rope." His voice was raised to be heard above Au's screams.

"I'm wearing it, for Christ's sake," Cobb shouted.

"What?"

"Untie me!"

"Oh, yeah, yeah."

Cudlipp cut Cobb's arms and legs free and used the rope to tie Snider's feet, while Cobb went to Tann and undid her bindings.

She was shaking, and she clutched at him.

"It's okay," Cobb said. "I think."

Outside, Jin Feng approached from the shadows, bent down over the body of Ng Soon, and took the ignition key from his pocket. Then he glanced into the window.

Fate had intervened, and Ma Wo-chien would be satisfied; although, had Feng been left to his own means — without the stupid intervention of the fool Cudlipp — the task would have been performed cleanly, and without witnesses.

A few seconds later, Cobb heard the sound of the rented yacht's engine. He looked out the back door and saw it moving away from the pier and throttling into high gear, moving out of the bay in front of a high wake.

"Let the sucker go," Cudlipp said. "They'll catch up to him."

Still ignoring Au, whose screams slowly lessened in pitch and intensity, Cudlipp grabbed Snider by the armpits and lugged him outside, depositing him in the daffodils. "Getting rid of the garbage," he said, returning.

Tann glanced nervously at Au, and when she saw his wounds, she blanched and stepped back.

"Don't worry about it," Cudlipp said. "He's had it. These bullets blow apart when they hit." He went up to Au. The Surgeon's eyes rolled toward his assassin, and their hardness began to fade behind a veil of approaching insentience.

"Sorry, Doc," Cudlipp said, "but I had to perform my end. Somebody else came up with a better offer. I'm a man of my word, too — if I get a better deal." He looked at his watch. "The plane's coming in anytime. It was due at noon. Jesus, the timing had to be tight."

Au's eyes glazed over. The scalpel and needles slipped from his hand and clattered onto the table.

Cudlipp grinned at Cobb. "Yeah, Mr. Cobb, now I hope you know what it felt like for me when Alice walked into that court-room last Monday. Sure did not feel very sweet. Got any beer in the icebox?"

"I think there's a dozen cold," Cobb said.

Cudlipp wandered into the kitchen and yelled from there: "What about you guys? Thirsty?"

"No," Cobb said. Tann said nothing. She sat on a chair and buried her face in her hands.

Cobb heard Cudlipp pop a bottle cap in the kitchen. "Sorry I had to rough up your lady a little bit," he called. "Hell, she almost killed me. Anyhow, I had to get a hold of your gun. They took mine. Distrustful bastards." He came from the kitchen happily beaming and holding a beer bottle. "Yeah, it was your old buddy Santorini. Sure you don't want a suck on this?"

"No. Thanks."

"Yeah, he set it up. I had to take my fucking life in my hands, but it's better than a sawbuck in the can, right?" He took a hard pull on the beer, and wiped his mouth with his hand. "Went up to see him on Wednesday. Santorini. Actually, he called me in, wanted to make a deal. What the fuck, I'm up against the wall. I got no choice. Not particularly happy about it. I got no love for you, Cobb, and you know that. But I can't turn it down. What it is, is this: I grease the Surgeon here — like, save your useless balls, not to mention your life — and he lets me go to Australia, agrees not to extradite, agrees not to estreat on my bail. I get exile. You get to live. Shit, it's a deal."

Cudlipp winked and patted his breast pocket. "Got me a set of I.D. here, passport and all. And thanks to our late friend here" — he waved an arm in Au's direction — "I got myself a stake. Flying off to Sydney tomorrow. But Jesus, what a hassle." He shook his head and looked mournfully at the wound in his leg. "Guess I have to get this patched up first."

Cudlipp took another long drink from the bottle, emptying it. "God damn," he said, "I needed that."

He went into the kitchen, and Cobb could hear the icebox open and close.

"You're pretty close to Santorini, right?" Cudlipp called out.

"Yes."

"He can be trusted to come through hey?"

"He can be trusted."

There was a great roar of engine as the police Cessna buzzed the house.

Saturday, the Twenty-fifth Day of March, at Three O'Clock in the Afternoon

After the bones of Cobb's cheek and wrist were set, he was allowed to go from the hospital. He met Tann and Santorini in the waiting room, and they walked out together, past a newspaper kiosk. He could see the front-page banner line: "ORIENT CONNECTION BROKEN, DRUG RINGLEADER SHOT." Below was a picture of Cobb, and the story of Au's death.

They continued down the hospital steps into their cars. Nobody spoke. Then Santorini smiled and put his arm around Cobb's shoulders.

"Some opera, huh?" he said. "It wasn't supposed to drag out like that, Fos, but they took Cudlipp's gun away from him in the first scene. He had to play it by ear."

"Yeah," said Cobb.

"So," Santorini said. "How do you feel?"

"Great, goddamnit. Outrageous." He *was* feeling good, despite his injuries and his nausea and chills. "Hey, Eddie, I have a little speech. There's a line from Bacon somewhere: 'We are told to forgive our enemies. But we are not often told to forgive our friends.' I forgive my friend. Thanks. That's the speech."

"Well, gee, hey, Fos, when you're feeling better, let's get together for a little piss-up. Like old times."

"If your lordship pleases."

"Aw, no formalities, Fos. Just call me 'Judge.' I guess you know there'll be an opening now in my office. I'll be out of there in a couple of weeks, and you have first claim. Unless you plan to take up Smitty's partnership offer."

"I have some other ideas," Cobb said. "Try this for size: 'Cobb and Tann, Solicitors.'"

"Has a nice ring to it," Tann said brightly.

Santorini shrugged. "Maybe I can send some business your way."

Cobb managed a crooked smile. "No thanks, Eddie."

Three days later, at nine o'clock in the morning Hong Kong time, Ma Wo-chien dispatched Jin Feng from his study with a wave of his hand. Feng bowed low and left. Ma Wo-chien snapped open a metal box of small Ritmeesters and lit one. He smoked for a while, staring out the window at churning clouds, which spewed rain in wind-driven sheets. His fleet of junks bounced and tossed in the waters of the harbor below.

Ma sighed. There had been losses. There would be gains.

Such was business.

ABOUT THE AUTHOR

After working his way through law school as a journalist, William Deverell became one of Canada's most celebrated trial lawyers, serving as counsel in more than a thousand civil rights and criminal cases, including more than thiry murders — prosecuting as well as defending.

His first novel, *Needles*, won the $50,000 Seal Prize in 1979 and the Book of the Year Award. Since then he has published ten bestsellers, including *Kill All the Lawyers*, *Trial of Passion*, *Slander*, and *The Laughing Falcon*, and a true crime book, *A Life on Trial: The Case of Robert Frisbee*, based on a sensational murder trial he defended.

Trial of Passion won the Arthur Ellis prize, for the best Canadian crime novel, and the Dashiell Hammett award, from the International Crime Writers Association, for literary excellence in crime writing in North America. His novels have been translated into ten languages and sold worldwide.

He created the CBC's long-running TV series *Street Legal*, which has run internationally in more than 50 countries, and adapted many of his works both to screen and radio. He has served as Visiting Professor of Creative Writing, University of Victoria. He is former executive director and president of the B.C. Civil Liberties Association, and twice was acclaimed as chair of the Writers' Union of Canada.

He lives on Pender Island, British Columbia, and winters in Costa Rica. Please visit his web site at www.deverell.com